Climates of Migration

Climates of Migration

Ecology, Literature and Propaganda

Dominic Thomas

ANTHEM PRESS

Anthem Press
An imprint of Wimbledon Publishing Company
www.anthempress.com

This edition first published in UK and USA 2026
by ANTHEM PRESS
75–76 Blackfriars Road, London SE1 8HA, UK
or PO Box 9779, London SW19 7ZG, UK
and
244 Madison Ave #116, New York, NY 10016, USA

British Library Cataloguing-in-Publication Data
A catalogue record for this book is available from the British Library.

Library of Congress Cataloging-in-Publication Data: 2025938413
A catalog record for this book has been requested.

ISBN-13: 978-1-83999-626-9 (Hbk)/978-1-83999-627-6 (Pbk)
ISBN-10: 1-83999-626-9 (Hbk)/1-83999-627-7 (Pbk)

Cover Credit: Image by Midjourney, prompted by Adam Lomeli, based on
'LAION-5B' dataset, 2023

This title is also available as an eBook.

For Erin

Was it a good discussion?
Oh yes.
We discussed the future, you see.
What remains. What remains.

Christa Wolf, *What Remains*

CONTENTS

ACKNOWLEDGMENTS

I am deeply thankful for the unyielding support and indispensable insights provided by friends and colleagues. Those collaborations, conversations, exchanges, support and friendship inspired me to write this book.

My deep gratitude goes to France's Région Grand Est, the Eurométropole de Strasbourg and the University of Strasbourg for the award of the Gutenberg Prize and a Gutenberg Excellence Chair in Ecology and Propaganda. This provided an exceptional opportunity to further develop the ideas explored in this book, questions that frame the *Ecology and Propaganda—ECOPROP* research project at that institution. The Primary Research Investigators, Professor Ninon Chavoz and Professor Anthony Mangeon, in the *Unité de Recherche 1337: Configurations littéraires*, have contributed in immeasurable ways, and I am immensely grateful to them for their intellectual generosity and hospitality. The Dean of Humanities at the University of California, Los Angeles, Professor Alexandra Minna Stern, provided essential support, and I would like to express appreciation for the generosity of the donors who established the Madeleine L. Letessier Chair in French and Francophone Studies.

I would also like to express my gratitude to the remarkable artists—Claas Gutsche, Yinka Shonibare and Ai Weiwei—and institutions—the Humboldt Forum (Berlin), National Maritime Museum (London), Národní galerie v Praze (Prague) and the Getty Research Institute (Los Angeles)—for granting me permission to reproduce various images. Earlier versions of selected material included in this book were previously published in somewhat different form in various edited books and journals, and are included with kind permission: "Fortress Europe: Identity, race and surveillance," in *Race, Violence, and Biopolitics*, edited by Alessandro Corio and Louise Hardwick, *International Journal of Francophone Studies* 17, no. 3–4 (2014), 445–68; "African Cartographies in Motion," in *Literature and Cartography*, edited by Anders Engberg-Pedersen (Cambridge, MA: MIT Press, 2017), 299–322; "The Aesthetics of Migration, Relationality, and the Sentimography of Globality," in *Race and the Aesthetic in French and Francophone Cultures*, edited by Alessandro Corio and Louise Hardwick, *L'Esprit créateur* 59, no. 2 (2019), 165–79; "French

Colonialism: The Rules of the Game," in *Visualizing Empire: Africa, France, and the Politics of Representation*, edited by Rebecca Peabody, Steven Nelson and Dominic Thomas (Los Angeles, CA: Getty Research Institute Books, 2021), 85–96; "Erasure," in *The Berlin Journal*, no. 36 (2022), 66–68; and "Migrations, Narrations, the Refugee Condition," in *Politics of Times: Imagining African Becomings*, edited by Achille Mbembe and Felwine Sarr (Cambridge: Polity Press, 2023), 235–42.

I am am also deeply grateful to the anonymous readers of the manuscript for the meaningful suggestions they kindly provided, all of which helped reframe several arguments. It has been such a pleasure working with the editorial team at Anthem Press. Together, they expertly steered the manuscript through every stage of the publication process.

FIGURES

PROLOGUE

Erasure: From Colonial-Washing to Greenwashing

Everything faded into mist. The past was erased, the erasure was forgotten, the lie became truth.

George Orwell[1]

The black body was Europe's first unit of energy.

Lesley Lokko[2]

The planet has a history.

Dipesh Chakrabarty[3]

As a child I was intrigued by those glass bottles in which small ships could be found, vessels whose seafaring days following ceremonial launches had come to symbolic ends. I did not share this curiosity with anyone, nor do I remember ever soliciting explanations to the obvious question of how they had actually ended up in there. This reluctance to seek answers came with the full knowledge that the mental speculation provided by the mystery would be ruined by a dryly technical response. Today, a simple internet search reveals that these are categorized as *impossible bottles*, a traditional craft with roots in the eighteenth century, that there are several ways of placing a model ship inside a bottle, and that they can be found on display in maritime museums around the world. Of course, there are other childhood tales and unsolved enigmas, many of which have continued to shape my life. One of the earliest I pondered was whether the ubiquitous concrete wall that surrounded the family home in West Berlin was designed to keep people *in* or *out*. The watchtowers were less ambiguous, as were the armed border guards. Yet, somehow, the hidden promises to be found on the *other side* captivated my interest, promises that countered the dominant narrative. As German sociologist Steffen Mau has also observed, "On a political level, building a wall often acts as a targeted antidote to anxiety-inducing discourse. [...] Being locked up creates a feeling of security (but paradoxically also the opposite, namely a threatening *climate*)."[4]

These early imaginative excursions came to mind while visiting the Humboldt Forum in Berlin shortly after it was inaugurated in September

2021. On that occasion, I first saw the boat that was transported to Berlin in 1904 from the South Pacific Island of Luf, a German colonial possession in Papua New Guinea's Bismarck Archipelago. Acquired by Eduard Hershey (navigator and captain) and Maximilian Thiel (trader) on behalf of the merchant company Hershey & Co. in 1903, the disassembled vessel was shipped shortly thereafter to Germany.[5] Initially on display at the Ethnologisches Museum (Ethnological Museum) in the Dahlem district, it was subsequently unhoused and rehoused during construction in 2018 in the reconstructed imperial structure that contains the Humboldt Forum. The 50-foot outrigger, handsomely decorated, remains a subject of controversy. Much like the ships of my childhood, sealed in bottles, the Luf boat was lowered into the building, thereby confining it in what the *New York Times*' architecture critic Michael Kimmelman aptly described as a "fake Baroque palace [...] a manufactured charm, erasing traces of the bad years of the twentieth century."[6] The small island of Luf after which the boat is named was the target of vicious, relentless and "countless crimes," and as such "is an extremely instructive representative example of the colonial violence done to Indigenous peoples in tens of thousands of other cases."[7] Unfortunately, "in the cold concrete mausoleum where the splendid Luf Boat is interred, visitors learn next to nothing about how the vessel functioned, how sophisticated its construction is, what its ornamentation means, how the caulk was produced, how its builders lived, what nautical skills they possessed, or how, for millennia, they were able to sail hundreds of miles upwind across the South Seas."[8]

These matters are all the more disquieting given that the late nineteenth-century merchant and showman Carl Hagenbeck aspired, in this same European capital, to display Germany's African colonies, as commemorated in the Berlin quarter of Wedding (often referred to as the *Afrikanisches Viertel*), where one can still wander down Afrikanische Straße, Togostraße, Kongo Straße or Koloniestraße. Carl Hagenbeck also promoted *human zoos*, placing non-Western people (often naked) on display in enclosures so that they could perform and entertain visitors, themselves caged in the ideologies and myths that served to justify colonial expansion. Their superiority remained unchallenged, comforted and reaffirmed by the staged hierarchy between observers and objects. *Extraction* and *provenance*, henceforth everlastingly betrothed.

The Humboldt Forum has been front and center in public debates on cultural heritage and the repatriation and restitution of cultural artifacts pillaged during the era of colonialism, and continues to struggle to reconcile *museological practices* with *historical reckoning*. Various panels displayed throughout the permanent exhibition recognize that "museums are increasingly focusing on the critical reappraisal of holdings from colonial times and the violent methods by which they were acquired." Yet, as John M. Coetzee once wrote: "I

Figure 0.1 Luf Boat (960 × 1520 × 650 cm, late nineteenth century), Oceania exhibition of the Ethnologisches Museum (Ethnological Museum) of the Staatliche Museen zu Berlin (National Museums in Berlin) at the Humboldt Forum. Author photograph, 2021.

say to myself, we are all sorry when we are found out. Then we are very sorry. The question is not, are we sorry? The question is, what lesson have we learned? The question is, what are we going to do now that we are sorry?"[9] Is it adequate to simply acknowledge a reprehensible past for culpability to be erased and for that gesture to open up different futures?

Glass, much like history, is fragile; walls are never permanent. This was the fate of the iconic Palace of the Republic (designed by East German architect Heinz Graffunder) that was demolished to make room for the reconstructed Hohenzollern royal and imperial Berlin Palace. The former was inaugurated more than four decades earlier on April 23, 1976, by the government of the German Democratic Republic. It became the seat of the People's plenary chamber (*Volkskammer*) and the center of gravity for cultural, sporting and social gatherings. German reunification got underway after the collapse of the Berlin Wall in 1989, inaugurating multiple processes of erasure in order to advance the imperative of forging common identities and a sense of shared belonging, the failed legacy of which continues to be evident in the asymmetrical relationship and lingering inequalities between what were temporarily two separate Germanies. As Dominic Boyer has argued, the "East/West

distinction remains a powerful axis of social imagination, a residue of the
Cold War politics of memory and identity."[10] With this knowledge in mind,
how does one begin the process of confronting the truth, evaluating extraction and provenance and charting a path toward memorial evidence and
recovery, all while simultaneously recalibrating dynamics between centers
and peripheries and evaluating the concentric circles that ripple across these
historical terrains?

The (fake) Berlin Palace rests on unstable layers and foundations. As with
tectonic shifts or plate motions, these will continue to crackle until the assessment of historical narratives is undertaken in a meaningful way, "especially
in Berlin, a city in which the Cold War played out also on an architectural
level," as Daniel Jütte has noted.[11] Indeed, "Walter Benjamin's interwar characterization of glass as 'the enemy of secrets' took on a dark, unintended
dimension. Transparency came to symbolize the conflation of public and private, of individual life and collectivist mass culture."[12] The Humboldt Forum
shop now offers replicas—for a staggering €3,895—of the thousands of ceiling
lights that once hung in the Palace of the Republic. One cannot help but be
reminded of the comment made by the main protagonist (Richard) in Jenny
Erpenbeck's novel *Go, Went, Gone*: "There's no better way to make history disappear than to unleash money, money roaming free has a worse bite than an
attack dog, it can effortlessly bite an entire building out of existence."[13] These
are mockeries, contemptuous and insulting copies of the originals that were
suspended in what was then referred to fondly as "Erich's lamp shop," in recognition of Erich Honecker, General Secretary of the Central Committee of
the Socialist Unity Party. But these are also caricatures of the past that ignore
East German sensitivities and downplay anti-capitalist impulses, privileging
instead consumerist mentalities similar to earlier historic attempts aimed at
commodifying ethnographic collections, stripped of cultural meaning, leaving objects denuded and reduced to static positions. These are also gestures
that sideline what Christoph Tannert has called "critical rehabilitation," of
the kind found in the "trace elements" inscribed into Claas Gutsche's large
monochrome linocuts on fine Japanese paper and that imply "remembering and overcoming the past in equal measure."[14] As Anne Wesle has written, Claas Gutsche's "works retrace among other topics the intra-German
past, and thus, in a broader sense, invoke themes of collective memory and of
commemorative culture" while paying attention to the "historical trajectory
of a collective consciousness."[15] In *Erasure* (2013), Claas Gutsche features the
Palace of the Republic, and the

light bulbs also play a prominent role in Gutsche's composition, where a
stylized circular garland of corn frames the negative space from which

something has been effaced, the empty aperture drawing in the eye on the left-hand side. The something that has been expunged and to which the work's title only alludes, is the hammer and compass-symbols within the GDR's coat of arms. During the period before the completion of the reunification process, a decision went ahead that all national emblems of the GDR in or on public buildings were to be dismantled during the first week of June in 1990. In the case of Gutsche's image (which combines diverse source material), the omission of the hammer and compass forecasts the total demolition of the building.[16]

Stefanie Gerke's research on ruins is enlightening in this regard, pointing to ways in which "the emptiness that had marked this site after the dismantling of the Palace, just like the empty frame had marked its façade for many years, is being overwritten."[17] Likewise, Judith Schalansky's volume of essays, *An Inventory of Losses*, offers a powerful reminder that "the art of forgetting is an impossibility because any allusion represents a presence, even when it refers to an absence" and that "fundamentally, every item is already waste, every building already a ruin, and all creation nothing but destruction."[18]

Walls—whether imaginary or concrete—continue to define twenty-first century life. Erasure was implicit in the sudden effacement of the Berlin Wall, not as a physical *presence*, but rather as an *obstruction* to circulation.[19] In fact, the German Democratic Republic itself stands as an *inventory of losses*, a country that "disappeared in the course of just a few weeks," vanishing into a "deafening silence," "suddenly wiped out."[20] But this, as Wendy Brown cogently argues, "permits us to consider whether and how contemporary walls work as symbols of collective and individual containment, as fortifications for entities whose real and imagined borders globalization places under *erasure*. [...] When does the fortress become a penitentiary?"[21] New technologies operate in a similar fashion, and truth has been distorted and instrumentalized, such that we now also speak of *firewalls* designed to monitor network traffic between the *inside* and *outside*. Access to information streams is often curtailed, and these mechanisms have been accompanied by new forms of surveillance, legislative and technological measures designed to regulate, limit and restrict access to content, control and monitor downloads and file-sharing, while introducing new forms of activism through leaks and anonymous postings. A new glossary of terms related to disinformation and misinformation now influences every facet of contemporary life. Likewise, new software allows for documents and information, records of experience, to be removed from hard drives with system erasers or data destruction software, thereby wiping away history.

In recent years, we have seen a resurgence of attention accorded to colonialism and postcolonial legacies. Discussions pertaining to historical

Figure 0.2 Claas Gutsche, *Erasure* (2013), Linocut print on Paper, 168 × 237 cm.

accountability and responsibility have emphasized the connection between actions in the past and unpredictable symptoms that manifest themselves in the present. These have been most evident in the public space with the toppling, spray-painting or beheading of statues that have glorified or honored racist figures, signs and symbols of a painful history.[22] The Orwellian dystopia warned of this polarization: "One could not learn history from architecture any more than one could learn it from books. Statues, inscriptions, memorial stones, the names of streets, anything that might throw light upon the past had been systematically altered."[23] But these are also prevalent in the multiple ways in which certain individuals and groups continue to bemoan the loss of a supposedly glorious past, refusing to relinquish their entitlement, clinging to the belief that they are deserving of everlasting privilege.

In an era of fake news and post-truth, or perhaps, given that the radical right is winning the discursive war about truth itself (and persists in exploiting polarizing rhetoric), it might make more sense to think in terms of post-*fact* rather than investing in truth or a *beyond* it. As we learned from the Ministry of Truth's slogan in George Orwell's novel *1984*, "Who controls the past controls the future: who controls the present controls the past."[24] All of these questions can be inscribed in the broader postcolonial context and accelerated proliferation of technocratic rhetoric deployed in response to migration, developments that deliberately seek to obfuscate the human element. As the sociologist Alessandro Dal Lago explained, a "tautology of fear" has been nourished according to which foreigners and others "constitute a threat," thereby compelling "the authorities to act" and implement a corresponding security apparatus that comprises camps and detention facilities.[25] These are incarnations of the bottles I alluded to, now accoutered in barbed wire, built for the clandestine, undocumented and illegals captured at sea and elsewhere. Having survived perilous ocean crossings in the guise of "a sort of Berlin wall across the Mediterranean and into the Atlantic"[26]—circumscribed in Hakim Abderrezak's neologism "seametery"[27]—migrants now find themselves submerged in a sea of acronyms, abbreviations, decrees, treaties, directives, declarations, policies, strategies and regulations, a lexical inventory structured according to exclusionary concepts and principles which French lawyer Claire Rodier has called "the business of xenophobia."[28] European countries have adopted migration management schemes that outsource the processing of asylum claims to third countries outside of Europe. Likewise, the United Kingdom, having successfully lifted the drawbridge to "Brexit Britain" and unleashed a variety of supportive slogans—*Take Back Control!* and *Stop the Boats!*—sought to implement equally unconscionable measures by sponsoring deportation flights to Rwanda, a destination thousands of miles away that the asylum seekers targeted *did not* leave and have *never* called home.

The mindset that enables the planning and enacting of such operations has deep roots in colonialism. The erosion of democratic institutions and principles, growing mistrust of journalists and influence of illiberal populists determined to restrict media freedom, weaken constitutional and juridical standards, subvert elections, disenfranchise voters and encourage voter apathy, all of which have been intensified by disinformation. This has coincided with increasing evidence of migrant-blaming and recourse to dehumanizing statistics. These archipelagoes of the mind are prevalent in Fortress Europe, now "surrounded by a moat that acts as a safeguard against the unwelcome Other,"[29] a mainland that conveniently forgets that the European Union includes departments, regions, collectivities and lands in the Caribbean and the Americas, the Pacific, the Indian Ocean and Antarctica. They resemble the vacuumed glass bottles I so admired as a child, shelters for people who have withdrawn like mollusks into their protective shells, erecting barricades to shield themselves from imagined predators in an age-old dynamic of power. "Why is it," Jenny Erpenbeck asks, "that the opening of the border in 1989 was something wonderful, but today voices cry out for new and stronger borders?"[30]

During my aforementioned visit to the Humboldt Forum, I asked an official guide how the museum was handling claims for restitution. The answer was telling: "Such technical questions have become irrelevant since the boat is now permanently enclosed within the institution's walls." Thankfully, Aly Götz's book, *The Magnificent Boat*, has highlighted the deep irony of that response: "Because of its size, the Luf Boat had to be transported to the Humboldt Forum while the building was still unfinished. The vessel was hoisted through a gap that had been left in the shell of the building [...] Should the boat be taken back to Papua New Guinea in the future, the building's wall would have to be reopened. But this would hardly be an insurmountable obstacle. After all, the city of Berlin has fond memories of walls being opened."[31]

Given my disclosures relating to ships in bottles in the opening lines of this Prologue, readers will be able to imagine the sheer delight I experienced when I discovered Yinka Shonibare's installation, *Nelson's Ship in a Bottle*, initially perched in 2010 some 60 feet in the air on Trafalgar Square's fourth plinth (May 24, 2010 to January 30, 2012), overlooking the capital of the former British Empire, "one of a number of works in which Shonibare refers to specific seafaring vessels."[32] Today, the ship has found a home at the National Maritime Museum in Greenwich, and the visitors' guide indicates that "*Nelson's Ship in a Bottle* is a scaled-down replica of Nelson's flagship HMS Victory, on which the Admiral died during the Battle of Trafalgar on 21 October 1805. It has 80 cannons and 37 sails set, as on the day of battle. The richly patterned sails were inspired by Indonesian batik, mass-produced by Dutch traders and sold in West Africa."[33] Yinka Shonibare has himself described how "a ship in a bottle is an object of wonder. Adults and children are *intrigued* by its mystery," as indeed I was.[34]

All of these questions will be explored in the container that is *Climates of Migration*. These terms provide the organizational pillars, but the interplay between them is not meant to be understood in a literal fashion. This is not a book specifically about climate migrants, but rather, as Wole Soyinka stated in 2005 with reference to a lecture he delivered, "Climate of Fear," the conjunction of terms "is meant to trigger off those associate devices [...] so that *climate of fear, climate of terror*, will surface in the mind without much conscious effort," similarly to the title of Dipesh Chakrabarty's book *The Climate of History in a Planetary Age*.[35] My own title aims to achieve analogous objectives, and the plural "climates" allows for a consideration of the various ways in which the term is commonly deployed in a figurative non-literal sense in order to signify "atmosphere." Accordingly, it is attached to anxiety, change, disinformation, fear and violence. In many ways, therefore, *Climates of Migration* is a book about *narratives* and *storytelling* and how these conjointly operate over a longer history of colonial conquest, one that lingers in the afterlives of empire in debates on identity politics, nationalism, responsibility, restitution, climate, racial and social

Figure 0.3 Yinka Shonibare, *Nelson's Ship in a Bottle*, 2010, 280 × 250 × 500 cm. © National Maritime Museum, Greenwich, London. © Yinka Shonibare CBE. All Rights Reserved, DACS/ARS, NY 2025.

justice. "These aporias constitute a *colonial ecology*," as Malcom Ferdinand has shown, "maintaining the artificial separation between the material becoming of the planet and non-humans and the social and political future of human beings."[36]

The call for new disciplinary frontiers in order to address these questions has been heeded by a consequential number of artists and scholars, in conversation with, and as outgrowths of, the pathbreaking work produced by earlier generations working on environmental questions. For example, art historian Estelle Zhong Mengual has called for a complete reframing of the anthropocentric way of seeing the world, Achille Mbembe encourages us to embrace a "planetary consciousness," Malcom Ferdinand has outlined a decolonial "world ecology," Philippe Rahm advocated for a "climaticist" framework in architecture, Baptiste Morizot evoked a "crisis of sensibility" and Ursula Heise underscored that "the task of ecocriticism with a cosmopolitan perspective is to develop an understanding and critique of these mechanisms as they play themselves out in different cultural contexts so as to create a variety of ecological imaginations of the global."[37]

Climates of Migration privileges comparative *interdisciplinary* (migration studies, environmental humanities, eco-feminism, decolonial and postcolonial studies, nationalism), *transhistorical* (colonial, postcolonial, political and conceptual frontiers), *transnational* (Belgium, Cameroon, Congo, France, Germany, Italy, Ivory Coast, Mali, Martinique, Mauritius, Mayotte, Netherlands, Nigeria, Senegal, United Kingdom) and *multigenre* approaches (literature, media discourse, art, propaganda, visual culture, policymaking), and concludes with an analysis of the interaction between ecology and propaganda in the context of technological innovation. The comparative framework is helpful in expanding and improving the understanding of the particular characteristics of the different branches explored. Conclusions are applicable to other regions of the world given the overarching context in which the "colonial Anthropocene" and contemporary phenomena allow us to conceive of "planetary climate change and environmental destruction as a spatial and temporal structure with accelerating consequences, one that spans more than five centuries of colonial domination."[38] Indeed, as Amitav Ghosh has argued, "The Anthropocene has reversed the temporal order of modernity: those at the margins are now the first to experience the future that awaits all of us," and this therefore calls for recalibration.[39] In this regard, the voices of women artists, theorists, eco-feminists, decolonial feminists, scholars, filmmakers, activists, *artivists*, policymakers and writers are a crucial component of *Climates of Migration*.[40] As Sara de Wit has argued, "By comparing the ways in which the contemporary discourse on gender and climate change adaptation unfolds for the Global South with earlier gender and (environmental) development discourses, [...] vital lessons can be learned about the historical mis-representation, reproduction, and fixation of certain ideas about gender and the agentive possibilities it affords and forecloses."[41] These are not stand-alone issues but rather of relevance to the overall project and conclusions. Across chapters, these questions surface in discussions pertaining to the activities of international organizations and policymaking institutions such as the EU, UNHCR (the UN Refugee Agency), International Organization for Migration (IOM) and the United Nations International Panel on Climate Change, in assessing gender-based violence at the border and in the analysis of the interface with migration, racism and xenophobia. Environmental migration, like other types of migration, is a gendered process.

The physical environment in which species live, and the ecological context that pertains to the relationship between organisms and their environment, are increasingly important issues. Global warming and climate change are the result of the planetary *derangement* caused by the dismantling of sustainable practices and accompanying degradation of biodiversity. In *Climates of Migration*, I have endeavored to use the terms in the appropriate way as they pertain to the context under discussion. This relationality is contained in "world ecology," what Malcom Ferdinand designates as "the preservation of a world between humans and with non-humans,"[42] and foundational to

Baptiste Morizot's dynamic according to which it becomes possible to "recon-struct paths of sensibility to living beings in general."[43]

The prerequisite for this to occur entails a *perspectival shift*, one in which the recognition that "the background is no longer just a background" is essen-tial.[44] As Estelle Zhong Mengual insists, "It is a question of taking as subjects of privileged attention those who had until now been taken into account as simple elements in a given context or as a decor for human actions: non-humans, and in particular the living, conceived not as things, but as agents. And of focusing on the relationships between them and humans."[45] This means acknowledging that colonial conquest and domination were shaped by the misplaced belief in mankind's capacity to assume the Cartesian aspira-tion of being the *masters and possessors of nature*, a paradigm whereby, as Baptiste Morizot explains, "we consider living beings primarily as a backdrop, as a reserve of resources available for production, as a place of healing, or as a prop for emotional and symbolic projection. To be merely a backdrop and a prop for projection is to have lost one's own ontological consistency."[46]

The ensuing *scramble* for resources was motivated by the mistaken belief that these were bountiful and limitless, a catalyst for the insatiable desire "to subdue and dominate nature by means of technology and machines," itself an unsustainable logic.[47] Indeed, awareness of the limitations of planetary resources defines what French economist and historian Arnaud Orain has elaborated in terms of a "confiscated world," one in which a "finite capi-talism" operates as "a vast naval and territorial enterprise of monopoliza-tion of assets—land, mines, maritime zones, enslaved people, warehouses, submarine cables, satellites, digital data—carried out by nation-states and private companies in order to generate rentier income outside the com-petitive principle."[48] Intrinsic to these questions is of course the history of racialization, most notably in terms of the ways in which certain popula-tions were deemed inferior, constructs that have survived in what Amitav Ghosh defines as a stubborn "imperial optic."[49] This emphasis on the longer history of imbrication between European modernity and contemporary planetary circumstances was perfectly encapsulated in the words (included in one of the epigraphs) of Lesley Lokko, Ghanaian-Scottish architect and novelist, in reference to the "Laboratory of the Future" exhibit she curated at the 2024 Venice Biennale of Architecture: "The black body was Europe's first unit of energy."[50] In the exhibition, "decarbonization" was "entwined with decolonization," in what Oliver Wainwright judiciously described as "an intentionally difficult show that explores the toxic landscapes and social scars that riddle the continent's postcolonial lands."[51] These are different embodiments of the various interdependent ecosystems explored in *Climates of Migration*.

The disruption to the global ecosystem is thus multidimensional, and these components, elements and patterns serve to map out the investigation into the two pillars—*climate* and *migration*—in the individual chapters framed according to various ecological frameworks: colonial games, migrant ecologies, ecological relations, ecological frontiers in literature and ecology and propaganda. Together, they emphasize continuity and connectivity between chapters.

In Chapter 1, we begin by tracing the tentacular planetary reach of European colonial powers, during an era when overseas travel was rarely an option. Yet, Europeans were encouraged to travel through the imagination and accordingly stimulated by the immersive experiences offered at World's Fairs and Colonial Exhibitions. Sophisticated propagandist mechanisms promoted the benefits of having colonies and glorified processes of conquest and expansion that were aimed simultaneously at molding young minds and bolstering patriotic fervor. The conjunction between "nationalism-capitalism" was privileged, one that has been resuscitated today in the extractionist anti-environmental crusade launched by far-right leaders globally.[52] Certainly though, in the nineteenth century and thereafter, the lessons to be learned were manifold, concerning as they did a recognition of the importance to the economy *of*—and dependency *on*—colonies, while implanting a deep familiarity with goods and products. The expeditions were enabled by new technologies and findings in astronomy, mathematics and physics, while other innovations (including the radio, film, chromolithography and electronically operated presses) enhanced communication and dissemination and provided citizens with the associated ingredients that were adventure and danger. To this end, a number of board games were produced during this era, featuring various soft and hard commodities associated with each region of Empire and providing important insights as to how people interacted with material culture. We will explore these in order to assess how the precarious balance between chance and strategy capitalized upon the experiential realities of colonial assignments, and how the design of the games replicated in this regard the defining elements of the colonial enterprise, while also of course mobilizing support for the expansionist drive. As Roger Caillois recognized in his book *Man, Play and Games*, there are games in which one "is influenced by play" and "man can check the monotony, determinism, and brutality of nature. He learns to construct order, conceive economy, and establish equity."[53] This highlights the contradictions and ambiguities of Empire, while also emphasizing the *ecolonial* dimension, a term that encompasses the ecological impact and that is associated with empire-building and land expropriation.

Dipesh Chakrabarty reminds us that "the planet has a history" and that "the climate events of this era, then, are distillations of all of human history," according to Amitav Ghosh's instructive interpretation.[54] Colonial expansion was justified through what I have described as *colonial-washing* strategies framed by indoctrination and the imperatives of the civilizing mission. The scramble for resources disrupted indigenous knowledge systems by unmooring and untethering populations from the land and multispecies ecosystems.[55] The ecologies of the "nature-space" relationships came under attack, and colonialism was ultimately about "imposition as the silencing of local knowledges and *erasure* of the other. [...] All these endeavors relied on a narrative of emptiness, of nothingness," as Daniel Macmillen Voskoboynik has shown,[56] denigrating "those who invented neither powder nor compass," as Aimé Césaire so brilliantly described the undertaking.[57]

Agricultural and extraction practices—monocultural and substitution crops, for example—contributed to anthropogenic global warming. Communities were removed or driven off their lands, displaced and compelled to migrate elsewhere, and as Malcom Ferdinand has argued in *Decolonial Ecology: Thinking from the Caribbean World*, "it is the same body that experiences the degradation of the planet's ecosystems *and* global social inequalities and political discrimination."[58] The *terraforming*—"molding" of the "land"—Amitav Ghosh explains, yielded narratives that "draw heavily on the rhetoric and imagery of empire, environing space as a 'frontier' to be 'conquered' and 'colonized'."[59] Questions of mobility—imaginative and physical—were therefore central to the production and visualization of Empire, and today, border control mechanisms and defending sovereignty can be traced back to this era. These are the questions to which we will turn in Chapter 2.

French philosopher Bruno Latour made significant contributions to the field of environmental studies, drawing attention to the multifarious ways in which a renewed consciousness of the importance of collective action and political engagement were urgently needed in order to confront emerging crises. In one of his last published works, *Down to Earth: Politics in the New Climatic Regime*, he convincingly demonstrated the various ways in which climate change had bent the arc of politics in new directions: "We can understand nothing about the politics of the last fifty years if we do not put the question of climate change and its denial front and center."[60] The centerpiece resides in the eco-colonial and migration nexus. As Hein de Haas explains, "changes in the dominant geographical direction of global migration since the end of the Second World War" mean that "at least from a European perspective, immigration may *appear* to be at an all-time high."[61] This is precisely why "the migratory crisis [is] so difficult to conceptualize," as Bruno Latour has succinctly shown, because "it is the symptom, to more or less excruciating degrees, of an ordeal common to all: the ordeal of finding oneself deprived of land."[62] The response to shifting migration patterns has been overwhelmingly defined by fear-mongering and scapegoating which in turn have influenced the negative characterization of displaced subjects. In what follows, the discussion focuses on the extensive recourse that has been made to climate metaphors in order to amplify anti-immigration rhetoric—swamped, swarm, floods, storms, waves, inundations, tides, flows, hurricanes, tsunamis—collectively delineating the parameters of an invasion narrative that alleges cultural, political and social saturation and submersion. Conflating climate change with these metaphors suggests a seamless twinning with the *ills* of immigration, grafting a pernicious meaning on the process (migration) *and* the people concerned (migrants)—in other words, a "disaster nationalism" that "effortlessly joins the dots between environmental collapse, the rise of the far right."[63]

The immediate consequence of weaponizing migration in this manner is that "every surge in unsolicited border crossings is extrapolated into the future, creating the usual migration panic about impending migrant invasion."[64] In the associative context of climate change, this logic operates optimally since it coincides with a diagnosis of catastrophic global warming and long-term projected impact. These narratives of "catastrophe" associated with uncontrollable, menacing and threatening phenomena that disrupt and overwhelm societies, blaming "the most downtrodden," serve to legitimize borders, frontiers, ramparts and walls under the pretext of furthering nationalist and protectionist responses, and these representations can only be generative of nativistic rhetoric rather than shining a light on "the system responsible."[65]

Exploring the ways in which national and European identities have been shaped by colonialism will improve the understanding of these various developments and how both facets of the "immigration" question—migration and post-migration—continue to define the political landscape. This means being attentive to changing election patterns, to the influence of far-right and populist parties, EU policymaking ("Green Deal" and "New Pact on Migration and Asylum of the EU"), the management of migration "crises" and lingering disagreements and polemics pertaining to the categorization, definition and recognition of *climate migrants* and *climate refugees*. Indeed, one finds a perfect synchronicity with the future impact of climate change and "a widely shared belief that climate change will lead to mass migration."[66] *Climates of Migration* encourages an approach in which displacement is understood as a "cognate phenomenon" in order to emphasize, as Amitav Ghosh has done, that "climate change is but one aspect of a much broader planetary crisis" involving "climate change, mass dislocations, pollution, environmental degradation."[67]

Alarmist positions that appeal to emotions have nevertheless proven effective. These are bolstered by disinformation and misinformation, conspiracy theories (such as Great Replacement and "white genocide," prototypes of a misplaced fear of *erasure*) and the instrumentalization of data, together undermining coordinated solutions to global warming and downplaying climate change. These factors have been prevalent in France and Germany, most notably in the former where the National Front / National Rally have proven especially adept at exploiting the intersection between immigration / national identity and ecological issues through "patriotic ecology." This is an equational relationship between land, territory and identity, one in which the structural pillars are provided by a protectionist component that replicates colonial mindsets, augmented by persistent attacks on environmental policies which, like the conventions and treaties pertaining to international migration are presented as undermining national sovereignty. Analogous far-right positions have been increasingly mainstreamed, even normalized, influencing policymaking at the EU, developments echoed in Ursula von der Leyen's (President of the EU Commission) linkage between climate change and migrant boats in the Mediterranean. Chapter 2 addresses these entangled questions in a concerted manner, a context in which a disquieting narcissistic nationalism associated with governments, politicians and policymakers encourages disidentification and isolationism. This apparatus also erases personal narratives, stories in which the artists and writers to which we turn our attention in Chapter 3 endeavor to foster modes of empathy, measures that become all the more essential at a time when the prevailing framework has been aimed at suppression.

Building on the conclusions of Chapter 2, and reappraising the coexistence of insular and open thinking and complex and simplistic reasoning, the focus in Chapter 3 shifts toward an engagement with categories such as empathy, sympathy, affect and emotions, and considers how cultural productions enhance relationality rather than disidentification and detachment. Two strands intersect here. On the one hand, Estelle Zhong Mengual encourages us to reflect additionally on how we might "become sensitive to other forms of life,"[68] whereas Achille Mbembe reminds us that we coexist in an "earthly community," in which resides "the possibility of a different aesthetics, a different politics of inhabiting the Earth, of repairing and sharing the planet."[69] These models serve to highlight the real-life consequences of policymaking on individuals and groups, and how works of art and literature play a key role in challenging the logic of official decrees and policies by focusing on intentionality and perspective while also foregrounding the human experience and thereby reversing the rationale informing decision-making. Artistic and literary works are able to deploy a creative composition that can confront shifting political realities, mobilize consciousness and foster modes of identification and new *ecological relations*. And they have the capacity, as T. J.

Demos has shown, to present contrasting perspectives on the "dehumanizing abstractions that invite invisibility and ignorance, and worse, xenophobia and racism."[70]

The focus on literary responses continues in Chapter 4 through an in-depth analysis of an emerging corpus of works by African writers for whom transhistorical violence motivates political commitment based on scrutiny and witnessing, documenting, recording and calls for accountability. Historically, African literature has been a literature of contestation, and today, authors are increasingly engaging with environmental questions, culminating in what Cheryll Glotfelty has described as a "greening" of fiction.[71] The discussion therefore showcases the distinct ways in which African literatures have been transformed as a result of the reassessment of the long-standing consequences of environmental ecocide, thereby contributing to a renewal of writing and the delineation of an African Anthropocene. These conclusions are relevant to the genealogy of African literature in which the appropriation of land, exploitation and extraction are ubiquitous. The works considered thus establish connections between colonial-era land exploitation and contemporary agricultural practices, examine how extraction was leveraged, while situating these discussions in the broader context of climate change and linking environmental derangement with population displacement as a consequence of these actions.

Chapter 5 builds on various overarching strands explored throughout *Climates of Migration*, most prominently with a focus on new technologies of communication and extraction, but also in terms of the interplay between ecology and propaganda. Data collection is, invariably, a form of extraction, optimized by algorithms, yet one with a historical particularity located in the fact that the extraction practices also opportunistically target populations in the Global North. Answers are sought to a number of important questions: How has recourse to propaganda been used in order to further an anti-ecological agenda—denouncing warnings concerning global warming as *fake news* or promoting a lifestyle founded on the exponential use of industrial technologies—*and* how have pro-ecology positions centered on an unrelenting effort to prevent the systematic destruction of the environment and aimed at raising awareness and consciousness as well as encouraging behavior modification operated? These questions demand of us that we remain attentive moving forward to emerging phenomena such as "technocolonialism," in which, as Mirca Madianou has noted, "the tenacity of imperial formations and the often occluded legacies of colonial domination [...] technocolonialism highlights that refugees and other humanitarian subjects are disproportionately affected by the convergence of digital developments, capitalism, and colonial legacies."[72] The *climate* is one of uncertainty, raising questions about regulation and the boundaries of free speech, questions to which we will turn in the concluding Epilogue. As Jenny Odell has remarked, "Capitalism, colonialist thinking, loneliness, and an abusive stance toward the environment all coproduce one another."[73]

Climate denialists continue to obstruct and demotivate climate action through governmental, corporate or other entities, and disinformation plays a central role in this dynamic. There is a pattern of deliberate obstructionist actions and of conspiring to mislead the public in order to undermine efforts geared toward climate change policymaking through lobbying, public relations firms, supporting legislation, false advertising, lack of corporate accountability and transparency. How does one begin to counter disinformation, and what examples are there of effective strategies? And how does one convince policymakers to relinquish futile efforts aimed at distinguishing between economic migrants, asylum seekers, refugees, climate migrants and climate refugees, categories which the individuals and groups concerned rarely have the privilege to argue over in the face of desperation. Jenny Erpenbeck drew attention to these disjunctures, clarifying that "like all paragraphs of all laws, [this] serves not only to *include* certain particular 'cases', but also to *exclude* other cases."[74] Merely "looking in the rear-view mirror," as David Van Reybrouk has demonstrated, "will not suffice [while continuing to draw] on the available resources. [...] In persisting to colonize the Global South, a long ordeal of migration, discrimination and disintegration awaits us."[75]

Ultimately, disproportionate attention has been granted to repression rather than to identifying solutions and adopting sustainable measures pertaining to the environment and migration. Addressing planetary challenges begins with debunking various myths, challenging coordinated disinformation and misinformation campaigns and relinquishing narratives built around overwhelming outcomes. As David Theo Goldberg has pointed out, "It's not just that the rate of reproducibility is dangerously debilitating. It is now that the conditions of possibility for reproducibility themselves are being undermined. And those eroding conditions of possibility further exacerbate existing climatological conditions in ways destined to heighten the challenges."[76] Similarly, Hein de Haas has convincingly shown that "migration policies have often failed or been counterproductive because they are based on a series of false assumptions, or myths, about the nature, causes and impacts of migration" and because "politicians [...], interest groups and international organizations perpetuate a series of myths as part of *deliberate* strategies to distort the truth about migration. Such propaganda is part of active efforts to sow unjustified fear and misinformation."[77]

Instead, a revitalized planetary consciousness provides a path toward meaningful change, transitions premised on our ability to abandon a "belated eurocentrism," ramparts of the mind defined by a "relentless drive to separate, to erect walls, all kinds of walls and fortresses to transform roads into borders, identity into enclosure, freedom itself into private property."[78] Bottles can contain ships, but they cannot contain people. On these ships, the people are absent, their stories taken to the ocean bed from shipwrecks, drownings and destroyed vessels. The expression "Das Boot ist voll" (The Boat is Full) has been evoked once again in the context of the "ecological-nativist paradigm" to describe nation-states' migrant absorption capacity, tainted as it is with the treatment of Jewish refugees during World War II.[79] The hallmarks of the Mauritian-French writer Nathacha Appanah's writing are the expressive and poetic language, all the more paradoxical given the context, but also its poignancy: "As long as there are seas, as long as there is misery, as long as there are dominators and dominated, I have the impression that there will always be boats to transport those who dream of a better horizon."[80]

Chapter 1

ECOLONIAL GAMES

Between colonizer and colonized, there is room only for forced labor, intimidation, pressure, the police, taxation, theft, rape, compulsory crops, contempt, mistrust, arrogance, self-complacency, swinishness, brainless elites, degraded masses.

Aimé Césaire[1]

Climate change is global-scale violence, against places and species as well as against human beings. Once we call it by name, we can start having a real conversation about our priorities and values. Because the revolt against brutality begins with a revolt against the language that hides that brutality.

Rebecca Solnit[2]

The current ecological crisis, more than a crisis in human societies on the one hand, or in living beings on the other, is a crisis in our relations with living beings.

Baptiste Morizot[3]

The Earth is at man's entire disposal and available for him to do with it as he wishes and at his own discretion. Now, henceforth, it is a matter of imagining other ways of inhabiting, sharing, repairing, and ultimately of taking care of it.

Achille Mbembe[4]

Writing to his representative in London in 1876, King Leopold II of Belgium could hardly conceal his exuberance at the potential for enrichment offered by the abundant commodities and resources available in what would become his personal possession in the guise of the Congo Free State, a territorial configuration almost eighty times the size of the Kingdom of Belgium which he ruled from 1885 to 1908: "I do not want to miss a good chance of getting us a slice of this magnificent African cake."[5] A few years later, German Chancellor Otto von Bismarck, echoing his Belgian counterpart, announced the terms of the continental parceling at the conclusion of the proceedings at the *Kongokonferenz* (Berlin Conference) he had convened November 15, 1884 to

February 26, 1885, a partitioning enshrined in the General Act of the Berlin Conference on West Africa, of which Article 2 is indicative of the scope:

> All flags, without distinction of nationality, shall have free access to the whole of the coastline of the territories above enumerated, to the rivers there running into the sea, to all the waters of the Congo and its affluents, including the lakes, and to all the ports situated on the banks of these waters, as well as to all canals which may in the future be constructed with intent to unite the watercourses or lakes within the entire area of the territories.[6]

Although these geopolitical realignments further consolidated long-lasting relations between the African and European continents, the asymmetrical nature and the contemporary legacies of these arrangements necessitate closer scrutiny. The absence of African representatives at the negotiating table serves as a glaring reminder that the decisions reached effectively erased and marginalized stakeholders. Those present were consumed by their rapacious appetite for the spoils on offer, and the arrangements agreed upon translated into an escalation and intensification of accumulative, exploitative and extractive practices on the African continent.

Colonialism is of course defined by uprooting, displacement and subjugation strategies, outgrowths of measures deployed by the ruling classes in Europe who had previously disrupted the sustainable modes of the peasantry. Eric Holt-Giménez has explained how these were decisions with transnational ramifications:

> Slavery, indentured servitude, and genocidal dispossession laid the foundation for the emergence of capitalist agriculture, a new form of production and consumption that emerged in the transition from agrarian to industrial society. Beginning with the enclosure of the commons in Britain and the forced migration of the peasantry to urban factories and the colonies, from as early as the sixteenth century, the agrarian transition has always entailed a violent restructuring of environment, production, and society.[7]

Private ownership regulations gradually transformed the organization of communal existence during the eighteenth and nineteenth centuries, systems that converted existing labor practices in order to maximize the exploitation of *bodies* and the *land*. These resulted in long-term damage to the ecosystems they had acquired, conquered and occupied. Modernization and urbanization of course further exacerbated the impact, and economic market demand and supply paradigms (promoted at colonial exhibitions and world fairs) were embraced. These served to justify the shift to plantations and mono-cultural cash crops, land was cleared to these ends by adapting it to models that created short-term optimal conditions for profit margins while simulta-neously satisfying the demand for commodities in European markets. Citing Richard Drayton's description of empire as "a campaign to extend an eco-logical regime," Daniel Macmillen Voskoboynik describes how "the fiction of negation and discovery, was used to justify the clearance of native habitats and inhabitants"[8] and how "the model was simple: exhaust the land, aban-don it and clear new land."[9] The scramble *for*, and pillaging *of*, resources, were a component of a broader global expansionist drive which was to have a dramatic impact on the environment, disrupting physical and species habi-tats and ecosystems, but also the broader ecological context and interaction between organisms.

The quantifiable symptoms of these actions were climate change, transge-netic bioengineering, desertification, deforestation, dispossession, soil erosion, pollution, chemical contamination, the excessive release of greenhouse gases into the atmosphere, ocean acidification, sea level rise and global warming, attributable to exploitative rather than environmental management and sus-tainable practices attentive to indigenous knowledge systems. The inventory of terms that describe the resulting *planetary derangement* include depletion, deterioration, devastation and impoverishment, while also focusing our atten-tion on *planetary displacement* as emerging migratory phenomena relating to "climate displacement," "environmental migrants," "climate migrants" and "climate refugees," are delineating the contours of twenty-first century con-cerns and challenges.[10] The goal of this chapter is therefore to examine the propagandist narratives that provided the cultural, economic, political, reli-gious and social scaffolding upon which colonial enlargement was conceptu-alized and justified. This will make it possible to assess how these mechanisms ultimately heightened the vulnerability of the environmental and ecological framework.

Ecolonial Terraforming

The term *ecolonial* is proposed here as a way of circumscribing the explicit conjunction between the *ecological* and the *colonial*. It offers, as Jessica L. Horton has suggested, a configuration that enables the examination as to how "the containment of Indigenous people compounds the damage wrought by extractive industries by limiting their capacity to adapt with the land"[11] and accurately conveys the insatiable appetite for resources and disregard for human life. The implementation of mechanisms aimed at distinguish-ing between the anthropos and the earth, while also seeking to domesticate both, "locates causality," as T. J. Demos reminds us, "in the long unfolding of capitalist reason," defining the parameters of extractive capitalism as they are erected on the promise of exponential growth and availability of earth's finite resources.[12] The scheme was supported by "a shearing of subjects from geography," as Kathryn Yusoff underscores, "and the reinstantiation of those subjects into a category of geology that recoded them as property, whereby extraordinary possibilities in relation to the earth were wiped."[13] As such, it constitutes an outgrowth of the foundational and motivational impulses of the slave trade, delimiting as Achille Mbembe has argued, "the world of raw extraction. Racial capitalism is the equivalent of a giant necropolis of capturing and gathering, selling and buying. It is the world of raw extraction."[14]

Climate change remains a source of polarization, even though there is consensus in the scientific community pertaining to human responsibility for global warming. In assessing anthropogenic climate change, some scholars have called for additional nuance when it comes to attributing responsibility for human influences—the result of human actions as "geological agents"[15] which scientists have identified. Among the most prominent is T. J. Demos who, in his book *Against the Anthropocene: Visual Culture and the Environment Today*, has been reluctant to privilege the term "Anthropocene"—widely used to designate the historical time period during which the dominant actions on climate and the environment are ascribed to human activity—but this is not because the term somehow fails to "register[s] the geological impact of colonial and industrial activities on Earth's natural systems," but rather because it inaccurately attributes responsibility to humans as a generalized category, rather than specifically targeting the organized perpetrators, and to whom "culpability for ecocide is assigned."[16] Amitav Ghosh offers a concrete example of the total colonial disregard for the human and the nonhuman: "The landscapes of [the Indonesian Banda] islands were places of dwelling that were merged with human life in ways that were imaginative as well as material [but for the Dutch East India Company] had no meaning except as resources that could be harnessed to generate profit."[17]

Remoteness was instrumentalized and identification with overseas colonies fostered. Additionally, the relationship with nature meticulously conceptualized, together forming the impetus for the exploration, conquest and exploitation that left ineffaceable traces in terms of the degradation, damage, destabilization, destruction and disruption of ecosystems. This combination of *ecolonial* actions defined the entangled histories between regions, the result of exchanges and interactions, and certainly, as Lynn White's work has shown us, "scientific knowledge means technological power over nature [and] its acceptance as a normal pattern of action may mark the greatest event in human history since the invention of agriculture, and perhaps in nonhuman terrestrial history as well."[18] In its various incarnations and specificities, as Jan Nederveen Pieterse reminds us, European colonialism comprised a vast geographic space whose coordinates spanned the globe, with "control extended over 84 per cent of the earth's surface."[19]

Migration *and* environmental questions are inextricably linked. Empire-building consisted of an inventory of mechanisms that transformed the dynamics between the human and nonhuman world. Foremost among these were the complex propagandist strategies to which European powers had, to varying degrees, recourse. These endeavored to bridge the distance between the *here* and the *elsewhere* by instilling curiosity and nourishing patriotic fervor—instruments shaped by a "colonial culture"—a concept developed by historians Nicolas Bancel, Pascal Blanchard and Sandrine Lemaire in order to address the multidimensional mechanisms that permitted the "creation of a cultural environment, flooded with representations of the colonies, [and that] had a massive impact on the collective unconscious within the metropole, and its perception of the colonies."[20] These intermedial instruments—radio, print, visual, musical, film, performance—targeted adults and children. Additionally, commodities, ephemera, games and toys contributed to the formation of an understanding of overseas territories, privileging selective narratives and worldviews. In turn, these imparted information pertaining to biodiversity and resources while simultaneously encouraging conscious bias toward racialized indigenous populations and furbishing tools of oppression.[21] For example, in picture postcards as late as the 1950s, one could find a "standard composition" featuring "orderly plantations carved out of the wilderness and natives at work under European supervision. The key image was that of natural abundance harnessed through European discipline and control," in which the asymmetrical relationship between humans and nature was strikingly evident.[22] These mechanisms were especially operational in the board games to which we will turn our attention later in this chapter.

Masters and Possessors of Nature

French mathematician and philosopher René Descartes' influential *Discourse on the Method of Rightly Conducting One's Reason and of Seeking Truth in the Sciences*, published in 1637, succinctly summarized the aspirational drive for conquest and domination by accentuating mankind's capacity to assume the status as "masters and possessors of nature," fortified by monotheistic traditions that contributed to delinking man from nature. These were more specifically illustrative of what Estelle Zhong Mengual elucidates as "the very particular way in which moderns conceived of the living and non-living world, from the sixteenth century onwards, as separate from the human world, thought of as inanimate matter, governed exclusively by quantifiable causes, devoid of meanings (other than mathematical), and identified with an exteriority, composed of objects and not subjects."[23] This anthropocentric perspective was buttressed by an unwavering conviction that the planetary ecosystem, as Mohamad Amer Meziane contends, resided in "a belief in the existence of *this world* as the only real one: the certainty that it is here below, on the earth, that salvation can be realized, through *unlimited* enjoyment ensured by a continuous growth in riches" thanks to the colonization of "subterranean worlds."[24] The transition toward a reliance on fossil fuels enabled more ambitious expansionist efforts and enhanced the extractive potential. These proved to be the catalyst for a relentless process that exacerbated environmental degradation, loss of biodiversity, and that therefore compromised the global ecosystem and established the genealogical roots of the contemporary climate crisis.

A significant component of nation-building entails establishing, contesting and defending national territories, and subsequently fine-tuning these mechanisms through the implementation of control and surveillance strategies designed to monitor and safeguard these frontier spaces. Colonial territories were no different in this regard, and cartographic instruments contributed to varying degrees to the process of compartmentalizing existing communities according to boundaries that continue to be contested. Certainly, the Berlin Conference of 1884–1885 reaffirmed the centrality of Europe and contours of the African continent, but more recent border control policies in the EU and the militarization of external borders aimed at safeguarding Fortress Europe have interrupted planetary circulation within continents *and* between regions.

The underlying forces—curiosity, passion for adventure, greed and competition—furnished the drive for imperialistic enterprises whose realization became increasingly conceivable, feasible and even attainable as a result of these momentous technological advances. Systematic remappings of the world gradually took place, achieved by stimulating interest for distant lands, thereby enlisting support for the implementation of policy and motivating individuals to contribute to these undertakings. Imperceptible, subtle steps were taken that gradually demarcated available and underexploited lands, opportunistic rhetorical devices that embraced prevailing characterizations of incompetent indigenous populations. These narratives synchronized ignorance of indigenous knowledge systems with racial hierarchies in order to further capitalist ambitions and gains. Colonialism indiscriminately harmed the life forms it came into contact with, prioritizing commerce as the gateway to civilization. As Baptiste Morizot puts it, "Once living beings were debased ontologically, that is to say considered as endowed with a second-order existence, of lesser value and lesser consistency, and thus transformed into 'things', human beings discovered that they alone truly existed in the universe" and "the hidden violence of Western naturalism, which in fact aims to justify exploiting all of nature as a raw material lying to hand for our project of civilization—it means treating others as matter ruled by biological laws, refusing to see their geopolitical promptings, their vital alliances."[25] This perspective on nature is of course based on a false premise; it is tantamount to *a lie*, a contradiction in terms, an inoperative duality informed by a "central paradox," as William Cronon has reasoned, because it "is not a pristine sanctuary where the last remnant of an untouched, endangered, but still transcendent nature can for at least a little while longer be encountered without the contaminating taint of civilization. Instead, it is a product of that civilization, and could hardly be contaminated by the very stuff of which it is made."[26]

Decolonial Perspectives and Strategic Convergence

In *Decolonial Ecology: Thinking from the Caribbean World*, Malcom Ferdinand describes the "double fracture" which is "revealed through the technical, scientific, and economic modernizations of the mastery of nature, the effects of which can be measured by the extent of the Earth's pollution, the loss of biodiversity, global warming, and the associated persistence of gender inequality, social misery, and the 'disposable lives' that are thereby created."[27] In this analysis, the term "persistence" is key, since contemporary discussions of migration and environmental issues have not always accounted for longer transhistorical models whereby "the logic of land use remained the same: *intensive exploitation of the land as a resource serving the ends of commercial export and the financial enrichment of a few overseas shareholders and local colonists*" and "a bridge of justice is built across the environmental and colonial fracture, making non-humans count politically and legally as well as seeking justice for the colonized and the enslaved."[28] The term *ecolonial* is thus helpful in expanding the kind of intersectionality foregrounded in decolonial works and works on black ecologies.

Reiterating the degree to which a shared experience of the damaged earth—one that integrates an indigenous knowledge or traditional ecological knowledge (TEK) perspective—is a prerequisite step.[29] These frameworks are important, especially given the tendency and risk of romanticizing indigenous knowledge systems. Certainly, the "dystopian" universe evoked by Kyle Powys Whyte has emerged as an incontrovertible concern.[30] One dimension that is crucial to emphasize concerns the multidimensional ways in which ignorance of indigenous knowledge functioned. On the one hand, as Harriet Mercer and Thomas Simpson have indicated, "the omission or devaluation of climate-related Indigenous and local knowledge by scientific elites was at times deliberate and part of wider programs of conquest and control,"[31] whereas on the other, as Baptiste Morizot reiterates, the colonial presence was assembled in such a way as to facilitate actions aimed at "suppressing, controlling and channeling the wild animals, insects, rains and floods," namely the assumption of positions diametrically opposed to those occupied by "natives" that fostered "an attention to the interweaving of other life forms."[32]

Exporting *Grandeur* and Postcolonial Legacies

In France, "colonialism was seen as a mark of civilization, of national grandeur, of science and progress," and according to the prevailing narrative, "the nation, which emerged out of the French Revolution, brought *liberty* and not *oppression, development* and not *exploitation,* to the peoples it was 'liberating.'"[33] However, the dual task of convincing the French population of the merits of overseas expansion *and* enlisting their support for the enterprise so as to transform France "from an exclusively hexagonal society (with the exception of a few colonial territories inherited from the Ancien Regime) to an imperial culture" was a complex one, and considerable propagandist resources were devoted to this objective.[34] School-age children were targeted, coupling *pedagogy* with *propaganda*, and thereby effectively shaping mentalities and mapping consciousness. The molding of young minds and indoctrination project were inseparable from broader nationalist imperatives, instilling a fervent sense of patriotic duty, such that "this blend of pedagogy, patriotism, and nationalism helped to cement the idea that colonialism was consubstantial to the Republic."[35] But the lessons to be learned were manifold, concerning as they did a recognition of the importance to the French economy *of*—and dependency *on*—colonies, implanting a deep familiarity with products and goods, while also stimulating the associated ingredient of adventure and danger. These elements helped marshal the ensuing scramble for Africa, a veritable political game at which only the most adept, creative, inspired, motivated and strategic at outsmarting and outmanoeuvring the competition stood to benefit exponentially from various deals, negotiations and treaties. As we shall see, analogous frameworks were deployed in the design of board games, where players competed with opponents and shared common and specific goals and outcomes, namely victory and defeat along with the accompanying territorial and resource accumulation. In many ways, the precarious balance between chance and strategy, a fragile arrangement at best, capitalized upon the realities of colonial assignments. Game design sought to replicate the defining elements of the colonial enterprise, namely entertainment, unpredictability and intrigue. As Elizabeth Heath has shown, "These structures of thought, first formed through fantastical imaginings and playacting, served as the cognitive foundation of an imperial identity with roles for metropolitan men and women and their colonial doubles."[36]

The first French Minister of the Colonies (this ministry has been folded in to the responsibilities of the Ministry of the Interior and Overseas) was appointed in March 1894—offering a rather homogenous and hypermasculinized view of the world, one that lacked in diversity and was shaped by monolithic ideas. The fact that the 65 ministers appointed to this role were all male emphasizes this point. The Agence Générale des colonies (General Bureau of the Colonies), established by decree on June 29, 1919, was in charge of overseeing propaganda in the aftermath of World War I and was "omnipresent in all facets of French society, which helps to explain why the colonial fiction was possible."[37] It functioned as a "seduction machine" designed to stimulate "national interest in support of imperialism" and effectively "nationalize the colonial idea," with the consequence that

> from the spectacular but ephemeral expositions to the insertion of the colonial ideology into daily life through textbooks, food, games, and calendars, the empire was everywhere. At school, at home, or at work, the French were acquiring a specific national and colonial culture. This was in part thanks to propaganda's manifold qualities. The best tactics were employed to convince the middle and working classes that the nation was not limited to metropolitan France—the Hexagon—but included 'Greater France'.[38]

Operating as a public information tool that served to "justify its endeavors in the colonies," itself bolstered by a "discourse of imperial greatness,"[39] the Agence Générale des Colonies simultaneously educated the general public and school-age children through resources aimed at curricular enhancement.

Analogous mechanisms characterized the colonial policies of other European nations. The Deutsches Historisches Museum (German Historical Museum) in Berlin curated the *German Colonialism: Fragments Past and Present* exhibition on this history (October 14, 2016 to May 14, 2017). As Ulrike Kretzschmar (Director of the Exhibitions Department) wrote in the exhibition catalog, "An exhibition cannot claim to be exhaustive [but] will provide a wealth of inspiration for a topical critical debate about the colonial past and will raise public awareness about its long-term consequences."[40] The exhibition's wall panels underscored the objective of fostering wider public debate while also addressing, in unambiguous terms, how colonialism was elaborated and justified: "Colonialism as a form of violent foreign rule was legitimized by a racist ideology of European superiority" and "By endeavoring to set and implement a clear line between the rulers and the ruled, the colonizers continually reasserted their own identity." These efforts are to be inscribed in a much broader European and global context focusing on colonialism, engagement with the past, postcolonial legacies and structural and systemic racism. In Amsterdam, for example, the Tropenmuseum launched a new permanent exhibition on Dutch Colonialism in 2022, "Our Colonial Inheritance."[41] This represents a commitment by the museum to *retell* the history of the Dutch West Indies Company (founded in 1621), revisit the role of the Transatlantic trade and the multiple legacies of these engagements, while also providing a space devoted to the perspectives of populations from now sovereign nations such as Indonesia and Suriname in order to remind visitors of "the resilience, creativity and opposition of colonized countries and people."[42] Invariably, this has entailed addressing the impact of these activities and important questions relating to provenance:

> A large part of our collections was acquired during the colonial period. This was a period characterized by grossly unequal power relations and violence. As a consequence, some of the objects we care for, including objects in this exhibition, may have been obtained through looting or in other dubious and unjust situations. The museum is actively doing research to clarify the provenance of its collections.

The vocabulary has been carefully measured and the objective is *truth-telling* (examples include "grossly unequal power relations," "violence") and establishing a narrative that is *fact-based* ("looting," dubious," "unjust") and that moves away from the misinformation associated with the myth-making that was used to justify expansion. In another panel devoted to "Exploration," one reads that:

> From the fifteenth century onwards, developments in shipbuilding and navigation intensified contact between different cultures, now possible across great distances. The first contact between societies was seldom peaceful: European merchants fought their way into Asia and coerced local traders into unfavorable agreements. Everyday violence, extortion and racism were all a result of the European urge for expansion. The Dutch Republic was deeply complicit in this. Shipping whetted an insatiable appetite for products from afar, influenced the arts, and increased knowledge of cultures and customs that were considered both alien and exotic.

Once again, there is no ambiguity in the referential terms: "seldom peaceful," "fought their way," "coerced," "unfavorable agreements," "everyday violence," "extortion" and "racism." Finally, the economic and environmental legacy is addressed in "Wealth from Overseas" and acknowledgment that impacted populations continued to draw on the Indigenous knowledges denigrated or ignored by colonial powers:

> Producing these commodities came at the price of environmental destruction. Mountains were excavated for minerals, forests felled, wetlands drained to make way for plantations. Our addiction to these products continues. We can trace our current environmental crisis back to such global patterns of large-scale extraction and exploitation of natural resources. Even within the conditions of the colonial system, some people continued to engage with the natural world in less exploitative ways. Maroons across the Caribbean used African and Indigenous knowledges to sustainably manage and care for their environment, including their small agricultural plots.

In an earlier publication, *The Netherlands East Indies at the Tropenmuseum: A Colonial History*, director Lejo Schenk wrote that "a museum collection serves as a gateway to an endless number of stories."[43] However, since the publication of this work, the impetus for decolonizing museums has transformed the process of evaluating collections and reflecting on the ways in which *narratives* and *stories* are told. As the editors Wendeline Flores and Wayne Modest have emphasized, "The title, *Our Colonial Inheritance*, was carefully crafted. By using the possessive pronoun 'Our', together with 'Colonial', we wanted to push beyond what for some people in the Netherlands, but also across Europe and North America, was a normalized rhetoric of denial, a distancing of the slavery and colonial pasts [...]. In this account, slavery and colonialism was not simply a temporal other, a past beyond any possible memory, but it was something that happened in a somewhere else, an over there."[44] The new exhibition "is curated as part of the museum's ongoing critical reflection on, and intervention in, the growing national and international discussions on European colonialism, its histories and afterlives in the present" while reminding readers that the museum was established in 1864 as the Colonial Mission to "support the Dutch colonial project" and accordingly "serve as an *etalage* for the display of products of a colonialism practiced overseas; an important part of its role being to educate a visiting Dutch public into the ideological underpinnings of colonialism."[45] These strategic choices and initiatives are the product of decolonial and postcolonial alliances, examples of how institutions can be proactive in embedding historical reassessment and charting a roadmap through meaningful commitment to change and re-orientation, yielding a more *accurate* historical account—one that foregrounds *accountability* and *acknowledgment* of structural inequality.[46]

Heading south-west to the French capital and to the 12th arrondisssement, one finds the home of the Palais de la Porte Dorée (designed by the architect Albert Laprade and initially known as the Musée permanent des colonies), constructed for the 1931 Colonial Exhibition. Subsequently transformed into the Musée de la France d'Outre-mer, then the Musée des Arts africains et océaniens, it was later repurposed as the Musée national des arts d'Afrique et d'Océanie prior to its rebranding as the Musée national de l'histoire de l'immigration (National Museum of the History of Immigration) in 2007. Though partially refurbished on the inside, the building is known for its remarkable bas-relief façade by French sculptor Alfred Auguste Janniot. As the museum website explains, it "[features] a series of allegories, in the midst of abundant fauna and lush flora, this 'stone tapestry' measuring 1,130 m^2 exalts colonial wealth," albeit one from which "the figure of the colonist is absent from this ideal portrayal. The exotic imagery, presenting an enthralling vision of a peaceful world seen as a land of celebration, is free of violence: there is no reference to forced labor and abuse. This is an illustration of the theme of abundant lands, where man lives in harmony with a lush and generous nature."[47] Indeed, one finds "the entanglement of the seemingly contradictory themes of a wild and exuberant nature contrasted with an explored and valued continent," as Dominique Taffin has shown, that "dialectically establishes the image of an Africa destined to be tamed by the European genius."[48] A plaque outside the museum offers some insight as to that history:

> Portrayed as Abundance, France sits on the throne at the top of the staircase. Colonial riches are spread at her feet, from Africa on her left and Asia on the right. For educational purposes, various inscriptions link each territory to the goods and raw materials it produces [...] The sculptural style of the 1920s and 1930s was used for imperial propaganda: muscular and imposing figures, wild and lush nature, ethnic faces that were recognizable and simplified according to the ethnographic codes of the time.

Furthermore, as Maureen Murphy has argued, "The bas-reliefs, ordered according to geography, illustrate the benefit of the colonies to the metropole," and in turn the frescoes themselves found inside the building "France's influence in the world."[49] Linking as it does labor with environmental exploitation, the sculpture conceals and erases the contributions of colonized subjects and migrant workers to France's wealth overseas *and* domestically. This has survived as a transcolonial dynamic, one that continues to shape postcolonial debates on immigration and national identity. In many ways, the building itself, and in particular the elaborate façade, stand as a precursor to the kind of visual interplay evidenced in the board game designs we will examine.

Elsewhere, in Germany once again, the colonial question has informed institutional and public debates, including important activist measures aimed at connecting this history with contemporary racial legacies.[50] Arguably, though, the most public debate on these issues took place in the context of the Humboldt Forum, inaugurated in 2021, and home to the Ethnologisches Museum (Ethnological Museum). German historian Götz Aly has admonished attempts by the authorities and curators of this past, notably in his scathing critique of the Humboldt Forum's inconsistent actions and handling of questions related to provenance. Firstly, for him, the transcolonial framework could not be ignored, given that the "men who ran the German museums [during the colonial era] knew all too well about the atrocities that were going on. [...] That was the reason behind the urgency with which they went about their tasks. If their museums were to be filled with ethnographic objects, it would have to be soon, before everything was destroyed," and secondly, "the curators of the current ethnological attraction in Berlin display ignorance toward Humboldt's methodology of observation, collection, and investigation of deeper contexts. The exhibition in the Humboldt Forum has nothing to say philosophically, scientifically, or historically."[51] Similar controversies informed the inauguration of the Quai Branly Museum in Paris in 2006, when President Jacques Chirac (a museum now renamed after him as Musée du quai Branly—Jacques Chirac) claimed that "France wished to pay homage to peoples to whom, throughout the ages, history has all too often done violence. Peoples injured and exterminated by the greed and brutality of conquerors. Peoples humiliated and scorned, denied even their own history. Peoples still now often marginalized, weakened, endangered by the inexorable advance of modernity. Peoples who want their dignity restored."[52] In 2018, newly elected President Emmanuel Macron commissioned a landmark report—*The Restitution of African Cultural Heritage: Toward a New Relational Ethics*—that was prepared by Senegalese scholar and writer Felwine Sarr and French art historian Bénédicte Savoy on the restitution of objects that were "pillaged," "plundered," "stolen" and "illicitly exported" during the colonial era.[53] This shifting memorial landscape is indicative of the political stakes of a history that is nowhere near being foreclosed.

A History of Subjugation and Climate Change

In *The Nutmeg's Curse: Parables for a Planet in Crisis*, Indian writer Amitav Ghosh establishes a connection between colonialism and the dynamics of climate change and environmental planetary crisis through an analysis of the Dutch East India Company's military conquest of the Indonesian Banda Islands in the early seventeenth century.[54] As he powerfully demonstrates, "Colonization was thus not merely a process of establishing dominion over human beings; it was also a process of subjugating, and reducing to muteness, an entire universe of beings that was once thought of as having agency, powers of communication, and the ability to make meaning—animals, trees, volcanoes, nutmegs."[55] One chapter in particular, "The Brutes" (inspired by Sven Lindquist's 2007 book *"Exterminate All the Brutes": One Man's Odyssey into the Heart of Darkness and the Origins of European Genocide*), serves to underline how "the idea of extermination was central, not marginal, to Western elite culture" and that maps therefore often serve as a record of cultural erasure, "exterminatory violence," a historical misremembering that has often resulted in the perpetrators being "commemorated in roads, parks, poems, and history books," in other words culminating in the privileging of certain narratives over others.[56]

As we will be able to gauge from the analysis of the logic informing the board games, "narratives are grounded not in abstractions, but in the ground itself, in the soil of particular places."[57] Compelling accounts of this transformation are to be found in Olivette Otele's book *African Europeans: An Untold History*, in which she has delineated how

> the mass demonstrations led by Black Lives Matter and consequent debates about racism have highlighted both the need to expand knowledge about the histories of people of African descent and the urgency with which we must revise the teaching of colonial history in the Global North. *African Europeans* is a response to these needs. It aims to provide multiple histories as a starting point to learn about the past and to dismantle racial oppression in the present.[58]

Colonialism is defined by the drive for territorial conquest and land expropriation, and anti-colonialism and the struggle for independence is therefore concerned with reclaiming territorial autonomy. Empire-building was premised on profit-making, justified by the burgeoning European need for "indispensable raw material for industrialization"[59] and an entrenched belief that what they saw before them was "an untended garden open to the enterprises of Man."[60] Given that transition from slave labor to indentured labor "did not put an end to commerce in Africa," a point made by Catherine Coquery-Vidrovitch, "imports of raw materials essential to the metropolitan French industry only intensified exchange, which increased ten-fold during the first half of the nineteenth century," and the import-export monopolies were controlled by the Compagnie Française d'Afrique Occidentale (CFAO) and the Société Commerciale de l'Ouest Africain (SCOA), whereby "the French Empire [...] was considered more as a reserve of resources, to be exploited by France as needed," at a time when "French society was consuming all things colonial," including cotton, coal, rubber, vegetable oil, peanuts, rum, sugar, chocolate, ivory, coffee.[61] The colonial project was about resource acquisition and ever-expanding distribution networks, including *between* colonies and protectorates, exponential growth patterns across a map of the world that resembled bleeding ink dispersing and spreading over the surface on which it has been accidentally spilled.

This was a process supported by labor mobility on a global scale, sourcing workers in China, India and the African continent, among other regions, so as to mitigate various labor shortages that resulted from population displacement measures, exterminations or massacres, practices that remain evident in state-sponsored (and often selective) immigration mechanisms. Migration and environmental degradation therefore share a long-standing symbiotic link. These are the entangled histories about which Nathacha Appanah has written in *La mémoire délavée* (Faded memory). In this memoir of her grandparents' migration to the island of Mauritius, referencing indentured labor and the coolie trade (known in French as *l'engagisme*), we find a story of a "global transhumance, an organized and multidimensional migration dictated by Europe's colonial expansion but also by the endemic poverty in the countries involved. [...] Having left their home countries and after weeks at sea, these new workers are committed to working the land after these crossings."[62] As early as the sixteenth century,

> navigators, geographers and scholars from all over Europe were in quest of Eden. They were convinced that by sailing the oceans they would end up finding it, somewhere on this earth. Not surprisingly, their quest met with failure. It did, however, enable them to discover islands with luxuriant vegetation, to experience nature as never seen before, in the Canaries, the Mascarene Islands, St Helena, Mauritius. These paradise islands would be their Eden and they set about colonizing them over the course of the seventeenth century.[63]

Together, these factors rendered exploration, conquest, land dispossession and dehumanization inseparable, dismissing in favor of the Occidental gaze a range of indigenous knowledge systems and cosmogonies and yielding the kinds of conditions Estelle Zhong Mengual has described that were "favorable to the relationships of domination and exploitation of the living world."[64] These exchanges were monitored through the methodical management of "exchanges between humans and non-humans" and "as its main discursive scene," as Malcom Ferdinand outlines, "the Plantationocene exposes the singular relationships that a minority on the Earth used to impose one type of worldly arrangement with non-humans: one of compulsive and standardized exploitation. It highlights the disturbances of biodiversity and ecological degradation caused by the plantations."[65] The geometric coordinates were relatively straightforward: acquisition, appropriation, investment, exploitation, extraction, consumption, returns and profit. The outcome of these orchestrated agricultural and extractive practices that included deforestation, disruptive agricultural monoculture, the privileging of substitution crops, and misguided land management, were therefore all the more *predictable*. This was a system promoted at world fairs, one that compromised soil fertility and exacerbated pollution-based activities.[66]

As such, the colonial *mission to civilize* launched by the European powers was also framed as an ecological mission since the dismissal of indigenous knowledge systems as archaic was implicit to the rationale informing racial hierarchies.[67] The words of French statesman Jules Ferry before the Chamber of Deputies on July 29, 1885, provide the scaffolding and foundation of this racialized ecology: "I repeat, that the superior races have a right because they have a duty. They have the duty to civilize the inferior races." Furthermore, this language establishes clear distinctions between populations (natives and savages) that were presented as lacking civilization, inadequacies that a civilizing mission might partially remedy over time, although these would be conveniently differed in the immediate future and ultimately proved insurmountable in the afterlives of colonialism as they morphed into new exclusionary categories, masquerading as nativist, protectionist and nationalist rhetoric.

The interface between land exploitation, underdevelopment of land resources and amputation of generational knowledge transmission have precluded, severed and voided sustainable relationships with the land through the substitution of capitalistic production practices. The resulting impact on global warming is measurable. As Lori M. Hunter and Raphael J. Nawrotzki have suggested, it is "imperative that we measure and integrate consideration of the environment's interaction with other factors in shaping migration" particularly in relation to cumulative environmental degradation as exemplified by land scarcity, degradation, air pollution and whether as a "direct cause" or "monocausal phenomenon" or alternatively "in indirectly in combination with other factors."[68]

Propaganda and Ecological *Re-story-ation*

In Chapter 5, our attention will turn to some of the ways in which propaganda has been used in order to further an anti-ecological agenda *and* pro-ecology

positions aimed at raising awareness. There are of course heated debates relating to the specific timeline that pertains to "awareness" of human responsibility for global warming, from age-old land management practices to the
early nineteenth century when the industrial revolution was jumpstarted,
onward to the oil crisis in the 1970s or the 1992 United Nations Conference
on Environment and Development.[69] We shall devote greater attention to
these contemporary discussions later in *Climates of Migration*, but suffice to
say that the colonial era offers numerous precursors when it comes to ascertaining ecological awareness, as carefully elaborated propaganda campaigns
were deployed in order to promote overseas expansion and enhance resource
exploitation. As Guillaume Blanc confirms, "The more the colonization programme advanced, the more the paradise islands inevitably deteriorated.
During the course of the eighteenth century, naturalists, botanists and agron-
omists began to be aware of the scale of the catastrophe."[70]

Ample and incontestable evidence therefore exists when it comes to the
degree to which calculated actions were taken that impacted the environment. What we can be certain about, as Deborah Coen has authoritatively
demonstrated, is that "imperial expansion transformed colonial environments in far-reaching and irreversible ways. [...] depleted natural resources,
disrupted ecosystems, and introduced invasive species, often leading to the
extinction of native ones."[71] Although the actual impact on public opinion
was minimal, the anti-imperialist counter-exposition staged in Paris in 1931
by the Surrealists and Communist Party nonetheless drew attention to the
exploitative nature of colonies, a position that countered the official attempt at
promoting the benefits to France.[72] The latter encouraged *attachment* through
identification with the colonial mission, but also *detachment* when it came to
the dehumanizing elements that threatened the prevailing sense of Western
entitlement that propaganda helped secure. Ecology concerns relationality
between living things and their habitat, and colonialism was determined to
undermine that bond.

In France, iconographic materials produced from the early days of the
Third Republic (from 1870 onward) provide unique insights into the colonial
past and accordingly help us to "better understand how generations of colonizing and colonized subjects were conditioned by these imaginaries and how
they continue to impact society today."[73] The visual apparatus "immersed" the
country in a "colonial bath," and each image participated in the elaboration
of a social imaginary through which the national community "constructed
itself."[74] The objective was to encourage each French person to "join in the
imperial enterprise, to enlist and mobilize support for expansion overseas,
and recruitment posters featured construction projects The idea of a 'Greater
France' and of the 'civilizing mission' spanned several generations."[75] Fairs

and exhibitions—such as the Crystal Palace Exhibition (London, 1851) or Exposition Universelle (Paris, 1855)—were especially impactful given that in "the mid-nineteenth century, when very few Europeans traveled overseas, an average person with a shilling or a franc and a spare day could step into the cultures of other continents in their nation's empire" at these sites, and "find exhibits and other materials that glorified and promoted the benefits of their empires."[76]

At the 1931 Colonial Exhibition staged around the Lac Daumesnil that stood at the center of the Bois de Vincennes on the eastern outskirts of Paris,[77] "imperialism was not a subtheme, but rather the explicit purpose; visitors could, as the government's slogan advertised, take a 'Tour du monde en un jour' (Around the World in a Day), touching down on continents and oceans that represented the breadth of France Overseas."[78] Extolled in the caption to Victor Jean Desmeures' exhibition poster, the "separation between [...] colonizers and the colonized, is striking," as "the 'white' onlooker [in the shadow of the guardian tricolor French flag], the only 'race' not actually included in the image, serves to reinforce the hierarchical colonial gaze, and reminds onlookers that these [stereotyped indigenous] populations are 'different' to the French."[79] This iconic image, among hundreds of others that proliferated at the time, portrayed colonization as a crucial component of "an intrinsically glorious France, building patriotism and national pride, while also establishing a fusional relationship between metropolitan and overseas territories: the myth of a 'Greater France' finds itself embodied in the images themselves."[80] Promotional and publicity campaigns were launched for a wide variety of products, including the famous Banania powdered drink, but also for rice, cocoa and tea, systems of colonial extraction that privileged these monoculture commodities. The impact was quantifiable, and "polling in the late 1930s shows approximately 90 per cent support for the Empire," and products whet the appetite for aggrandizement.[81] Propaganda set out to "conquer French tastes," a dual process premised on changing "consumption habits" (intense lobbying from the Union of Rice Exporters was one such example) while simultaneously expanding markets and often diverting or reassigning production from one colony to another.[82] This visual apparatus succeeded in helping "to crystallize an idea of France's relationship to the colonies. An image is but the visible part of a symbolized idea, a means through which, in this case, the realities of colonization could be distorted."[83] The modes of behavior were not unique to French colonies, and as Mariana P. Candido has shown, were also deployed by Iberian powers whereby "these ideas (pertaining to land as a space of belonging and maintaining contact with previous generations), however, were challenged by the arrival of European powers during the modern era, who expropriated land and justified it" and "possession of territory and control of its inhabitants and natural resources were the ultimate goals."[84] These schemes were shortsighted, privileged single-crop production, and had the devastating impact we know of today.

The British context is equally compelling. In *Propaganda and Empire: The Manipulation of British Public Opinion, 1880-1960*, John MacKenzie describes how "colonial exhibitions were a celebration of the white man's successful transplantation to the farthest reaches of the globe, and his creation there of societies modelled on European lines. They were the peripheral expression of the larger-scale celebrations of the mother country, epitomizing local control of the environment and its resources."[85] Similarly to France, the desired impact was achieved through multiple outlets, including theater, cinema, exhibitions, toys, books, youth literature and magazines, fueling patriotism and a "consciousness of imperial and military destiny" from which the authorities "were able to dress economic benefits in idealistic garb, substituting moral crusade for mercenary motive, romance and adventure for political and military aggression. The values and beliefs of the imperial world view settled like a sediment in the consciousness of the British people."[86] Propagandist mechanisms successfully shaped mindsets through *narratives* and *storytelling*. The resource exploitation and extraction practices they engendered did not take into consideration stewardship of nature, thereby setting them on a collision course. As botanist Robin Wall Kimmerer so powerfully demonstrated in *Braiding Sweetgrass: Indigenous Wisdom, Scientific Knowledge and the Teachings of Plants*, "the land shows the bruises of an abusive relationship. It's not just land that is broken, but more importantly, our relationship to land. And as Gary Nabhan has written, we can't meaningfully proceed with healing, with restoration, without 're-story-ation'. In other words, our relationship with land cannot heal until we hear its stories."[87] The reality of course was that the uneven relationships that defined colonial relations stifled reciprocal engagement, and "only Europeans, it was thought, were sufficiently intelligent and technically resourceful enough to make meaning of the natural world."[88] Central therefore to this perspectival recalibration, to remedying historical attempts aimed at silencing and to meaningful *re-story-ation*, are questions of ecological restoration and reclaiming.

Quantitatively, Germany was less dependent on colonial propaganda, but this does not mean that it did not endeavor to indoctrinate and inculcate citizens with colonial attitudes. To this end, Götz Aly's *The Magnificent Boat: The Colonial Theft of a South Seas Cultural Treasure*, provides an extraordinarily powerful critique of German colonialism.[89] Focusing on "colonial possessions" in the southwestern Pacific Ocean—known as German New Guinea—Götz Aly documents how colonists established plantations between 1884 and 1914 Exports included phosphate, gold, natural rubber and cocoa, and the most important product was copra (dried coconut) which was used to make margarine and soap. Framed as a mission aimed at "civilizing, missionizing, and protecting," this was a story of "colonial subjugation" defined by "selfishness, greed, violence, and capriciousness."[90] Extensive recourse was made to conscripted or forced laborers and introduced monocultural production that did "not meet local food needs" and were exclusively for the "benefits [of] distant shareholders who had made the initial investment possible" and constituting "monstrous moral and legal arrangements, [that form] the matrix of modern extractivism."[91] Ultimately, "Germans destroyed the means of subsistence of hundreds of thousands of men, women, and children" and "allowed the Indigenous population to perish from starvation or disease so that the colonists could transform the [island] into a profitable coconut plantation" that was "aimed at encouraging modern modes of production, economic exploitation, and profit."[92]

Belgian colonial actions in the Congo Free State also tell a story of exceptional violence and expropriation, and this history has been documented in works by Adam Hochschild and David Van Reybrouck.[93] As with other colonial powers, the propulsive force was for "raw materials to feed the Industrial Revolution," such that "by the turn of the century, the État Indépendant du Congo had become, far and away, the most profitable colony in Africa. The profits came swiftly because, transportation costs aside, harvesting wild rubber required no cultivation, no fertilizers, no capital investment in expensive equipment. It required only labor."[94] Not surprisingly, in 1960, when Patrice Lumumba was appointed prime minister in his newly independent country and threatened control over resources, "His speeches set off immediate alarm signals in Western capitals."[95] Only 62 years later on June 20, 2022 did Belgian prime minister Alexander De Croo officially apologize for Belgium's role in his assassination on January 17, 1961, stating that colonization "established an unequal relationship, in itself unjustifiable [...] a pernicious system that shamefully tarnished the history of our country" and marked by "enslavement, occupation, exploitation and despoilment."[96]

The conclusions are therefore analogous to what Malcom Ferdinand has described in the Caribbean context, namely that the "agricultural plantation economy devotes most of these lands to the export of monocultures, without providing for the food needs of the inhabitants of the islands."[97] These practices completely neglected sustainable agrarian practices, and as Bill Grammage has argued, endorsed processes of dispossession that "upended the lives of many species" and resulted in "erasure," since "gone are the stories [...] gone knowledge of land, sea and sky, the skill to care for every habitat, to grow local crops and husband native animals, to feel truly at home."[98]

The Colonial Game

Cartography—the graphic design and representation of geographic areas and the creation of maps to chart and describe the physical world and earth's surface—proves to be especially important. Extensive recourse was made to maps in order to provide information about the colonies and representations of colonized peoples, many of which have survived into contemporary societies and are reflected in current mindsets. These stimulated the imagination and appeal for remote spaces, overseas and otherwise unremarked, concomitantly fortifying a sense of familiarity and appetite for adventure and travel in an era when such experiences were not widely available to the vast majority of people. With scientific claims to accuracy, maps were often distorted for political ends, exploiting a broad range of communicative strategies in order to further ideological goals. Examples include the maps affixed to the walls in French school classrooms that featured an oversized mainland France located front and center, thereby emphasizing its importance, and surrounded by smaller, scaled-down and peripheral regions, themselves dispersed across a global empire over which Republican ideals and values radiated.[99]

Board games—among other ephemera—provide insights to a range of *ecolonial* issues. Questions of travel—imaginative and physical—were central to the production and visualization of Empire. Board games mirrored geopolitical dynamics, and participants understood that they were assuming the role of protagonists in the unfolding game of power. Jan Nederveen Pieterse cites the words of Ethiopian Emperor Tewodros II in this regard, a sovereign who perfectly understood the nature of the "game": "First traders and missionaries, then ambassadors, then the cannon. It's better to get straight to the cannon."[100] During French colonialism, attention to such matters was pivotal in disseminating and encouraging identification with "France overseas," a source of tremendous pride. School systems are of course universal mechanisms developed to educate and prepare new generations of active contributors to a given society, and it is not surprising that considerable efforts would be devoted to enlisting support for the colonial enterprise in educational establishments. The games under consideration were produced over fifty years after the Berlin Conference, yet a similar logic characterizes the conceptualization and treatment of non-European territories: remoteness, economic opportunity and adventure. As Sandrine Lemaire has made manifest, "imperial power is a recurring theme in the majority of textbooks from the 1920s until the 1950s. Students were thus invited to explore the history of their country, which featured a glorification of colonial battles and heroes, the works of 'civilization,' modernization, and examples of which they could be proud."[101] Whatever benefits could be gained from such activity, these were inseparable from France's constructed generosity.

French direct rule was organized around the principle of a civilizing mission, namely "a representation of French uniqueness and the belief in a special link between France and the world."[102] Such efforts were by no means new, and "'Overseas' colonization was therefore not a departure from the past; in fact, it inscribed itself in a consubstantial continuation of the construction of the French nation, and then, as a kind of legacy, of the Republic."[103] Rather, these measures served to establish a very particular relationship, one in which "France was a great nation because it possessed colonies,"[104] a connection in which the two components were inextricably linked. Likewise, board games adhered to these norms, extending classroom lessons into the extracurricular domain where "students were thus invited to explore the history of their country, which featured a glorification of colonial battles and heroes, the works of 'civilization,' modernization, and examples of which they could be proud."[105] These elements functioned in conjunction with other mechanisms that related to the production of empire, such as the "colonial culture" ecosystem. Whether in the weekly editions of popular magazines or elsewhere, the image disseminated was of a dynamic empire committed to improving the lives of "natives" while also pursuing economic activity, a "reality completely at odds with efforts on the ground in the actual colonies."[106] In the Netherlands, as Gloria Wekker has shown, efforts were made to imbibe moral principles and inculcate school-age children with a sense of moral responsibility, "Knowledge of the other got transmitted to the metropole by travel and narratives of imperial citizens in the colonies; by photography and racial images on all kinds of colonial products."[107] I describe these measures as *colonial-washing*, in other words analogous efforts to corporations today adopting greenwashing strategies.

As one of the panels at the Deutsches Historisches Museum exhibition discussed earlier reminded viewers, "The world of colonial images in the German Empire shows that visual relationships are also power relationships. Photographs, consumer goods, and advertising all transmitted themes of colonial conquest and racist stereotypes. Through such images of themselves and of others, consumers and viewers learned colonialist patterns of interpretation that have retained their potency to this day." Similarly, and as with any board game, conquest was a defining characteristic, and "confronting colonization is to deconstruct the discursive practices that made it possible" and that were "vigorously promoted in what is today the last republican institution meant to bind the social body: the school system."[108] Large-scale disruption resulted from these actions and initiatives, precisely because "at a time when Africa needed to be developing industrial farming techniques," as

Kehinde Andrews suggests, "to provide food and resources for the continent, precisely the opposite was occurring [...] Cotton, rubber, oil palm, cocoa, coffee and more were procured to be exploited away from Africa, with huge profits going to European companies."[109]

The toys and games distributed during the interwar years "made the discovery and conquest of colonial lands fun," as Nicolas Bancel claims, while spreading "a clear political message on the empire and its people" and reaching into "the familiar and intimate universe of family, neighbors, and friends."[110] Furthermore, "this world introduced children to unheard-of adventure, through which they developed new relationships to space. [...] Conquest was a game, without any apparent consequences, a game that contributed to the construction of a mentality meant to prepare a young elite for the challenges of colonial life and the defense of the empire. These games of courage were preparing the youth to help reestablish France's power and conserve its empire."[111] The games called upon new literacies, and innovative concepts in design and technology strengthened the concomitance between emotion and visualization, randomness and unpredictability, education and ideology, and inserted a convergence between interactivity and strategy. As with colonialism itself, popular culture contained the power to convince "by means of narration, fabulation, and dream."[112] Indeed, as Ian Bogost has argued, "rhetoric in its contemporary sense refers to both persuasion and expression," and although his focus is specifically on video games, the "procedural rhetoric" he describes should be understood as applicable and "encompassing any medium—computational or not—that accomplishes its inscription via processes."[113]

Games were also in dialogue with other narrative devices such as adventure stories and colonial fictions that reached substantial audiences. As Carly A. Kocurek noted in Walter Benjamin's text "The Storyteller" (1936), play "occupies an uneasy space between the real and the fictional and is deeply enmeshed with narrative strategies" and "the most skillful storytellers are not unlike the most skilled game designers, and there is a meaningful overlap between storytelling and play. [...] Storytelling, as Benjamin describes it, is fanciful in that it is less interested in factual information and explanations than it is in the imparting of wisdom, morals, and deeper truths."[114] As with the above-mentioned "Tour du monde en un jour" (Around the World in a Day) poster designed by Victor Jean Desmeures for the 1931 Colonial Exhibition, colonial-era games also focused attention on the perspective of the onlooker and, according to Charles Forsdick, "play creates identification with nation and empire, and confirms the French player's privileged citizenship within larger colonizing structures, with the right to travel through and profit from the colonies engrained in the game's fixed rules"[115] and serves, as

Yann Holo explains, to "awaken the child's imagination from a very young age, play a considerable role and add an element of fun to discovery of the Colonial Empire [and] spread all the stereotypes about Africa and pass on prejudices about Black people to young people."[116]

Numerous examples exist in other European colonial contexts. "By the end of the [nineteenth] century," John MacKenzie has shown, games "were being produced very cheaply, and were used as teaching aids" and the "entwining of economic and moral purpose appears in all history and geography books [...] interlocking parts of economic imperialism."[117] Germany, like France, also made widespread use of toys and games. David D. Hamlin, in his book *Work and Play: The Production and Consumption of Toys in Germany, 1870-1914*, describes how these were used "to justify the use of brutal force by the German colonial troops" with the consequence that the "African population was systematically demonized and reviled, such that they were no longer really accepted as members of the same human species."[118] Elsewhere, in *Raising Germans in the Age of Empire: Youth and Colonial Culture, 1871-1914*, Jeff Bowersox draws a distinction with the French context arguing that "young Germans were less interested in instructional tools or patriotic messages, but [...] depended on accepting the generally received notions of civilized and uncivilized used to justify European expansion; this binary was essential to developing exciting, adventurous, even subversive worlds. As they embedded these hierarchies in their play, young people played their own important role in assembling Germany's jumbled colonial culture."[119]

When a German cigarette manufacturer in Dresden released a photo-mechanical print card collection album named *Deutsche Kolonien* in 1936, the images were instead commemorative, featuring "the German colonial empire lost as a consequence of World War I" and some 270 "color collecting cards [were] pasted onto full-page black and white lithographed illustrations of colonial scenes, offering multiple glimpses of scenery, architecture, military action, indigenous peoples, artifacts, wildlife, and agricultural products of the various colonies."[120] Much like the French context, it is the interplay between adaptability, adventure, discovery and unexpected encounters that heightens interest and inspires new generations. However, as Jeff Bowersox asserts, underpinning the adventure narratives is the persistent depiction of "uncivilized peoples who squandered their natural resources or lived in outright indolence,"[121] in other words populations with no perceived legitimacy in maintaining proprietorship over lands whose resources they inadequately managed. Comparative analysis therefore of the French and German context reveals the expediency of games in conditioning mindsets, disseminating information and soliciting patronage and sponsorship for imperialist conceptions of territorial conquest as the basis of European supremacy.

Gaming Empire

A number of games were released in France in 1941, and these included a two-sided board game featuring the *Jeu de l'Empire Français* (The French Empire Game) and the *Course de l'Empire Français* (The Race for the French Empire). These games represent an empire that had burgeoned to 24 times the size of mainland France. A decade after the impressive propagandist venture that was the 1931 Colonial Exhibition and that aimed at improving awareness of and bolstering support for the vast French Empire, these board games shared analogous purposes. As Alice L. Conklin and Julia Clancy-Smith have indicated, games and toys distributed during the colonial era

> raise questions about the place of the colonial past in the writing of
> France's history. The insertion of empire ideologically, commercially,
> and pedagogically into all realms of French daily life, from children's
> games and juvenile literature to religious activities, mass entertainment,
> leisure, tourism, advertising, legal categories, language, and so on, and
> the state's vigorous role in promoting empire contrasts with the relative
> inattention to colonial questions in mainstream historical scholarship in
> France until the past decade or so.[122]

These games, designed by the accomplished illustrator Raoul Auger (1904–1991), contained a wealth of information about France overseas. As Jan Nederveen Pieterse makes clear, "The journeys of exploration did not simply produce 'knowledge', they were also large-scale operations in myth-making, and they unfolded in a kind of western (and Eurocentric) 'tunnel vision' that was to culminate in European colonialism."[123] But in addition to these factors, one cannot overstate the degree to which these games, commissioned by the Economic Bureau of the Colonies under the Vichy regime were the result of "a major, well-conceived, and organized marketing campaign."[124] It is of course worth underscoring that this was an era far removed from the realities of the postcolonial world in which technological transformations would dramatically improve access to and affordability of travel, thereby bringing these remote places into close proximity. Thus, what previously had been mostly restricted to the realm of the imagination now found itself within reach for growing numbers of Europeans.

When the Vichy regime redoubled its efforts to rekindle public interest and support for empire, this occurred with two particular concerns in mind. Firstly, addressing the particular circumstances of a nation destabilized by German occupation under the aegis of a military administration. "The colonies gave the impression that France had not lost its place as a leading power within the world order," as Pascal Blanchard and Ruth Ginio have explained, "in spite of the defeat by the Germans."[125] And secondly, as the expression of concern with the proliferation of anti-colonial and independence movements in the British and Dutch empire (notably in India and Indonesia). This is precisely the context in which the French colonial games were designed, featuring Marshal Pétain, the chief of state in the collaborationist regime and the nation's guide and compass in uncertain times. Propagandist materials highlighted France's global presence, and these efforts were accompanied by major public cultural and sporting events such as La semaine de la France d'outre-mer (July 15–22, 1941) and the Quinzaine impériale (May 15–31, 1942).

A selection of these games was included in the *Connecting Seas: A Visual History of Discoveries and Encounters* exhibition (December 7, 2013 to April 13, 2014) at the Getty Research Institute in Los Angeles. The ingredients or defining characteristics and qualities of any respectable board game are to be found here—namely, curiosity, passion for adventure, greed and competition—and the message was clear, as outlined in a French geography school textbook published in 1913: "It is thus essential that French youth be familiarized with the resources from the vast territory over which *our* flag waves. They must learn about the living conditions, their chances of success, and also the potential risks encountered by colonials in *our* overseas possessions."[126] The French Empire was massive and diverse, and board game designers devoted considerable effort to functionality, to the process of capturing that geographic coverage so that the players' experience would be enhanced, thereby replicating the sense of adventure and discovery that was synonymous with the real-life experience of those who were fortunate enough to venture beyond the shores of the mainland. Alice L. Conklin and Julia Clancy-Smith have reminded us that "similar colonial games were produced in France from the late nineteenth century on: embossed, cut-out paper soldiers. [...] All celebrated conquests of foreign lands in the form of mass-produced playthings for French children, whether at home or abroad. Intertwined with the imperial messages was a blatant commercialism, since the toys often contained advertisements for foods, or even alcoholic beverages."[127] The "Game of the Goose" is widely considered the earliest commercially produced board game (fifteenth-century), and descriptions and playing instructions abound; it is a game traditionally played on a spiral-shaped board with consecutive numbered spaces and a number of hazard spaces— challenges and obstacles—that either accelerate or slow down the player's goal of reaching the last square or tile ahead of the playing partner(s).[128] The *Jeu de l'Empire Francais* and the *Course de l'Empire Français* have been described as follows by Isotta Poggi:

Made in France at the outbreak of World War II, the game sought to educate children about the colonial world supporting the French economy. With tokens printed in vivid colors to represent places and natural resources in regions colonized by the French, from North Africa to Oceania to southeast Asia, this game encapsulated the mighty business opportunities that lay ahead for adventurous explorers willing to embark for faraway colonial lands. As described in the rules at the center of the board, the underlying purpose of the game was to admire, through play, the greatness of the French colonial undertaking. The colonization of a land was symbolically achieved first by hoisting the French flag on its soil, then by the establishment of a hospital, a school, and ultimately a harbor. But the ultimate winner was to export the rich natural resources of the colonies back to France by boat. Images on the game provide a vivid picture of the vast variety of resources, including animals, plants, and minerals, that the colonies provided to France from all around the globe.[129]

Careful attention has been paid to the graphic design elements, an effort to combine cartography and mapping in order to foreground a perspective and particular message about the overseas locations featured, and each game comprises two carefully demarcated circuits.

In the *Jeu de l'Empire Français*, two tracks are available: red and white tiles contain various obstacles such as overturned canoes, missed train connections, an iceberg, mechanical problems with an aircraft, lost identity papers, as well as climatic factors (monsoon rains, high winds and sand storms) that can impede progress and must be overcome, whereas blue tiles offer a fast track and can expedite the journey to the final location. The rules of the game section (printed in the top right-hand portion of the central inset) inform players that "each square is ascribed a particular meaning. In this way, as players make their way around the board, they will discover the beauties, resources, and attractions of imperial France, but also a series of obstacles." In the quest to travel the length and breadth of the empire in the shortest possible time, the journey begins in the French southern port city of Marseille, and 84 tiles later, the victorious player-adventurer arrives in the north of France in another port city, Le Havre, having covered an impressive physical distance throughout France's prodigious empire. This is a dice game, and progress is based on the number rolled. Competitors are promised they "will enjoy the beauty, attractions, hazards encountered in the various lands of imperial France." The imagination will be stimulated, their interest piqued and excitement guaranteed from the sense of perilous adventure.

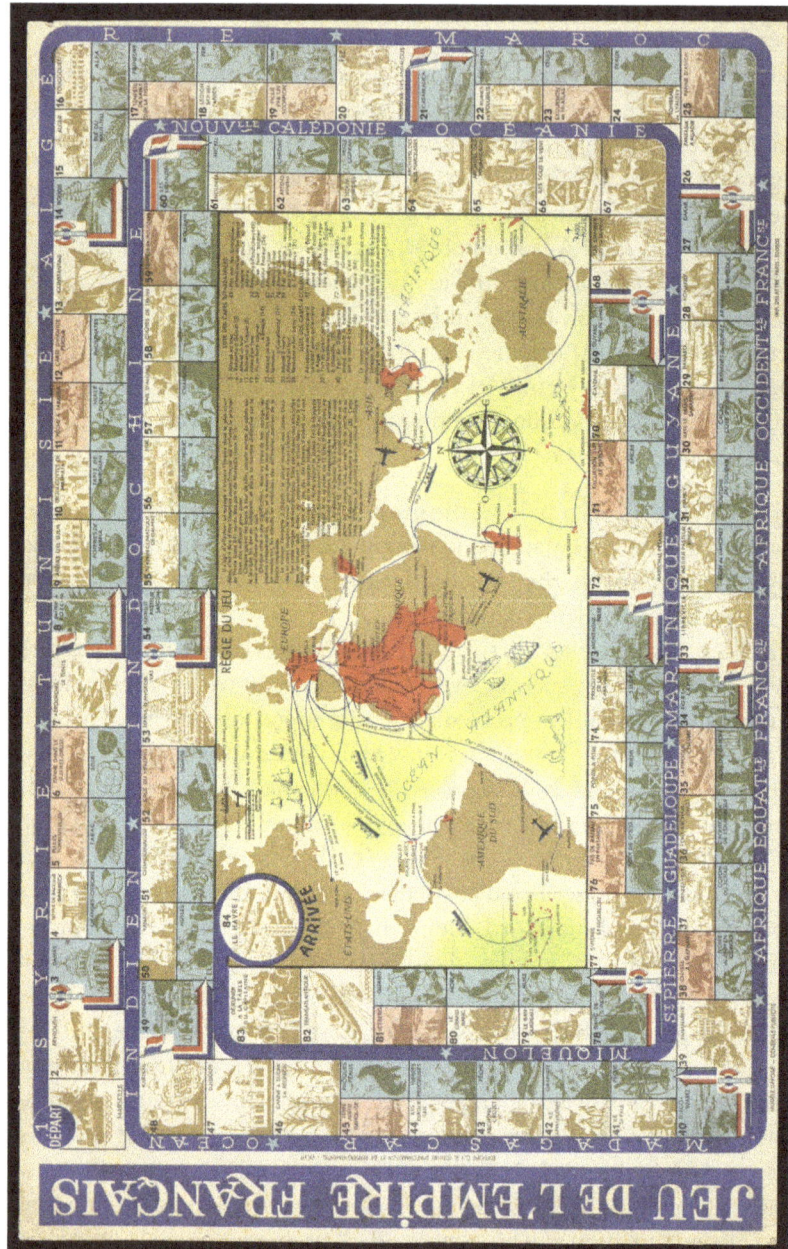

Figure 1.1 Raoul Auger, Imprimerie Delattre, 1941, *Jeu de l'Empire français* (The French Empire Game), two-sided game board, color lithograph, 32 × 50 cm, Getty Research Institute, Los Angeles.

With the exception of tile 72, devoted to the effigy of Marshal Pétain, the tiles contain illustrations of France's global empire in French Equatorial Africa (AEF), French West Africa (AOF), Indochina, New Caledonia, Guadeloupe, Martinique and elsewhere, and players familiarize themselves with colonial cities such as Algiers, Tunis, Dakar, Fez, Bamako, Saigon, Brazzaville, Djibouti, Pondicherry and Nouméa. Specific geographic regions are identified with architectural sites (the Temple of Angkor Wat) or products, cocoa in the Ivory Coast, hardwoods in Gabon, bananas in Guinea, and elsewhere one finds nickel, iron, coal, gold, silk, tobacco, cotton, rubber, spices, rice, rum, olive oil, sugar cane and coconuts. The design concept promotes an associative process, connecting concepts and ideas while facilitating the navigation of semantic space. As research in cognitive sciences has revealed, this type of thinking enhances creativity, problem-solving and decision-making.[130] Together, these skills improve competitiveness through augmented strategic capacity. The games considered here combine the interplay between images and text—similarly to memory card games or collection cards that stimulate concentration, visual recognition and recall—and cultivate retrieval processes and pedagogic retention, encouraging associative memory between colonies of exploitation and specific products, resources, ethnic stereotypes, landscapes and botanical elements.

The Colonial Food Regime

In 1896, Ambroise Jeanneney published a book, *Ce que produisent nos colonies: leçons de choses et lectures*, in which he attempted to provide an exhaustive inventory as a record of what each colony produced, stating that "it is crucial for you to know which goods come from our colonies in order to fully grasp why the homeland has made such heavy sacrifices in order to conquer these distant countries."[131] Thus, intrepid explorers set out to conquer and discover, and the most valuable tiles consolidated the underlying lessons. Yet, success was premised on deploying a range of aptitudes, and "the explorer's audacity and merit in successfully taming the environment" is achieved by overcoming climatic and meteorological adversity thanks to technological advances and individual prowess.[132] These games thus function as knowledge dissemination portals, refining pedagogy and reinforcing linkages with school lessons and textbooks, while also affirming participants in their allocated roles as *masters and possessors of nature*.[133] In *L'école des colonies*, French author Didier Daeninckx examined images and plates that offered a wealth of information on colonial territories, often replicating the information found in the various tiles on the board games.[134] For example, one learns in a caption that "due to its immense natural resources, whose methodical exploitation will be enhanced by the railway under construction, the Ivory Coast is expected to achieve great economic prosperity, impeded however by the insufficiency of the indigenous workforce."[135] Information is divided between *products* (corn, sorghum, millet, potato, peanut, sesame, vanilla, coffee, cocoa, cotton), the *rainforest* (mahogany, ebony, baobab, kola tree) and *mineral resources* (gold, iron, lead, copper), and the message is clear in terms of France's dependency on its colonies. The evidence points to the "intricate and overlapping set of Eurocolonial worlds" described by Arjun Appadurai, and as Eric Holt-Giménez has explained, the "colonial food regime" was implemented and "as Western Europe industrialized it came to depend more and more on the colonies in the Global South for food and raw materials" while "prohibiting the colonies from industrializing, forcing them to buy the empire's own manufactured goods."[136] Prominent chocolate manufacturers during the colonial era were notable for the brand identities they developed featuring the global French empire. They achieved their promotional goals through intermedial platforms that together emphasized consumption practices and implicit adherence to the value of Empire itself. These included trading cards, school supplies, games, posters, and collectible albums.[137]

Board games necessitate motion—they are defined by a glossary of directional moves, backward or forward, steps, leaps—not unlike the logistics of how "transportation companies offer passage on certain routes and not others."[138] Landscapes are transformed as a result of technological resourcefulness, converted by the European presence and production yields augmented as indicators of progress attributed to colonial practices. This enabled the delineation of "sharper distinctions between 'civilized' Europeans and 'uncultured' Africans," as discussed in Philipp Lehmann's book *Desert Edens: Colonial Climate Engineering in the Age of Anxiety.*[139]

In the *Course de l'Empire Français*, participants living under Vichy-occupied France are generously offered by Marshal Pétain (to whom tile number 42 is devoted, a winning tile since any player fortunate enough to land on it is immediately expedited to the final tile numbered 50 and declared victorious!) the opportunity to travel around the world as they visit the length and breadth of the French Empire. This corresponds to "a major, well-conceived, and organized marketing campaign directed at French youth, the Vichy regime created a 'kingdom' of distraction."[140] Planetary circulation is possible thanks to "France's impressive aerial and maritime network" (Rules of the Game). There are two departure tiles (Marseille or Toulouse) and separate blue or red tracks, and the journeys culminate respectively in either Le Havre or Marseille, from where air travel will transport the winner to Paris. Each circuit comprises "special" tiles that can speed up or slow down progress—a player on the blue circuit must miss a turn for landing on certain tiles as they

Figure 1.2 Raoul Auger, Imprimerie Delattre, 1941, *Course de l'Empire français* (The Race for the French Empire), two-sided game board, color lithograph, 32 × 50 cm, Getty Research Institute, Los Angeles.

await refueling, as a lock raises or lowers a boat to a higher or lower part of the canal, or await a connecting flight, and fall back a number of spaces as a result of passport control. A similar fate awaits players on the red circuit. As indicated in the Rules of the Game, different circuits feature examples "of great French people, glorious aviators, aviation pioneers, esteemed navigators, soldiers and leaders of the French Empire." As with the *Jeu de l'Empire Français*, players gain familiarity with the vast array of French overseas possessions, thereby narrowing the concrete and imaginative gap between the here and the elsewhere. This is also a lesson in geography and geopolitics, and tiles incorporate information on local architecture and décor while endeavoring to emphasize the complex transcolonial and transnational networks whose connectivity has been enhanced by technological advances and recourse to fossil fuels, allowing the expansionist dream to come to fruition in concrete terms. Individual tiles share points of commonality with postage stamps, an analogous representational logic. To this end, the games perfectly encapsulate official policies, while encouraging the conscription of French youth eager to serve overseas and propagate the value-system.

Another game, the *Jeu des échanges France—Colonies*, is all the more convincing in this regard, conceptualized in such a way as to mainstream the ideals of the authorities as players accumulate wealth by building a house, hoisting the French flag, and gradually expanding the larger infrastructure with hospitals, schools, and similar institutions to facilitate the export of products from the colonies. The game states: "It is the immense richness of the colonies that makes France great" (GRI exhibition label). This game follows a different set of organizational principles and reward paradigms. Players now distribute elegantly designed colorful tiles arranged by geographic destination. The central panel includes the instructions and rules of the game. The purple territorial markings demarcate "France and its empire." The guidelines prompt participants to engage in a collective process of "admiration" for "France's colonial *œuvre* in all its grandeur." Adding a paper chip or token marked "Colonies" (Colony) is to lay claim to that territory as one's own and to be able to "cultivate" it. To add a "Drapeau" (Flag) is to build a hospital or a school, whereas a "Bateau" (ship) allows the player to transport the goods back to the metropole. The players are "colons"—settlers or colonists—and the colonies themselves are divided equally among the two, four or eight players. When trading begins, the goal is to match through color codes the outstanding chips with their respective colonies, flags and corresponding ports. The game is entertaining, but it is also about emotional stimulation, enticing players to "feel" what it is like to be on location, on the ground in one of these colonies, competing for crops and various products, including bananas, rice, sugarcane, tea, cotton, gold or diamonds, across the globe in Guinea,

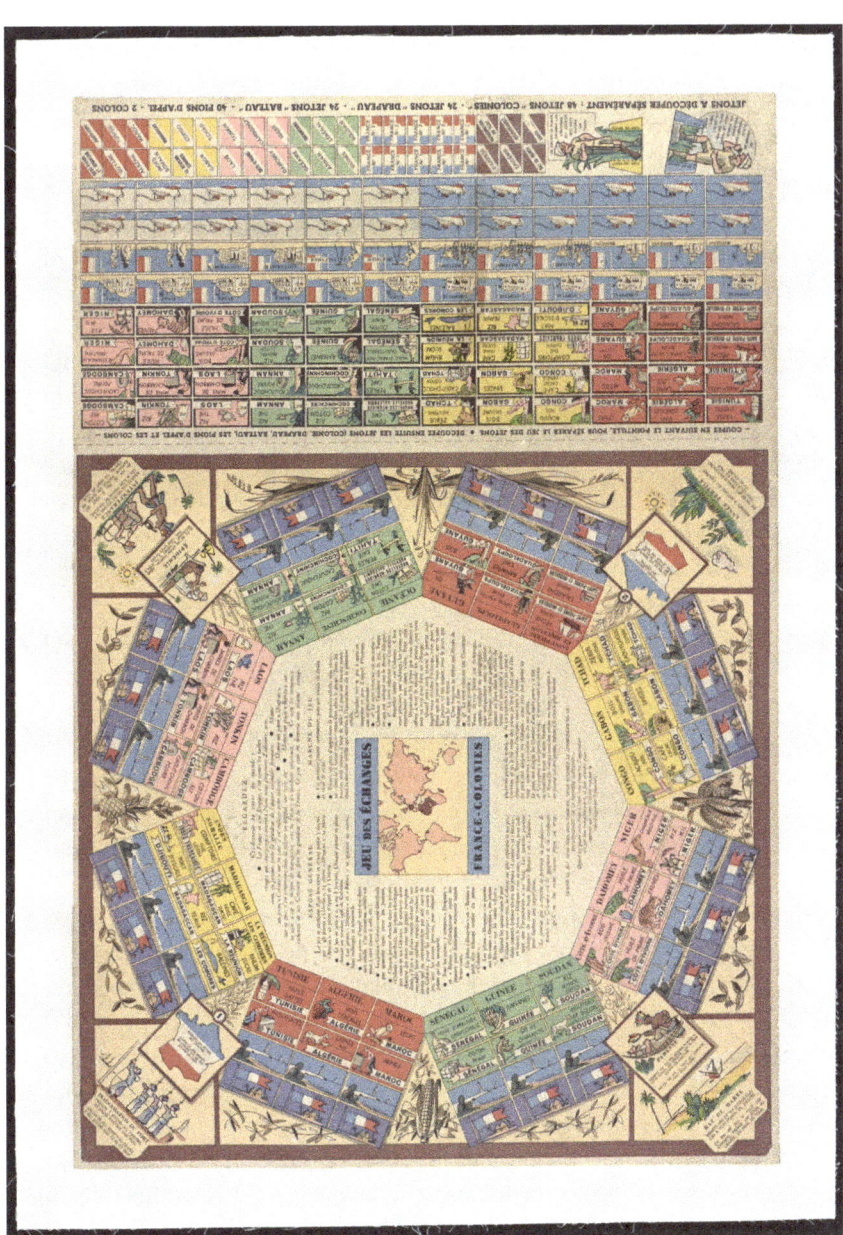

Figure 1.3 *Jeu des échanges France—Colonies* (Trading Game), 1941, Office de publicité et d'impression, lithograph on linen, 58.1 × 81.9 cm, Getty Research Institute, Los Angeles.

Morocco, Cochinchina, Guadeloupe, Saint-Pierre and Miquelon, Réunion and Comoros, or Laos and Cambodia. The ultimate winner will be declared once all their colonies are settled and the export of goods and products is underway. The logic therefore replicates the spirit of the relentless scramble for resources, fulfilling the aspirational ideals inventoried by Jan Nederveen Pieterse as "strategic considerations," "national grandeur," "economic gain," "expansion" and "pre-emptive imperialism."[141]

The appetite for accumulation and exploitation stimulates participants. In game theory development, this is defined as the Player Experience of Need Satisfaction (PENS), and a "complete theory of motivation in the arena of gaming must not simply catalog observations of player behavior (e.g. 'players like carrots' or 'players pursue challenges') but should also be able to describe the underlying energy that fuels actions in the first place (i.e. our 'motivational lightbox')."[142] These games reward a spirit of ownership and proprietorship and aim to cultivate and nurture identification with the impressive nature of the colonial project itself. Considerable energy is devoted to the goal of ensuring that the "colonial imaginary transcended the confines of the classroom in order to provide distractions for children. [...] Games transmitted official discourse and in doing so multiplied the ways in which young people were exposed to imperialism."[143]

These games also reproduced the organizational logic that had informed the conceptualization of the 1931 Colonial Exhibition. In that instance, maps guided visitors around the empire and assigned areas and enclosures to given geographic spaces, much in the same way as the tiles would later do in the board games. In the games, players made their way around the French Empire, whereas visitors at the exhibition followed "an itinerary from the civilized splendors of Paris to the savage beasts of the zoo, with educational lessons in colonial geography and ethnography along the way."[144] Both employed techniques aimed at arousing the imagination and galvanizing escapist propensities, illusory quests to emulate the hazardous exploits of those compatriots enlisted to serve the colonial enterprise. The games and maps emphasized the idea of taking a tour and accordingly helped curate and shape their adventure around the world, predominantly to expose them to the promise of the awe-inspiring "Plus Grande France" (Greater France) and achievements of the civilizing mission. The spectacular array of architecture and of arts and crafts were juxtaposed with an educational dimension that made it possible to establish connections between people, products and global territorial spaces.

The particular attention given to food products was fundamental, strengthening the connection between metropolitan France and its overseas colonies, and implicit was the concomitant increase in patriotic adherence. As Pascale Joassart-Marcelli has explained, "The movement of food, going hand in hand with human migration, has been a central feature of this history [...] paying attention to the flows of food commodities, the evolution of food cultures and practices, and the political and economic forces and technologies shaping these global exchanges" reveals how "its scope, organization, and impacts have changed dramatically over time, culminating in today's global, industrial, corporate, capitalist, and neoliberal food system."[145] Generations of young people responded enthusiastically to these adventures. Yet, a deep irony lingers, one that originates in the (arguably predictable) discrepancy between the concerted effort in evidence in the board games to provide information on sourcing and the absence of attention to the ways in which these activities compromised the relationship to the land and biodiversity and eroded the understanding of what a sustainable food supply chain would entail. This is all the more apparent given that, as Séverine Kodjo-Grandvaux has argued, "The contemporary ecological crisis is the result of this excessive exploitation."[146]

Colonial practices are directly responsible for the transition from subsistence production to industrial farming and to the increase in monocultural and substitution cash crops, resulting in growing economic asymmetries— food insecurity, inability to compete in the global market place, development policies, limited access to subsidies, borrowing and indebtedness, deregulation, currency devaluation, reliance on structural adjustment programs— and the disproportionate percentage of GDP associated with agriculture and food exports heightening vulnerability to world price fluctuations and transnational agrifood corporations.[147] As David Van Reybrouck has argued, the ecocidal impact is clear given that "global warming has been, and continues to be, caused primarily by the richest countries located in the temperate regions of the planet, and it predominantly affects the poorest countries in the tropics."[148]

The New Scramble

Recognizing these outcomes and realities is necessary in order to ascertain, comprehend and evaluate the lasting impact of European colonialism. Many of the devices implemented during the colonial era in games, international exhibitions, architecture and advertising relied heavily on iconographic paradigms that remain prevalent, whereby the "habits and spaces [of ethnic minorities] continue to be represented by fruits and scents in many advertisements, be they for tourist destinations or the display of cacao, bananas, coconut trees, vanilla, or sunny beaches. These representations send the nonwhite

French back to the geographic, climatic, or cultural causes of their failure to integrate into the nation."[149] The legacy of these adventures are to be found in the neocolonial alignments associated with *Françafrique*[150] and the activities of the International Organization of Francophonie (OIF), heightening perceptions of "lingering neocolonialism," in other words of "a tradition or a system that goes against all principles of transparency and democracy, fueling inequity and corruption, and safeguarding oppressive dictatorial regimes."[151]

The transhistorical dimension of resource exploitation has received considerable attention, notably when it comes to pinpointing human rights abuses and the adverse effect of current actions on the environment. Writing in the *New York Review of Books* about mining and conflict minerals in the Democratic Republic of Congo, Nicholas Niarcos describes how "corruption and unscrupulous extraction practices contribute to what economists call the 'resource curse' and to a seemingly endless cycle of penury."[152] And more recent works provide evidence of the disruptive nature of these practices. To this extent, contemporary extraction practices amount to a new "scramble for Africa" as players eager to gain access to critical mineral resources essential to twenty-first-century industries enter the fray. As we shall see in Chapter 4, several contemporary African authors have turned their attention to these questions.

Guillaume Blanc has written extensively about the ways in which colonial and postcolonial environmental conservation practices in Africa have had disastrous consequences for local populations, compounding existing problems and accelerating the degradation of ecosystems. In *The Invention of Green Colonialism*, he contends that vigilance is necessary in terms of tracing transformations over a longer history, namely that "the whole issue of worldwide ecology is influenced by the colonial past."[153] Scientific research supports these arguments and conclusions. For example, Harriet Mercer has tracked how climate scientists increasingly associate climate change with colonialism and points to concrete developments. These include the release of the International Panel on Climate Change's (IPCC) report[154] in 2022 in which "for the first time in the institution's history [it] included the term 'colonialism' in its report's summary. Colonialism, the report asserts, has exacerbated the effects of climate change. In particular, historic and ongoing forms of colonialism have helped to increase the vulnerability of specific people and places to the effects of climate change."[155] Credit for the inclusion of this crucial component can be given to Indigenous groups and non-Western nations who have campaigned "for the recognition of the unequal effects of climate change on different groups of people."[156] Of particular note is Section B.2. of the "Summary for Policymakers," in which one can read: "Vulnerability of ecosystems and people to climate change differs substantially among and within regions [...] driven by patterns of intersecting socioeconomic development, unsustainable ocean and land use, inequity, marginalization, historical and ongoing patterns of inequity such as colonialism, and governance" and Section B.2.4: "Present development challenges causing high vulnerability are influenced by historical and ongoing patterns of inequity such as colonialism, especially for many Indigenous peoples and local communities."[157]

Together with members of the "Making Climate History" research team at Cambridge University,[158] Harriet Mercer and Thomas Simpson have released a comprehensive study that convincingly demonstrates the correlation between colonialism and climate change and "the role of modern European empires as key drivers of climate knowledge throughout the early modern and modern eras."[159] Five pillars serve to define the impact assessment: (i) reliance on the knowledge and labor of Indigenous and local peoples in efforts to understand climatic change over time and space; (ii) actively erased or devalued the contributions of Indigenous and local peoples' knowledge if it did not suit their ideologies and ambitions; (iii) built infrastructures for measuring and conceptualizing a global climate system as part of their efforts to expand their strength, wealth, and influence; (iv) made particularly deep investments in climatic research when they sought to expand across contiguous land masses; and (v) laid the foundations for enduring unequal power dynamics in the collection, analysis and presentation of climate science data.[160] This research is in dialogue with an increasingly important field of research concerned with the environmental legacy of colonialism. Attention has been given to the long-term consequences of natural habitat disruption attributed to carbon emissions, pollution, cultural erasure and greenhouse gas emissions. Together, these factors have compromised soil fertility and accelerated species extinction and resulted in resource depletion, poverty and growing inequality, all of which are drivers of population displacement. However, these also serve to "highlight the imperial and colonial power dynamics that still shape climate science, as well as neocolonial dynamics that continue to inflect new climate data and theories."[161] Nishtha Singh has shown how colonialism was premised on an "exploitative economic model that thrive[d] on natural and human domination. Colonialism also led to the disappearance of ancient and important cultural traditions that could have helped to contain the devastation of nature that is at the root of climate change," and as a logical outcome of these asymmetrical power relations, "colonial powers of yesterday and capitalists of today have benefited, more or less directly, from unsustainable practices and exploitation" and those "who contributed the least to ecological destruction will most likely be unable to adapt and endure the most substantial impacts and pay the highest costs."[162] What we can be certain of, as Amitav Ghosh has submitted, is that "the terrain [is] fighting back," and that "as we watch the environmental and biological disasters that are now unfolding across the Earth, it is becoming ever harder to hold on to the belief that the planet is an inert body [...] the climatic changes of our era are nothing other than the Earth's response to four centuries of terraforming."[163]

The Terrain Is Fighting Back

The impact of colonialism on the environment is multidimensional, damaging landscapes, disrupting ecosystems, dismissing and ignoring indigenous knowledge and wisdom, depleting natural resources and compromising biodiversity. These detrimental changes which can be attributed to European expansion and exploitation have resulted in deforestation and soil degradation, outcomes related to agricultural practices that include large-scale plantations and monoculture farming that substituted new practices for sustainable local farming systems. Ascertaining the relationship between the past and the present, computing for the "distillations of all of human history,"[164] are expedient steps in order to address the afterlives of ecolonial activity. These are all the more urgent given that incontrovertible evidence points to the fact that "European settlement produced massive ecological shifts," and as Neel Ahuja maintains, "these forces have historically embedded the sustenance and reproduction of national economies in processes that deplete ecological capacities, displace people from traditional homes and lands, and render rural people dependent on long-distance markets."[165] Various protest and resistance movements have continued to emerge in response to these historical legacies, notably in the French Overseas Department of Guadeloupe where the Collective Lyannaj Kont Pwofitasyon (Collective Against Extreme Exploitation) solidarity movement was launched in 2009.[166] These, and analogous forms of protest, resistance, and solidarity, are anchored in what Yarimar Bonilla has identified as a seemingly ineradicable system of production, ultimately never able to satiate those "European alimentary tastes" that nourish the "absurd colonial frame," and yet, for "ecological regeneration" to occur, these "colonial archaisms" must be necessarily relinquished.[167]

As we will see in the next chapter, intra- and extra-continental migration in which climate change is a component has increasingly interjected itself into conversations and debates on immigration.[168] Today, *migrant ecologies*, just like any other category of migration, pertain to the movement of a species to a different environment. Accordingly, new categories have emerged in an attempt to address this phenomenon: "climate migrants," "climate refugees" or "environmental migrants." These developments require further attention, above all because they are tethered to disquieting nationalisms and because, as Saskia Sassen has observed, "They point to larger histories and geographies in the making. Further, they tell us about the gravity of conditions in their places of origin."[169] Charting the coordinates of the journey ahead will necessarily entail revisiting the rationale that shaped the colonial adventure, one in which, as Bruno Latour has argued, Europe has "the greatest responsibility in the history of the ecological upheaval."[170]

In Chapter 17, titled "Of the limits of the penal branch of jurisprudence," in *An Introduction to the Principles of Morals and Legislation*, English philosopher and jurist Jeremy Bentham famously posed the question of the applicability of moral rights to nonhuman animals: "The question is not, Can they reason? Nor, Can they talk? But, Can they suffer?"[171] Philippe Descola, in *Beyond Nature and Culture*, proposes an "extensionist ethics" that would make provisions for nonhumans in the form of a "moral consideration that used to be attached solely to humans," a dynamic "in which the emphasis is placed on the responsibilities of humans in the preservation of a balance between ecosystemic communities."[172] As the spectacle of nature grieving and suffering unfolds, uninhabitable lands, contaminated waterways and compromised air are *fighting back*, assaulted by toxins, pollution, reduced oxygen, excessive CO_2 and despoliation, and are articulating their plight through tornadoes, storms, rising sea water levels and the proliferation of catastrophic incidents, gathered together in an orchestra of loud cries, screams and expressions of unconscionable pain. As Aimé Césaire wrote in 1939, concerned with attuning to the world around him, "I would go to this land of mine and I would say to it: 'Embrace me without fear [...] And if all I can do is speak, it is for you I shall speak.' And again I would say: 'My mouth shall be the mouth of those calamities that have no mouth, my voice the freedom of those who break down in the prison holes of despair'."[173]

Chapter 2

MIGRANT ECOLOGIES

We can understand nothing about the politics of the last fifty years if we do not put the question of climate change and its denial front and center.

Bruno Latour[1]

So that is how to create a single story, show a people as one thing, as only one thing, over and over again, and that is what they become. It is impossible to talk about the single story without talking about power. [...] How they are told, who tells them, when they're told, how many stories are told, are really dependent on power.

Chimamanda Ngozi Adichie[2]

Viewing present ecological disasters including climate change as an outgrowth of colonial forms of labor, production, and energy use helps us understand something about how race, as a flexible regime of colonial power and profit, and racism, as the structured management of group vulnerability to premature death, have shaped ecologies of migration.

Neel Ahuja[3]

The government of human mobility might well be the most important problem to confront the world during the first half of the twenty-first century.

Achille Mbembe[4]

"The wind of change that carried my own parents across the globe in the twentieth-century was a mere gust compared with the hurricane that is coming."[5] In making this assertion on October 3, 2023, former UK home secretary Suella Braverman did not hesitate to embed climate alongside migration invasion metaphors in repeated assertions aimed at heightening anxiety around global population movement patterns. The transhistorical connection with Empire was evident, drawing as she did on the words of Conservative Party prime minister Harold Macmillan who, in his address to Members of both Houses of the Parliament of the Union of South Africa in Cape Town on February 3, 1960, had asserted that "The wind of change is blowing through this continent," in what he deemed an apt description of the ongoing collapse of the former British Empire at the time. As we shall see, recourse to climatic metaphors in order to describe migratory pressures and national collapse exploits the general consensus that climate change and global warming are *negative* developments. As Katherine E. Russo has argued, "The use of topoi related to natural disasters, chaos and catastrophe and intensification strategies were found to emphasize ideas of security and safety [...] In this manner, the symbolic images of climate and environmental refugees may be read as an example of how the fantasy of border control is connected to the affective state of paranoia—a perception of white injury where worrying becomes the dominant affective mode of expressing one's attachment to the nation."[6]

There are, of course, numerous precursors to the aforementioned rhetoric. After all, Winston Churchill had no qualms championing the use of the slogan "Keep England White" as the Conservative Party headed for a General Election in 1955. Later, on April 20, 1968, Enoch Powell (Member of Parliament for Wolverhampton South West) shared his anti-Commonwealth immigration stance at the Conservative Association meeting in Birmingham, an intervention that became known as "The Rivers of Blood Speech." On this occasion, he claimed to relay the concerns of a growing number of his constituents: "In this country in fifteen or twenty years' time the black man will have the whip hand over the white man" and "whole areas, towns and parts of towns across England will be occupied by different sections of the immigrant and immigrant-descended population [...] It is this fact above all which creates the extreme urgency of action now, of just that kind of action which is hardest for politicians to take, action where the difficulties lie in the present but the evils to be prevented or minimized lie several parliaments ahead." Thus, he concluded, "As I look ahead, I am filled with foreboding. Like the Roman, I seem to see 'the River Tiber foaming with much blood'."[7] He was, of course, bemoaning the sense of displacement that accompanied the recalibration of previously asymmetrical power dynamics between the colonizer and the colonized and that were interwoven into the fabric of European consciousness and ingrained in the scaffolding of Empire. Ultimately, he voiced a fear of *being displaced by the displaced*, in other words, *of being landless on his land*. These types of constructs have yielded a rather stubborn conflation between Europeanness and Whiteness, forms of racial prejudice that continue to be exploited by far-right commentators and groups. Indeed, as Bayo Akomolafe has powerfully argued, "Tug at the web of white fragility and xenophobia today [...] and you'll awaken deeply held fears about the scarcity of space. [...] What masquerades as pure hate is actually not *pure* at all – nothing is pure *anything* at crossroads. Instead 'hate' in this instance is an ecosystem of unresolved anxiety, centuries of displacement and wandering, the dark animus

and schadenfreude gained from maltreating others believed to be ontologically inferior to you, and the longing to be truly met and embraced as the
world experiences its ongoing upheavals. To summarily denounce this hate
– while in keeping with what moral authorities must do – is, quite ironically,
to lose an opportunity to excavate the shared histories, mangled hopes and
desperate inclinations dwelling under the surface of things."[8]

In *Down to Earth: Politics in the New Climatic Regime*, Bruno Latour illustrated
the various ways in which climate change has bent the arc of politics in new
directions: "We can understand nothing about the politics of the last fifty
years if we do not put the question of climate change and its denial front and
center."[9] Central to his observations was the seismic decision made during his
first term in office by President Donald Trump on June 1, 2017, to withdraw
from the Paris Climate Agreement (shortly after his second inauguration
ceremony on January 21, 2025, he re-exited the accord that his predecessor
had reinstated), a step that provided unequivocal assurance that henceforth,
"Everyone now knows that the climate question is at the heart of all *geopolitical*
issues and that it is directly tied to the question of injustice and inequality."[10]

One of the important ways in which this chapter merges with the previous discussion concerns the relationship between land and the environment.
Agricultural land use conformed with settler colonial models, processes that
upended the ecologies on which people depended. These "ecosystems of relations," as Patrick Chamoiseau[11] and Felwine Sarr have shown, are structured
around a relationality "based on this principle of war, conquest and appropriation" which calls for a shift in mindset that would enable people to "consider nature not as a resource that we exploit, but as a place that shelters us
and offers us life, as a living and inexhaustible library from which we learn."[12]
What has changed, however, is the direction of population movements, and
in this reconfigured framework, those who "had been subjected to the impact
of the 'great discoveries', of empires, modernization, development, and finally
globalization [...] knew quite well what it meant to be chased out of one's land.
They had no choice but to become experts on the question of how to survive
conquest, extermination, land grabs," whereas now, "the great novelty for the
modernizing peoples is that this territorial question is now addressed to them
as well as to the others."[13]

As we saw in the previous chapter, "subsum[ing] agriculture to the needs
of industry" directly influenced climate change and compromised foodways,
compelling populations to rely on global food systems, while also fostering
a dependency on World Bank and International Monetary Fund loans.[14]
Similarly, neocolonial initiatives aimed at modernizing agriculture, notably under the aegis of the Green Revolution (1960–1980), ended up, as Eric
Holt-Giménez's work demonstrates, "flooding the global food market with

food. The oversupply drove prices steadily downward. [...] This squeezed borrowing countries that had counted on high prices in global markets to pay back their development loans. [...] Countries began defaulting on their loans, sending the Global South into a profound economic crisis and creating an unpayable foreign debt."[15] The business model implemented by the World Bank and International Monetary Fund compelled African governments (among others) to enact economic liberalism and development politics that embraced structural adjustment programs, measures that voided the prospect of instituting food sovereignty while expanding food insecurity as dependence and reliance on supplies from the Global North.[16]

These policies, as T. J. Demos indicates, "help to maintain a global system of economic and political inequality that drives the cycle of migration."[17] In French colonies in Africa, for example, a new currency was introduced—the "CFA franc," an acronym that corresponded to Colonies françaises d'Afrique (French Colonies in Africa)—and initially distributed in the colonies. The contemporary incarnation—the Communauté financière en Afrique—is a common currency circulating in the Union économique et monétaire ouest-africaine (West African Economic and Monetary Union, UEMOA) and the Communauté économique et monétaire de l'Afrique centrale (Economic and Monetary Community of Central Africa, CEMAC), configurations that essentially replicate the post-independence nation-states that made up the previous colonial divisions between the AEF (Afrique Equatoriale Française / French Equatorial Africa) and AOF (Afrique Occidentale Française / French West Africa).[18] "The effect of 'reconditioning' the terrain represented by these countries for an expansion of new forms of advanced capitalism," Saskia Sassen has asserted, resulted in the "immiseration and expulsion of growing numbers of people who cease to be of value as workers and consumers." [19] Communities in which people were born and raised gradually became uninhabitable.

Framing Colonialism: Climate Change and Migration

Although belated, recognition in 2022 by the United Nations Intergovernmental Panel on Climate Change (IPCC) of the role of colonialism in "dangerous anthropogenic interference" was an important step: "Vulnerability of eco-systems and people to climate change differs substantially among and within regions, driven by patterns of intersecting socio-economic development, unsustainable ocean and land use, inequity, marginalization, historical and ongoing patterns of inequity such as colonialism."[20] As Cajetan Iheka has argued, these conclusions underscore the degree to which European colonial powers were "complicit in ecological degradation," and more importantly why "Africa deserves special attention in the energy humanities [...] because the continent discloses the most visceral social and ecological costs [...] environmental devastation resulting from resource extraction alongside existing and speculative infrastructures of finitude suitable for a diminished planet."[21] Climate change is connected to displacement within national, international, intracontinental and extracontinental contexts. The interplay between land exploitation and population displacement is, of course, a relationship with a very long history. Climate change has introduced a number of variables as well as an acute level of unpredictability. As Parag Khanna has argued, "those countries least responsible for climate change" are today most impacted by it, compelling a reckoning with the absurdity of circumstances given that, as Amitav Ghosh forewarns us, "The Anthropocene has reversed the temporal order of modernity: those at the margins are now the first to experience the future that awaits all of us."[22]

The increase in greenhouse gas emissions in the atmosphere during fossil fuel combustion is caused by anthropogenic human activities, and the resulting pollution has been documented. Similarly, the nefarious impact of colonial policies on the land and the accompanying environmental damage was already a concern for indigenous populations, botanists, chemists and physicists who monitored atmospheric changes and indicators of degradation over several generations. At the Earth Summit in Rio de Janeiro (Brazil) in 1992 (and subsequently, at various COP conferences, or in international treaties such as the Kyoto Protocol or the Paris Climate Agreement), as the architect Philippe Rahm has argued, "human responsibility for global warming and its disastrous ecological and human consequences came to be officially recognized around the world" and was initially discussed with sense of urgency and recognition of the need for action and a coordinated planetary response.[23]

In just the past decade, positions have evolved dramatically in terms of evaluating the relationship between climate change and migration. Emphasis on "multi-causality" and "variable factors" positions climate change at the center of discussions, but this can actually complicate the assessment of the impact because "climate change is mainly generating slow-onset, incremental environmental degradation," as Roger Zetter has explained.[24] The risk, according to Maurice Stierl, is that "by reducing migration to seemingly easily discernible factors, it is unable to comprehend the complexity of contemporary migration."[25] Important steps therefore need to be taken in order to ascertain the global impact of these changes but *also* in countering false narratives pertaining to the climate change-migration nexus. Equally important is the recognition that the contemporary focus is an outgrowth of earlier patterns, important considerations, as France's leading demographer Hervé Le Bras has underscored: "Climate variations did not wait for the present era to influ-ence migration."[26]

   Although anthropogenic pollution is widely accepted, climate change and global warming remain polarizing issues. Scientific indicators point unam-biguously to environmental *deterioration*, although a lingering issue is the rela-tive absence of political or scientific consensus when it comes to establishing the relationship between climate change and migration. Scientific data over-whelmingly rely on estimates shaped by common methodologies that seek to establish an equational alignment between population density, popula-tion growth and expected rises in sea level. Ultimately then, any attempt at achieving a long-term prognosis of the climate-migration continuum must invariably emphasize the unpredictable and "highly speculative" nature of developments, factors which together, as Hein de Haas, Stephen Castles and Mark J. Miller have argued, mean that "it is not possible to make a direct link between climate change, environmental stress and large-scale migration."[27] In a context characterized by "the relative lack of academic research on links between migration and climate change," as Neel Ahuja maintains, "concern about global warming as a driving force in the current displacements is grow-ing, and crisis thinking is quickly generating depictions of Black and Brown migrants from Africa and Asia fleeing shrinking zones of habitability."[28]

   Having said this, climate and migration are emerging as increasingly important fields of interdisciplinary research with significant cultural, politi-cal and social ramifications. But it also remains a fact that the political instru-mentalization of climate and migration has complicated the analysis of the phenomenon in often unexpected and unanticipated ways. The purpose of this book is not to conclusively arbitrate on these issues, but rather to disen-tangle some of the strands and stakes evident in these divisive debates. At the same time, the objective is also to highlight the multifarious ways in which "the overlapping and ever-shifting contexts of climate change," as Andrew Baldwin and Giovanni Bettini have demonstrated, "might be used to *politicize* migration."[29] How these questions are framed is therefore crucial. Increasing recourse is being made to categories such as *environmental migrants* and *climate refugees*, in scholarship, but primarily by politicians, policymakers and inter-national organizations. Amitav Ghosh has also indicated how these terms "have been embraced by many displaced people," although his experience is that although migrants are "well informed about climate change [...] none of them believed that their journeys had been driven primarily by environmen-tal disruptions."[30] As we shall see, emphasizing the deep interconnectedness between climate change and migration is important, but perhaps less so than the recognition that a conjunction of factors—that include extreme weather events, sea level rise, compromised agricultural land and food security, water scarcity, ecosystem disruption and conflict—shape, and will increasingly continue to shape, displacement patterns.

The most frequent recourse to this, or related terminology, is to be found in the language used by various international organizations. Certainly, the 2018 Groundswell report produced by the Climate Change Group of the World Bank proved incredibly distracting and unhelpful when it came to identifying and implementing meaningful strategies and solutions to the planetary climate change challenge.[31] For example, the "Preparing for Internal Climate Migration" report made the claim that "internal climate migrants are rapidly becoming the human face of climate change. [...] without urgent global and national climate action, Sub-Saharan Africa, South Asia and Latin America could see more than 140 million people move within their countries' borders by 2050."[32] Three years later, in the updated 2021 report, "Acting on Internal Climate Migration," that figure had increased substantially, and climate change was now referred to as "an increasingly potent driver of migration," one that "could force 216 million people across six world regions to move within their countries by 2050."[33] As Hein de Haas reminds us, these figures have absolutely zero correlation with sociological factors, given that "most people living in the poorer countries of the world do not have the resources to move over larger distances."[34]

These questions are also, of course, gendered. In fact, as Neel Ahuja has claimed, women stand in as "the embodiment of climate change's human impacts."[35] Connections are to be found throughout this chapter, notably in the discussion of Great Replacement conspiracy theories as they pertain to reproductive rights and "questions about who should procreate more and whose procreation is alarming and should be halted," as Sarah Bracke and Luis Manuel Hernández Aguilar have argued.[36] Feminist theorists such as Judith Butler, Elsa Dorlin and Françoise Vergès have emphasized the body as the privileged site for the interplay between identity and power, notably in the context of colonial and postcolonial frameworks as they relate to the interface between gender, sexualized violence, migration, racism and xenophobia.[37] Elsewhere, in a report published by the IOM, one finds emphasis on the reality that "far from being gender-neutral, climate change, and the use of migration as a coping mechanism, will have specific gendered impacts [...] While it is difficult to make predictions about how communities will adapt to climate change, the nature of migration as a result, and repercussions for gender dynamics and women's lives, it is essential nonetheless to recognize that climate change will have gender specific impacts, and, critically, to mainstream a gender perspective into climate change discussions."[38]

Carolyn Merchant's *The Death of Nature: Women, Ecology and the Scientific Revolution* remains an indispensable reference, juxtaposing as it does the precarious equilibrium between "nurturing and domination."[39] "The meta-phor of the earth," initially presented "as a nurturing mother was gradu-ally to vanish as a dominant image as the Scientific Revolution proceeded to mechanize and to rationalize the world view," and then the "second image, nature as disorder, called forth an important modern idea, that of power over nature. Two new ideas, those of mechanism and of the domination and mastery of nature, became core concepts of the modern world" and "the new images of mastery and domination functioned as cultural sanctions for the denudation of nature."[40] Frantz Fanon drew attention to the dehumanizing effects of colonialism and racism in *The Wretched of the Earth*, and the notion of "wretchedness" has proved helpful in discussions on gender discrimination and gender-based violence in the context of climate change and migration.[41] As Frances Pine and Haldis Haukanes have pointed out, we find ourselves in somewhat perplexing circumstances, "a moment of polarization in Europe (and beyond) in which on the one hand progress towards inclusion and equal-ity (gender, sexuality, reproduction, labor) is being made in terms of both policy and popular understandings and discourses, and on the other hand ideologies of exclusion, separation, and right-wing nationalism are effervesc-ing, fueled by strong populist movements and sentiments that are reinforced and legitimated by state policies of regulation."[42] Explanations may very well reside, as Kyle Powys Whyte has shown in the context of indigenous climate change studies, whereby climate change emerges as "both a gendered form of colonially imposed environmental change, and another intensified episode of colonialism that opens up Indigenous territories for capitalism and industri-alization that occurs through gender violence."[43]

Women migrants face specific forms of discrimination, as confirmed by studies conducted by the UNHCR (the UN Refugee Agency),[44] confirm-ing the role of climate change in "exacerbating the vulnerabilities and ine-qualities experienced by women, particularly those who live in rural areas or the Global South and those who are Black, Indigenous, or other people of color."[45] Camille Schmoll's research, published in *Les damnées de la terre. Femmes et frontières en Méditerranée*, focuses on women and the Mediterranean migration route, a dimension emphasized in the title of the above-mentioned book in which the term "damnées" (the "wretched") appears in the femi-nine plural.[46] Official migration data underestimates the number of women migrating while inadequately accounting for such factors as vulnerability and mortality rate, inaccurate and incomplete data that downplays historical vul-nerabilities and disparities that together contribute to the "invisibilization of women."[47] In fact, most of the newly available data reveals near parity between female-male migration levels, with women more often than not out-numbering men when it comes to regional and intranational displacement or movement. The IOM has described the phenomenon in terms of a "feminization of migration."[48]

Inspired by the work of Arjun Appadurai, Camille Schmoll redeploys the notion of a "moralscape," identifying a number of "frontiers" between "deserving / undeserving" human beings, and fastens on "other hierarchization processes" pertaining to "border work" and "gender work."[49] The border is an intrinsically violent space, and as Ursula Biemann's extensive and groundbreaking work has shown, the border "becomes materialized not only in architectural and structural measures but also in the corporate and social regulations of gender."[50] These observations extend to some of the feminist critiques alluded to earlier, since "women's bodies are the site of multiple social norms and forms of regulation and discipline, and offer an important framework for understanding and apprehending migration policies. Migration is, without a doubt, a test of the body."[51] Camille Schmoll calls for changes in the way in which migration is discussed, insisting upon "comparative and intersectional" approaches, "comparative, because the connection between different regional and historical contexts allows us to account for the complexity of different types of migration and their variation according to places, timeframes, origins, and destinations" while an "intersectional perspective makes it possible to show how female positions are intertwined within multiple power relations, in terms of gender, but also class, sexuality, ethnicity, race, physical ability or generational."[52] Scholars have drawn attention to the "sensationalist" and "stereotypical ways" in which gender is framed, and fiction writers have explored various challenges associated with migration, such as the impact on communities and families left behind, humiliation, sexual violence, vulnerability and intimidation.[53]

The ethical and moral dimension of these questions is often sidelined, privileging instead alarmist projections—the scaffolding for which draws upon questionable data or is informed by a willingness to exaggerate and inflate statistics or misrepresent data—that simultaneously draw attention to the uncertainty and unpredictability of climate change and migration while also amplifying the threatening dimension of these prognoses.[54] Ultimately, these serve to justify the need for a range of enforcement and humanitarian mechanisms. The evidence confirms this, notably in the proliferation of "repression, surveillance, and violence [...] as the preferred forms of adaptation" rather than actually seeking to address the politicized causes of climate change and addressing the "collision of political, economic, and environmental disasters" which Christian Parenti describes as "catastrophic convergence."[55] The emphasis on security adaptation is itself premised on a flawed logic. Climate change and global warming are planetary issues that necessitate an articulated and coordinated response, and though many see salvation in impregnable fortresses, there exists no wall capable of selectively protecting only the few. Ironically, those that seek protection in order to *escape from the invasion*, neglect that in reality, the imagined *invaders would first have to evade*, something which most are unable to do since they are more often than not "trapped, often with any hope of escape, they bear the brunt of the shock of terrestrial life on a damaged planet" as Achille Mbembe asks us to bear in mind, and secondly because movement actually entails "cross[ing] lines and barriers."[56] Addressing planetary challenges begins with granting climate change the attention it warrants, debunking various myths and reckoning with carefully coordinated disinformation and misinformation campaigns.

The Afterlives of Imperial Fantasies

The campaign for the United Kingdom's withdrawal from the European Union (Brexit) relied heavily on disinformation strategies. These actions were aimed at misleading voters, most notably in terms of the persistent assertions and claims that the EU's migration policies were responsible for uncontrolled immigration to the island. Recourse to such malicious propagandist strategies, although not unique to the context of climate change and migration, has become especially prevalent in that domain. The question, therefore, of their intentionality is important, and Hein de Haas does not hesitate to describe these mechanisms as examples of propaganda: in the first instance, they "perpetuate a series of myths as part of *deliberate* strategies to distort the truth about migration. Such propaganda is part of active efforts to sow unjustified fear and misinformation," and in the second, self-fulfilling outcome, translate into "failed" or "counterproductive" migration policies precisely "because they are based on a series of false assumptions, or myths, about the nature, causes and impacts of migrations."[57] These devices have been shored up by crisis and invasion narratives. In Christopher Priest's 1972 dystopian novel *Fugue for a Darkening Island*, readers bear witness to the "impact of hundreds of thousands of [...] refugees flooding into the country," arriving in "small boats and dinghies, offloaded out at sea from the larger ships. [...] The African continent had become uninhabitable, and millions of refugees were spreading out around the world."[58] Although the initial response in the novel was overwhelmingly humanitarian, the "polarization of attitudes was accelerated [and] schisms in the country grew deeper," and eventually "agitators from the extreme right wing attempted to stir up racist feelings against the new arrivals."[59]

The racial discourse that shaped colonialism continues to thrive in the postcolonial temporal era, and both climate change and migration find themselves interlaced and instrumentalized to analogous exclusionary ends. This is an emotional debate, thereby increasing its potential for manipulation, one in which researchers seeking to produce "scientific" data and statistics are confronted with a Sisyphean task. Indicative of this is the oft-repeated research conclusion that juxtaposes an "idea" with "facts": "the *idea* that migration is at all-time high has gained the status of an almost unquestionable truth," yet "the *facts* tell quite a different story" since, "over the past decades, global migration levels have remained remarkably stable."[60] Ultimately then, interpretation begins with recognizing that directional shifts in migration patterns since the end of World War II have inaugurated "a form of propaganda that is deliberately designed to sow panic and fear [and that promotes a] fabricated and recycled idea that the West is besieged," in other words arguments reducible to simplistic correlative tautologies that "amalgamate[s] into the dominant idea of a 'migration crisis'" shaped by "a series of global, economic, demographic and environmental crises."[61] Indeed, as Paul Gilroy has repeatedly demonstrated, the "racisms of Europe's colonial and imperial phase preceded the appearance of migrants inside the European citadel. It was racism, not diversity, that made their arrival a problem."[62]

Among the most impactful statements in this regard have been those made by Donald Trump. Originating with the slogan "Make America Great Again" (MAGA), tactics and terminological choices have consistently described immigration as a threat—*terrorism* (the travel ban on Muslim-majority countries), *criminality* ("bad hombres" from Mexico and *undesirability* (people originating from so-called "shithole countries"). When discussing immigration and "caravans" at the Mexico-US border in an interview that Raheem Kassam streamed on the conservative right-wing media source *The National Pulse* (September 27, 2023), he stated that "nobody has seen anything like we're witnessing right now. […] It's poisoning the blood of our country," or as one of his presidential campaign X accounts (@TrumpWarRoom) tweeted on August 13, 2024, "Import the third world, become the third world." These "ecologies of waste," a construct used by Elizabeth M. DeLoughrey in *Allegories of the Anthropocene*, reveal "how state hierarchies contribute to the positioning of certain people as matter out of place" and how "relegating human beings to waste is a dehumanizing and deeply entrenched social and political practice of capitalism, empire, and neoliberal globalization."[63]

As things stand, it would be more accurate to state that we find ourselves confronted with an *anti-immigration crisis*, one that heightens the precariousness and vulnerability of migrants, and in which, as Valeria Bello has argued, "prejudice, and not migration, is a global security threat."[64] It only takes a cursory glance to realize that the category "immigration" has expanded exponentially to the extent that it now encompasses threats presented by race, country of origin, gender identity, religion, cultural incompatibility, terrorism, demography, climate, health and so forth. Alongside these, recourse has been made to increasingly vague categories that include illegal, irregular, clandestine, undocumented, unauthorized, unwanted and criminality, collectively representing a danger, menace and threat to the homeostasis of the nation-state, and that therefore necessitate demonstrable countermeasures. The consequences of such rhetoric were strikingly evident in the attacks by mobs of white people that took place in various cities in the United Kingdom during the summer of 2024 in the aftermath of the stabbing of three young girls in the seaside town of Southport. These occurred following inaccurate claims that the assailant was a Muslim asylum seeker, rather than a British Christian born in Wales to Rwandan parents. As David Olusoga remarked, "They are not looking to address inequalities but to target those whom they will never accept as fellow Britons. In doing so, they, and those swept up in the chaos they foment, are willing to tear apart the nation to which they preposterously claim to be patriots."[65]

Objecting to immigration has become more widespread, though few political parties would survive politically without it. Mobility is transactional, shaped by projection, a contingency that Italian sociologist Alessandro Dal Lago understood very well, illuminating discussions with his insightful analysis whereby

> every discrimination or persecution of internal or external foreigners occurs through recourse to mechanisms of the victimization of the aggressor and assigning guilt to victims. The aggressors are usually the "victims" of wrongs that must be righted or the weaker citizens abandoned by the institutions, and who band together to enact their own justice. Those who are attacked or discriminated against are the foreign bodies, invaders, corrupters or enemies of a defenseless society.[66]

The concerted attention to immigration since the 1990s—a time frame that coincides with growing attention to climate change since the Earth Summit held in Rio de Janeiro in 1992—has been built around a "tautology of fear" that emerges as the contrary to inertia, launching instead an acceleration of frightening and ominous narratives that "demonstrate[s] the reality of that which is being decried."[67] This rhetoric of fear drives what the distinguished lawyer and immigration advocate Claire Rodier has aptly described as the "business of xenophobia," a perpetual enforcement and protective operation since "always more, always better, always more costly," and because at the end of the day, "in the game of cat and mouse, the cat does not necessarily have an interest in eliminating its prey."[68] Military invasions are premised on the objective of occupation and subjugation. By mobilizing these associations in the context of immigration, one ends up invariably stipulating the need for militarized borders while implanting a dependency on new technologies, the catalyst for a fiercely competitive and extremely lucrative market for developers, contractors and manufacturers, state and private sectors, that calls for constant equipment and infrastructure upgrades, satellite imagery, buoys equipped with infrared sensors and hydrophones, early warning systems and drones, as well as a proliferation of barriers, borders, fences, frontiers, ramparts and walls. The message is clear: "We will protect you."[69] These investments and responses are aimed at reassuring, since, as Achille Mbembe explains, "By inventing for all intents and purposes an enemy and in making fear of this enemy into the cornerstone of everyday life and culture, the objective has been to accord legitimacy to the role of the authorities as the enforcers of protection and security."[70]

This is of course a transcolonial matter, one in which the world continues to be perceived through an "imperial optic" reliant upon "certain continuities that structure experience from the vantage point of Western colonialism and its ongoing colonial present."[71] In the Prologue and in Chapter 1, we considered the ceremonial launches of ecolonial ships for distant shores. Patrick Chamoiseau encourages us to keep this historical context in mind since, unlike their European migratory predecessors, immigrants do *not* arrive in gunboats; the so-called invasion is *not* "military," in other words, "they come with no flag, banner, or coat of arms."[72] Nevertheless, these are recurring tropes, mutating concepts that coalesce into new narratives that nourish racism and migrantphobia. Ultimately, as Anthony Mangeon has shown, invasion is "never anything other than the concrete expression of a phantasmatic obsession with the increased presence of the Other in our world, and which could lead to its overthrow."[73] Concepts such as "Fortress Europe" (a World War II propaganda term that has been redeployed to refer to the EU's border and detention apparatus) and organizations such as the European Border and Coast Guard Agency (Frontex, formerly the European Agency for the Management of Operational Cooperation at the External Borders of the Member States of the European Union) and the European Border Surveillance System (Eurosur), which tracks "illegal" immigration, have inserted themselves as guarantors of security and guardians of European identity. But at the heart of this resides a narrative, one in which history and memory serve a broader nostalgia, as a container for a sense of loss and the accompanying desire for a commitment to restoring the circumstances of a bygone era. In the United Kingdom, for example, as Paul Gilroy argued in *Postcolonial Melancholia,*

The political conflicts which characterize multicultural societies can take on a very different aspect if they are understood to exist firmly in a context supplied by imperial and colonial history. Though that history remains marginal and largely unacknowledged, surfacing only in the service of nostalgia and melancholia, it represents a store of unlikely connections and complex interpretative resources. [Revisionist accounts] obstruct the development of multiculturalism by making the formative experience of empire less profound and less potent in shaping the life of colonizing powers than it actually was. This popular, revisionist output is misleading and dangerous because it feeds the illusion that Britain has been or can be disconnected from its imperial past.[74]

This type of nostalgia was evident when UK prime minister Theresa May invoked a "global Britain" in the context of Brexit negotiations, summoning a bygone glorious era when the sun never went down on the British empire.

To this end, decolonization has endeavored to restore territories and valorize universal equality, positions that stand diametrically opposed to colonial notions of hierarchy and superiority. The latter have been invalidated, yet othering processes remain operative. Anti-colonial alliances attempted to disassemble prevailing structural inequities, but new personifications of these are today evident in the interface between nationalism and nativism. In France, for example, the universality of the foundational values of the Republic, namely Liberty, Equality and Fraternity, have been questioned because of their uneven application in colonies, a questioning that has persisted given the inability to reconcile the imperative of colorblind policies with tenacious racial profiling and discrimination. According to historians Nicolas Bancel and Pascal Blanchard and sociologist Ahmed Boubeker, "we live in an era in which identity labels and conflicts have reached a level of violence similar to that found in French society during the colonial era."[75] Colonialism was also, of course, built around the insidious alliance between identity and erasure; the very premise of equality remains inconceivable to some, and this is evident in the enduring traces of colonial mindsets in European societies. Former European colonial powers have yet to disentangle themselves from the colonial narrative that delineated the contours and status of modern European nation-states. Caryl Phillips gives a clear and lucid account of this: "Europe's absence of self-awareness seems to me directly related to a lack of a cogent sense of history. [...] But history is also the prison from which Europeans often speak, and in which they would confine black people. It is a false history, an unquestioning and totally selfish one, in which whites civilize and discover" and "Europe must begin to restructure the tissue of lies."[76]

Europe on Edge

In theory at least, given the coexistence of national and supranational identities in the "family of democratic European countries" that make up the EU, multiple identities shape the interplay between member states. However, the contours of the collective "we" in the family portrait remain unclear.[77] A combination of anti-EU and anti-immigrant rhetoric has had a deep impact on politics and resonated with voters, yielding protectionist national policies and increasingly restrictive immigration legislation. Parties across the political spectrum now find themselves eager to demonstrate the effectiveness of their policies and proposed solutions to a national population to whom they are ultimately electorally accountable. Politicians have sought to capitalize on this dimension by alluding to a supposed erosion of the nation-state, assigning blame to supposed out-of-control non-Western immigration and charting a path toward recapturing, reclaiming and reconquering power through restrictions on mobility.

Certainly, the globalized nature of human interaction has contributed to the loss of exceptionality of the nation-state while concurrently reviving calls for cultural, political and social recalibration. Over the past twenty years, both national and European parliamentary elections have been symptomatic in this regard, and numerous far-right, extreme-right and radical-right parties have made significant advances in terms of support, often outperforming traditional mainstream parties. In spite of their oppositional positions and because of variations in the process of distributing electoral outcomes in their respective national representative bodies, these EU-skeptic or EU-soft parties have often been able to achieve levels of electoral recognition in European parliamentary elections that they usually do not otherwise enjoy in national elections.

The question of European identity remains a contested one, and recent developments have only served to further highlight the lack of consensus when it comes to demarcating its parameters. Comprehensive efforts have been made to harmonize policy between EU member states and build a sense of shared identity. This has been informed by a complex process shaped by the tenuous relationship between insiders and outsiders, exclusionary mechanisms that define identity construction in negative terms rather than the outcome of efforts aimed at consolidating feelings of belonging through recourse to affirmative points of commonality.[78] In other words, a persistent tension exists between an ambiguous "we" and "us." Categories such as "Third Country Nationals" or "Non-EU foreign nationals," alongside age-old racial and religious attributes, serve to bolster the idea of non-Europeans circulating among a privileged multigenerational citizenry. Far-right parties have been especially adept at exploiting these cultural and social divides and are successful at promoting the incontrovertible appeal of protectionist and anti-immigration arguments. Their policy agendas have now, to varying degrees, been appropriated, instrumentalized, mainstreamed, or normalized, compelling parties across the political spectrum to contend with these questions.

Significant changes have taken place incrementally in European politics. Two notable examples are France and Germany. Both systems had, historically, been dominated by major parties, yet are now increasingly fragmented. We have witnessed the erosion of "big" parties and the proliferation of smaller ones. These developments have translated into increasing divisiveness, polarization and voter disaffection (low turnout and high abstention rates), while of course rendering coalition formation increasingly complex and volatile. Breakthroughs of movements and new political groups have been recorded in Austria, France, Germany, Hungary, Italy, the Netherlands, Poland, Romania and Slovakia, among numerous other countries.[79] In the 1970s, anti-immigration agendas were seen as *extreme* far-right or *radical-right* positions, but today, immigration is usually a defining issue in national elections. As Cas Mudde has argued, the 2023 Dutch General Election marked a "turning point in Geert Wilders' path to Dutch electoral triumph [...] Not only is the far right now part of the political mainstream, it is an increasingly dominant part of it."[80] Harsh anti-immigration rhetoric has become progressively more palatable, the result of the growing acceptance of such positions.[81] In Germany, for example, different political parties have invoked the need for a "firewall" against the far-right Alternative for Germany, but the significant encroachment and ultimately success in elections have made such assertions increasingly unsustainable.

Blaming migrants and refugees for society's ills partially explains Donald Trump's successful transformation of the Republican Party, much in the same way as the Conservative Party in the United Kingdom converted immigration into the most salient issue motivating "leave" supporters in the Brexit referendum. Political figures such as Boris Johnson ("Take Back Control" and "Get Brexit Done") and Rishi Sunak ("Stop the Boats") did not hesitate to employ catchphrases and slogans during the Brexit and subsequent general election campaigns.[82] The objective was to embolden racism and migrant-phobia, and as home secretary, Suella Braverman often exaggerated statistics to heighten the "danger narrative," on occasion in contradiction with international law.[83] Speaking at the American Enterprise Institute for Public Policy Research (AEI) in Washington, DC on September 26, 2023, she equated the United Kingdom and Mediterranean context with that of the United States' southern border, and reiterated a number of platitudes about invasion and threats to the West. Uncontrolled illegal immigration was presented as "an existential challenge for the political and cultural institutions of the West" and "unless we act, it will only worsen in the years to come" and "become one of the top five global risks in the next decade, ahead of national resource crisis, geoeconomic confrontation, and environmental disasters."[84]

Together, these ascriptive categories and labels serve to reinforce the peripheral status of various individuals and groups, building on generalizations and stereotypes, while simultaneously emphasizing distance and insurmountable differences through polarizing rhetoric. "How was I to reconcile," Caryl Phillips ponders, "the contradiction of feeling British, while being constantly told in many subtle and unsubtle ways that I did not belong."[85] Individual positions are thus entrenched in identities that must be protected at all costs in order to initially safeguard the national family and by extension the European one as well. As such, this question is reframed as an extinction threat—a dimension to which we will return shortly in the discussion pertaining to patriotic ecologies—whereby nationalistic proclivities rejoin environmental species protection, jointly requiring proactive measures and concrete actions aimed at securing the longevity of a species poised for substitution and supplantation, in other words, replacement.[86]

In the 2022 French presidential election, over sixty years since the majority of the French Empire achieved independence, every major candidate made statements about colonial history in a fierce process of one-upmanship.[87] These debates, certainly not dissimilar to those found elsewhere in Europe, occurred in a society in which decolonization has been impeded by lingering hierarchies and neocolonial practices, perpetuating age-old asymmetries and displaced notions of *grandeur*. As Salman Rushdie has asked with reference to analogous matters in the United States and the United Kingdom, "When exactly was that? What is the date to which we are looking backwards? Was it, for example, when there was slavery? Was it before women had the right to vote? Was it before the civil rights movement? Exactly which is the American greatness to which we must return?"[88] He encourages the reader to recognize that "the thing about the golden age is that it never existed" and that when applied to "the Brexit catastrophe," one lands upon "another golden age myth, which is: 'England used to be this glorious country and it could be that glorious country again, if only we could get rid of all these foreigners'."[89] This menace has been exemplified in the writings of far-right British journalist Douglas Murray who, in *The Strange Death of Europe: Immigration, Identity, Islam*, resorted to the three "I"s contained in his book title to describe the ills of twenty-first-century society.[90]

Patriotic and Border Ecologies

In *The Next Great Migration: The Beauty and Terror of Life on the Move*, Sonia Shah emphasizes the importance of accounting for the part that racialization plays in the climate change migration nexus, stressing that "creatures and peoples [were] conflat[ed] one with the other" and that "scientific ideas that cast migration as a form of disorder were not obscure theoretical concerns. [...] They were widely disseminated in popular culture."[91] Historically, a correlation is to be found between the work of naturalists and the interest in the classification of species, offering convenient ways to distinguish "between 'us' and 'them'."[92] During the eighteenth century, racial taxonomies and pre-anthropometric techniques contributed to the "systematic and scientific classification of races."[93] Reflections on climate played an important role in scientific discourse, and as such, climate metaphors contain residual markers of these investigations. Frantz Fanon was of course no stranger to such questions and dissected these constructs in *The Wretched of the Earth*: "This compartmentalized world, this world divided in two, is inhabited by different species. [...] Looking at the immediacies of the colonial context, it is clear that what divides this world is first and foremost what species, what race one belongs to. [...] The ruling species is first and foremost the outsider from elsewhere, different from the indigenous population, the 'others'."[94]

Rejoining these historical patterns, Margaret Thatcher made immigration a central campaign issue, explaining in an interview on Granada TV's *World in Action* broadcast on January 27, 1978, that "people are really rather afraid that this country might be rather swamped by people with a different culture."[95] As Brigitte Nehrlich has shown, recourse to this "type of talk divides and polarizes people. It also stigmatizes 'the other'. Migrants are framed as invaders, criminals, a calamity and as posing a threat to decent, law-abiding, patriotic people," and resorting to nativistic rhetoric in this manner as the self-appointed "defender" of the nation is designed to achieve this outcome.[96] The outgrowth of this circular logic is that the "crisis narrative is further reinforced by the common use of [...] apocalyptic vocabulary" and the associative context of climate change operates optimally, as Hein de Haas explains.[97] The significant problem with this thinking is that it marginalizes what is so obviously true as to be indubitable, namely that "global warming is the most pressing issue facing humanity," yet "to link this issue with the specter of mass migration is a dangerous exercise based on myth rather than fact," all the more so because "the environment is but one of the many factors that shape migration, and this effect is indirect rather than direct."[98] What is crucial to emphasize is that vulnerability will be enhanced by "rising global temperatures," and that these, as Neel Ahuja confirms, "will increase the incidence of heat-related deaths, disease, food insecurity, and destructive weather, affecting poor countries most severely due to already overstressed infrastructures."[99]

Additionally, such frameworks also tend to obfuscate regional specificities, often underestimate community resourcefulness and do not adequately distinguish between intra- and extra-continental migration.[100] Furthermore, they downplay the colonial and neocolonial impact on environmental degradation, thereby weakening the link between those factors and the broader context of displacement. More recently, as Andrew Baldwin and Giovanni Bettini have argued, "privileging climate change as the main 'agent', 'determinant' or 'trigger' of migration. [...] obscures the always historical circumstances that lead people to migrate [...] the countless other counter-histories," effectively "superseding these counter-histories in favor of the perceived primacy of climate change, by reducing mobility to climate."[101] These questions are all the more fascinating precisely because of the sizeable challenge they present when it comes to deciphering how they have reconfigured contemporary politics. Environmental questions are increasingly cross-party issues, no longer reducible to exclusively left-leaning entities, resulting in an overall blurring of positions that one cannot always easily define along strict party lines and affiliations.[102] The far-right nevertheless remain, as Antoine Dubiau has shown, "more concerned with the defense of a way of life hooked on fossil energies than on the current ecological devastation,"[103] and as Christian Parenti explains, "climate-change denial" and "xenophobia" are aligned.[104]

Balša Lubarda's research, published in *Far-Right Ecologism: Environmental Politics and the Far Right in Hungary and Poland*, indicates how "the data from the European Parliament has shown that the far-right involvement in climate debates has been continuously increasing. Such an increase was informed both by the climate crisis and the related environmental issues on one hand, and the need to engage with salient debates to win (predominantly younger) voters on the other hand."[105] What we do find, though, as Bernard Forchtner has argued, is a persistent articulation between ethnonationalism and the natural environment, "linking membership in the nation to biological / racial and / or cultural traits" shaped by "the natural environment (and concerns over it) [evident in a] full-blown ecological worldview which stresses the interconnectedness of flora, fauna, the nation and its homeland."[106] In fact, as Andreas Malm has argued, "ecology is the Border," and to make this point references the positions of the former National Rally MEP Hervé Juvin, who justified borders for identity and ecological reasons, invoking the right to "defend his biotype against invasive species," whereby *green nationalism* offers both autonomy and protection.[107] In France, the National Front and its successor National Rally have platformed patriotic ecology as an integral component of its broader de-demonization strategy aimed at reforming the party's image and reputation and widening the appeal of their policies. This new pillar can be inscribed within the larger nationalist agenda under the aegis of green nationalism, exploiting the intersection between immigration and national identity and ecological issues, something which its current president Jordan Bardella has reiterated in terms of an "environmental and immigration challenge."[108] The appeal is equational: land, territory and identity. As Salomi Boukala and Eirini Tountasaki have shown, the "conception of nationhood is linked to a synthesis of blood, culture and territory."[109] The protectionist component replicates colonial mindsets since it "presupposes a distinction between a superior France and the 'Others' [...] that are excluded from the imagined community of the culturally and naturally superior French nation and territory."[110] Certainly, this appropriation of environmental issues by the French far-right compels us to monitor the ecofascist dimension, since when it comes down to it, as David Theo Goldberg has powerfully argued, "Green here is bleached white, soaked in the red blood of others. Blood and soil, race and nature: the battle cry of the ecofascists."[111]

The geography of Europe is important in tracking differences not only between parties on the left and the right but also between ideological branches. These differences are also reflected in the supranational alignments at the European Parliament, where elected members are seated according to their ideological profiles rather than national affiliations. Beyond the obvious instrumentalization of environmental questions for electoral expediency, recourse to climate catastrophe narratives amplifies such a discourse and has the potential to be recuperated by those expressing a concern with "protecting the 'authentic' species of the land" and combined with "nostalgic appreciation of the past environments [...] articulated as a lament for lost traditions, landscapes, but also territories."[112] These positions have been bolstered by persistent attacks on EU environmental policies and the Green Deal, which, like the conventions and treaties pertaining to international migration, are seen as undermining national sovereignty. In the pamphlet produced for the 2022 presidential elections, "L'environnement pour une écologie française" (The Environment for a French Ecology), the National Rally described these mechanisms as "climatic terrorism" and threats to "national independence," concluding that "ecology is incompatible with open borders and infinite individual mobility."[113] This reveals a synergy between denialist and negationist positions and the greening of nationalist policies, one in which grievances and suspicion of globalization and international solutions remain front and center.

The *Greening* of Hate

Demography, climate change, global warming, racial identity and reverse colonization all appear in the inventory of terms pertaining to Great Replacement conspiracy theories. These are based on unfounded fears of white erosion through racial mixing that can be traced to nineteenth-century racist ideologies. These continue to fuel and feed off collective anxieties that are key elements in the ecofascist playbook. As Sindre Bangstad and Maria Darwish have shown, "racism and racial fantasies pertaining to 'white replacement' are intrinsic to contemporary ecofascism. But what is particularly noteworthy for the contemporary form of racism, which is inherent to ecofascism, is the emphasis on biological diversity and the rendering of *nonwhite* immigrants as racialized minorities as 'foreign, invasive' species."[114] This is all the more paradoxical given that those "populations that were instrumental in advancing European colonialism, settler colonialism, and extractive racial capitalist formations and populations that sometimes also perpetrated actual colonial genocides are now cast as being under existential threat by formerly colonized and racialized populations. It is, in other words, impossible to think of ecofascism without also thinking about colonialism and settler colonialism."[115]

These paradigms have provided the contours of Great Replacement theory, which frames immigration as a concerted and deliberate effort to replace and substitute dominant White populations with ethnic minorities. It has taken a number of forms, more recently in the reinvigorated prevalence of the term "remigration" that proposes the return of non-ethnically Europeans to countries outside of Europe. Enoch Powell's assessment of immigration remains prominent in the oft-repeated claims articulated by the far-right, eager to counter what they see as the systematic dislodging of White Europeans.[116] The choice of words draws attention to specific connotations, symbolic associations and a social imaginary grafted onto a broader discursive realm in which myths, narratives and propaganda collide.[117] Ultimately, there is nothing surprising about the uptake of these conspiracy theories since, as Julia Ebner has shown in *Going Dark: The Secret Lives of Extremists*, the particular appeal of the concept is especially powerful given how it amalgamates "all four features of a violence-inciting ideology, so-called 'crisis narratives,'" namely "conspiracy, dystopia, impurity and existential threat. The idea is that Europeans are being replaced with racially and culturally distinct migrants (impurity) by a cabal of global elites and complicit actors in governments, tech firms and media outlets (conspiracy), leading to the gradual decay of society (dystopia) and the eventual extinction of whites (existential threat)."[118] German politician Thilo Sarrazin has described how "Germany is abolishing itself," French leader of the nationalist Reconquête! (Reconquest!)

party has evoked a "French Suicide," and Douglas Murray has been relentless in his criticism and denigration of Muslims and migrants, arguing that "Europe is committing suicide," thereby rejoining the conclusions reached by Enoch Powell half a century earlier.[119] Interestingly enough, the vocabulary of immigration has inserted itself into the technological domain, such that new categories are perpetually evolving in order to circumscribe evolutions in generational timescales, whereby digital immigrants (born before the widespread adoption of technologies) are contrasted with digital natives (who have lived alongside technological change) and digital migrants or digital refugees whose lives and professional environment have been disrupted by technological transition. As such, the online far-right ecosystem on which Julia Ebner's research has focused, provides invaluable insights into the multiple ways in which digital platforms increasingly provide safehavens for extremists, most notably in a context in which there has been a reversal or weakening of control over the monitoring of disinformation and misinformation as an outcome of technology leaders aligning themselves with far-right leaders and interfering in politics.[120]

A common stance has been to exploit climate change and population growth to justify repressive and restrictive immigration policies. This is symptomatic of the obstinate survival of Malthusian theories "in contemporary debates on migration, climate change, and even degrowth."[121] Speaking on CNews (a French network reputed for its support of far-right positions) on September 7, 2023, Éric Zemmour claimed that "Today, there is a continent, Africa, which is pouring into another, Europe. This migratory invasion is the challenge of the century."[122] Here, we have an example of liquid metaphors suggesting saturation and submersion. As Bram Frouws has underscored, "Within the migration-climate nexus, using water metaphors, the fear of large numbers of migrants and refugees and unsubstantiated claims about millions of people migrating due to climate change, turns out to be a particularly persistent narrative to mobilize action."[123] But there is also a deeply ironic dimension provided by decisions made initially during the 2016–2020 Trump presidency: "Trump denied climate change, yet proposed building a US-Mexico wall, which (according to the US military's own predictions) would be useful to stall future climate migration. […] In each case, a plausible response is made to climate change: not *as a climatic phenomenon*, but as a general social crisis requiring the imposition of an authoritarian state."[124] Fears concerning a "population bomb" and "looming scarcity" end up attributing responsibility for climate change to migrants, individuals and groups disproportionately impacted by the historical actions and decisions of actors in the Global North, and that, as Sam Moore and Alex Roberts remind us, "have contributed almost nothing to global climate change."[125]

German journalist and philosopher Carolin Emcke has argued in *Against Hate* how "everything only confirms the haters' own projection—and even their own aggression can be idealized as self-defense."[126] And Michel Agier has evoked the idea of a "postcolonial fear" expressed through the prism of colonial optics and racial bias: "This fear is therefore aimed at those among others who were once colonized, dispossessed, separated by apartheid or enslaved. Any foreigner arriving from these parts of the world will be seen through the filter of this fear, as the dangerous emissary of a vengeance that the Western world anticipates and fears."[127] These are to be inscribed in a longer history, punctuated by race theories and eugenics,[128] and are prominent in contemporary debates on nationality, suspicion of dual-nationals and stigmatization of former colonial subjects and their descendants such that "trying to insert those memories into the general memory often meets with hostility and rejection."[129]

In Chapter 1, we explored the mechanisms that contributed to environmental degradation as a result of "capitalist property systems [that] created widespread conditions for human displacement and racial disposability,"[130] questions to which Neel Ahuja turns his attention in *Planetary Specters: Race, Migration, and Climate Change in the Twenty-First Century*, offering invaluable insights into the ways in which "the specter of future mass migration due to planetary ecological change thus configures migrants as embodiments of environmental processes."[131] These are shaped by inconsistency: as the European Parliament declares a climate emergency, climate change denialists and skeptics are forced to tweak their positions and exploit the fractures in general thinking. As philosopher and sociologist Zygmunt Bauman has observed, "'Fear' is the name we give to our *uncertainty*: to our *ignorance* of the threat and of what is to be *done*" and "to prevent a catastrophe, one needs first to *believe in its possibility*."[132] When applied to contemporary issues, "its story [that of natural disasters] is told in the words all too familiar to us: in the language of boundary breaking, invasion, conquest, annexation, colonization,"[133] categories that have captured the attention of scholars such as Jean-Pierre Dupuy who has considered catastrophe and doomsaying in terms of the emergence of the "sudden intrusion of the newly possible into the realm of the once-impossible."[134] This way of framing responses to climate change alarmism shares points of commonality with the plethora of narratives deployed relative to immigration. In some instances, they represent deliberate efforts aimed at heightening anxiety and uncertainty in order to "reinsert them into an existential and civilizational dynamic that grants them a form of legitimacy,"[135] while also producing predictable outcomes such as worsening global warming as a direct result of inaction.[136]

"Just like super-typhoons, rising seas, and heat waves," Todd Miller has argued, "border build-up and militarization are by-products of climate change."[137] The implication, of course, as Betsy Hartmann has suggested, is that "blaming immigrants for climate change is the latest iteration of this greening of hate."[138] The irony is to be found in the uncompromising nature of these ramparts, since the "same countries constructing unprecedented border regimes" are today, citing Harsha Walia, "[deploying these] against those whose very recourse to migration results from the ravages of capital."[139] Linking climate change and migration has, as we have seen thus far, become a common paradigm, yet although "experts agree that climate change is affecting mobility," as Kira Walker contends, "the relationship between these two things is not straightforward, as it is often portrayed, but complex, multi-causal and context specific."[140]

The existing United Nations 1951 Convention and 1967 Protocol definition of a refugee and right to protection concerns the "well-founded fear of being persecuted because of reasons of race, religion, nationality, membership in a particular social group, or political opinion."[141] Increasing calls have been made to expand this definition because it is seen as inadequate in the context of twenty-first-century challenges and vulnerabilities. Nigerian environmental activist Ken Saro-Wiwa (whom we will discuss in Chapter 4) invoked the notion of "indirect genocide" as a way of describing the premeditated actions of oil companies as they inflicted "conditions of life calculated to bring about its physical destruction in whole or in part," as stated in the United Nations Convention on the Prevention and Punishment of the Crime of Genocide (UNPCG) of 1948. Simon Behrman and Avidan Kent, for example, have argued for "a new regulatory order."[142] But as Sumudu Anopama Atapattu has explained, this has historically represented a conundrum since "people rarely move solely for environmental reasons. [...] Climate change acts as a threat multiplier. Due to this reason, it is often hard to establish the causal link between migration and climate change, obscuring the impact of climate change on migration."[143] Linguistic uncertainty highlights the complexity and lack of consensus, and the coexistence of an inventory of terms with different referential qualities complicates the process of achieving an accurate definition of the phenomena described. These include descriptors such as cross-border disaster-displaced persons, climate-displaced persons, environmentally displaced persons, climate refugees or environmental refugees—and these are just some of the terminological categories found in scholarly and policymaking documents.

The European Parliament published a brief in 2021, "The concept of 'climate refugee': Towards a possible definition," in which "the significance of the nexus between climate change-induced disasters and displacements has been acknowledged."[144] Although motivated by the imperative of "effective management of environmental migration [in order] to ensur[e] human security," the category "environmental migrants" is enshrined in the IOM's policy statement as "persons or groups of persons who, predominantly for reasons of sudden or progressive change in the environment that adversely affects their lives or living conditions, are obliged to leave their habitual homes, or choose to do so, either temporarily or permanently, and who move either within their country or abroad."[145] Dina Ionesco (Head) and Mariam Traore Chazalnoël (Senior Policy Officer) at the Migration, Environment and Climate Change Division at the IOM have underscored how

> the IOM's flexible mandate and operational capacity allow development of activities pertaining to both forced and voluntary forms of migration, linked to both climate change and environmental degradation. [...] Without negating the weight of the negative consequences of migration linked to climate change, it is important to also develop a framework that is not only based on an alarmist view that reduces migrants to agentless individuals and migration as a negative phenomenon to be curtailed or combatted.[146]

Even though, rhetorically, there has been an attempt to achieve an equilibrium between humanitarian and political priorities, what stands out is a reluctance or even outright refusal to utilize the category of refugee in terms of climate and environmental factors because recourse to "such terms could potentially undermine the international legal regime for the protection of refugees."[147] This is not the same as arguing that definitional challenges are rendered more complex by the multicausal dimension; instead, this framing appears to relegate the interventionist and protectionist responsibility to only security concerns. As we shall see a little later, analogous strategies are evident in EU policymaking, and ultimately one is left with more questions than answers. As T. J. Demos has asked, "How might we conceive alternative representational systems that enable the juridico-political recognition of climate-based migration according to an expansive definition of what climate means" given that "the climate refugee, by definition, represents an intangible figure, a relentlessly conceptually mobile one, owing to the impossibility of disaggregating its sources of displacement?"[148]

"Every day, we see that conflict, climate change and instability are pushing people to seek refuge elsewhere," so claimed the president of the European Commission, Ursula von der Leyen.[149] Indeed, such thinking has shaped the formulation of EU environmental policy in a more general manner,[150] and the Green Deal itself specifically, whereby "climate change and environmental degradation are an existential threat to Europe and the world. To overcome these challenges, the European Green Deal will transform the European Union into a modern, resource-efficient and competitive economy."[151] Yet, somewhat paradoxically, "Europe is the fastest-warming continent," and the "climate risks Europe is facing are driven not only by increases in climate hazards, but also by how prepared societies are for them."[152] However, these legislative documents conceal disquieting positions on these urgent matters, a Eurocentric racial unconscious that undermines long-term solutions. This was exemplified in the words of Josep Borrell, EU High Representative for Foreign Affairs and Security Policy, who stated on October 13, 2022:

> Europe is a garden. We have built a garden. Everything works. It is the best combination of political freedom, economic prosperity and social cohesion that the humankind has been able to build—the three things together. [...] The rest of the world is not exactly a garden. Most of the rest of the world is a jungle, and the jungle could invade the garden. [...] Europeans have to be much more engaged with the rest of the world. Otherwise, the rest of the world will invade us, by different ways and means.[153]

As the Migrant Rights Network has argued, this statement serves to underscore how "Western knowledge systems are deemed 'superior'," and the insinuation of "backward" and "primitive" populations is impossible to sidestep.[154] The characterization of "migration" and "nature" as somehow interconnected and indissociable entities and processes has culminated in what Kira Walker describes as a reluctance "to step up climate action" while "further entrench[ing] xenophobia and racism and contributed to the fortification of Fortress Europe."[155] Likewise, when "used intentionally or unintentionally," as Brigitte Nehrlich has shown, "such conceptualizations dehumanize people in a variety of ways, turning them into objects or animals, or depicting them as people that are morally inferior compared to others."[156] What permeates then from these objectionable comments is the sketch of an undesirable "invasive species" defined by metaphorical devices related to climatic and medical factors, together instrumentalized to interrupt mobility.

A climate of fear and uncertainty pervades, complicating feelings of belonging in the EU. Recourse to increasingly harsh immigration policies and border control mechanisms has cultivated exclusionary frameworks and coincided with an escalation and intensification of dehumanizing initiatives. These "dehumanizing, toxic metaphors and fear-invoking language," as Bram Frouws has highlighted, "influence cognition and behavior."[157] The technocratic vocabulary of institutional policymaking further compounds the negative perceptions of migrants. As I have argued elsewhere, this vocabulary is "being learnt by Europeans and non-Europeans alike, because it helps organize our perception of migration within and into Europe. The issue of sharing referentiality is as crucial as the mastery of already identified languages and a shift is clearly occurring as a new lexicon is installed according to exclusionary concepts and principles."[158] Associating climatic metaphors related to floods, storms, waves, inundations, tides, flows, hurricanes, tsunamis and swarms with migrants stimulates depersonalizing and dehumanizing emotional responses. This situation is aggravated by the accumulation of additional designations and terms that exist alongside media images of individuals and groups scaling walls, crossing river borders, breaching fortifications, assaulting ramparts, walls and fortifications. Together, these migrant-scapes give credence to the idea of uncontrolled immigration, of "invading hordes," writes Adrian Favell, "who, with their peculiar practices and origins and predilection for crime and moral turpitude, would never be able to assimilate," overwhelming bureaucracies and highlighting the enduring nature of the danger or threat to the national community.[159] The consequences and impact are real, and as Bram Frouws has explained, when "migration is conflated with forced displacement and mentioned in one breath with a range of bad outcomes" and is then adopted by "those aiming to securitize the migration debate in order to limit asylum and control immigration," then these "climate/migration linkages [...] encourage greater fortification of borders and more restrictive policies."[160] Together, these define a *greening of hate* and a *greening of security*.

EU agencies such as Frontex and Eurosur have implemented a security apparatus designed to strengthen a common immigration policy. Policy initiatives such as the European Pact on Immigration and Asylum are designed to coordinate immigration policy, the main pillars of which remain in place today: "to organize legal immigration," to "control illegal immigration," to "make border controls more effective" and to "create a comprehensive partnership with the countries of origin and of transit," while encouraging "the synergy between migration and development."[161] Likewise, the Schengen Agreement that abolished checks and controls at the EU's common internal borders and allowed freedom of movement and a common area of security and justice was gradually expanded in order to address new forms of population mobility and changes in global migration patterns.

Underneath this lies a deliberate and conscious attempt to consolidate the cohesiveness of a European identity as the outcome of reinforced exclusionary agreements. These are shared by signatories and effectively juxtapose those residing within and outside Fortress Europe. The EU relies on an integrated border management strategy, and Frontex is responsible for issuing an annual risk analysis.[162] This reporting reproduces the logic of the agency's purpose, namely to oversee "the management of the EU's external borders and the fight against cross-border crime" while demonstrating the effectiveness of the measures adopted and outlining "the evolving risks and challenges at the European Union's external borders, reflecting Frontex's commitment to secure and humane border management."[163] The May 2024 report is organized around a number of indicators—"overarching risks"—that include "cross-border crime and terrorism" while also referencing "threat multipliers such as climate change" and providing questionable conclusions.[164] This corresponds to what Charles Heller, Nicholas De Genova, Maurice Stierl, Martina Tazzioli and Huub van Baar have described as the "spectacle of statistics," whereby "the strategic use of statistics generates the homogenized and aggregate representations that are decisive for erasing the individuality and political subjectivity of people on the move as well as effacing their collective struggles and hardships, and thus for portraying 'unauthorized' border crossers as a menace."[165] Likewise, Louis Imbert has demystified the foundational premises of such self-defining mechanisms, according to which "the agency [Frontex] defines and constructs the problem it is supposed to help combat. The analysis serves to legitimize its role and justify its budget."[166] The sections featuring climate change reference "apocalyptic scenarios," and the predictable result has been that "once integrated into the official communication of the European institutions, the idea of crisis spreads."[167] These arrangements have resulted in the intensification of control over Third Country nationals or migrants, confirmation that the European *family of nations* continues to edit the official portrait.[168]

Peripheral Geographies and Rights

In 2020, the European Commission opened negotiations on the new Pact on Migration and Asylum of the European Union, and an updated version was agreed upon in December 2023. Over the past fifteen years, the EU has faced a number of significant challenges, including losing a member to Brexit, increasing divisiveness and polarization as a result of pressure from far-right agendas and ongoing Russian aggression in Ukraine. These disruptive factors shaped the revised pact, and comparison between the 2008 and 2024 versions is revealing. The four main pillars of the new pact are: (i) Secure external borders, (ii) Fast and efficient procedures, (iii) Effective system of solidarity and responsibility and (iv) Embedding migration in international partnerships.[169] There is ample evidence of conciliatory language, emphasis on "social cohesion" and "solidarity," concessions to "frontline states" (Greece, Italy, Spain) or obstructionist members (Hungary). In fact, asylum and migration have become such a "polarizing issue in European politics" in the area of "legislation on migration and asylum" that, as Ankita Dutta has explained, "the new deal was passed through a qualified majority voting (QMV) instead of unanimous voting," with a number of countries "abstaining," "rejecting the pact" or "seeking substantial concessions."[170]

Embedded in the pact, one finds corresponding terms: "harmonized asylum processes," "solidarity mechanism," "principle of solidarity," "fair sharing of responsibility," "harmonized regulatory framework," "disproportionate responsibility," "adequate capacity," "common procedure," "uniform" and "streamlining procedural arrangements."[171] This language resides under the umbrella of burden sharing, accentuating asylum procedure regulation and asylum and migration management regulation. In this context, the commitment to a "humane and effective return policy" remains questionable, and the claim that new regulations will be "fair," "efficient," "comprehensive" and "sustainable" is equally so.[172] These are contradictory constructs, even oxymorons, since the pact dissociates the repressive measures from the particular circumstances and stories of the individuals and groups targeted. Overall, the document is fundamentally dehumanizing while heralding new forms of insensitivity couched in protectionist and securitarian vocabulary molded by xenophobia and racism.

Ursula von der Leyen did not hesitate to release a "10-point plan for Lampedusa" on September 17, 2023, in the context of a sudden influx of migrant boat arrivals on the Italian Mediterranean island.[173] Once again, the response was focused on prevention and deterrence: "manage," "step up returns / surveillance," "facilitate readmission," "support the prevention of departures," take measures to limit, and "apply swift border and accelerated procedures" were just some of the constructs deployed. More specifically, this entailed "undertaking a renewed, concerted outreach to the main countries of origin of the new arrivals," the implementation of efforts aimed at "improv[ing] cooperation and facilitat[ing] readmission" in order to "ensure the swift implementation of returns," "support the prevention of departures by establishing operational partnerships on anti-smuggling with countries of origin and transit," "limit the use of unseaworthy vessels [disabling of recuperated boats and dinghies]," "apply swift border and accelerated procedures" and "increase awareness and communication campaigns to disincentivize the Mediterranean crossings." As late as Point 8, one learns of plans to "continue working to offer alternatives such as humanitarian admission and legal pathways," almost as an afterthought, but then immediately thereafter in Point 9, the ultimate objective is reiterated, namely to "increase assisted voluntary return from countries of transit."

Additional evidence of the exclusionary nature of these policies is provided by the renewed commitment to outsourcing the management of migration and the expansion of externalized borders.[174] Specialists, most notably Claire Rodier, have pointed to the ways in which these measures reinscribe age-old power dynamics and reaffirm a "sense of superiority," actions that are once again transcolonial in nature, whereby "by imposing on its allies the role of gatekeeper makes it possible to carry over a hold inherited during the colonial era over the definition of borders."[175] In addition to toughening border control mechanisms aimed at restricting entry pathways, the redistribution and processing of migrants are increasingly outsourced to subcontractors with the goal of interrupting crossings. Historically, these have involved privileging development and trade partnerships with countries that have included Albania, Egypt, Libya and Tunisia, among others (the United Kingdom and Rwanda Migration and Economic Development Partnership, a deportation scheme, after initially being ruled unlawful, was ultimately abandoned by newly elected prime minister Keir Starmer in July 2024). Whether they admit to these or not, the benefits to policymakers and governments are multiple, including deterrence, reducing migrant visibility *in* Europe, while offering plausible deniability with regard to the risk of "mistreatment [migrants] often suffer in distant countries with lower standards than in Europe" and therefore "freeing the European Union from the obligations imposed by European laws."[176] Asylum seekers, migrants, and refugees have witnessed an erosion of their fundamental rights, and therefore access to protection. *Out of sight, out of mind.*

Once again, the reactive nature can only be understood in the context of pressure from outspoken far-right parliamentary groups, elected officials and member states, and Ursula von der Leyen has been heavily criticized for the EU's protectionist and securitarian response, equating her words and actions with a capitulation of sorts to far-right agendas and talking points. Francesca De Benedetti ascribed these actions to a "right-wing drift: the more proper term would be the 'Melonization' of Von der Leyen,"[177] drawing a parallel with Italy's far-right prime minister Giorgia Meloni—she would subsequently extend this analogy through a reference to Hungary's prime minister Viktor Orbán, arguing that "Meloni Is Orbánizing the European Union."[178] After all, as president of Fratelli d'Italia (Brothers of Italy), a right-wing populist party that has partial roots in neofascist movements and parties, Giorgia Meloni brandished a provocative general election campaign slogan in 2022, "Italy and Italians first!," *Di patria da onorare, Di terra da amare, Di identità millenaria da difendere*—Of a homeland to be honored, Of land to love, Of a thousand-year-old identity to be defended. The cornerstones of nationalist ideology are front and center in terms of the profile she offers—"I am a woman, I am a mother, I am Italian, I am a Christian, and you can't take that away from me"—components of an identity declined throughout the campaign, inviolable and non-negotiable, in other words the prototypical ingredients of what she defines as *Italianness*.

At the height of the so-called 2015 "migration crisis," then German Chancellor Angela Merkel famously stated on August 31, 2015, *Wir haben so vieles geschafft, wir schaffen das*—We have managed so much, we can manage this. How, one might ask, was a government official's plea for empathy so blatantly disregarded? Eight years later, *Der Spiegel* magazine's headline (September 23, 2023) rekindled that statement by the former chancellor: *Schaffen wir das noch mal? Der Deutsche Streit über die Asylpolitik*—Can we do this again? The German dispute over asylum policy. The answer was of course resolutely negative, and the initial concern with migrants themselves had seemingly receded into the rear-view mirror.

Observers and policymakers started to characterize these circumstances as a migrant or refugee "crisis." Meanwhile, the right-wing populist party, the Alternative for Germany, having failed to reach the 5 percent electoral threshold in the 2013 German Federal Election, exploited these circumstances. As they headed into the 2017 Federal election, they campaigned almost exclusively on an anti-immigration and anti-Islam platform, a strategy that proved successful since they emerged as the largest opposition party in the Bundestag with 94 seats and 12.6 percent of the vote, a feat they repeated in the 2025 Federal election. The AfD has consistently polled as one of the leading parties in Germany and has proven adept at siphoning votes away from what had been, historically at least, the mainstream parties. A direct correlation between their prominence and support for anti-immigration measures and identity is evident. When Joachim-Friedrich Merz, the leader of the Christian Democratic Union (CDU) and now German Chancellor, made headlines (September 4, 2023) at the annual Gillamoos "Volksfest" (folk festival held in the Bavarian town of Abensberg) announcing that "You are Germany! Not Berlin, not Kreuzberg! Gillamoos is Germany!," juxtaposing rural White Bavaria, in other words the "real Germany," with diverse and multicultural urban Berlin, there was little doubt as to how stigmatizing and scapegoating immigrants would remain attractive moving forward, preferring to broker in blame while flirting with far-right positions rather than promoting empathy.

Greening Migration

Ursula von der Leyen's 2023 State of the Union Address, titled "Answering the Call of History," provides important insights into the EU's immigration and environmental policies as well as the conjunction between anti-immigration views and climate skepticism:

> Every day, we see that conflict, climate change and instability are pushing people to seek refuge elsewhere. I have always had a steadfast conviction that migration needs to be managed. It needs endurance and patient work with key partners. And it needs unity within our Union. This is the spirit of the New Pact on Migration and Asylum. When we took office, there seemed to be no possible compromise in sight. But with the Pact, we are striking a new balance. Between protecting borders and protecting people. Between sovereignty and solidarity. Between security and humanity. We listened to all Member States and focused on all routes. And we have translated the spirit of the Pact into practical solutions. [...] We stepped up border protection. European Agencies deepened their cooperation with Member States.[179]

Far-right, sovereigntists and national conservatives do not hold a majority in the European Parliament (as of June 6–9, 2024 they accounted for 187 of the 720 elected members), but they nevertheless exercise a disproportionate influence and have endeavored to undermine the European Green Deal. The EU's inability or unwillingness to adequately counter these efforts has led some observers to qualify the circumstances as "backtracking."[180] An article in *Le Grand Continent* ponders, given that "nearly half" of these elected officials in these parliamentary groups "deny global warming or at least its human origin" and that "the others are overwhelmingly climate relativists, acknowledging the existence of climate change without actually integrating this issue into their policies," the extent to which they will be successful in eroding the commitments outlined in the EU's Green Deal.[181]

These positions intersect with, arguably, the most prominent international detractor of environmental concerns, namely Donald Trump. In August 2024, various claims and statements—available in the materials circulated in the conservative right-wing Heritage Foundation's 2025 Presidential Transition Project (Project 2025)—reiterated calls for reducing environmental and climate change regulations.[182] As we have heard repeated all too often, climate regulation is driving support for populism.[183]

Recent realignments in the global geopolitical landscape have further exacerbated the plight of migrants, displaced as they have been by conflict, persecution, repressive dictatorships, social upheaval and the deterioration of the environment. The IOM has recommended "efforts to strengthen its capacity to develop and implement a comprehensive approach to migration in the context of climate change, environmental degradation and disasters due to natural hazards," and outlined four Priority Areas of Engagement: (i) IOM migration policy role, (ii) IOM knowledge provider role, (iii) IOM operational role and (iv) IOM convening role.[184] Yet, numerous politicians and policymakers have warned against overemphasizing climate change, especially in terms of expanding recourse to categories such as climate migrants or refugees that might increase responsibility under international law. Meanwhile, "many developing countries have urged the EU to afford climate migrants the status of refugees."[185]

The Crossroads of Civilization and Nurturing Identification

Arjun Appadurai showed us "the contradiction between the idea that each nation-state can truly represent only one ethnos and the reality that all nation-states historically involve the amalgamation of many identities."[186] The monolithic path forward is narrow-minded and evidence of short-term thinking, and "these questions of inhabitation and interconnection, of mutuality, sustainability and durability, of the interlacing of human history and Earth's history are," as Achille Mbembe has argued, "far from abstract concerns. In fact, the ongoing long-term planetary environmental changes have only further dramatized them, and there is little doubt that they will be at the center of any debate on the future of life and the future of reason in this century."[187] Social justice and racial justice initiatives share important points of intersection with environmental justice and claims for an equitable and sustainable future.[188] Indeed, legal actions against multinational corporations should be seen as harbingers of things to come.[189]

Jenny Erpenbeck and Juli Zeh, two of the most critically acclaimed German authors writing today, have both turned their attention to immigration and climate change. In *Go, Went, Gone*, the former explored the "refugee crisis,"[190] whereas the latter, in *About People*, featured a main protagonist seeking to reconcile the seemingly diametrically opposed concerns of "turning Europe into a walled fortress" while simultaneously advocating "in favor of protecting the environment."[191] Juli Zeh's observation was telling, namely that "the sole certainty is that everyone is afraid, and everyone thinks their own fear is justified. Some are afraid of foreign infiltration, others of climate catastrophe."[192] How can we convert these feelings into compassionate and empathetic responses? These are questions that will guide the analysis and discussion in the next chapter. Indeed, as Baptiste Morizot has suggested, "For a migrant to move me, for his fate to distress me, I must realize that the fact that he is *him* and that I am *me* is a contingent fact: I could very well be him and he could be me."[193] But he also encourages us to think additionally about these relational questions. How, for example, does the word *other* necessitate further scrutiny given that this

> very small adjective, so elegant in its cartographic reconfiguration of the world: it alone reframes both a logic of difference and a common belonging. It traces bridges and open borders between the beings encountered in experience. Nobody will lose anything in the process. It certainly does not allow us to make any in-depth progress when it comes to similarities and differences. It simply makes it possible to naturalize an adequate logic, to avoid a gross error in biological taxonomy, to incorporate (as a civilization) a mental map with far-reaching political repercussions, and to internalize (as individuals) one more quiet truth, one that will join the roundness of the Earth, heliocentrism, evolutionism, the toxicity of neoliberalism, and the idea that democracy is the worst political model [...] except for all the others.[194]

However, rather than intensifying regulations on circulation, Claire Rodier draws attention to the human element of contemporary migration, nurturing forms of identification.[195] Likewise, Wendy Brown has observed, "What we have come to call a globalized world harbors fundamental tensions between opening and barricading, fusion and partition, erasure and reinscription."[196] Calling for more inflexible surveillance strategies and implementing supplementary entry and circulation restrictions will do little to address the underlying symptoms and prevent any possibility of spawning genuine solutions to the challenges inside and outside Fortress Europe. Circling back to one of the epigraphs, in which Achille Mbembe was cited claiming that "the government of human mobility might well be the most important problem to confront the world during the first half of the twenty-first century,"[197] his words are worth paying attention to as he indirectly completes his observation: "Instead of marketing fictions and inflaming dark passions and hysteria, we should take seriously the question of the future, reactivate our critical faculties and rehabilitate reason, because if we do not rehabilitate reason, we will not be able to repair the world or learn how to share the planet."[198]

In 2023, during an official visit to France, Pope Francis devoted a number of public interventions to what he observed as growing insensitivity to migrants: "Too many people, fleeing conflict, poverty and environmental disasters in their search for a better future, find in the waves of the Mediterranean Sea the ultimate rejection. [...] We find ourselves at a *crossroads of civilization*. Either the culture of humanity and fraternity, or the culture of indifference: let everyone fend for himself or herself."[199] To me, this was precisely Chimamanda Ngozi Adichie's message in "The Danger of a Single Story":

It is impossible to talk about the single story without talking about power. [...] How they are told, who tells them, when they're told, how many stories are told, are really dependent on power. [...] The consequence of the single story is this—it robs people of dignity. It makes our recognition of our equal humanity difficult. It emphasizes how we are different rather than how we are similar.[200]

Chapter 3

ECOLOGICAL RELATIONS

A writer is someone who pays attention to the world.

Susan Sontag[1]

This collapse leads to a loss of ethics, and when ethics fails, beauty falls.

Patrick Chamoiseau[2]

How can we become sensitive to other forms of life? And how do we transmit this sensitivity to others?

Estelle Zhong Mengual[3]

I want art to be able to do more than point; I want it to have a heart that beats and responds to the world.

Kehinde Wiley[4]

When Joseph M. W. Turner's *The Slave Ship* (Slavers Throwing Overboard the Dead and Dying, Typhoon Coming On) was exhibited at the Royal Academy in 1840, the impact of this painting at the height of the Industrial Revolution proved to be transformative, amplifying a debate on the atrocities of slavery on the occasion of the World Anti-Slavery Convention being held in London. The massacre that had occurred aboard the British slave ship *Zong* in 1781 (the subject of Turner's painting) proved to be consequential, fueling outrage while also standing as an important precursor in the context of debates on climate change, and "as a landscape painter his artworks show a sensitive awareness of the effect that the industrialized world was having on the environment."[5] Artistic and literary works offer alternatives to racist and xenophobic media and political discourses and have an important role to play in critical thinking. They are able to deploy a creative apparatus that can confront shifting political realities, mobilize consciousness and foster modes of identification. This has become all the more essential at a time when a criminalizing, debasing and often dehumanizing logic dominates, one that is fueled by the disquieting narcissistic nationalism associated with governments, politicians and policymakers, and that ultimately encourages disidentification and isolationism and suppresses empathy.[6]

Viet Thanh Nguyen stresses that "refugees are people who are just like us until these calamitous situations displace them"[7] and that the protection of refugees provided by the 1951 United Nations Convention and 1967 Protocol remains the international standard in this regard. Although he has expressed reservations as to the correlation between "empathy" and "political engage-ment," he nevertheless takes the opportunity in an edited volume of essays, *The Displaced: Refugee Writers on Refugee Lives*, to emphasize why artistic prac-tices are so vital, precisely "because a writer needs to know what it feels like to be an other," in other words to "conjure up the lives of others, and only through such acts of memory, imagination, and empathy can we grow our capacity to feel for others."[8] How, therefore, can aesthetic projects enable association and connection, improve relationality, stimulate empathy, under-standing, sympathy, consideration, pity and compassion? How can artists and writers operate individually or collectively in order to elicit and nurture identification and provide the impetus for mobilization? These concerns and questions are intrinsic to Viet Thanh Nguyen's own motivations for writing, more precisely in terms of the processes through which art and literature are able to *conjure up the lives of others*, and therefore stand to provoke and stimulate reactions and responses from observers and readers.[9] As we shall see, a range of mechanisms are employed, aimed at enlisting audiences in a process of conscientization in relation to the cultural, political and social contradictions of the world we live in.

David Palumbo-Liu's book, *The Deliverance of Others: Reading Literature in a Global Age*, provides some helpful indicators, pointing to how empathy operates in a broader historical framework as a mechanism that can potentially help define "the relation between the self and the other," thereby "mobiliz[ing] empathy for others and [enhancing] our ethical capabilities."[10] This under-standing of empathy is also helpful in complicating assumptions relating to "commonality" and "communicability" that have the potential to "imply commensurate relations between selves and others."[11] Naturally though, as he explains, "we cannot be the other, but we can try to imagine what her or his situation would make *us* feel like. [...] What norms, assumptions, presump-tions, what notions of mimesis, what norms of 'human behavior' do we intui-tively draw on to make sense of our bold statement that 'we feel your pain'?"[12]

These approaches necessarily involve different sequences and levels of intensity, feelings that cover the range of the emotional spectrum. Amy Coplan and Peter Goldie, in *Empathy: Philosophical and Psychological Perspectives*, have underscored how important it is to "take care to be sure what we mean by the term [empathy] when making our own claims and arguments," and they caution against seeking "to regiment the term into one single mean-ing."[13] Consensus is hard to achieve given that the terminology is understood very differently by art and literary critics, in philosophy, as well as in other fields such as neuroscience. My concern here is with artists and writers whose work seeks to elicit empathy because, as Graham McFee argues, empathy is "relational in a stronger sense than, say, even sympathy" given that "in empathy, I am seeking to enter into your emotional state, if only in imagi-nation."[14] There is of course some overlap between empathy and sympathy, but more often than not the two remain distinct, even inconsistent. Martha Nussbaum, in *Upheavals of Thought: The Intelligence of Emotions*, discusses these processes in terms of an "imaginative reconstruction of another's experi-ence," arguing ultimately that "if there is any difference between 'sympa-thy' and 'compassion' in contemporary usage, it is perhaps that 'compassion' seems more intense and suggests a greater degree of suffering, both on the part of the afflicted person and on the part of the person having the emotion. [...] Sympathy, like compassion, includes a judgment that the other person's distress is bad."[15]

For Hannah Arendt, relationships with others are a precondition to mean-ingful existence and necessarily intersect with collective responsibility, to the extent that relationality provides the structural basis for human rights.[16] But these relationships are also, by definition, *perspectival*, and Johannes Lang has argued that "it seems problematic to assume that empathy requires identifica-tion or a perception of similarity" and that this "form of imagination is quite the opposite of identification; it requires instead an ability to transcend the limitations of one's own perspective and one's own self-interest in order to put oneself in the place of another."[17] This distinction is especially relevant to the circumstances of asylum seekers, migrants and refugees since, as Rebecca Adami elucidates, the "political agency of individuals in terms of claiming or enacting their human rights is today dependent on the recognition of such political demands by states that are willing to realize rights and freedoms for their citizens and for people living under their jurisdiction, where the political space of citizens and non-citizens is limited within the legal borders of democracies."[18] We are certainly not going to resolve all of these issues here, primarily because such a wide range of philosophical traditions govern the application of emotions in moral philosophy. Instead of adhering to a monolithic framework with which to explore these multiple usages, accord-ing attention to the artists and writers and the particularities of their crea-tive work, public statements and writings will be helpful in delineating the coordinates and contours of the ensuing analysis. Afterall, "artworks are," as Amy Coplan and Peter Goldie demonstrate, "like actions, the product of, and expressive of, people's feelings and intentions. [...] Not only are these characters the intentional products of the artist; they also have a life of their own, so to speak, which is in many respects just like ours, and which is there to be understood, and, perhaps, empathized with."[19]

The previous chapter explored the afterlives of empire, persistent economic asymmetry, lingering racial dynamics and the ways in which colonial and environmental processes have shaped conversations and policies in the migration-climate nexus. One of the secondary effects of border externalization and of outsourcing migration management beyond Fortress Europe has been to promote distance at the cost of proximity. The interchangeability in media and public discourse of categories such as asylum seeker, migrant and refugee have deliberately confused the issues at stake and limited structural responses, while also deflecting and transferring accountability, obligations and responsibility away from international human rights laws.[20] These observations serve to highlight the real-life consequences of decision-making processes on individuals and groups, and works of art and literature therefore play a key role in challenging the logic of these official decrees and policies by focusing on intentionality and perspective and also in foregrounding the human experience while reversing the rationale informing these decisions. Deborah R. Coen has described these modes of connectivity in terms of "scaling," whereby "scientific judgments about the significance of human actions in relation to planetary processes have not derived from a unique perceptual faculty, nor from personal wisdom. [...] Scaling is therefore a somatic learning experience—but it is not performed by individuals in isolation. In order to orient ourselves with respect to distant places or past times, we rely on the knowledge of others."[21]

Perspective, Representational Logic and Humane Connectivity

The question of perspective is of paramount importance. In the film *Havarie* (2016) by the German director Philip Scheffner, a 3 minute 36 seconds cell phone video clip shot by amateur photographer Terry Diamond, that was originally uploaded to YouTube and titled "Refugees," is extended and stretched to 5,400 frames using slow motion to a 93 minute film. The video features an inflatable dinghy and was shot at a distance from the deck of a cruise ship, emphasizing location and positionality, but most importantly perspective. Anat Tzom Ayalon's insightful essay on the film describes how the "photographer understands that photography fails to get across the experience of the people on the boat and apparently the film follows his profound words, attempting to create a new perspective" and that "the change of temporality undermines the image's indexical status, and creates a displaced perspective, a new kind of ontology of ambivalence and uncertainty."[22] Likewise, as Brigitta Wagner has written

> The still frames of a vacationer's shaky cell phone footage [...] reveal a boat that sometimes seems to approach and sometimes recede from the camera, while the blue sea, the vessel, and the distant, indistinct human forms aboard function as a painting, a deferred hermeneutic exercise, something at once familiar and unknowable. The boat anchors the spectator's gaze as diverse languages and viewpoints on the soundtrack and in the subtitles discuss the waters, the plight of refugees, other maritime forms of migration and transnationalism on cruise and container ships, the desire for Europe, memories of crossing, of home, loss, and longing.[23]

Philipe Scheffner has described how the question of perspective was front and center in the production process: "You can identify with that person and understand that he or she has had a hard life. But as you're doing that, you very rarely question your own perspective. You feel empathy for that person, which is good. I'm not saying that it's a bad approach. But at a certain point, I said, 'But what about *our* perspective? What do we actually see in these images that are right there in our living rooms? And how can we include the questioning of our own way of seeing these images?'"[24] His perspective thus addresses a potential hazard implicit to such projects, one to which T. J. Demos has pointed, arguing that "the tendency of the traditional documentary project: to engender a compassion for the struggling and disadvantaged that conveniently overlooks the viewer's situation and potential complicity in the unequal political and economic arrangements that drive migration in the first place."[25]

Documentary filmmaking that questions immigration policies entails risk-taking. In *The Burning: The Untold Story of Africa's Migrant Crisis* (2023), American filmmaker Isabella Nathani-Alexander documents how "the colonial period stripped away Africa's natural resources and left it fractured into European designed states," and that "behind every statistic is a name, a face, and a story."[26] But the very process of attempting to document or draw attention to migration entails walking a fine line between objectivity and a hierarchical gaze. "Depictions unsettle," Brad Evans has argued, "because their intimate portrayals foster humane connections [and these] are crucial to any understanding of power relations. How we narrate images is in fact crucial to the authentification and disqualification of the meaning of lives."[27] This is complicated by the deeply polarized cultural, political and social age in which we live, one in which every facet of coexistence is complicated, and "notions such as compassion, solidarity and generosity are now viewed as a diminished, downgraded and philosophically devalued terminology," Felwine Sarr has written, and "this crisis is tied to ways in which we imagine the relationships we establish with our fellow human beings, our environment and living things in general."[28]

However, this also means that there are inherently counterproductive steps that may hinder empathetic responses by reactivating power dynamics. Federica Mazzara has paid particular issue to this complicated matter:

> The deployment of moral sentiments in contemporary politics [...] presupposes a relation of inequality, because when compassion is expressed in the public space, it is invariably directed from above to below, which is from the more powerful to the weaker, the more fragile, the more vulnerable, those who can generally be constituted as victims of an overwhelming fate? Within this supposedly alternative framing, migrants, and more specifically asylum seekers and refugees, have increasingly come to be understood and presented as "precarious lives", according to a pattern that mobilizes compassion rather than justice.[29]

The premise of migrant or ecological justice consists in drawing attention to individuals and groups with shared experiences of discrimination (racialized, ecological and destruction of biodiversity). But the real danger resides in the fact, as T. J. Demos maintains, that "the dominant media's visualization of refugees in general [is] detached from complex structural determinations" and that "these fictions easily become weaponized, fueling and perpetuating extremist political rhetoric, further detaching migration from its compound determinants."[30] As we saw in the previous chapter, repressive actions are bolstered through recourse to language defined by detachment, one which obfuscates the repressive nature of the official international responses and that ultimately, as Christine Ross has argued, migration in the context of the EU is "not about 'citizens' over here and 'migrants' over there but about coexisting citizens with and without rights."[31] This was evident in the New Pact on Migration and Asylum of the EU and the 10-point Plan for Lampedusa in which measures designed to interrupt passage were foregrounded, the imperative being to privilege demonstrable obstructionist steps. These are preventive measures, defined by projection, whereby "to protect the migrants is first and foremost an act of protecting ourselves, by confining, securitizing and sanitizing the others through practices of hospitality/exclusion."[32]

Migratory and Sensory Pathways

Susan Sontag wrote extensively about processes of identification and the complex mechanics involved in "regarding the pain of others," notably when it comes to assuming a degree of responsibility: "So far as we feel sympathy, we feel we are not accomplices to what caused the suffering."[33] At the end of the day though, reactions and responses are interpretative, personal and shaped by a range of factors. Chinese artist, dissident and activist Ai Weiwei has attempted to provoke responses to migration issues, issues that have received considerable attention in his numerous installations and films. There is, however, no consensus in terms of how his work has been received. For example, in *Safe Passage*, exhibited in Berlin in 2016 in the immediate aftermath of the so-called "migrants' crisis," Ai Weiwei "recycled" thousands of life jackets recovered in Greece. Federica Mazzara found that the "monumental commemorative artwork" communicated the idea "that the number of arrivals is beyond capacity, massive and unprecedented," thereby "reinforc[ing] the 'spectacle of statistics' in line with governmental discourse."[34] The messaging was certainly open to interpretation. Some saw in the work a catalyst for action, while highlighting how governments are, as T. J. Demos has argued in a different context, "complicit in the very production and management of migration."[35] My position, developed later in this chapter, is shaped primarily by an exhibition in Prague in which Ai Weiwei installed a large-scale inflatable dinghy. On that occasion, and in that particular space, I found Ai Weiwei's engagement with migration compelling, precisely because it was situated as an outgrowth of personal experience. This motivated audiences to reckon with questions of accountability while simultaneously interrogating the rhetorical strategies deployed by Frontex and evident in various EU declarations and policies.

These aforementioned mechanisms of detachment and disidentification have survived into contemporary politics. Donald Trump, on March 16, 2024, stated on the presidential campaign trail: "I don't know if you can call them people. In some cases they're not people, in my opinion," and then shortly thereafter (April 2, 2024), he referred to migrants as "animals" and "not human," adding: "The Democrats say, 'Please don't call them animals. They're humans'. I said, 'No, they're not humans, they're not humans, they're animals'." But herein lie the potentialities of a migratory aesthetics, what Mieke Bal has described as a "congruence between the relationality in the making and that within the society [...] inflecting this relationality toward the specific domains of aesthetics and migrancy. [...] Both terms are programmatic: different aesthetic experiences are offered through the encounter with such traces. Migratory aesthetics is an aesthetic of geographical mobility beyond the nation-state and its linguistic uniformity."[36] To this end, as Christine Ross has argued, the crucial point is that "migratory aesthetics is articulated not so much in the messages artworks convey about migration than in the works' devising of a sensorium that makes ways of coexisting perceptible and changeable."[37]

Relationality and Familiarity

The affective emotional element is therefore central to the process of representation since for meaningful symmetry to be attained, relationality needs to be multidirectional and take into account the range of ways in which the "articulation" of "other histories of victimization" may occur, but also greater interconnection and reciprocity.[38] This deserves special attention given that these processes are invariably racialized, especially in the context of African migration. As Achille Mbembe contends, "Blackness and race have played multiple roles in the imaginaries of European societies" and "have constituted the (unacknowledged and often denied) foundation, what we might call the nuclear power plant, from which the modern project of knowledge—and of governance—has been deployed."[39] The grievances of politicians and leaders have become bolder, as exemplified in recourse to increasingly nativistic and nationalistic rhetoric. The permanent inscription of difference and otherness solidifies the contours of insurmountable differences and serve to justify transhistorical hierarchies, deferring belonging *ad infinitum*. Suspicion is mapped onto others, suggesting that they ultimately might not even be similar species, certainly in terms of the absence of commonality. After all, *they* are not *like* us, mindsets evident in campaign slogans such as the French far-right's "On est chez nous" (This is our house *or* We are in our home). These concerted efforts aim to weaken emotional connection, as with the oft-repeated phrase "On ne peut accueillir toute la misère du monde" (We cannot take in all of the world's poor), initially uttered by French prime minister Michel Rocard in 1989, a declaration whose effect was "to neutralize any degree of affection in each one of us" and substitute a form of rationality in which, rather than attachment, othering and therefore distancing are foregrounded, the very incarnation of a "national preference."[40]

Similarly, one finds extensive recourse to animalistic language, accounts of predatory behavior, a propensity for uncontrollable violence, in other words a permanent and recurring menace. *They* are not *like* us, because *they* are *not* quite human. Beyond the realm of migration, such ingrained mindsets are especially harmful in the face of ecological crisis, a crisis that does not distinguish between centers and peripheries, all the more so given that "this Earth is our shared roof and our shared shelter [and] we have to share it as equitably as possible."[41] This sense of entanglement conveyed by Achille Mbembe resonates with French art historian Estelle Zhong Mengual's reflections on "sensitivity." "How," she asks, "can we become sensitive to other forms of life? And how do we transmit this sensitivity to others?"[42] We find here a conjunction between distance and proximity, but one that acknowledges the in-common as a relational concept that appeals to our collective imaginary. Baptiste Morizot has drawn on genealogical notions that play on *familiarity* and *familial* relations, reminding us that "all living beings, in fact, are for us both alien and kin, familiar aliens; in the old French sense, the word *'familier'* means that they are part of extended family, but their otherness is in certain respects undeniable, like that of civilizations from another planet."[43] This extends into a comprehensive analysis of the notion of "diplomacy" in order to explicate what he describes as a prevailing "crisis of sensibility," a crisis which is also a *crisis of empathy*:

> By "crisis of sensibility" I mean an impoverishment of what we can feel, perceive, and understand of living beings, and the relations we can weave with them—a reduction in the range of affects, percepts, concepts and practices connecting us to them. [...] This impoverishment of the scope of our sensibility towards living beings, of the forms of attention and of the qualities of openness towards them, is both an effect and one of the causes of the ecological crisis we face.[44]

This is what he ascribes to a "logic of relations" and "where the character of the diplomat takes on its full force: in the gallery of characters invented by human culture, there are few who have this logical dual feature of coming from one side, while being able to structurally place themselves at the service of the relation."[45] This is especially helpful to the framework of *Climates of Migration* and the reason why I cite him at length, since in apprehending the dynamic at work in the exclusionary discourse on migration, nationalism defines the parameters of and protectionist positions whereby "one's own side was [...] what required closed empathic identification (flag, anthem, homeland) and the prohibition of all empathetic movement towards the opposite side (the enemies from the nation next to ours are cockroaches, we are swamped by migrants, foreigners are barbarians)."[46]

These are the kinds of mediation that artists and writers propose, encouraging audiences to rethink and reimagine affiliation and to experiment with relationality. "The framing of the stories we hear, read, and see has an effect on eliciting our identification with the plight of others," as Ato Quayson suggests.[47] These are the journeys toward the other which art and literature entice us to embark upon. Assuming these positions presupposes a radicality of sorts, one that is positioned in opposition to prevailing assumptions, one that delineates an alternative narrative in the refusal to look the other way, and one that is committed to formulating a response that unquestioningly renounces processes that degrade humans and nonhumans through a persistent pattern of "denigration" that "deadens human sensibilities."[48] Instead, the resulting resuscitation of an empathetic response and reawakening of relatability make the ineluctable mechanics of othering untenable. This is where art and literature enter the imaginative and public realm through "empathetic writing" in order to confront the "indifferent or hateful gaze, and policies based on fear and rejection" which produce "this mask of inhumanity and absence from the world."[49] These elements define the work of Senegalese painter Alioune Diagne, featured at the 2024 Venice Biennale, illustrating the connection between migrations and "escalating poverty, resources depletion, racism and mutual dependence, some poignant scenes emerge from the works, shedding light on contemporary disasters happening in total indifference."[50]

Patrick Chamoiseau and Michel Le Bris brought together a group of writers to concentrate on migration in the face of what they saw as "indifference," the "defeat of human generosity" and "institutional shipwreck" of EU policymaking on these questions.[51] The authors who contributed to the volume *Osons la fraternité* (Daring to be Fraternal) offered a glimmer of sensibility, aspirational change in which both physical and mental barriers and fortresses would disappear as new forms of sensibility emerged. Wilfried N'Sondé reformulated usage of the word "sans"—*without*—used in French to categorize the "sans-papiers," those *without papers*, the undocumented whose circulation is interrupted, in the conjunction "Sang frontières"—*blood borders*—to designate fences and borders.[52] Elsewhere, activists and artivists have launched exhibitions (Documenta 14 in Kassel, Germany and the Venice Biennale 2024—"Foreigners Everywhere"), festivals, participatory exercises (on the Island of Lampedusa, for example), and forms of "planetary solidarities."[53]

Journeys and Post-journeys: Borders of the Mind

The association between the dual components that are imagining and feeling occurs when psychological and physical reactions coincide. This interaction is the object of Alejandro González Iñárritu's virtual reality installation, *Carne y Arena* (Flesh and Sand), subtitled "Virtually present, physically invisible" (2017), a piece that was conceptualized as an immersive experience aimed at triggering empathic responses. It is also a work that emphasizes the transnational context in which border enforcement and management takes place. As Fatima Bhutto has explained, "each visitor must enter and travel through the director's landscape of the Mexican-American border, by themselves, helpless and undefended. [...] Virtual reality is built somewhere between the borders of the real and imaginary, between the truth and a lie."[54] Literature offers numerous examples of such dynamics, and as Susan Feagin has argued, the "necessary condition for empathizing with a character in a literary work is that one simulates the relevant mental process of that character [...] it is the structural properties of a process that account for, at least to some extent, the affective or phenomenological 'feel' of the experience, and hence for the types and degrees of understanding one may have of a character with respect to the mental process being simulated."[55] This experience is achieved by positioning participants in what amounts to an interregnum, an interval space, one that locates them concurrently at the border of the imaginary and the real, thereby replicating metaphorically the harsh conditions associated with crossing the physical border between Mexico and the United States. The installation sought an affective response by attempting to simulate a physical experience, an aesthetic project aimed at fostering identification that encourages audiences to imagine how they too might have recourse to such desperate and extreme measures as a way of safeguarding themselves and family members. As Gregory Currie has shown, one must note how "there are ranges of (bodily) simulation-based activities which are directed towards works of art or aesthetic objects more generally and which may contribute to aesthetic engagement with those objects."[56]

Viet Thanh Nguyen interpolates readers, asking them to consider the challenges facing refugees as they undertake the demanding endeavor of remembering and of recovering memory. In many instances, this process entails imagining a narrative that is not anchored in specific memories, but instead composed of disparate elements, scattered in a constellation of memorial undertakings: "I do not remember many things, and for all those things I do not remember, I am grateful, because the things I do remember hurt me enough. [...] I have to remember, *or sometimes imagine*, not just what happened, *but what I felt*."[57] The question of experience is key to memory, but in fact, individuals end up confronting the challenges of displacement and erasure that accompanies mobility. A number of these memories are unique, precisely because they are anchored in the experiential. However, they do not stand alone, necessarily composed as they are by *other* memories that are not constructed only by experience. These memories are paramount to the process of relationality, indispensable to inspiring bystanders—who more often than not share neither the experience nor the memory—to reflect nevertheless on the extent to which similar imaginative steps could bring them closer. Frances Stonor Saunders argues that "all borders—the lines and symbols on a map, the fretwork of walls and fences on the ground, and the often complex enmeshments by which we organize our lives—are explanations of identity.

We construct borders, literally and figuratively, to fortify our sense of who we are; and we cross them in search of who we might become."[58]

When it comes to the representation of migrants, images of boats sinking in the Mediterranean or of Central American "caravans" are now regular occurrences. These have been observed, filmed, recorded and documented, they constitute *evidence*. This evidentiary mode is of paramount importance, but the problem resides in the reality that the experiences captured are those of populations whose individual stories are often rendered indistinguishable. Artists and writers can therefore complement this uniformization by challenging anonymization through individualized narratives in a productive dynamic that stands to yield a more encompassing, and therefore accurate, picture of the sociopolitical issues at work.

Ai Weiwei has produced a number of important works on global migration, questioning what happens when those from "over there" come "here," and designating the dual facets of migration as the "journey" and the "post-journey," insisting that "establishing the understanding that we all belong to one humanity is the most essential step for how we might continue to coexist on this sphere we call Earth. I know what it feels like to be a refugee and to experience the dehumanization that comes with displacement from home and country. There are many borders to dismantle, but the most important are the ones within our own hearts and minds—these are the borders that are dividing humanity from itself."[59] Among his most powerful work was a major installation at the Národní galerie v Praze (Prague National Gallery, March 17, 2017 to July 1, 2018), *The Law of the Journey*. The transhistorical overlapping histories and systems are evident in Ai Weiwei's installation, drawing analogies between the context of the Zong massacre featured in the aforementioned painting by Joseph M. W. Turner when African slaves were thrown overboard, and the twenty-first century context of migration in which repeated drownings are the outcome of the confrontation with an unforgiving nature and Europe's institutional "failure."[60]

The installation resembles a real-life watercraft and thereby establishes a link between the evidentiary mode as exemplified by media coverage of migrant crossings and EU maritime patrols, alongside artistic representations. Museum visitors were confronted with a 70-meter / 230-foot-long inflatable black PVC rubber dinghy watercraft, a simulation or replica, suspended in the exhibition from the ceiling and overcrowded with 302 black plasticized human figures. The choice of materials, the stitching, and of course the rubber itself, a material known for tearing as a result of the propagation of a cut or tear, are symbols of nature's overwhelming force and operate conjointly to transmit a sense of fragility suggested by the imminent tearing of the fabric. The indistinguishability and interchangeability of the figures in the dinghy

Figure 3.1 Ai Weiwei, "The Law of the Journey," Národní galerie v Praze (National Gallery, March 17, 2017 to July 1, 2018). Courtesy of Ai Weiwei Studio. Author photograph, 2017.

are striking, as is their replaceability and substitutability, their infinite demultiplification, their anonymity and loss of individuality, swollen bodies clad in lifejackets, always already hinting at a pending drowning, swollen pre-carcasses, a premonition of a death to come, poised to be engulfed, sucked under water in an ocean eager to further swell the bodies, pre-wretches of the Mediterranean in transhistorical dialogue with Frantz Fanon's wretched of the earth, bodies that will eventually be washed up on the shores of Europe, a fortress that long ago lifted the drawbridge, determined to privilege a securitarian apparatus rather than counter the prevailing false narratives pertaining to invasion and crisis. Passengers desperately hold on to the sides as they cling to hope in the struggle for survival. A raft afloat, precariously suspended as if riding the crest of a massive wave. The signs throughout the exhibit reaffirm this by warning visitors not to walk under the installation lest it collapse, *Prosíme, nevstupuite pod lod / Please do not step under the boat* [...] hands reaching out, extended to observers, hoping someone will grab them and steer them to safety.

In Ai Weiwei's installation, the sea of faces is literally floating, suspended above the sea of words engraved into the tiled floor below and inscribed on the exhibition panels. These excerpts are inspired by works by influential intellectuals and writers, most notably Václav Havel (the acclaimed author and transition politician who served as the last president of Czechoslovakia and first president of the Czech Republic [1989–2003] and in whose birth city the exhibition was held), Franz Kafka (the German-language author born in Prague in 1883), and contemporary global figures such as Adonis, Edward Said, Hannah Arendt, Zadie Smith, Nawal El Saadawi and Samar Yazbek, alongside figures from antiquity such as Homer. Václav Havel's words reverberate throughout the exhibition space, "The salvation of this human world lies nowhere else than in the human heart, in the human power to reflect, in human meekness and human responsibility."[61] Together, these voices serve as reminders of historical antecedents, records of some of the darkest chapters in world history, links with a present unfolding before our eyes as new generations of refugees surface. Conceived in response to the so-called European "migrants' crisis" of 2015, Ai Weiwei's words appear prominently in one of the exhibition panels: "There is no refugee crisis, but only human crisis. In dealing with refugees we've lost our very basic values."[62] These words, spoken in this instance by one of the leading contemporary artists in response to a humanitarian disaster, resonate with the intellectual ethical legacy of many of the most important thinkers, aimed at instigating action and fostering compassion and tolerance. His words mark an important shift in positionality, a challenge to the empty technocratic language of the EU, a rhetorical gesture encouraging new perspectives on age-old questions.

Ai Weiwei's projects are a product of fieldwork and research, an outgrowth of personal experience with displacement, the artist as *act/art-ivist*, including to the Greek island of Lesbos located in the northeastern Aegean Sea where migrants started arriving in 2015.[63] As the exhibition curators, Jiř í Fajt and Adam Budak, have explained, *The Law of the Journey* is a

> multi-layered, epic statement on the human condition: an artist's expression of empathy and moral concern in the face of continuous, uncontrolled destruction and carnage. Hosted in a building of symbolic historical charge—a former 1928 Trade Fair Palace which in 1939-1941 served as an assembly point for Jews before their deportation to the concentration camp in Terezín—it works as a site-specific parable, a form of (public) speech, carrying a transgressive power of cathartic experience, but also a rhetoric of failure, paradox and resignation. Like Noah's Ark, a monumental rubber boat is a contemporary vessel of forced exodus, floating hopelessly within the immense, oceanic abyss of the Gallery's post-industrial, cathedral-like Big Hall.[64]

The connections with earlier writings on these and related questions are especially compelling: "Set for a journey across the unknown and the infinite,
an overcrowded life raft carries 'the vanguard of their people,' as Hannah
Arendt described the illegal and the stateless in her seminal 1943 essay, 'We
Refugees'," and "Law of the Journey" is a "call for action and condemnation
of the ignorance and blindness of the political and civic apparatus."[65]

Ai Weiwei's work engages in a transhistorical conversation with the quo-
tations from historical voices carved into the flooring, deposited on the seabed beneath the installation, notably from Homer's *Odyssey*, "If any God has
marked me out again for shipwreck, my tough heart can undergo it," since, as
Ai Weiwei has written elsewhere,

> Whether my status is seen as that of an artist, an activist, or a citizen,
> I always seek to integrate these various roles and create an effective
> interplay between form and language in my explorations, documen-
> tary recordings, and exhibitions. [...] Artistic creation, being so per-
> sonalized, commonly stands in stark opposition to a state's agenda, and
> my work typically has an antagonistic dependence on the will of the
> group and the will of the state. No one can rid themselves of the imprint
> of their era's language and culture, and art serves simply as a pioneer
> for collective reflection: it offers a chance for a group, or a nation, to
> become alert to an issue, and to enhance its awareness of things.[66]

In the case of Ai Weiwei, this dialogue is framed around an inventory of inter-
related terms that include exile, migration and identity. A range of notions
are summoned in relation to the human odysseys captured in the installation:
displacement with no possibility of return, denunciation of hegemonic nationalism, humanitarianism, survivalist determination and resilience in the face
of adversity, an interplay between image and text. In his discussion of works
of art that impact representation and perspective in meaningful ways, T. J.
Demos registers a range of defining components, including hybrid qualities
and disruptive factors, qualities that he has identified in Ursula Biemann's
recourse to the "video essay" which "joins images and writing, but also,
more complexly, presents images as a form of writing and writing as a form
of images."[67] Exploring these circuits of interconnectivity can help further
elucidate what is at stake in *producing* art and assessing its impact, yielding
"new modelings of affect."[68] In *Sahara Chronicle* (2006), for example, Ursula
Biemann "generates a transformative experience by extending the dislocat-
ing forces of migration into a mode of address that shifts perspectives and
thereby creates its political effect: to transform the act of migration into a
political demand for equality and participation that challenges the global

system of social inequality and geographical exclusion in which migration takes place."[69]

Ai Weiwei enacts a form of mediation between historical time frames, highlighting the coordinates of migration (colonial, neocolonial, globalization), while initiating a transhistorical dialogue with writings that have focused on refugees, the Holocaust, dictatorship, sophisticated state surveillance and censorship, in other words histories that have unearthed and unlanded populations in the past and that continue to do so in the present. His life has been haunted by analogous experiences, as described in *1000 Years of Joys and Sorrows: A Memoir*. He draws on this past and his fieldwork in refugee camps, and capitalizes on his cultural and political capital as a global artist with the full understanding that his work reaches a transnational audience. These factors afford him institutional space in which to deploy this influence and shed light on important political and social issues. Indeed, the compositional elements of his work foster what Baptiste Morizot defines as "interdependences," namely "the possibility of bringing out new arrangements, new mediators, invisible alliances, communities of concern. Then the diplomat of relation becomes something else: the creative voice of interdependences. Without this creativity, all we do is reach a basic, weary compromise between the two sides, we do not invent the right relationship, fair and relevant, and constantly renegotiated: adjusted consideration."[70] Two linguistic registers clash, swirling in the turbulent waters much like the friction generated by variations in ocean currents and temperatures. Words of inspiration and hope that are diametrically opposed to the cold, desensitized and indifferent vocabulary of the administrative machine, defined as it is by statistics, figures, documents, deportation and expulsion decrees. The tension is dissociative, "the ignorance of violence" as Achille Mbembe has phrased it is compounded by forms of "ignorance that serve to justify abandonment and indifference, contained in the fact that no one takes issue with the treatment of others in ways that would not otherwise be tolerated."[71]

This process of enhancing compassion in readers is what Martha Nussbaum so persuasively elucidated in *Poetic Justice: Literary Imagination and Public Life*, attributing value to this paradigm, since "the very form constructs compassion in readers, positioning them as people who care intensely about the sufferings and bad luck of others, and who identify with them in ways that show possibilities for themselves."[72] As the exhibition curators explain, "the exhibition's title alludes to Walter Benjamin's reading [1934] of Franz Kafka's 'Das Gesetz der Fahrt', a route of unexpected reversals and distortions that derange casual connections between origins and destinations, wishes and fulfillments, annunciation of messages and their reception."[73] Ai Weiwei finds inspiration in this, arguing in turn for the role of artistic practice: "As artists

[...] we are always working in a dangerous area and questioning existing judgments, [whether] moral, philosophical or aesthetic. [...] Art has to be relevant. Relevant means making the people whose life and moral judgments are so fake at least feel uncomfortable about it."[74] Ai Weiwei's dramatic engagement with human vulnerability deliberately targets exhibition visitors, compelling them to reckon with the arbitrary and perilous nature of human existence and to unsettle their consciousness in the process. Indeed, as Gualtiero Zambonini has documented, the "oft-heard slogan" in Germany *Das Boot ist voll* (The Boat is Full), "conjured up the image of the country being stretched to capacity."[75] Instead, Ai Weiwei's work seems to ask the following questions: Where is the boat—*geolocation*? Why is it here—*geopolitics*? How will we process these migrants—*bureaucracy*? How can *they* become *we*—*empathy*? What are the parameters of *humanity*? As Christine Ross has described this process, "Humanism—the imperative of humanism in the aftermath of its loss in economically privileged societies—is what the migration works are ultimately set out to assert, and the mobilization of the viewer's empathy is the vehicle to restore that humanism."[76]

Chiara Brambilla makes an extremely valid point, drawing attention to the ways in which "this relationship is politically ambivalent" since it contains the potentiality of "[depriving migrants] of their political subjectivity and agency."[77] Ai Weiwei though demonstrates an awareness of these pitfalls, and Christine Ross has discussed how his "migration-related installations" are "also calls for empathy," describing how they "result from that deep identification; they are empathically made and are made to be empathically experienced by the viewer."[78] In the Prague installation, "faceless human figures on which viewers could mentally project their own faces" created circumstances in which "empathy [was] explored as the most powerful affective state to reach humanistic awareness—the awareness that these beings are humans, just like 'us'."[79]

Having said this, these tensions and ambiguities are important. T. J. Demos, with reference to Ai Weiwei's documentary film *Human Flow* (2017), argues that "we also need to take matters deeper in terms of interrogating the causes of the oppressive conditions that make life miserable for multitudes and that propel displacement."[80] This is what motivated Glenda R. Carpio to question the usefulness of the term "empathy" itself, since "migration needs to be understood as a global phenomenon, one that, much like global warming, is produced by the actions of institutions that permeate every level."[81] The tenuous relationship contained in the interplay between identification and recognition of the underlying structural matters are essential, necessitate additional attention, even though "public consensus about empathy's efficacy as a political and moral tool is strong."[82] These critiques are certainly pertinent, but in *The Law of the Journey*, Ai Weiwei adopts a methodical approach to the refugee condition, one that privileges a multidimensional framework that relies on conversations and interviews with migrants, different forms of dialogue that are structured around an interchange between textual and visual elements. A questioning thus pervades the exhibition in the explicit interpellation of the audience and in the manner in which this responsibilizes visitors. This culminates in the transcription of a longer history, one that is defined by transhistorical interconnections and experiences in which associative mechanisms reintroduce a planetary archive of displacement, exile, migration, oppression and persecution.

For Ai Weiwei, the answers reside in connectivity, in the individual imaginative capacity to put oneself in someone else's shoes, to understand another, to empathize, in other words to cross the bridge over to the other: "The border is the refusal—with the curtain drawn—to talk to each other and to seek to understand each other. This is why borders are often there only to maintain our ignorance: they betray our inability to grasp what is really happening on the other side."[83] Artistic expression and practice and political commitment have charted that trajectory for Ai Weiwei, and as an artist he has accepted the challenge posed by Susan Sontag in one of the epigraphs to this chapter, according to which, "A writer is someone who pays attention to the world,"[84] responding by asserting that "As a human being, as a citizen, but also as an artist, I have to ask myself how to deal with this experience of suffering, how to make it evident and transmit something fundamental to my contemporaries."[85] Rather than remaining cloistered behind a wall, "fatally locked in our own point of view," cultivating the alternative, as Juan Gabriel Vásquez suggests, corresponds to an exercise in courage, since "adopting another's point of view is one of the most difficult tasks there is: it requires strong doses of imagination and moral flexibility, curiosity and foresight."[86] Though reluctant to wholeheartedly embrace the concept of empathy, Hannah Arendt nevertheless proposes "to occupy the place of the other, to penetrate their point of view through the imagination," the dictinction or nuance residing in what she outlined in the essay "Truth and Politics," namely that "the more people's standpoints I have present in my mind while I am pondering a given issue, and the better I can imagine how I would feel and think if I were in their place, the stronger will be my capacity for representative thinking and the more valid my final conclusions, my opinion."[87]

Capsized Dreams

On the one hand, one finds attempts to stimulate identification, whereas on the other, determined efforts are channeled toward disidentification. As we saw in Chapter 2, there exists a glaring discrepancy between concerns for human rights and justifications for vigilance and enhanced repressive systems. This securitization of empathy implies a rupture and disconnection, and the resulting isolation and withdrawal it produces flows into emotional detachment, dispassionate positions and an inability to engage. The objective is to discourage empathy, nurturing dissociation and ultimately indifference.[88] Furthermore, this leads to insular thinking and simplistic reasoning. Media images and widespread dissemination on the internet and social media contribute to this, and T. J. Demos has referenced the "numbing, anaesthetizing capacity of such images," citing Jacques Rancière's expansive body of work on "intolerability."[89] Human rights have been sidelined in favor of emotional responses that have helped galvanize nativist and protectionist agendas, "a conjunction between 'fear' and 'charitable sentiment.'"[90] Artists and writers endeavor to provide a counterpoint.

Pending catastrophic collapse and unstoppable outcomes also shape discussions on climate change and have contributed to empathy erosion. Hakim Abderrezak's groundbreaking research on the Mediterranean has helped explain some of these forces at work.[91] For example, the neologism "seametery" has been especially powerful in this regard, a term that is "meant to capture the oxymoronic nature of the sea in which liquidity has become synonymous with immobility precipitated by preposterous and rigid policies that have transformed a *sea* into a *cemetery*."[92] These tropes of liquidity, which we have considered previously, have been exploited by politicians. Matteo Salvini, in his prior role as Italian minister of the interior, suggested that "a 'sieving' of outsiders is necessary for the sake of 'saving' an alleged monolithic cultural identity on the verge of extinction."[93] Public discourse pertaining to "desert trash" and "border trash" also introduces "a frantically xenophobic visual inventory of border trash topographies" since their "unequivocal fate is the dump / morgue."[94] By the same token, there is also a terminological concurrence between "violence against the environment, in the case of mighty, nonbiodegradable plastic" and the "violence directed primarily against immigrants [...] the frailty and death of disenfranchised humans."[95] Together, the screening, sorting and triaging that define "borderscapes"[96] have contributed to "compassion fatigue"[97] and concomitantly "desensitized the public" and resulted in the "habituation to the spectacle of death."[98]

In the face of the incontrovertible challenges associated with twenty-first-century migration, both within and between continents, artists, filmmakers and writers are increasingly responding by rethinking humanity from an expanded global framework, one that contains the potential to spawn what Patrick Chamoiseau describes as a "relational ecosystem."[99] What, we may ask, is at stake in such a reconceptualization of the question? Italian filmmaker

Andrea Segre is active in the organization ZaLab, an association whose "aim is the production, distribution and promotion of social documentaries and cultural projects" for individuals and groups that "otherwise wouldn't have the means to express themselves, and who through our laboratories become authors of their own stories."[100] ZaLab offers an invaluable example as to how relationality, through the democratization of perspective, can be achieved. These initiatives broaden the scope of reference by showing "how easy it is to become a migrant [...] an asylum seeker or a refugee [...]. Thinking backwards is necessary to be able to feel at the center of your actual history."[101] Numerous films have come out of these fruitful partnerships, notably *A sud di lampedusa* (South of Lampedusa, 2006) in which attention is given to perilous desert journeys, *Mare chiuso* (Closed Sea, 2012) on the Libyan conflict and the impact on population displacement, and *L'ordine delle cose* (The Order of Things, 2017) on the EU's response to migration. The goal of course, as Achille Mbembe has shown, is nothing less than "reaffirm[ing] the innate dignity of every human being and of the very idea of a human community, a same community, an essential human resemblance and proximity" and delineating in the process new forms of coexistence and relationality.[102] Erri De Luca has asked, "Do the treaties make allowances for shipwrecks?"[103] To which one could add: Do they justify capsized dreams?

Other writers have devoted works to the question. Points of commonality are to be found in Nathacha Appanah's novel *Tropic of Violence*, a work that transports the reader to the northern Mozambique channel in the Indian Ocean in order to tell the story of migrants arriving on the French island of Mayotte (a French overseas department/region and single territorial collectivity in the Indian Ocean and, geographically, one of the nine outermost regions of the EU), aboard the precarious *kwassa-kwassa* fishing boats (often referred to as "boats of death").[104] In June 2017, French president Emmanuel Macron derided these, stating that those operating between the archipelago of Comoros and the island Mayotte in the Indian Ocean "aren't doing too much fishing, but they are bringing in plenty of Comorian [a play on the fish by that name], and that's not the same thing." Elsewhere, in *The Silence of the Choir*, Senegalese novelist Mohamed Mbougar Sarr interweaves the novel with the stories of individual migrants, physically set apart from the rest of the text in the form of gray pages.[105] Immigration introduces difference, but in this work each encounter compels individuals to rethink their positions. The "Ragazzi [the name used for the migrants] and Sicilians were not the same," Mohamed Mbougar Sarr initially writes, and "at first it was only the differences between them—gaping—that stood out glaringly in the light. The differences in their bodies and in what those bodies showed, their faces and what they expressed, their expectations and what they hid, their past lives and what they concealed."[106] But then he takes the line of questioning further, adding "What could they have had in common at that point? A shared space, a shared feeling of foreignness to each other, the prospect of a shared future, whatever it might be. They were all human, and they wanted to live."[107]

Jason deCaires Taylor's underwater installations in the Atlantic Ocean are located at the Museo Atlántico in Lanzarote. Included in the permanent exhibition is *The Raft of Lampedusa*, aboard which are featured thirteen refugees, a work inspired by Théodore Géricault's nineteenth-century painting *The Raft of the Medusa* (1818-1819).[108] The installation conjures Italy's southernmost island, a major entry point to the EU for migrants coming from the African continent. As Susan Smillie wrote, "On the seabed off the coast of Lanzarote, British artist [sculptor] Jason deCaires Taylor [created] an extraordinary series of underwater artworks, concrete figures representing desperate refugees and selfie-taking tourists that are transformed as they become slowly colonized by marine life."[109] This process of awakening feelings yields a topography, a landscape upon which one can map a *"sentimography* of globality,"* associating *sentiments* with *topography*.[110] The street artist and activist known as Bansky has also been inspired by this same painting, adding in 2015 a monochromatic stencil on a wall in Calais, *Refugees Waving to a Luxury Yacht*, in the French port city that overlooks the Strait of Dover, an area in northern France in which migrants have congregated for the past thirty years in the hope of crossing to the United Kingdom.[111] Christine Ross has described how the black stencil "features an imperiled group of people on a sinking raft, hailing an indifferent luxury yacht or ferry boat just on the horizon. [...], by appropriating the work, Bansky can be said to have rehistoricized present-day migration within the deeper history [that] ends up disclosing the persistence of European colonialism despite abolitionism."[112] There is also an obvious intermedial connection with the film *Havarie* (2016) by the German director Philip Scheffner discussed earlier, whereby one is encouraged to "engage perceptually, sensorially, sensibly, cognitively, corporeally with the distressful conditions of migration."[113]

Cohabitation in an Uninhabitable Earthly Community

On June 16, 2016, during the Brexit campaign, the far-right UK Independence Party (UKIP) published an anti-immigration poster, "Breaking point: the EU has failed us all," featuring a long queue of migrants. This was a deliberate attempt to instill fear, since the photograph was actually of Syrian refugees approaching the Croatia-Slovenia border in 2015.[114] These political methods are designed to reduce empathy for displaced populations, and also to incite political and racially motivated violence. Since then, the Hungarian government has recycled the same image to similar ends, and in the United States, President Donald Trump has not hesitated to have recourse to analogous tactics and terminology. Ample evidence of compassionless actions and policies are to be found elsewhere. In Italy, Matteo Salvini abused his authority as minister of the interior and prevented humanitarian rescue boats from disembarking. In all of these examples, human dignity is compromised.[115]

Artists and writers have advocated for, and found inspiration in, politically committed practices. Their work has an important role to play in critical thinking, in deploying a creative apparatus that can confront shifting political realities, raise consciousness and endeavor to foster modes of identification. In the next chapter, we will consider how an emerging corpus of African writers have adapted literary practices in order to document and denounce the long-standing consequences of environmental ecocide on the continent. Indeed, as T. J. Demos maintains, "By foregrounding speculative imagination, these creative ecologies not only critically expose oppressive structures but also open up emancipatory futures, new worlds beyond catastrophic climate breakdown, colonial domination, and social injustice."[116]

In any case, as Saskia Sassen has made clear, "There are no easy solutions" since "'sending them back from where they came' is often not an option. What was once home is now a war zone, a new private gated community, a corporate complex, a plantation, a mining development, a desert, a flooded plain, a space of oppression and abuse."[117] But how then does one find ways to cohabit an uninhabitable "earthly community"?[118] Philippe Descola hints at a path forward through "an ecology of relations" which, "like modes of identification, relational modes are integrating schemas; that is to say, they stem from the kind of cognitive, emotional, and sensorimotor structures that channel the production of automatic inferences, orientate practical action, and organize the expression of thoughts and feelings according to relatively stereotyped patterns."[119] Almost two centuries have elapsed since Joseph M. W. Turner's *The Slave Ship* was exhibited at the Royal Academy in 1840. In 2023, Inaugural National Youth Poet Laureate Amanda Gorman published a response to the devastating spectacle of the capsized migrant boat Adriana off the coast of Greece that resulted in more than six hundred deaths.[120] In her attempt to better comprehend the significance of, and generalized indifference to, this latest human tragedy, she made the connection to a longer history of forced maritime transplantation, evoking "a haunting that is almost heritage: humans squeezed onto a boat by their traffickers, crushed skin to skin, bone to bone, throats gasping in the breaths of a hundred suffering others, enduring or perishing in the hellish conditions of starvation and dehydration as the vessel churns them away from their homeland."[121] Though a historical and imaginative distance separates the "two historical occurrences" that are the transatlantic slave trade and contemporary migration, "they share the cruelty and global apathy that allowed them."[122] As with *The Slave Ship* painting, Amanda Gorman's writing seeks to reinscribe consciousness and responsibility for her twenty-first century fellow humans: "The purpose of an elegy is to mourn the dead. But I also recognize it as a chance to move the living, to mobilize us to care, in every meaning of the word. To look into the wreckage and, piece by broken piece, find something much like ourselves."[123]

Chapter 4

ECOLOGICAL FRONTIERS
IN LITERATURE

Hear the call of the ravaged land
The raucous cry of the famished earth
The dull dirge of the poisoned air
The piteous wail of sludged streams [...]
Nature succumbs to th'ecological war.

Ken Saro-Wiwa[1]

Literature in the era of global warming might be deemed a relatively new phenomenon given that the formal consideration of climate change and global warming is itself historically recent. However, the conjunction between ecology and literature and the interplay between the environment and creative practices have for a long time been distinguishing features. As Édouard Glissant wrote in 1981, "The relationship with the land, one that is even more threatened because the community is alienated from that land, becomes so fundamental in this discourse that landscape in the work stops being merely decorative or supportive and emerges as a *full character*. Describing the landscape is not enough. The individual, the community, the land are inextricable in the process of creating history."[2] Eco-criticism and eco-feminism are now established scholarly fields as a result of groundbreaking works on these questions. There has also been a profusion of innovative works in fields such as art history, philosophy, history, political science and sociology, including recent works that have called for a rethinking and overhaul of the existing theoretical apparatus in order to foreground environmental approaches. In this context, the notion of frontiers has been important, its etymology referring to borders, boundaries, partitions and separation—or to the extreme limits of knowledge—conquest, exploration, expedition and unchartered territories. I turn in this chapter to the multiple ways in which transnational African literatures have engaged with environmental questions, thematically "greening" fiction—a relationship Cheryll Glotfelty framed "as a critical stance, ecocriticism has one foot in literature and the other on land"[3]—and been transformed by this engagement, while also offering new literary frameworks with which to consider the long-standing consequences of environmental exploitation and degradation on climate change on the continent.[4]

The ability to identify various agents and determinants is premised on accounting for the intricacies of the ecologies we have explored thus far in a transhistorical context—colonial, identity, migrant, aesthetic—and necessarily entails attuning to what Baptiste Morizot has described as the "spectacular crisis in our productive relations with living environments, visible in the extractivist and financialized frenzy of the dominant political economy."[5] As Ursula K. Heise reminds us, "climate change poses a challenge for narrative and lyrical forms that have conventionally focused above all on individuals, families, or nations since it requires the articulation of connections between events at vastly different scales."[6] In terms of bibliohistory, there are abundant examples of works pertaining to how the land—acquisition, appropriation, expropriation, extraction—defined existence. Even when a correlation between climate change and ecological mutations was not explicitly articulated, authors nevertheless incorporated reflection on the nefarious impact of long-standing policies on their surroundings, noting, for example how "everywhere there were decimated herds, the remains of animals that were not quickly hidden like those of men, and which rotted in the sun, filling the already suffocating air with a fetid odor of death. And he had even seen oxen kill themselves, yes, by throwing themselves into the bottom of dry wells, preferring, they who are called beasts, death to the desperate life without water."[7]

Environmental questions are therefore inextricably linked to this history; likewise, contemporary practices stand as indubitable examples of uninterrupted colonial arrangements. These conclusions are also relevant to the genealogy of African literature in which the land, exploitation and extraction practices are ubiquitous. In Chapter 1, we mapped out how colonial expansion and territorial conquest resulted in the systematic destruction of ecosystems and indigenous knowledge while disrupting cosmogonies. As Kathryn Yusoff has shown, "Nature narrates the colonial story, through its vast mines, its desecrated rivers and emaciated territories. Across continents, mangroves, grasslands, rainforests and wetlands were cleared to make way for quarries, plantations, ranches, roads and railways."[8] Literature can chart the path to collective awareness and action, extending aesthetic and relational elements. In a lecture delivered in 2010 and titled "The Polluting of the World and the Silence of African Writer,"[9] Ivorian author Tanella Boni's main argument has been characterized by Janice Spleth "as an environmentalist manifesto for African writers."[10] The trailblazing nature of the intervention came from the call to reckon with the "environmental damages caused at our doorstep," insisting on the assumption of responsibility.[11] As such, the examples I have selected for analysis make no claim to exhaustiveness, but they do showcase the distinct ways in which writers have explored new ecological frontiers, how this has contributed to the renewal of writing, revitalization of cultural constellations and accordingly framed new modes of expression.

The board games discussed earlier featured various categories of commodities, raw materials or agricultural products associated with different regions of the European empire. These were mass-produced on colonial plantations *above ground* and extracted *below ground* for the benefit of exports. Together, they transformed European modes of sustenance, disrupted traditional food-ways and fueled the industrial revolution. In France, the Eiffel Tower, built for the Exposition Universelle of 1889, stood proudly as the tallest building in the world at the time and served as a symbol of technological superiority and *grandeur* that helped consolidate the expansionist idea and accelerate the implementation of their enhanced extraction capacities. Neocolonial policies further exacerbated the destructive and disruptive actions of colonial powers, heightening food insecurity and vulnerability, intensifying inequality and poverty and ultimately displacing communities from their land. Nature served as a backdrop to the colonial narrative and "a reserve of resources available for production."[12] Estelle Zhong Mengual has proposed a reappraisal of this asymmetrical relationship, challenging us to "reinvent our relations and the attention we give to the living" and to move beyond categories established in natural history during the eighteenth century that "instrumentalized nature for commercial and agronomic ends, activities that were complicit with colonial destruction."[13] In *Littérature et écologie. Le Mur des abeilles*, Pierre Schoentjes observes that "it is clear that environmental issues have come to the forefront of contemporary thinking" and that "novels that problematize environmental issues will multiply exponentially in the future."[14] Although his focus is restricted to French literature, analogous conclusions would apply to the various literary ecosystems found in the libraries of the *world republic of letters* or in *world literature in French*, and could also be extended to the corpus of African literary works explored in this chapter.[15] In this regard, in *Un nouveau sentiment de la nature*, Michel Collot expands the framework by rejoining Édouard Glissant's aforementioned words, pointing to ways in which "for the colonized peoples," landscapes were "also the emblems of a cultural identity whose defense went hand in hand with that of their environment."[16]

Framing Ecologies

Alexandre Gefen has asserted that "ecological writing will be for the twenty-first century what politically committed writing was for the twentieth."[17] I share this assessment, one that I would not hesitate to extend to cultural production in a more general manner. The only slight reformulation I would add would be to underline how specific *engagement* with ecological questions now stands as an unassailable form of *political commitment* and *artivist* practice. I would also maintain, as Ursula K. Heise has, that "the task of ecocriticism with a cosmopolitan perspective is to develop an understanding and critique of these mechanisms as they play themselves out in different cultural contexts so as to create a variety of ecological imaginations of the global."[18] Political commitment has been a pillar of African literature, though one that has also proved divisive. Guinean novelist Camara Laye was the subject of harsh criticism in an article published in the journal *Présence Africaine* in 1955, "Romancing Africa," by Cameroonian writer Mongo Beti, who was disturbed by what he perceived as the "monstrous absence of vision and depth of the Guinean's book [...] Particularly for those who, in the final analysis, believe that the century demands of the writer—believe that it is a categorical imperative—that he refuse gratuitous art, that he reject the idea of art for art's sake."[19] In this case, Mongo Beti fastened on what he deemed an inadequate focus on colonial violence, evidence of a reluctance to embrace a specific model of political commitment. Historically though, African literature has been a literature of contestation—anti-colonial, oppositional, feminist—the cornerstones of which have been military dictatorship, kleptocracy, civil conflict, migration, genocide and today environmental ecocide.

Some critics have argued that African literature has been disproportionately shaped by an overemphasis on political and social issues, leading them to bemoan the *literariness* of African writing, as if somehow aesthetic and politics were not reconcilable, or that they could only thrive within Eurocentric interpretive grids. In reaching these and analogous conclusions, they have not been adequately attentive to Black ecologies, in other words to the various ways in which works, as Alex A. Moulton and Inge Salo have shown, "evince agencies, epistemologies, and poetics (e.g., storytelling, songs, poetry archives) that are monuments to capacious and protean Black life and life-making practices."[20] Furthermore, such assessments are, quite simply, not substantiated by the evidence offered by the *bibliodiverse* nature of global African voices in which one finds ample evidence of writings infused with multiple cosmogonies, cultural practices, histories and languages, and defined by avant-gardist, experimental and trailblazing characteristics.

Guy Ossito Midiohouan has traced the genealogy of the role of the environment in African literature, distinguishing between the long-standing "importance of the environment in literary creation" and a more recent "awareness of the problems posed."[21] Indeed, if an earlier framework focused on the relationship between nature and spirituality, subsequently on encroaching colonialism and urban development, then one finds today evidence of a turn toward anthropocentric reckoning. This has heightened consciousness of "the disruption of environmental balance and accelerated the degradation of nature."[22] Environmental considerations have therefore reconfigured African writing, drawing attention to transcolonial factors such as compromised bio-diversity, systemic racism and weakened infrastructure, thereby maintaining its pertinence as an interlocutor of societies as *things fall apart* and new para-digms are contemplated in order to secure sustainable futures. "In short," as Amitav Ghosh has claimed, "the great, irreplaceable potentiality of fiction is that it makes possible the imagining of possibilities."[23]

The environment has been an important element in writing *about* Africa and Empire more generally. Joseph Conrad's *Heart of Darkness* (1899), E. M. Forster's *A Passage to India* (1924), and André Gide's *Travels in the Congo* (1927) come to mind as immediate references, combining observations on trade practices and the operations of the colonial concessions while provid-ing descriptions of the landscapes and natural resources. Alongside these, labor practices and transformations in technology accelerated extraction, but also simultaneously disposability and expendability. The construction of the Congo railway was a cornerstone of such developments, connecting the capital Brazzaville to the Atlantic port city of Pointe-Noire, a project that started in 1921 and was completed in 1934.[24] Diverse and distinct ecosystems have also made it possible to designate environmental singularities based on geographical criteria, offering insights into eco-diversity and tracking envi-ronmental changes, but also altering the anthropocentric dimension.[25] In Emmanuel Dongala's (Republic of the Congo) writings, the forest features prominently, whereas the desert is omnipresent in Abdelkebir Khatibi's (Morocco) work. Similarly, awareness of climate change and environmental collapse is not the only lens through which to think about the environment in literature. The environmental impact (today, one would speak of "carbon footprint") of travel narratives and adventures that followed in the footsteps of explorers as a consequence of the growing influence of boats, ships and railways as steam-powered locomotives and vessels came into use during the nineteenth century and inaugurated the beginnings of mass tourism. Emma Carenini, for example, in *Soleil: Mythes, histoire et sociétés*, evokes how "the ships from colonial expeditions returned from Africa, Asia and the New World laden with innumerable riches […] At the dining table, people wanted before them exotic foods that only grew in the sun: bananas, pine-apples, coffee or chocolate," and so "they brought the sun into their living room."[26]

The focus on environmental questions has, rather, expanded the oppor-tunities for "political commitment and formal and narrative renewal,"[27] and as Ato Quayson has demonstrated, there are innumerable ways in which

African literatures are engaging today with environmental questions.[28] These forms of commitment are inscribed in a longer history since that history has been overwhelmingly concerned with the question of land—conquest, colonial occupation, expropriation of resources, degradation and of course *displacement*. In Chapter 2, we extensively reviewed the multicausal factors attributed to "climate" and "environmental" migrants and refugees. These are complex, and therefore "narrating this story is a real challenge," as Ben De Bruyn has argued, yet works of literature "encourage readers to consider climate and migration crises as democratic challenges rather than savage spectacles."[29] African literatures have examined the afterlives of colonialism and privileged environmental questions—they provide compelling examples of "literature through the prism of the Anthropocene."[30] Even when these factors are not the primary focus of a work, authors will allude to climate change and attribute migration to a destabilized ecosystem, "Our entire environment has changed. [...] Our land has become a waiting room leading to hell [...] Nature has also known its share of misfortune. Stripped of its fauna, it has been reduced to a battlefield, and each of its plots resembles a tomb" (Khalil Diallo), describing the impact on society (Djali Amadou Amal), or referencing the climate of uncertainty (Diadié Dembélé).[31]

The works considered in this chapter are categorized according to four pillars. These serve to delineate the range of environmental questions around which African writers have converged: (i) Resource exploitation, (ii) Extraction, (iii) Petro-politics (iv) and Ocean and marine pollution. To a certain degree, this breakdown replicates several different "timescale of *epochs*"— including the Plantationocene, Capitalocene, Extractocene, Petrolocene, Plasticene and Anthropocene Ocean—yet, I have avoided this organizational structure because, as Andrew Curley and Sara Smith have convincingly argued, "Cenes bound time and space while generating *linear* narratives about the past and present. They impose abstract and singular timescales on diverse places, overwriting variegated experiences and temporalities. When combined with human history, cenes emphasize attributes of human activity or certain standpoints to stand for everything and everyone in that time."[32] Having said this, the writers included might be considered to have heeded Amitav Ghosh's call: "This is the great burden that now rests upon writers, artists, filmmakers, and everyone else who is involved in the telling of stories: to us falls the task of imaginatively restoring agency and voice to nonhumans. As with all the most important artistic endeavors in human history, this is a task that is at once aesthetic and political—and because of the magnitude of the crisis that besets the planet, it is now freighted with the most pressing moral urgency."[33]

Chocolate Nation

Fermented cocoa beans—often referred to as "green gold"—are cultivated for processing plants or commodity trading houses and were mass-produced in colonies for export. Like many other products, they played a significant role in financing the Industrial Revolution and remain among the most highly consolidated and lucrative industries. Gauz' (born Armand Patrick Gbaka-Brédé) and Samy Manga, respectively Ivorian and Cameroonian, have written extensively about this history. For Gauz', the soft commodity has deep roots in his family genealogy, and he has devoted two novels, *Comrade Papa* and *Cocoaïans*, to exploring this history.[34] His interest in the question is shaped by his status as a witness to the devastating impact of climate change on biodiversity and land degradation.[35] This is attributed to European frontier expansion and the shift to monoculture plantations that resulted in expanding deforestation. Rising temperatures and extended droughts negatively impact the health of the Theobroma cocoa tree, factors that drive increasing regional deforestation as farmers seek alternative cultivation areas.[36] To put things in perspective, data from the Food and Agriculture Organization of the United Nations indicates that 64 percent of the Ivory Coast's land is devoted to cocoa bean production (together with Ghana, they account for approximately 60 percent of the global supply), and agricultural activity has resulted in "deforestation, soil erosion and climate change" and has "altered the country's fragile ecosystems and affected agrifood chains and rural farming communities."[37]

On May 2, 2016, Gauz' delivered a lecture, "Les rêves de Kong de Binger" (The Dreams of Kong de Binger) at the Collège de France (widely considered France's most prestigious research institution with a history beginning in 1530) at the international conference "Penser et écrire l'Afrique aujourd'hui," organized by the writer Alain Mabanckou.[38] He began by explaining how he had stumbled upon a tombstone during a visit to the Montparnasse cemetery on which the inscription read as follows: "Louis-Gustave Binger, explorer of the great bend of the Niger river, who *gave* the Ivory Coast to France."[39] The name rings a bell, and he soon realizes that the town of Bingerville must have been named after him. Louis-Gustave Binger first set foot in the region (today's Ivory Coast) around 1891, part of what Gauz' refers to mockingly as the "*scramble* in the jungle," reaching by foot the strategic northern trading city of Kong (from which his nickname originates) and was subsequently appointed the "inaugural" governor (he was in fact preceded by Marcel Treich-Laplène in an equivalent role) of the new French colony of Ivory Coast in West Africa in 1893.[40] Gauz' establishes a connection with the site in which he was speaking on this occasion, an institution that had commemorated in 2015 the one hundredth anniversary of the birth of French philosopher Roland Barthes, himself elected to the Collège de France in 1975. As it turns out, Roland Barthes' mother, Henriette Binger, was no less than Louis-Gustave Binger's daughter, and therefore his "Grandfather gave [...]"[41] For Gauz', this is not a negligible story, since "for me, my Africa of today is written in what History does not say, in that History that has nothing to say about Kong's dreams [...] Africa was colonized by those dreams, and we will decolonize it by dreaming as well."[42]

He revisits the transcolonial dimension of this history in the novel *Comrade Papa*, "founded," as Ninon Chavoz has explained, "on the interweaving of two narratives"—the French "exploration" and "conquest" of the Ivory Coast by the historical explorers and colonial administrators Marcel Treich-Laplène and Louis-Gustave Binger recounted by a "fictional character named Maxime Dabilly"—and the postcolonial "convergence" that occurs when a young mixed-race child named Anuman Shaoshan Illitch Davidovitch growing up in Amsterdam is sent to the Ivory Coast to join the revolutionary struggle and discovers that Maxime Dabilly was none other than a great-grandparent.[43] Gauz"s storytelling aptitude, as demonstrated in the above-mentioned lecture and the novel *Comrade Papa*, is effectively generative of a new approach to colonial history. His attentiveness, intuition and sensitivity to the questions under investigation highlight the interpenetration of narratives and the complex web of genealogical "filiations"—of lies and silences as "the fruit of a sexual relationship"—enabling a disentangling and more accurate historical account.[44] As Marie Poinsot has argued, the novel is able to simultaneously "denounce the imperial project of political and economic conquest" and "address what colonization has brought about in terms of encounters, discoveries of personalities," such that "these intertwined stories present several contradictory facets of colonization, and the cultural and identity influences that result from it and link Europe and Africa."[45]

An entire chapter is dedicated to the "caractère colonial" (colonial temperament) related to this experience. In the original French, the heading includes the expression "Y'a bon," translated by Frank Wynne as "Uncle Tom" in an attempt to preserve in English the derogatory history of the term that implies a form of docility, subservience and submissiveness, one that was extensively theorized by Frantz Fanon in works such as *Black Skin, White Masks*.[46] Initially launched in 1915, the nationalist publicity campaign for the chocolate powdered drink "Banania" featured a smiling African infantryman (known as "tirailleurs sénégalais") enjoying "the most nourishing of French foods," which, as David Murphy has shown, "the *tirailleur* utters his pidgin French slogan 'Y'a bon'." Indeed, "an awareness of its racist charge is not new: even Léopold Sédar Senghor, the great poet of Negritude, whose writing and politics consistently sought to overcome the divide between colo-nizer and colonized, angrily declared in a 1948 poem, 'I will tear down the Banania smiles from every wall in France'."[47] Gauz' does not miss the oppor-tunity to rekindle this association in the context of resource exploitation, and in so doing, transforms the protagonist Dabilly into a kind of amalgam of Marcel Treich-Laplène and Louis-Gustave Binger.[48] Upon landing on the shores of Grand-Bassam, he immediately takes in the array of trading houses and warehouses, registering the company names: Compagnie Française de l'Afrique de l'Ouest, Swanzy & Co., Société Commerciale de l'Ouest Africain, Compagnie Commerciale des Côtes d'Afrique and the Compagnie Française de Kong.[49] These enterprises represent the economic infrastruc-ture of empire, the incarnation of the extractive logic animating colonial board games. Dabilly is given instructions, framed as *duty*, "We have a duty to accelerate the arrival of settlers," which leads him to ponder whether the "we" in fact "refers to the French Republic" or the "trading house" itself.[50] The answer surely resides in the interchangeability of the referent given the symbiotic link between the overseas presence and the imperative of bolstering patriotic *grandeur*, since after all, "In the colony, people profiteer."[51]

The book *Cocoaïans (naissance d'une nation chocolat /* the birth of a choco-late nation), effectively offers a political history of chocolate. The genealogy of colonial conquest is reiterated and French military officers, explorers and administrators are back in circulation (Jean-Baptiste Marchand, Marcel Treich-Laplène) alongside cities named after military campaigns and expedi-tions (Treichville). Cocoaland becomes a laboratory for monoculture: "We're going to stick them all to cocoa farming. We're even going to specialize them in that. We've already tested it on the coasts. They've got the same tropical soil as in the Americas from where we brought the plants back from. These new lands will be a pantry where our food is produced."[52] Gauz' illustrates how the colonial authorities planned and implemented new food pathways while disrupting soil fertility and dismantling native ones. But this process also compromised indigenous knowledge systems and transformed identities, since "the cultures that we plant in the earth determine the culture that we plant in our souls. To no longer be who we were and to become that which we cannot predict, that is, in reality, the question that this plant poses to us."[53] Gauz' traces this history, pointing to the incremental steps—colonial, neoco-lonial, IMF and structural adjustment plans—which together resulted in the contemporary realities: "After the hypocritical counters and the elusive trade, a pernickety administrator is placed here, a devious soldier there. Then, the serious stuff begins."[54] There is an intertextual link with Camara Laye's novel *The Dark Child* (1954), in which Laye described the gradual changes unfold-ing: "But the world rolls on, the world changes, my own world perhaps more rapidly than anyone else's; so that it appears as if we are ceasing to be what we were, and that truly we are no longer what we were, and that we were not exactly ourselves even at the time when the miracles took place before our eyes."[55]

In the transfer from the French colonial presence to the independent Republic of the Ivory Coast, the changing of the guard is presented as a symbolic capitalist handover contained in the lowering of the colonial "blue-white-red" flag and the hoisting of the "orange-white-green" national flag.[56] In this regard, the date of 1893 is especially important, coinciding with Ivory Coast's official inauguration as a French colony and integral component in the puzzle of "European national development in the nineteenth-century,"[57] demarcating a before and after in terms of ascertaining the environmental impact. As researchers have shown, "in pre-colonial times (before 1893) Côte d'Ivoire probably hosted one of the largest elephant populations in West Africa," and the massive decline in wildlife can be attributed to colonial practices and forest agricultural clearing.[58] As the narrator explains to his daughter, "Yet, we are still at their mercy, as if nothing had happened in the meantime," and "although we have produced a third of the world's cocoa for years, we can't even make your chocolate bar."[59]

Although set in the imaginary country of Cocoaland (located, we are informed on the southern coast of West Africa, bordering the Atlantic Ocean, and with a surface area that corresponds precisely with that of Ivory Coast), what emerges is in actuality little more than an ironic or playful gesture since the context is clearly real-life Ivory Coast. This context serves to delineate an explicit indictment of persistent asymmetrical economic relations, albeit in a context in which the interchange between fiction and reality nevertheless culminates in a utopian future in 2031 in which alliances are forged in a newly established *Afridoukou*: "It's time for us to come together, to join forces and give meaning to the historical sacrifices made by our parents, our culture, our environment."[60] Gauz' invents the closed compound word "*cocoaïans*," an interplay between the much-coveted cocoa and the stimulant cocaine, a by-product derived from coca leaves, in the way that chocolate is made from the cocoa beans or seeds contained in the eponymous pods: "Our mission is to ensure that not a single bag of cocoa beans leaves this country. The West will have to buy chocolate powder from us exclusively, just as it buys cocaine powder."[61] For Gauz', the analogy just like the solution is straightforward, no less than a total recalibration between the exploitative (human and land) characteristics of production and distribution that would mitigate the infrastructural inequities associated with surplus value as the commodities are exported to production sites in Europe prior to entering the luxury chocolate market. In reality, "we would be talking about something else if we were the world's leading producers of chocolate rather than cocoa."[62] Elara Bertho has powerfully deconstructed the underlying logic: "We have not emerged from the extractivist exploitation system in which African countries sell raw materials at low cost while having to buy manufactured or processed products at high prices. [...] This is not accidental but rather due to a continuous mechanism of colonial predation that has never actually come to an end."[63] As such, the country that is Ivory Coast is a "Cocoaland," designated as such in the subtitle, "the birth of a chocolate nation," although in actuality, as Elara Bertho suggests, it is "more of a cocoa *nation* than a *chocolate nation*."[64]

The Bitter *Taste of Cocoa-Washing*

In *La science des sorciers de Koba* (The Science of Korba's Sorcerers), Cameroonian author Caroline Meva's central protagonist Almega, pursuing studies in Australia, returns to his native (imaginary) Balanga and finds "powerful states, myriads of human beings, like infernal machines or armies of magnan ants, were poisoning the atmosphere and emptying the earth of all vital substance, nibbling away and carrying away piece by piece large sections of the protective bubble, thereby mortgaging away any chance humanity might have of survival on earth."[65] In a 2023 interview with the author, Baltazar Atangana asked Caroline Meva to respond to his observation that environmental questions are increasingly found in literature, and that her own work could be categorized as "literary activism." For Caroline Meva, "literature is interested in all subjects in life, notably environmental problems, and offers solutions that can serve as a springboard for observers and decision-makers of today and tomorrow" and fully subscribes to the need for a "committed novel."[66]

Samy Manga, also from Cameroon, who self-describes as an ecological militant, has focused on the appalling environmental effects associated with resource frontiers relating to land appropriation and enhanced resource exploitation. Together, these have rendered ecosystems increasingly fragile as a result of the destruction of habitats and biodiversity, rising pollution and contamination. For some, this has been the catalyst for what is ultimately a choice of last resort, namely "continental exodus." This decision is motivated by a multiplicity of factors, though often reducible to environmental considerations. In *Chocolaté. Le goût amer de la culture du cacao* the word "amer"—bitter—serves to emphasize the devastating consequences of cocoa growing and farming.[67] Samy Manga reiterates Gauz"s position, as Chanelle Leclerc has shown, given that "cocoa was exported to Africa through colonization, where its cultivation was imposed on African countries because the climate and environment were favorable. We, in Africa, only provide cocoa beans to

Western countries without consuming it ourselves."[68] Having said this, he pays additional attention to a much longer history of dispossession, ventriloquizing through the central protagonist Abéna (a 10-year-old who works alongside his grandfather on the cocoa plantations) the roots of resource acquisition, for whom "it is obvious that since its entry into the royal court of France in 1615, cacao cultivation has become the banner of a sinister continuation of slavery, economic oppression, food conquest and the outrageous colonization of the African continent."[69]

Colonial culture and colonial propaganda constituted meticulously articulated efforts aimed at stimulating the appetite for colonial products and growing market demand, most notably for the chocolate manufactured in Europe. Destructive modes of land usage were implemented in order to meet commercial targets, forms of exploitation equated with "ecocide" (Samy Manga's term) and more specifically exacerbating "climate change."[70] Erasure was a consequence, the result of deliberate efforts at delinking cocoa pod farming, harvesting and fermentation from postproduction processes: "By ignoring the history of our lands, our suffering, our ruined dreams, our harsh daily lives and the thousands of dead that littered the plantations in the villages in the South, it is we who produce the seed for the rich with the sweat of our veins."[71] In recounting this history, Samy Manga attempts to reconnect the final product to the sequential stages that punctuated the trajectory from conquest to production, thereby offering a counter to the *sweet* taste of chocolate in the mouths of consumers. This is achieved by juxtaposing the *bitter* circumstances and atrocities committed in its name, thereby *spoiling* the digestive pleasure and drawing attention to *despoiled* lands and peoples. This alternative narrative rejoins Chimamanda Ngozi Adichie warning of the intrinsic "Danger of a Single Story," as Samy Manga concludes: "As long as the hunter tells the story, we will never know anything about animal resistance."[72]

Museums internationally have been pressured to account for the provenance of objects in their collections. They are questioned on their procurement strategies and acquisition history. This has been made possible because of the recognition that objects carry particular meaning, provide important connections to the past, and that restitution contains a restorative potential. Similar questions are being asked of agricultural production. Land exploitation is inscribed in a long history, one that has also weakened, eroded or erased cultural attachment. These questions are confronted in *La dent de Lumumba: Régicide contre la Colonie* (Lumumba's Tooth: Regicide Against the Colony), a work in which Samy Manga shines a light on the hypocrisy of governmental efforts aimed at reparations, reaffirming in the process the crucial importance of the transcolonial dimension of these questions.[73] Forms of transhistorical exploitation are inscribed in a continuous sequencing relating to an "eco-negrocide,"[74] one that includes "ten million elite souls torn from the Congo, ten million trees dug up for charcoal, ten million elephants shot with broken knees, ten million minerals extorted."[75]

Thus, attention is increasingly being granted to the ethics of product sourcing rather than promoting the idea of nature as an eternal commodity. In this regard, cacao production provides an especially compelling example of dispossession. Multinational chocolate corporations have been scrutinized for a range of questionable practices: recourse to child labor, deforestation, reliance on chemicals, fertilizers, pesticides and soil fumigants that contaminate soil and water systems and compromise health through exposure. Although protocols have been signed and commitments made to eliminate these, Samy Manga has convincingly demonstrated how such preventive measures have been undermined by advertising campaigns directed at improving brand image rather than actually mitigating abuses. "One only has to scratch the surface of these statements to discover the profound discordance with the reality of plantations in Africa," he writes, "the sole and unique aim [is that] of assuaging the conscience of these money-makers and that of millions of European consumers who do not want to ask themselves a crucial question: that of the origin of the raw material of their great taste pleasure."[76] The choice of Patrice Lumumba is not coincidental, an iconic figure assassinated in 1961.[77] As the independent country's first democratically elected leader, he had endeavored to recalibrate relations with the "Belgian, British, and American corporations" that, as Adam Hochschild has explained, "by now had vast investments in the Congo, which was rich in copper, cobalt, diamonds, gold, tin, manganese, and zinc."[78]

From the "colonial supermarket" to the "cocoa bean *business*," Samy Manga draws attention to disingenuous statements concerning the importance of the "fight against deforestation" when the "cocoa plantations fundamentally depend on the destruction of nature."[79] These propagandist agendas are tantamount to *greenwashing*, or perhaps what we might call *cacao-washing*. *Chocolaté. Le goût amer de la culture du cacao* thus offers a cogent appraisal of these developments; literature inserts itself in these debates as an act of resistance, documenting, recording and seeking accountability. To this end, Samy Manga's work establishes powerful points of commonality with the Nigerian environmental activist Ken Saro-Wiwa, who conjured the notion of "indirect genocide" as a way of describing the premeditated actions of oil companies as they *inflicted* "conditions of life calculated to bring about its physical destruction in whole or in part," as stated in the United Nations Convention on the Prevention and Punishment of the Crime of Genocide (UNPCG) of 1948. Samy Manga embraces a *call and response* dialogue with Ken Saro-Wiwa, the latter beseeching him to "hear the call of the ravaged land / The raucous cry of the famished earth / The dull dirge of the poisoned air / The piteous wail of sludged streams [...] / Nature succumbs to th'ecological war,"[80] and Samy Manga responds with these words:

> How can we forget those vast expanses of equatorial forests that have been raped, devastated, emptied of their beautiful tree species, their primates, their birds, their wild animals, their bees and their royal snakes? How can we not think of the hundreds of contaminated rivers, the poisoned soils, the ecosystems assassinated by the bulldozers of capitalism, the African biodiversity exterminated for the benefit of a single and unique plant.[81]

The Afterlives of Extraction

One finds other examples elsewhere on the African continent of what Cajetan Iheka has described "as sites of multigenerational violence" associated with extraction practices.[82] Congolese author In Koli Jean Bofane's novel, *Congo Inc.: Bismarck's Testament*, is an example of persuasive writing, underpinned by reasoning and evidence.[83] The work establishes an immediate and explicit correlation between the neocolonial nation-state "Congo Inc." and the colonial initiative that was the 1884–1885 Berlin Conference in the guise of "Bismarck's Testament."[84] This gathering transformed the global cartography of power relations and proved to be a determining moment in African and European history. The General Act served as the catalyst for the ensuing commercial "Scramble for Africa," updated here under the aegis of the corporate "Inc." King Leopold II of Belgium capitalized on these measures that granted legitimacy to his ambitions of imposing his rule over the Congo Free State from 1885 until 1908. The epigraph to the novel further underscores that connection, citing Chancellor Bismarck's closing speech to the delegates in February 1885: "The new state of Congo is destined to become one of the most important enforcers of the work we intend to accomplish."[85]

In Koli Jean Bofane's novel emphasizes rapacious planetary ventures through the inclusion of an online game fittingly named *Raging Trade*, effectively an updated form of the exploitative impetus featured in the propagandist trading games discussed previously that convey the transnational dimension of what Xavier Garnier has denoted as "the logic of globalized extractivism."[86] A striking correlation is established between the entertainment dimension provided by the online game and the geopolitical context examined in the novel. In Koli Jean Bofane offers the reader a near-exhaustive inventory of the damning history of the region, beginning with the

Berlin Conference, straddling both World Wars, then on to Hiroshima and Nagasaki, the Vietnam War, the sanguine history of decolonization, genocide and culminating in the nefarious activities of multinationals:

> The algorithm Congo Inc. had been created at the moment that Africa was being chopped up in Berlin between November 1884 and February 1885. Under Leopold II's sharecropping, they hastily developed it so they could supply the whole world with rubber from the equator, without which the industrial era wouldn't have expanded as rapidly as it needed to at the time. [...] Disposable humans could also participate in the dirty work and in coups d'état. Loyal to Bismarck's testament, Congo Inc. more recently had been appointed as the accredited supplier of internationalism, responsible for the delivery of strategic minerals for the conquest of space, the manufacturing of sophisticated armaments, the oil industry, and the production of high-tech telecommunications material.[87]

Pillaged, plundered, looted, despoiled, embezzled, stripped, ransacked, ravaged—each and every one of these synonyms remains pertinent to the unquenchable transgenerational thirst for Congo's natural resources. As David Van Reybrouck has written,

> It was almost too good to be true. Until then, the economic exploitation of the area had been aimed exclusively at its biological riches—ivory and rubber—but now a far greater wealth was found to be lying a few meters under the ground. [...] The discovery that the colony was sitting atop these immense mineral riches came, by the way, not a moment too soon. [...] It seemed like a historical déjà vu: in the same way that the rubber boom had arrived just in in time to offset the dwindling ivory trade, mining began just in time to replace the ailing rubber industry.[88]

In Koli Jean Bofane's canvas depicts a truly apocalyptic scene in which vultures congregate and compete to devour festering, putrid carcasses, ignoring the deleterious consequences of their choices, much like their predecessors gathered in Berlin. Togolese writer Kossi Efoui, in *La Fabrique des cérémonies*, captured the spirit of the conference: "This conference table where the pencils were sharp as knives."[89]

Blaise Ndala (born in the Democratic Republic of the Congo, but residing in Canada), in the novel *In the Belly of the Congo*, also describes "Léopold II's emissaries, sent to explore and then exploit the resources of the Congo basin," and among his selected epigraphs, includes the speech delivered on May 18, 1879, by Victor Hugo on the occasion of the twenty-first anniversary

of the abolition of slavery: "Forward, People! Claim the land as yours. / Take
it. From whom? No one. / Take this land from God. God gives the land to
men. / God offers Africa to Europe. Take it. / Where kings would bring war,
bring concord."[90] As with Gauz''s novel *Comrade Papa*, *In the Belly of the Congo*
is also structured in a multigenerational transcolonial timeline. Blaise Ndala
features the 1958 Brussels Universal and International Exhibition (Expo 58)
at which an "indigenous village"—*human zoo*—sponsored by the Belgian
Ministry of Colonies displayed African children, women and men in order to
showcase the civilizing achievements of Belgian colonialism.[91]

The DRC is one of the largest and most densely populated countries in the
world. The political instability that had become characteristic of the early
years of postcolonial transition subsequently defined Mobutu Sese Seko's
own period of military rule from 1965 to 1997, a much-satirized dictator
who became the embodiment of corruption, degeneracy and wickedness. As
Nicolas Michel has argued in his review of *Congo Inc.—Bismarck's Testament*,
the work in which "Congo's extravagance" has found a home.[92] The novel
meticulously traces the seamless continuation between the colonial and postcolonial scramble, the ongoing depredation of resources by multinational
corporate interests, coupled with, nourished and sustained by corrupt governance that has culminated in widespread civil conflict, human rights abuses
and environmental degradation.

Witness to this devastation is the main protagonist named Isookanga, who
devotes his days to making the necessary preparations for his exodus to the
capital and megalopolis Kinshasa. "The place of concentration and fission is
Kinshasa, laboratory of the future and, incidentally, capital city of the nebula,
Congo Inc."[93] He is able to connect to the outside world from his rural village
because of a telecommunications tower installed by Chinese business opera-
tives. Certainly, mobility and relocation are not in and of themselves new
developments in the library of francophone sub-Saharan African literature, a
library that proudly displays the emblematic stories of Fara in Ousmane Socé's
Mirages de Paris (1937), Laye in Camara Laye's *The Dark Child* (1954), Tanhoe
in Bernard Dadié's *An African in Paris* (1959), Samba in Cheikh Hamidou
Kane's *Ambiguous Adventure* (1961), Joseph in Daniel Biyaoula's *L'Impasse* (1996)
or Massala-Massala in Alain Mabanckou's *Blue White Red* (1998). These protagonists were seduced by the colonial project and postcolonial opportunities
they were promised in Europe, by what Christopher L. Miller has described
as the inherent "francocentrism," symbol of upward mobility.[94] As we know,
these entailed "ambiguous" journeys that were often defined by disillusion-
ment as protagonists demystified the false promises ascribed to colonialism.
However, what distinguishes Isookanga's case is that his goals are premised
on intranational migration.

In Koli Jean Bofane's novel certainly draws on the colonial background, but his main protagonist is instead lured away by advances in new technology and the growing exposure to globalization: "Now he couldn't do without the computer, and the online game Raging Trade had become his reason for living. Raging Trade was the recommended game for any internationalist wanting to know how to get into the business world."[95] In the multiplayer online gaming community, under his Lingala avatar *Congo Bololo* ("bitter" Congo), Isookanga confronts his ruthless adversaries—*Skulls and Bones Mining Fields*, *Uranium and Security*, *American Diggers*—to the soundtrack of American rap music:

> Isookanga now knew how American Diggers increased its points. It was GGAP, Skulls and Bones Mining Fields, and Kannibal Dawa that snuck off on the sly. All three of them had succeeded in opening secret accounts where they stored whatever they wanted: points, vouchers for weapons, offshore companies. Congo Bololo figured it was time to break up some of these agreements. Thanks to his sophisticated weapons, he had managed to repel Skulls and Bones into the same zone as the Goldberg & Gils Atomic Project. Suddenly their alliance had shattered in a gruesome way. The corner where they must have assembled their troops was bursting with gold, diamonds, and cobalt. What was bound to occur actually happened. To control the wealth, they started firing at each other. From the distance, Congo Bololo had witnessed the carnage and snickered. "In this game, Old One, I'm a raider. I recently annihilated everybody but one, Kannibal Dawa, who maliciously caught a second wind despite the losses I made him suffer."[96]

Prerequisites for success in most games include a combination of creativity, strategizing, perseverance and risk-taking. In the case of *Raging Trade*, players strive, through relentless battles, rampant pillaging and senseless killing, to amass resources. By the time Isookanga sets out from his village, the knowledge he has attained of the outside world comes almost exclusively from the time he has devoted to a game that rewards devious, malicious, dishonest and corrupt behavior. These may seem at first glance to be desirable credentials for anyone seeking employment in the extraction sector. However, like so many of his fictional (and real-life predecessors), Isookanga's adventure is also a form of extraction. His journey is simultaneously defined by a physical move toward an urban setting, but one in which a transition from innocence to insight and initiation occurs, the logical outcome of life lessons.

Journeying alongside Isookanga, the reader discovers the striking correlation between the online game and the challenges confronting the DRC on the larger geopolitical landscape. Colonial-era games aimed to reproduce replicas of real-life adventure, and the online video game played by Isookanga mirrors the chessboard of globalization and the rapacious acquisitions race for resources in a new postcolonial scramble for Africa. Both eras focused on the insatiable accumulation of goods and the pursuit of infinite profit. When asked by his Uncle, "But what is it exactly that you want to do?," Isookanga does not have to think twice before responding: "Globalization, computer technology, Uncle."[97]

Shortly after his arrival in Kinshasa, Isookanga meets Zhang Xia, a Chinese man endeavoring to resolve his own complicated personal issues, and who becomes a mentor of sorts: "Experience is a lantern that only sheds light on the path you've already walked."[98] Their interaction is far from unusual in a city in which the Chinese presence is by now a long-standing one. In *Sur les ailes du dragon: Voyages entre l'Afrique et la Chine (On the Dragon's Wings: Voyages Between Africa and China)*, Belgian author Lieve Joris described the extraordinary flow of goods and people between these two regions of the world.[99] In Guangzhou, for example, a major transportation hub in southern China, it is common to see shipping logistics companies using world maps on which the arrows point outward exclusively to destinations on the African continent (notably in the DRC, Angola, Kenya, Mozambique, Tanzania). And Chinese president Xi Jinping has been holding regular multilateral summits under the aegis of the Forum on China-Africa Cooperation (FOCAC) aimed at significantly increasing infrastructure and development projects, notably in terms of mining operations.

Isookanga remains steadfast, resolute, reiterating his commitment to "globalizing" in what is among the world's most active extractive zones.[100] As T. J. Demos has argued in a different, albeit related context, "the sourcing of rare earths for computer technology, server farm reliance on fossil fuel energy, and for the destructive disposal of e-waste—is exclusively environmentally damaging,"[101] and there is therefore a deep irony that applies to the gaming activities in *Congo Inc.—Bismarck's Testament*. This extends to a much broader indictment, one that implicates *all* readers, namely that "our planetary mobility," as Pierre-Philippe Fraiture reminds us, "has been made possible at the expense of the Congolese and if we can move around on roads (rubber) and on digital superhighways (coltan for cell phones) it is partly thanks to the DRC."[102] And these are, of course, following Malcom Ferdinand's tracking of historical developments, "Beyond agriculture, plantations also take the form of industries that extract the rare minerals that are found in computers and mobile phones and of the terrestrial and marine 'plantations' of oil wells. Whole segments of humans and non-humans are enslaved in order to continue this colonial inhabitation."[103] Thus, although Isookanga's uncle Old

Lomana sees things quite differently, it will take a period of maturation for Isookanga to change his perspective. Meanwhile, Old Lomana observes how triumphant globalization has further disturbed the eco-balance and driven the wildlife away:

> Since it was put up, that bit of metal had brought nothing but trouble. First of all, it had caused harm on the level of social peace because it had its detractors among the majority of the Ekanga population and partisans who were thrilled to finally join the modern world. Although one could ask in what way the antenna could possibly be of service to them—phone whom? surf what?—they would defend the iron tower like a member of their own family. Then there was the matter of subsistence, sustenance had turned on its heels. Now they had to go for miles to flush it out. Some people simply didn't look any further than the end of their nose. And his own nephew Isookanga was one of them. Nothing but nonsense. Modernity, modernity. Can you eat modernity?[104]

Initially, at least, these concerns are secondary to Isookanga. Gradually, though, he does begin to open his eyes and is able to observe how the city epitomizes the futile greed of the times: "It was simply a matter of being in control of the largest reserve of raw materials in the world, and may the best man win."[105] In Koli Jean Bofane's novel reckons with the harsh realities confronting the DRC (and elsewhere, of course, in the region and on the African continent), as well as the embedded corruption. This analysis is anchored in fiction, but the fictitious space ultimately resembles all too much the contemporary reality. This is a world fashioned by violence, a world that tests the limits of empathy and understanding, a deeply troubled world which, as Achille Mbembe has argued, "In a world set on objectifying everybody and every living thing in the name of profit, the erasure of the political by capital is the real threat. The transformation of the political into business raises the risk of the elimination of the very possibility of politics."[106] These (post) colonial globalized cartographies have produced new spatial and racial dispositions, reconfiguring cultural and social environments, but also reshaping economic systems in the process. Lingering disparities between the relatively prosperous areas of the world and those located in extraction zones in the Global South, where abundant resources are coveted, persist. Corresponding factors can help elucidate the multifaceted ingredients of today's neocolonial configurations—access to cheap labor, tax incentives, emerging market yields, distribution networks, foreign direct investment—at a moment in time when the *here* and the *elsewhere* have become imbricated in new and previously unanticipated ways. Yet, somehow, in the face of genocide, ethnic cleansing, civil conflict, ecocide, disease, coercion and gender-based violence, out of the horror, mutilation and dismemberment, In Koli Jean Bofane's novel strives to delineate the contours of a universe in which fiction can address indignation and gradually pave the way for moral imagination.

Congo Inc.—Bismarck's Testament is thus especially relevant precisely because of its engagement with the intricate nature of postcolonial African history. Many authors have adopted imaginary topographic backdrops, often a necessary step to bypass censorship, repression and violence, but In Koli Jean Bofane elects instead to concentrate on, and explicitly name, current political configurations. This makes it possible for him to draw attention to the role of multinational corporations, foreign investors and nation-states in climate change and environmental degradation, factors that disproportionately impact vulnerable populations, serve as catalysts for population displacement and increase the potential for conflict. Old Lomana has monitored these events and describes how "the village is having problems," how animals are being "forced out of their own region," people are sustaining work-related and occupational injuries involving machinery, "food is becoming scarce," and concludes that these factors can be explained by changing environmental conditions: "Something's happening in the ecosystem, Isookanga. Parameters are in the process of changing radically."[107]

Ecocidal Wounds

The DRC is home to the world's most significant mineral deposits, including bauxite, cobalt, coltan, copper, gold, diamonds, tantalum and uranium. These account for almost the entirety of exports, and the extraction industry has resulted in large-scale population eviction and forced displacement, environmental deterioration, human rights abuses and compromised social relations. Not surprisingly, these questions have received comparatively more attention in the DRC in contemporary literature and art than elsewhere. Although Sinzo Aanza does not explicitly embrace the label "committed writer," the Kinshasa native nevertheless concedes that "it is difficult to not be political when one writes about a country like the Congo."[108] In *Généalogie d'une banalité* (Genealogy of a Banality), he turns his attention to the inhabitants of a fictional neighborhood (the "Bronx") in Lumumbashi, the DRC's mining capital located in the southeast.[109] Below their abodes, residents, reputed for their resourcefulness, are busy digging holes in search of mineral resources, holes in a "burrowed land" that serve, as Cajetan Iheka has shown, to remind us "that mining is a process of excavation and extraction with nothing put back in return."[110] A parallel is also established intertextually with the "heart of darkness" chronicled by Joseph Conrad in 1899, a void that the civilizing mission would seek to fill through religious conditioning and pedagogic indoctrination. The "genealogy" Sinzo Aanza evokes is thus the outgrowth of the fractured and multiple voices whose interventions are broadcast on the eponymous national radio network.

As Justin Bisanswa has argued, "The novelist's skill consists in particular in making history emerge from below, told by those who often endure it, while, in the novel, they seek to transform it, by digging to find copper under their makeshift dwellings" and thereby "inviting a different history of the colonized and the powerless."[111] Pierre-Philippe Fraiture, who has written extensively about these questions, explains how the copper rush "became one of the defining moments of European expansion in Congo. From the outset, this enterprise had a definite international dimension. Of course, it was controlled from Brussels, but at the same time, it was built on an intricate network of agents from Europe and beyond who would set out to work towards the establishment of globalized operations."[112] For Sinzo Aanza, current circumstances can only be understood as derivations, extractions from a colonial history that has severed successive generations from the land: "We are no longer rooted, and we never will be again. We are trees that someone has cut down and that are rotting on the surface," such that "little by little, between incompetence, resourcefulness, cronyism, economic and political crises, weakness of the State, a putrid administrative culture was born here. And as a result, the country is in the shit."[113] Kafka, the school teacher, echoes these conclusions, since for him Congolese society is "entirely the creation of the colonial economic machine, this vast campaign of exploitation of the country."[114]

Sony Labou Tansi, writing from across the Congo River in Brazzaville, had also registered the importance of environmental conditions when, in 1973, in the "Note de l'auteur" (Author's foreword) to his play *Conscience de Tracteur* (Tractor Conscience), he used the word "cosmocide" ("Nous sommes les enfants du Cosmocide" / We are the children of Cosmocide).[115] These themes were dear to him, and he would continue to underscore how recognizing environmental peril had become unavoidable. Much later, in his last published novel, *Le Commencement des douleurs*, he reassembled these earlier positions through an etymology of pain and suffering, one in which "This land has gone haywire. She is forced to screech at the top of her lungs for it to be known that she is not happy with our nonsense. The cliff won't interrupt its squawking. The ocean wails, the mountain bellows, the sky screams all night long and the stones never stop sulking."[116] Sara Buekens makes an astute observation: "It is striking that natural signs follow the destructive activities of human society, almost like a force of punishment," and reminds us that "the natural environment remains heir to the historical past," so that "the order in which ecological disasters occur is by no means fortuitous, but responds to a chain of environmental causalities determined by the laws of geology, biology and climatology."[117]

Alice Desquilbet has also explored the intersection between Sony Labou Tansi's and Sinzo Aanza's writings, finding in the former an author who "paints a picture of a Congo gutted, pillaged and squandered, due to the increasing exploitation of forest and oil resources."[118] Elsewhere, she has demonstrated how the work of Chinese photojournalist Lu Gang on deforestation in the Congo, notably *Blood Wood* (2018), features "a close-up of the wound in the bark of a tree whose red sap actually looks like blood," montages in which "ecological preoccupation remains indissociable from social and political commitment."[119] Likewise, at the National Pavilion of the Democratic Republic of Congo at the 2024 Venice Biennale (May 17 to November 24, 2024), curated by James Putnam and Michele Gervasuti, the Biennale's theme, "foreigners everywhere," is refracted, since we now have an example of how "a land and people are being exploited by foreigners" and how the new scramble is conducted by "foreign companies [that] are 'rushing' to extract lithium [and] cause vast ecological damage."[120] The featured installation by Aimé Mpane, "Gold" (170 × 70 × 60 cm, 2021), contains a wheelbarrow, ebony wood, and acrylics, "comprising [molten metal] ingots carved from black Congo ebony, etched with the geographical coordinates of regions in Africa (and elsewhere) where the usurpation of gold has triggered conflict and war."[121]

Literature, Underground

Fiston Mwanza Mujila (born in Lumumbashi) published his debut novel *Tram 83* just over a decade ago to almost immediate critical acclaim.[122] Alongside Sinzo Aanza's *Généalogie d'une banalité*, as Pierre-Philippe Fraiture attests, Fiston Mwanza Mujila's "novel probes the limits of literature, its heuristic power, ability to render the truth, and translate lived experience, for beyond this schematic synopsis, this text captures the randomness of human encounters and the cacophony of verbal communication."[123] Together, "these two novels memorialize Belgian colonialism in Congo and Katanga" while offering "a dissonant and deliberately disjointed narrative" that "obliquely testifies to the cultural and environmental ravages wrought by neocolonialism and Sino-Western capitalism."[124] What emerges are new ways of engaging with environmental questions and concerted actions aimed at simultaneously transforming the process of writing. In Sony Labou Tansi's writings, the treatment of power in the postcolony compelled him to explore new ways of writing, identifying narrative structures and modes of linguistic experimentation capable of accommodating the violence he sought to depict.[125]

The afterlives of colonial extraction have become the focus of a new generation of writers (such as Sinzo Aanza and Fiston Mwanza Mujila) whose works provide evidence of new modes of writing in which "the complex imbrication of narrative voices on which this text relies mirrors the equally elaborate cartography of a city originally conceived to master Katangese geology."[126] Although politically committed and confrontational, the works are less *underground literature* than they are *literature underground*, a form of *extraction writing* defined by engagements with what Xavier Garnier calls "writings of the subsoil"[127] and that extends the shelves of libraries devoted to such concerns, alongside Émile Zola's novel *Germinal* (1885) that also explored the environmental impact of exploitative industrial capitalism. The aspiring writer Lucien, in *Tram 83*, embraces this model of literature and responds to the daunting task implied in this assumption of responsibility: "I think, unless I am mistaken, that literature deserves pride of place in the shaping of history. It is by way of literature that I can reestablish the truth. I intend to piece together the memory of a country that exists only on paper."[128] The cast of characters roaming the ecosystem he depicts are easy to distinguish: fraudsters who handle contraband, loot and embezzle, chaotic modes of existence that re-create the subterranean geological disruption: "At night they infiltrated the facilities, which were guarded by mercenaries, the chief's personal militia, and other security outfits. Clashes ensued, lasting for hours, accompanied by corpses. [...] Whether diggers or dissident rebels or for-profit tourists or students, the common denominator was the gold rush that began at the station whose metal structure."[129]

Pierre-Philippe Fraiture's research on artistic and literary practices in the DRC emphasizes the multiple ways in which extraction emerges as "a key term to understand Congo's geopolitical position and predicament since colonial times" thanks to the "rich, complex, multifaceted, and hitherto little-explored array of tropes and ideas" it presents.[130] As with *Tram 83*, Fiston Mwanza Mujila's second novel, *The Villain's Dance*, is also therefore an *extraction novel*.[131] Interspersed over 54 story sequences, navigating between Angola and the DRC, what rises to the surface is a polyvocal story of life above ground mediated through the prism of the insatiable quest for the riches that lie beneath their feet. One of the vibrant street kids, Ngungi, "became aware, to his cost, that the Union Minière, the mastodon, the vile beast, the monster—the one for which folk from all over had forsaken whatever dump they came from to climb aboard any old train to go shift the unctuous earth and melt copper—had sucked his blood down to the last drop."[132] And among the most notable figures is that of Tshiamuena (Madonna of the Cafunfo Mines) who enjoys the reputation as "an unparalleled raconteur. She would recap the same tale fifty times. And with each telling, the story took on a different flavor. A living, ancient eyewitness to this golden age."[133]

The innovative dimension of Fiston Mwanza Mujila's writing (himself a skillful *raconteur*) is to be found in the dialogue between these layers of activity and in conjunction with the intra-textual discussion of writing. From a seemingly disjointed, fractured and fragmented narrative, much like the eponymous "Villain's Dance" that animates the nightlife, choreographed performances deliver unity: "Amid the raging Hawaiian guitars, congas, cymbals, vibra-phone, sax, and bass clarinet, the fauna writhed to the rhythm of the Villain's Dance. [...]. Lifting your head, you began twisting your hips—gently at first, then energetically—while using the elasticity of your legs to descend and rise again, descend and rise again, hands whirling as if distributing money, a devilish grin on your face."[134] Ato Quayson, writing about *Tram 83*, describes—and these insights are pertinent to *The Villain's Dance*—how "the musicality that we see at the level of content is also superbly augmented by rhythms at the level of narration and it is here that the experimental innovativeness of Mujila's narrative style must be recognized. The rhythmic character of the narration is systematically structured around a series of repeated sentences, phrases, and sequences in a sometimes harmonious but often dissonant distributional matrix."[135]

In the poetry collection, *The River in the Belly*, Fiston Mwanza Mujila ponders whether "after taking our diamonds, copper, cobalt, coltan, and uranium, after torching our fields [...] will they also find a way to haul away the Congo River."[136] The transcolonial link with extraction is a recurrent theme, one which he also underlined in the "Author's Note" included in *The Villain's Dance*. This provides a helpful perspective on writing, one in which Fiston Mwanza Mujila acknowledges the influence of the prominent Belgian anthropologist Filip De Boeck, known for his groundbreaking research on the DRC. The latter has also collaborated with the Congolese artist, curator, photographer and filmmaker Baloji, who has explored colonial history and extraction.[137] In fact, Baloji's multimedia work has been crucial in terms of identifying "the roots of (neo)colonial extraction of the DRC's minerals" and "[initiating] new debates on the many human and environmental abuses this process has generated."[138] Vincent van Velsen, in his "Curatorial Essay" to *A Blueprint for Toads and Snakes: A Solo Exhibition by Sammy Baloji* (2018), describes how, "by way of his art, he explores the histories, present-day realities and contradictions inherent to the formation of Congo in general, and its southeastern province Katanga in particular [...] The colonial project together with the exploitation of these resources has marked the country and its people continuously."[139] And, as Pierre-Philippe Fraiture concludes, "Baloji's work strongly resonates with recent literary experiments from the DRC and the

Congolese diaspora. Works by [authors that] have also been underpinned by an ambition to delve into Congo's extractivist present past and focus on the central presence of the mine in this cultural landscape" and "the two activities, writing and mining, are conflated to examine Congolese culture in a local, national, but also global context" in an "anti-extractivist novel."[140]

Petro-Politics and Petro Fiction: Commitment with Consequences

Challenging multinational energy corporations and industrial-scale mining operations comes with serious consequences. Nigerian environmental activist Ken Saro-Wiwa was persecuted and eventually executed on November 10, 1995, by the Nigerian government as a direct result of environmental activism. The populations he advocated for were forced to leave their lands, their ecosystems were compromised and a vast array of human rights abuses were recorded. Climate justice and environmental justice intersected in this context, defining factors in what Cajetan Iheka attributes to "postcolonial trauma" and a range of "traumatic stressors" delimiting the boundaries of "sites of multigenerational violence inflicted on people and the nonhuman."[141] The work of Macarena Gómez-Barris, *The Extractive Zone: Social Ecologies and Decolonial Perspectives*, has been foundational in this regard, highlighting the acute competition for resources.[142] The story of the Niger Delta is deeply ingrained in this history "due in no small part to the British government's insistence that the oil industry be instrumental in Nigeria's economic future after independence,"[143] and subsequently adapted to postcolonial circumstances as multinational corporations orchestrated favorable extraction terms with corrupt governments eager to generate revenue. "The geographic expansion and systemic deepening of capitalist relations of production in the global South is, in many ways, an old history," as Saskia Sassen has maintained, and "this gradual destruction of traditional economies prepared the ground, literally, for some of the new needs of advanced capitalism, among which are the acquisitions of vast stretches of land—for agriculture, for underground water tables, and for mining."[144] Ken Saro-Wiwa organized the resistance to these arrangements under the auspices of the Movement for the Survival of the Ogoni People (MOSOP), founded in 1990 in order to promote democratic awareness and protect the environment of the Ogoni people in southeastern Nigeria.[145]

In their book on Ken Saro-Wiwa, Roy Doron and Toyin Falola provide an inventory of terms that have been used to qualify the direct impact of oil spills, gas flarings and pipeline failures. These include poisoned waterways, killed marine life, large parcels of land rendered unusable, dispossessed farmland, degradation of the region's ability to produce food, soil contamination attributed to oil penetrating the soil and entering waterways, crop destruction and emission-caused harm, compromised atmospheric quality and health problems.[146] Ken Saro-Wiwa spoke of this degradation, describing "the agony of trees dying / In ancestral farmlands / Streams polluted weeping" in his poem "Ogoni! Ogoni."[147] A collective of young poets from Gabon have also joined forces, publishing an anthology titled *Nos vers en vert* in which the title is a homophone, whereby the French words "vers" (verse) and "vert" (green) are juxtaposed in order to emphasize the articulated conjunction between literature and environmental action.[148] One of the contributors, Fath Kumbe Manduku, wrote that "Through despicable acts / Man is damaging the ecosystem / The climate is deteriorating / The seasons are merging."[149] Yet, it is, of course, a story of "collusion between the government and the oil industry" and "military government hoping to ingratiate itself with the petroleum industry."[150] Environmental questions have been the catalyst for organized protests and furnished the authorities with the justification they sought to implement repressive responses aimed at deterring, intimidating and ultimately silencing opponents.

Ken Saro-Wiwa did not back down, forcefully defending what Daisy Pullman has described as an "eco-nationalist Ogoni identity."[151] And he persisted in advocating for the recognition of the Ogoni condition as "indirect genocide" as defined by the United Nations Convention on the Prevention and Punishment of the Crime of Genocide since ultimately the government's negligence with regard to the environment "made conditions unlivable and destroyed the ability of the Ogoni to live as a society."[152] As Mark Dummett has shown, "The United Nations Environment Programme vindicated his [Ken Saro-Wiwa's] claim [...] that the people of Ogoni [...] had lived with chronic oil pollution throughout their lives."[153] In Chapter 2, we explored analogous arguments being formulated in order to expand the current UN definitions of refugees to incorporate "climate or environmental refugees" as outcomes of climate change as a displacement factor. Ken Saro-Wiwa's compatriot, Helon Habila, has also contributed to the library of "petro-fiction," notably in the highly acclaimed novel *Oil on Water* in which one finds an unequivocal reference to the execution by hanging of his fellow man of letters: "The weight of the oil tight like a hangman's noose around the neck of whatever life-form lay underneath."[154] As Olarotimi Ogungbemi has argued, "As African ecocriticism and petrol fiction continue to develop, they provide vital platforms for engaging with the environmental and social challenges posed by the exploitation of natural resources. Literature, in this vein, not only critiques the present but also paves the way for imagining a more sustainable and equitable future."[155] These questions have also been explored by numerous other authors, notably in Cameroonian writer Imbolo Mbue's *How Beautiful We Were* in which the impact of historical extraction and land degradation on the fictional village of Kosawa as a consequence of the actions of an American oil company is explored.[156]

Sandrine Bessora Nan-Nguema (who goes by the pseudonym Bessora) was born in Belgium to a Gabonese father and a Swiss mother. She completed a doctoral thesis at the University of Paris 7 in 2002 entitled *Mémoires pétrolières au Gabon* (Oil Memories in Gabon). In the Abstract, one reads that "Gabon's Petroleum memories began in the early 1900s. They are rooted in older memories from which they were fed. [...] Once again, all the human energies of the country were focused on this cycle, which 'petrolized' and urbanized the coast. This cycle reinforced the social hierarchies that pre-existed while adding new ones. [...] An oil ideology was emerging."[157] Shortly thereafter, she published the novel *Petroleum* and integrated her research findings into the story of extraction that resulted in the emergence of petro-dictators feasting on "l'or noir" (black gold) in Gabon.[158] As in the doctoral thesis, Bessora charted the incremental stages of extractive processes, beginning with the arrival of the first geologists in the region and thereafter linking, phonetically, "colonization" with "patronization," which, as Giulia Champion has shown, "further identifies the entanglements between colonial practices and petroleum extraction and trade," while also accentuating how the "longer history in imperial extractive forms of exploitation [...] have precipitated the consequences of anthropogenic climate change in formerly colonized spaces."[159] International oil companies operating in Gabon today are predominantly in offshore fields, and deepwater drilling is a major source of toxic pollution.[160]

Marine Eco-stories and Expeditions: *Underwater Dynamics* and *Surface Politics*

Wilfried N'Sondé (born in Brazzaville) is a prolific writer who has concentrated on a number of themes, including immigration, race relations, national and diasporic identity. His writing has now taken an environmental turn and considers the impact of climate change on the planet. In one example, *Femme du ciel et des tempêtes* (Woman of the Sky and Storms), Wilfried N'Sondé transports the reader to the Yamal Peninsula of northwest Siberia, where a scientific research team has gathered in order to examine the recent discovery below the permafrost in a section of the Arctic Ocean of the preserved corpse of a woman.[161] The shaman named Noum, who made the discovery, "immediately noticed her beautifully braided, tightly curled hair and was surprised by the dark brown color of her skin. She lay on the fragments of a finery composed of pearls and shells that had been carefully perforated.

The richness of the grave goods made him think that he had just discovered an African queen from a very distant past."[162] Affectionately named "the African woman of the Arctic," the team led by the medical doctor Cosima is committed to "saving a still wild ecosystem from the ravages of industry."[163] However, their activities threaten to get in the way of gas prospecting and extraction under the careful watch of the Moscovite Serguei hired to fend off detractors.

Wilfried N'Sondé has also participated in a number of collaborative artistic projects on these and related questions. *Homo Detritus* brings together photographs by Stéphane Gladieu and text by him that explore the pollution caused by industrial waste exported to the DRC, a volume in which one encounters "the alliance of detritus with poverty [...] carrying the rebellion of the invisible exiled to the periphery of the rich and sanitized center."[164] These questions are also explored in a second project, *Borders*, this time with the photographer Jean-Michel André. Here, Wilfried N'Sondé connects environmental degradation and migration, whereby the eponymous borders are reduced to "scars on landscapes" and "a blight on the horizon [that] lacerate the course of the winds and lend their breeze a funereal accent."[165] His interest in environmental questions rose to a whole new level with the publication in 2022 of the novel *Héliosphéra, fille des abysses, d'amour et de plancton* (Heliosphera, daughter of the abyss, of love and plankton) in the "Mondes Sauvages" series at Actes Sud edited by Stéphane Durand, a series that includes such important scholars as Estelle Zhong Mengual and Baptiste Morizot and emphasizes alliance, cohabitation and the in-common, terms that reverberate throughout Wilfried N'Sondé's book.[166]

The novel brings together artists and scientists seeking to "hatch an ecosystem of stories" and thereby accords cultural and political respect and value to their collaboration, while creating the conditions in which scientific "knowledge" can be "translated" by others "into sensitive and aesthetic knowledge."[167] Wilfried N'Sondé thereby offers a multispecies perspective and assesses the impact of anthropogenic climate breakdown. He is aligned with Baptiste Morizot's position that "the human way of being alive only makes sense if it is woven into the countless other ways of being alive that the animals, plants, bacteria and ecosystems all around us demand," namely an *"interspecies diplomacy of interdependences."*[168] One thus finds in *Héliosphéra, fille des abysses, d'amour et de plancton* a counter to what Amitav Ghosh criticized in Western ways of thinking, namely an "absolute distinction between the natural and the human [that] leaves no room for other-than-human beings to figure as protagonists in history or politics,"[169] as well as an attempt to redress the imbalance described by Timothy Morton, whereby "capitalist economics is also an anthropocentric practice that has no easy way to factor in the very things that ecological thought and politics require: non-human beings and unfamiliar timescales."[170]

The genealogy of *Héliosphéra, fille des abysses, d'amour et de plancton* is especially compelling since it is the outcome of an artist residency on the Tara Atlantic expedition: "The Tara Ocean Foundation is leading a scientific revolution around this ecosystem. [...] It uses this high-level scientific expertise and these sea voyages to raise awareness and educate young people and the public in general, to mobilize political decision makers at the highest level and to enable developing countries to access this new knowledge about the Ocean."[171] The commitment to conducting research in a complex marine ecosystem aligns with the experimental nature of the novel itself, an expanded framework that provides a space for the complexity of the scientific element. The exploration of new aesthetic terrain is itself infused with field research and incorporated into a book that is augmented with artistic and geometric illustrations rendered with microscopic precision by Margaux Bidat.

The ship-laboratory expedition gathered samples in the "Humboldt Current," a cold-water stream that flows north along the western coast of South America. As Nicolas Michel has explained, the South American coastal waters represent "one of the most important *upwelling* zones in the world," a water and nutrient displacement process essential to plankton activity.[172] The current itself owes its name to the influential explorer and naturalist Alexander von Humboldt, who had identified the phenomenon in his travel diaries to Central and South America between 1799 and 1804, notably in the multivolume *Cosmos: A Sketch of a Physical Description of the Universe* (1845).[173] As Aaron Sachs has explained, "Humboldt had discovered that the water of the bay at Callao, Peru, for instance, was [colder] presumably by taking temperature readings at every port he encountered."[174] The team of scientists Wilfried N'Sondé joined aboard the Tara, a 118-feet aluminum-hulled schooner with multiple masts (known in French as a *goélette)*, had been at sea for several years on the "Mission Microbiomes" project ("Understanding the invisible life of the ocean to protect our future"). He participated in the Chile leg of the larger mission, divided between the Amazon, Antarctic and Africa, whose objectives were framed by three research questions: "How does climate change disrupt ocean currents and the distribution of the marine microbiome? What impact does pollution and particularly microplastics have on the marine microbiome? How does the land fertilize the ocean?"[175]

Wilfried N'Sondé boarded the schooner in 2021, and his own mission as part of an artist residency was to "produce a work related to this experience."[176] As Nicolas Michel writes, "The book is not a depressing or guilt-inducing text, it is above all a spirited eulogy of life, one that ends on a note of hope: What if the symbiosis of phytoplankton and zooplankton was a lesson in universal love?"[177] Wilfried N'Sondé has described the impact of this residency and how it transformed his approach to writing, environmental questions, and perhaps more importantly, to the ways in which one can communicate more effectively on these crucial issues:

> My experience on the sailboat was very interesting. It's above all a human adventure. You have to get used to life on a boat which requires a lot of energy and social resources. Being with scientists from morning to night, I had the opportunity and the leisure to ask questions. I learned a lot about plankton and the ocean in general. I was able to write during my time on board, and even submit some of what I had written to the scientists and sailors. I'm very satisfied because the objectives I had when I came aboard have been accomplished, even beyond what I'd hoped for in developing the writing project. I gathered enough information for my corpus, at least to start. It's extremely encouraging. It was a very intense immersion, because it's not easy to live together on a boat in times of confinement. I stayed exactly 5 weeks on Tara without leaving, not even on a stopover.[178]

This entailed a perspectival change. Selecting two single-celled plankton as the main protagonists challenged the existing hierarchy between beings since, as Amitav Ghosh has argued, "If those nonhuman voices are to be restored to their proper place, then it must be, in the first instance, through the medium of stories."[179]

The choice of focusing on plankton was not an arbitrary decision. Phytoplankton play an important role in complex ocean ecologies and are crucial to the marine food web. Wilfried N'Sondé found inspiration in the symbiosis of phytoplankton (plants) and zooplankton (animals) in the way in which their existence is premised on a mutually beneficial alliance. This exchange summons alternative modes of communication and mediation. Asserting his respect for science was in and of itself a political statement that served to credibilize research findings pertaining to climate change in a broader context of acute polarization shaped by climate skepticism and anti-science lobbies that have sought to undermine scientific knowledge. *Underwater dynamics* thus find themselves juxtaposed with *surface politics*: "I am not saying we are all the same, but rather that we resemble one another. And that is not the same thing."[180] The plankton protagonists thus offer a modeling of sorts, and attention to them can yield meaningful lessons: "Drawn into a sensual vertigo, phyto- and zooplankton had erased the barriers found in the subdivision of the living world into irreconcilable species and kingdoms. [...] A fertile osmosis of the animal world and the plant world under the seal of the erasure of borders. [...] What no terrestrial mammal—including humans—would ever have succeeded in conceiving."[181] This resonates with earlier interventions Wilfried N'Sondé has made, most notably in terms of his visceral dislike for the "ethno-identitarian machine" that he sees as "a deadly poison" that distances us from the "essence of being and magic of words."[182]

In terms of the innovative qualities of Wilfried N'Sondé's novel, foremost among them is his ability to "deconstruct the novel of man as master and possessor of nature" and to "make a place for the non-human in literature," as David Bornstein has argued.[183] Detailed information is provided on marine life and on the importance of plankton as the basis of aquatic food webs, in absorbing carbon emissions and generating a significant portion of the atmosphere's oxygen, in addition to their place on the frontline of risk and vulnerability due to exposure to increasing emissions.[184] These were all requisite steps in enlisting the reader in the consciousness-raising dimension of his own experience at sea. Alongside the plankton that occupy center stage—Héliosphéra (a zooplankton, an aquatic microorganism that supports nutrient flows and plays a significant role in the transfer of materials and energy) and Xanthelle (a phytoplankton, a microscopic marine algae plant)—the cast of characters is reflective of the experimental nature of the novel and includes the scientist Ollanta Suarez and even a red balloon! Ollanta delivers scientific information and ventriloquizes through her actions and a set of intra-textual interventions the author's own experience at sea.

Ollanta's heritage is important and further emphasizes the historic dimension of the expedition. Her birth name conjures approachability, spirituality and ambition, and is also found in Inca culture to designate a revered warrior. Mapuche from her paternal lineage, the largest indigenous group in Chile, and with her mother being from Guadeloupe, her upbringing stressed and valorized a "harmony between humans and the mysteries of nature."[185] She builds on the long history of parental activism in the fight for social justice, the emancipation of women and against racism, and expands this track record with new intersectionalities that include environmental protection. The cosmogony from which Ollanta draws inspiration is shaped by indigenous populations and knowledge systems that were subjected to Dutch excursions to the region as early as the sixteenth century, and thereafter in the form of colonies and settlements. Further northeast, the Dutch West India Company established the plantation colony of Surinam, also unofficially known as Dutch Guiana.[186] In contradistinction to these earlier incursions—defined by conquest, exploitation and cultural erasure—Ollanta's expedition is concerned with mitigating the damage being done to ocean biodiversity as a result of global warming. She equates this history with her own sense of adventure, excitement and trepidation, as well as the prospect of discovery, "the feeling of stepping back in time and becoming a sixteenth-century explorer discovering an unknown land" such that "the schooner embodied the perfect blend of exploration, adventure and concrete action to work towards a better future for the planet."[187]

Pollutant Pathways

Somewhat paradoxically, the same waterways and currents that once guided explorers and navigators on their "discoveries" and "excursions" are the very same that transport detritus along new pollutant pathways as a result of human activity.[188] "Under the effect of ancestral marine movements orchestrated by the regular wind well known to sailors," Wilfried N'Sondé writes, "the trade wind which originated at the equator favored the phenomenon of accumulation and incessant residual circulation."[189] Equally paradoxical is the fact that these historical predecessors were able to embark on such ambitious journeys on the high seas because of new scientific discoveries (the work of physicists) and breakthroughs in technology (the compass) that helped guide them and map the world, even though they often got lost and *found* territories they had not been looking for.[190] The contemporary version of these new frontiers in technology are submersibles, sensors and sampling devices designed to improve deep-sea mineral resource exploration and extraction from the seafloor. "The landbound exploitatively pillage oceanic resources," as David Theo Goldberg has explained, "while caring less about the health of oceans as long as they keep giving."[191] The competition henceforth is between ocean exploration and extraction and conservation and preservation: "Sailors of yesterday like those of today, even the most seasoned, felt an absolute veneration for the treasures that the kingdom of the unexplored blue immensity held before their eyes, and for the secrets lurking everywhere in the abyss below their vessels."[192]

Ollanta and the scientific team collect samples to monitor levels of disintegrated plastic in the ocean and in planktons. Oxidation and sunlight are responsible for chemical breakdown, a sequencing that from an anthropocentric perspective goes from microplastics to nanoplastics. Although gradually these changes are no longer visible to the naked eye, the remnants remain identifiable thanks to microscopes, and research confirms the significant increase in these particles that are harmful to the entire ecosystem.[193] Elizabeth M. DeLoughrey's work has helped improve our understanding of the fundamental principles of ocean pollution, describing how the Plasticene introduced "the era of the 'technofossil', a new stratigraphic signal of the Anthropocene produced by plastics and other materials that are globally distributed."[194]

Wilfried N'Sondé, like the fictional scientist Ollanta, boards the Tara at a time that coincides with the global COVID pandemic and lockdown protocol. This is circumstantial, yet confinement on the Tara *and* on the ocean imposes detachment and insularity. This decentering proves to be generative of scientific deliberation at a time when an alliance was burgeoning between vaccine skeptics and climate denialists. The experience on the Tara is also climatic in that protagonists are far from any mainland and exposed to high temperatures, factors that heighten sensory stimulation. Meanwhile, the red balloon also continues on its own cartographic journey after bursting at a celebration in the French Alps. This event, which occurred years prior, has been carefully recorded through biographical chronicling and its movements mapped all the way to the southern Mediterranean waters and onward to the ocean in which the Tara finds itself: "However, once launched into the water, the remains of the red balloon—like all other objects—accentuated their degradation process under the effect of wind, ultraviolet radiation, salinity, the strength of the currents and the power of the waves."[195] The impact is cumulative and, in concert with other pollutants, magnifies the range of side effects—oxidative stress, compromised immunity, endocrine activity, digestive tract vulnerability, reduced biodiversity—ultimately "destabilizing the totality of the ecosystem."[196] David Theo Goldberg has summarized the stakes: "The Sea stands as the barometer of the planet's slow suffocation."[197] Ocean turbulence thus metaphorically reflects climate change disruption, circumstances in which the plankton have "enormous difficulty feeding and reproducing"[198] because of diminished aquatic oxygen levels while those above the surface are slowly being asphyxiated by what Achille Mbembe has called "the age of the world's combustion."[199] Indeed, as Jeff Goodell has claimed, *the heat will kill you first.*[200]

Wilfried N'Sondé therefore proposes an encompassing view of the world of the living by relinquishing anthropocentric positions in favor of a plankton-world view: "These microscopic beings, probably thanks to their incredible experience accumulated over hundreds of millions of years, sometimes showed capacities to unite that surpassed those of mammals. [...] Héliosphera aimed to transcend the boundaries that separated the animal and plant kingdoms."[201] This is a challenge of sorts, an invitation to abdicate our often entrenched positions in order to integrate a new awareness of planetary interconnectedness. Ollanta is galvanized by this message, and "she felt strangely familiar with these microscopic organisms and had convinced herself that they had a lot to teach her. Participating in such a research program also represented a kind of return to the sources, a dive into the very foundations of life."[202] These correspond to the forms of reciprocity and relationality that were discussed in Chapter 2 in the context of migration. In this case, they are magnified by the beautiful love story between Héliosphéra and Xanthelle, "Two diametrically different entities looking for one another, close to finding each other, they were going to tend towards the same mutually beneficial goal. A form of equitable assistance that would take the lovers on a common path. They would exchange favors, for shared satiety. In their future actions, each would favor, essentially privilege what would be beneficial for themselves and for the other. Both intrigued, still undecided, a bond was nevertheless being woven."[203] The key term here is "woven," introducing the principle of interweaving that frames Wilfried N'Sondé's novel, assembling geometries of duality and binarism, dissemblance and resemblance, convergence and divergence, similar and opposite, and identical and dissimilar. An inventory of terms interspersed throughout the novel (exceeding seventy in total) captures this duality and is indicative of the proliferation of amalgamation, synthesis, symbiosis and commonality, terms that suggest alignments rather than the kind of polarizing oppositionalities we have encountered elsewhere in *Climates of Migration.*

For Ollanta, "witnessing the process of planktonic symbiosis between an individual belonging to the phytoplankton and another from a population of zooplankton, an event very rarely observed by scientists" proves to be genuinely transformative.[204] She realizes there can be no turning back from the newfound equitable multispecies framework that she has identified: "The only thing she felt more or less certain of was that never again would planktonic individuals appear to her as mere rudimentary organisms or objects of study. Each of them contained within themselves all the magic and mystery of the living. As such, they all deserved to be considered with tenderness and respect."[205] Ollanta draws an analogy between what was imparted to her during her upbringing, knowledge shaped by the refusal to subjugate nonhuman life-forms and reduce nature to an object-background status. Instead, the Mapuche elected to position these side by side with human activity and, "unlike the newcomers, never had the ambition to control their environment, and they ignored the pretension to modify it by overexploiting it without limit."[206] In this instance, the word "exploitation" suggests the dual dimensions of its meaning and applicability to the environment, signifying to "exploit (develop) the land" (exploiter la terre) and "exploit (take advantage of) a people" (exploiter un peuple). Monocultures and industrial harvesting destroyed the land and displaced people. The precursors to ecological degradation and pollution were these earlier polluters, namely those that conducted exploratory expeditions and ecocidal actions, supremacist gestures aimed at desecrating the lands, traditions and peoples. "Plastic," Wilfried N'Sondé writes, "the child of modernity, polluted and arrived where ancient peoples described as primitive had long since disappeared. The indigenous populations had been exterminated, massacred by the colonists or decimated by diseases imported from Europe. Women, men and children for whom the arrival of 'civilization' had brought neither prosperity, nor wealth, nor comfort, but had instead been synonymous with death and annihilation."[207]

Ato Quayson reminds us that "stories are the social currency of our everyday lives, and what we need are more stories, not fewer. The more diverse stories we have and in as many forms and media as possible, the more we can guarantee that our sentimental education is not hijacked by the narrow-minded purveyors of false reality that try to pass it off as truth."[208] African writers have contributed in meaningful ways to this objective, adapting aesthetic frameworks in order to confront the incontrovertible questions of their era, while also adopting innovative conceptual modes that stand to amplify their messaging. Achieving an informed point of view on climate change must necessarily entail challenging alternative narratives, notably those evident in the architecture of conspiracy theories and misinformation campaigns that distract from environmental policy implementation, questions explored in the next chapter in the discussion on ecology and propaganda.

Chapter 5

ECOLOGY AND PROPAGANDA

Truth needs to be well engineered to be effective.

Jenny Erpenbeck[1]

What happens to humanity when on the one hand they believe what's online but on the other they are deeply distrustful of everything online?

Sibylle Berg[2]

The previous four chapters have explored various *ecologies* in the context of the interplay between environmental and immigration questions—ecolonial games, migrant ecologies, ecological relations and ecological frontiers. The path forward at this juncture consists in looking at how these intertwined ecologies have been woven into the fabric of contemporary propagandist discourse. Propagandist discourse can serve a dual purpose, humanizing migrants or instead furthering anti-immigration agendas. Likewise, analogous strategies have been operative in the context of environmental discourse, either promoting awareness of climate change or exaggerating denialist positions. What can the analysis of the ecology and propaganda nexus reveal? How has recourse to propaganda furthered anti-ecological agendas by describing climate change as a "hoax," denouncing the perennial "prophets of doom," or promoting a lifestyle founded on the exponential use of new technologies?[3] Or instead furthered pro-ecological positions centered on an unrelenting effort to prevent the systematic destruction of the environment and aimed at enacting social change by promoting awareness? As Sam Moore and Alex Roberts have shown, "Denialism has historically been propagated through institutions funded directly by fossil fuel capital" and "when denial is untenable [...] conspiracies are used instead," opening the door to propaganda which, as Peter K. Fallon has argued, offers the simultaneous capacity of "building (or diminishing) support for a specific piece of legislation, or policy" or in turn "warn them [the people] of the consequences of inaction on the climate."[4]

Mutating Propagandas

In 1928, Edward Bernays published the pathbreaking book *Propaganda*, a mechanism he described as "a consistent, enduring effort to create or shape events to influence the relations of the public to an enterprise, idea or group."[5] With ancestral roots in religious propagation going back to 1622, propaganda has functioned as an essential apparatus in the process of fostering political and social change. A distinguishing feature of Edward Bernay's analysis was to be found in the emphasis on "wise propaganda"[6] and its capacity to leverage social issues in positive ways—women's activities, education, social service and art and science. Additionally, cost was an important factor that explained propaganda's "concentrat[ion] in the hands of the few because of the expense of manipulating the social machinery which controls the opinions and habits of the masses."[7] Historically, propaganda has diverged from the trajectory he initially outlined: it has served as the staging for colonial expansion and the civilizing mission, was instrumental to the rise of Fascism, shaped Cold War relations, upheld American foreign policy doctrines and has shored up autocratic regimes by degrading democratic institutions. As we saw in Chapter 1, technological advances in printing and visual culture were embedded in colonial propaganda. But more recent developments, attributable to new technological inroads, have inaugurated transformational changes by increasing access to the tools of dissemination through social media platforms, while simultaneously enhancing the capacity for manipulating information. As Julia Ebner has shown, "Entirely new modes of *storytelling* have formed and shaped our virtual space as much as our real lives. [...] While centuries ago the creation of narratives was reserved for the most privileged in society, today anyone can spread their stories on a global level at incredible speed."[8]

The most significant outgrowths from propagandist precursors are to be found in the exponential proliferation of disinformation techniques. In the notion of "manufacturing consent" theorized by Edward S. Herman and Noam Chomsky, the emphasis was on the multifarious ways in which "the mass media are drawn into a symbiotic relationship with powerful sources of information by economic necessity and reciprocity of interest."[9] In 1964, Marshall McLuhan had already pointed to the impact of the media on social perceptions, arguing that "the effects of technology do not occur at the level of opinions or concepts, but alter sense ratios or patterns of perception steadily and without any resistance."[10] In this regard, the most dramatic shift pertains to the impact on democracy; this was of course key in Jacques Ellul's contribution to the field in his 1968 book *Propaganda: The Formation of Men's Attitudes*.[11] However, these lines of argument and interpretive grids have mutated and been superseded by newfound concerted efforts aimed at transmitting misinformation and which, as Peter Pomerantsev has shown, "At their most effective they can construct whole alternative realities, conspirational worlds where you have no responsibility."[12] The objective is to confuse, deceive and disorient, and "people trust what sounds right, and trust permits manipulation," as Timothy Snyder has demonstrated in *The Road to Unfreedom: Russia, Europe, America.*[13] Political messages are promoted with the help of memes, trolls and bots on social media platforms such as X, Facebook, Instagram, YouTube, TikTok and so on, and Russian propaganda and disinformation have been especially effective in this regard thanks to a massive state-sponsored machinery.[14] This example stresses the persistence of an "older monopoly [that] was based on centralized control of information," but as Peter K. Fallon indicates, a "newer monopoly—at this moment at least—is based on decentralization of power, an absence of control over information flow, and is an agent of entropy."[15]

How do we even begin to comprehend the amplitude of these transformations? The most convincing answers and explanations connect with many of the questions that we have explored in previous chapters, most notably in terms of the fundamental transhistorical societal organizational principles outlined by Pankaj Mishra in *The Age of Anger: A History of the Present*, as they pertain to the ways in which "individuals with very different pasts find themselves herded by capitalism and technology into a common present, where grossly unequal distributions of wealth and power have created humiliating new hierarchies."[16] These circumstances have been intensified by social media which, as George Monbiot and Peter Hutchison have argued, "accelerate the generation and spread of these fictions, sowing confusion and creating alternative realities faster than ever before."[17] Their collective success is premised on what Eva Illouz calls the "emotional life" of the messaging, heightening fear and resentment,[18] and "embraced" by extremists.[19] Post-truth strategies have created ripples, concentric circles reflecting the coordinated endeavors aimed at shepherding societies back toward a mythic era of unbroken traditional stability.[20]

Giuliano da Empoli's work on what he calls the "engineers of chaos" offers insights on "how a new kind of propaganda, adapted to the era of selfies and social media, has been reinvented" and is "transforming the very nature of the democratic game" as the accompanying conspiracy theories nourish populism, xenophobia, racism and migrantphobia.[21] The colonial-era board games explored in Chapter 1 encouraged patriotic fervor and as Sandrine Lemaire has argued, "Seduction and persuasion techniques aimed at commercial and political targets can be described according to the same pyramid on which one finds, from the structure's base to its peak, the different steps that constitute a doctrine, a program, slogans, and symbols."[22] However, unlike these antecedents, the new propaganda "game" is defined by algorithms that "feed principally on negative emotions since they are the ones that guarantee the greatest participation" and "In Europe as elsewhere, lies are popular because they are inserted into a political narrative that captures the fears and aspirations of a growing share of the electorate, while the facts of those who oppose them are inserted into a narrative that is no longer considered credible. In practice, for the followers of the populists, the veracity of individual facts does not count. What is true is the message as a whole, which corresponds to their experience and their feelings."[23] Many far-right parties, such as the Alternative for Germany and National Rally in France, have latched onto societal grievances (often connected to neoliberal policies) but predominantly exploited these by converting them to racially motivated resentment. Brexit was the epitome of such efforts and immigration served as the container for the emotional concerns of "Leave" voters. And as we have previously seen, propagandist slogans before and after Brexit such as "Take Back Control," "Get Brexit Done" and "Stop the Boats" were "part of active efforts to sow unjustified fear and information," while also helping to explain why "migration policies have often failed or been counterproductive because they are based on a series of false assumptions, or myths, about the nature, causes and impacts of migration."[24] Not surprisingly, these measures have coincided with autocratic tendencies. Anne Applebaum, in *The Dictators Who Want to Run the World*, describes how "autocratic information operations exaggerate the divisions and anger that are normal in politics. [...] In seeking to create chaos, these new propagandists, like their leaders, will reach for whatever ideology, whatever technology, and whatever emotions might be useful."[25]

Disinformation and propaganda have been prevalent in immigration debates and policymaking and in the "fabrication of the migration threat," as Hein de Haas explains in *How Migration Really Works: The Facts About the Most Divisive Issue in Politics*, a book in which the final section is devoted to "Migration Propaganda."[26] These developments have been especially prevalent in framing the complex phenomenon of climate migration, whereby the far-right have leveraged "the specter of future mass migration, and the need to set up border controls to prevent such an imagined deluge," approaches that have ultimately worked conjointly to "deflect" from "the human-made nature of many environmental hazards" rather than addressing accountability for the consequences of fossil fuel extraction, pollution, agricultural land spoliation and the resulting climate injustice.[27]

Climates of Disinformation: *Populism*, *Polarization* and *Post-truth*

Inflammatory rhetoric pertaining to identity and immigration has served to emphasize the peripheral nature of racialized populations who continue to be marginalized and othered in the name of reifying misplaced and misguided notions of national historical fortitude. The position is hardly original, which of course does not mean that it has not proven effective in fueling polarization. Extensive recourse has been made to analogous strategies by numerous commentators and politicians in Europe and elsewhere, although President Donald Trump has been a repeat offender in this regard. His outlandish remarks during the 2024 presidential race concerning Haitian immigrants and their propensity to eat pets—"They are eating the dogs, they are eating the cats, they are eating the pets of the people who live there"—are one such example, whereby "they" (the alleged immigrant pet eaters) are juxtaposed with the legitimate "people who live there." Although the claims were "completely untrue," the outcome was that "such disinformation amplifies existing xenophobic beliefs within the American psyche as a means of political gain,"[28] what French journalist Pierre Tevanian and lawyer Jean-Charles Stevens have described as a form of "prejudicial propaganda" in which one finds an "amalgamation" of concepts, stereotypes and myths with long-standing records that culminate in a dehumanizing "xenophobic propaganda."[29]

These rhetorical devices share points of commonality with the discourse that has emerged around global warming, especially in terms of intensifying divisiveness. As Amitav Ghosh has argued, this "has become one of many issues that are clustered along a fault line of extreme political polarization."[30] German-Swiss author Sibylle Berg makes an important point in this regard: "A divided populace is a controllable populace."[31] Moisés Naím, in *The Revenge of Power: How Autocrats Are Reinventing Politics for the 21st Century*, describes the "formula" that is shaping the new "playbook" of leaders and informing their "authoritarian proclivities" as they embark on "improving new tactics and reengineering old ones to boost their ability to impose their will on others," namely *populism*, *polarization* and *post-truth* (the 3Ps).[32] These three pillars rely "on a compact core of strategies to weaken the foundations of democracy and cement its malignant dominance" and "as they consolidate their power, they cloak their autocratic plans behind walls of secrecy, bureaucratic obfuscation, pseudolegal subterfuge, manipulation of public opinion, and the repression of critics and adversaries."[33] The scaffolding is assembled around groupings that include catastrophism, the criminalization of political rivals, using external threats, denigrating experts, attacking the media and eroding checks and balances.[34] The outcome is predictable, as "political rivals come to be treated as enemies. Contending sides no longer seek to accommodate each other in a quest for minimum viable governing arrangements."[35] As the German writer Juli Zeh has argued, the circumstances are such that it is "less about arguing a valid point and more about proving [one is] right."[36]

These abominable classifications are increasingly prevalent. Corresponding patterns have linked the respective domains of environment and health given the common experience of being targeted by anti-science groups and the proliferation of propaganda and fake news. French medical doctor Catherine Beauvais has published research on the "external determinants of people's beliefs linked to the media ecosystem and social media platforms and the internal cognitive and psychological determinants (confirmation bias, political partisanship, repetition and familiarity) as well as mixed sociological factors (selective exposure, echo chambers, false news fabrication and pressure groups)" that in combination "feed the fake ecosystem in that people may change from consumers to creators of fake news and vice versa."[37] Bǎlsa Lubarda's research on environmental politics and the far-right in Hungary and Poland accentuates "how interpreting unanticipated events is primarily relational and only then ideological, as ideological explanation can be sufficiently tweaked for the purpose of legitimization."[38] Daniel Macmillen Voskoboynik, in *The Memory We Could Be: Overcoming Fear to Create Our Ecological Future*, describes how "many scientists have themselves diagnosed a triple crisis in science: a crisis of public trust in science, a crisis in the quality and credibility of published science and a crisis in the political use of science," most notably in terms of how they have been "co-opted" in "climate misinformation campaigns."[39]

Political agendas have been advanced by climate denialists who are able to instrumentalize social media platforms in order to broaden their reach and attacks on scientists. By resorting to disdainful terminology, the new "enemies of society" are referred to as alarmists, doomers, fear-mongers, fanatics, terrorists and the list goes on. Swedish environmental activist Greta Thunberg has been the target of repeated attacks. Referred to in Italy as *gretini*—an Italian neologism that blends her first name with *cretini* (cretin)—she has also been denigrated by National Rally and Republicans Party legislators in France as the "guru of the apocalypse," the "Joan of Arc of climate change," the "Justin Bieber of ecology" and a "prophetess in shorts," *pirralha* ("little brat" or "pest") by Brazil's far-right politician Jair Bolsonaro, and Donald Trump has insulted her on multiple occasions through patronizing remarks which she subsequently, and adroitly, appropriated by updating her then Twitter bio with his language and copying his phrasing.[40] While aimed at intimidating and silencing detractors, such attacks also serve to highlight the prevalence of misogyny, what Cara Daggett has qualified as *petro-masculinity*, "a reminder that [misogyny and extractivism] emerged together and through each other, which means that gender anxiety now slithers alongside climate anxiety, and misogynist violence can sometimes explode as fossil violence."[41] As the former U.S. climate chief, John Kerry stated, "The populist backlash against net zero around the world is imperiling the fight against climate breakdown and must be countered urgently or we face planetary destruction."[42]

In this framework, a multidimensional security threat is invoked relating to immigration and global warming: on the one hand, the phantasms of the national defense establishment are fortified by their assessments of the impact of climate change on security[43] with the direct consequence that "migration is largely in military and paramilitary hands,"[44] and on the other, urgent attention is called for in order to address the perceived menace posed by eco-extremists and eco-terrorists. Together, they serve to justify demands for additional spending allocations in the ever-expanding "business of xenophobia" and "ecological security."[45] These positions are at best shortsighted and shaped by the misconception that "the West will largely be insulated from the worst effects of the planetary crisis" while mistakenly "project[ing] images of catastrophe into the future in a fashion that negates the possibility of confronting climate change in the present day."[46] Betsy Hartmann's research on the Pew Charitable Trust (an entity sponsored by the Sun Oil Company) tracks their gradual interest in "foreign policy issues related to the environment and [how they] would offer support for applied research on the linkages between population, environment and security […] in order to create the necessary alarm."[47] This course of action is designed to overwhelm and immobilize policymaking pertaining to immigration and environmental issues. In the case of the latter, this has led to "climate paralysis" and, as Laurence Tubiana has argued, "climate action has become a communications battle in which polarization serves as a useful rhetorical tool to mask inaction and maintain the deadly status quo in which we live."[48] Of note is the fact that the defense and security sector also have deployed sizeable communications and public relations services, and as Mathieu Rigouste's research on the "police of the future" has shown, "ecological crisis" and "climate risk" are growth industries that offer satellite and terrestrial communication while dedicating new technologies to threat and vulnerability assessments.[49]

Early in his first term as French president in 2017, Emmanuel Macron made a deliberate reference to President Donald Trump's nationalist slogan "Make America Great Again" in the aftermath of his decision to withdraw from the Paris Climate Agreement, proposing instead to "Make the Planet Great Again." Ultimately, though, his track record on climate action can best be described as lukewarm and inconsistent, as with the EU as well. Although the latter did approve the Green Deal in 2020 and passed the European Climate

Law in 2021,[50] thereby enshrining the commitment to reducing net greenhouse gas emissions by 2023 and becoming climate-neutral by 2050, they subsequently made concessions after labor action by farmers forced amendments to the Common Agricultural Policy (CAP).[51] The Biden administration successfully signed climate legislation into law (Infrastructure Investment and Jobs Act and Inflation Reduction Act) but also "approved more permits for oil and gas drilling on public lands than had even his climate-denying predecessor."[52] And former UK prime minister Rishi Sunak "retreated" from climate issues during his short time in office and did not even attend the UN Climate Week summit in September 2023.[53] The gathering was fittingly opened by the host UN Secretary-General António Guterres with the claim that "humanity has opened the gates of hell," prompting Mohamed Adow, the director of the Kenyan think tank Power Shift Africa, to remind everyone that "the climate crisis was birthed in the UK through its creation of the combustion engine."[54]

The Arsenal of *Post-truth*

Emphasis throughout *Climates of Migration* has been placed on the longer history of environmental degradation and on the kinds of arguments made by Harriet Mercer and Thomas Simpson, whereby "it has become a truism for historians that the modern field of climate science emerged out of processes of imperial and colonial expansion."[55] Although climate change is supported by conclusive scientific evidence, challenges to these are gaining traction. Developing countries, many of them former outposts of Empire, are disproportionately impacted by climate change. As David Van Reybrouck has insisted, "today's climate change is deeply colonial: it has been largely caused by the temperate zones from the northern hemisphere."[56] The sense of urgency is very real, yet denialist strategies have proven difficult to counter and particularly distracting when it comes to implementing consequential measures.

During the nineteenth and early twentieth centuries, technological innovation accelerated and expanded communication and dissemination. These enabled new forms of information transmission and manipulation, but the defining qualities of the apparatus shaping the twenty-first-century innovation continuum are disinformation and alternative facts. Sana Marin, during a state visit to New Zealand as prime minister of Finland, expressed her level of concern in a public statement: "I really worry about the dependencies that we have right now on authoritarian countries when it comes to new technologies, the digital infrastructure in our countries, and also the natural resources that we are dependent on" (November 30, 2022). Her assessment has proven accurate and the social network X is now considered the "largest source of disinformation"[57] and its owner-operator Elon Musk has evidently been *red-pilled*, self-anointing as aggregator of nationalist far-right conspiracy theories (such as [great] replacement theory, boosting false claims about election fraud) and spreading the messaging to his 200 million+ followers, thereby further degrading the platform. A proliferation of terms is symptomatic of this evolution and stored in the formidable arsenal of *post-truth*: fake news, conspiracy theories, smear campaigns, infowars, viruses, micro-targeting, adware, infodemics, cyber harassment and intimidation, doxing, worms, phishing, spoofing, spyware, deep fake technology, Trojans, malicious chatterbots, ransomware, bots, botnets and malware, among many others. In the French language, one even finds a felicitous term that encompasses this inventory—*intox*—a truncated version of "intoxication" that encompasses disinformation, fiction, lies and brainwashing, while also bringing into the fold the connotation of "poison" and "intoxicated," whose mental and physical impairments and side effects include disorientation and reduced cognitive control. These are new frontiers whose attributes and distinguishing features are contained in their inordinate capacity to deceive, foster suspicion and magnify polarization while being driven by a consumerist model and capitalist profit motives. The process of assessing their cultural, political and social impact has only just started. The climate is one of uncertainty, raising questions about regulation and the boundaries of free speech.

Zac Gershberg and Sean Illing have explained the degree of vulnerability that accompanies new technological apparatus, one that has permitted a metamorphosis in terms of "a free and open communication environment," but one that, paradoxically, "because of its openness, invited exploitation and subversion from within."[58] This has presented content creators, developers and regulators with a dilemma, one in which regulation has grown increasingly crucial given the obvious nefarious and even execrable abuses of these new platforms. In some countries, governments have imposed internet blackouts and media shutdowns, restricted access to information streams and content, launched cyberattacks and disabled VPNs. Yet, at the same time, resistance has been mobilized against regulatory mechanisms, which is of course hardly surprising given that these platforms have relied on the absence of control and regulation in order to burgeon. How much monitoring and oversight is warranted, will AI moderation assist with flagging disinformation content and tracking hate, and who will be anointed society's information gatekeepers?[59] This tenuous debate is one that is full of contradictions, but there is also an urgent need for improved monitoring and prevention of harmful content, something which the European Commission's "Digital Services Act" (DSA) has set specific targets for.[60]

Research on disinformation provides insights into digital markets and the relationship of these to the information dissemination precursors explored throughout this book, most notably in terms of the synergies between the public and private sectors that were particularly evident in the domain of colonial-era propaganda. Julia Ebner's research has, in this regard, been truly pioneering. In *Going Mainstream: How Extremists Are Taking Over*, she describes the emergence of "alternative media ecosystems" and the incremental growth of "hyperpolarized communities."[61] Among the most noteworthy features of these developments is the prevalence of climate change skepticism, an area in which "activists have built powerful global networks to bring their radical ideas to mainstream audiences. Their members span business, politics and civil society and have given rise to ecosystems of alternative science and biased journalism,"[62] and predictably, coordinated efforts "overlap between the climate change denier scene and white nationalist circles."[63]

Carlos Diaz Ruiz has conducted research on the relationship between disinformation and profit models on digital media platforms through "programmatic advertising, commercial content moderation, influencer monetization schemes, and algorithmic optimization."[64] The research examines the ways in which algorithms are "determining how users access data such as search results, user-generated content, and advertisements," and "shape consumer behavior" through a range of mechanisms, including "propaganda, astroturfing, conspiracy theories, fake news, and pseudoscience."[65] This is an incredibly dynamic field, confronting frontline researchers with the two-pronged challenge of advancing knowledge through analysis and data interpretation, while simultaneously remaining apprised of rapid technological evolutions such as big data and artificial intelligence.[66] Digital media platforms "maximize consumer engagement, including the time and attention spent on the platform. [...] Since highly engaging content is often emotional and controversial, content creators lean toward polarizing opinions as these will gather more reposts, comments, and shares."[67] The fossil fuel industry has been adept at exploiting new media platforms and "misinformation and disinformation" are literally and metaphorically *fueled* "by the fossil-fuel industry [that has] stalled climate action for decades," as corroborated by the conclusions of the Climate Action Against Disinformation Coalition (CAAD) 2023 report, "Climate of Misinformation: Ranking Big Tech."[68] On October 7, 2021, Google announced "a new monetization policy [...] that will prohibit ads for, and monetization of, content that contradicts well-established scientific consensus around the existence and causes of climate change."[69] Using a 21-point assessment system, the spectrum of findings ranged from ranking Pinterest as "leading the industry on policies that mitigate the spread of climate misinformation" to Twitter/X basically "lacking clear policies that address climate misinformation, having no substantive public transparency mechanisms, and offering no evidence of effective policy enforcement,"[70] obviously disconcerting conclusions given that the latter currently boasts an estimated 550 million monthly users.[71]

Petroknowledge, Carbopolics and Petro-pedagogy

Fossil fuel corporations have not had to look far and wide to find detractors refusing to acknowledge that climate change is a reality or to assign blame to human activity for fossil fuel extraction. Alternative facts and disinformation have played a central role in this regard.[72] Alliances have eroded efforts aimed at mitigating global warming, obstructed and demotivated meaningful climate action in quantifiable ways, and lobbied for withdrawal from the Paris Climate Agreement. They have also been successful in reversing bans on offshore drilling and in promoting anti-science policies, and successfully defunding and shrinking the EPA.[73] Unfortunately, as Sam Moore and Alex Roberts have written, not without a touch of irony, "Whatever happens with the climate, it will always be made worse by the arrival of far-right authoritarianism."[74] Other entities, such as the Climate Intelligence Foundation (CLINTEL), claim that "there is no climate emergency. Therefore, there is no cause for panic and alarm," and deny the opposite conclusions of the Intergovernmental Panel on Climate Change (IPCC).[75] This unwillingness to engage with the issues that confront humanity stands to ultimately generate even worse conditions than those predicted by scientific modeling.

To this end, a comprehensive, in-depth study commissioned by Greenpeace Netherlands that investigated the greenwashing strategies of European "fossil fuel interests" was published in 2022.[76] The scientific objective was to "expose digital climate discourse and deception," and Geoffrey Supran, Cameron Jickey and the research team at the Algorithmic Transparency Institute organized their findings according to five categories: Climate silence, Greenwashing, Misdirection, Nature-rinsing and demographic greening and misdirection.[77] Their groundbreaking research convincingly demonstrated how fossil fuel interests "have collectively waged a multi-decade, multi-billion dollar campaign of lobbying, disinformation, and propaganda to sabotage science, confuse the public, and undermine climate and clean energy policies" while adopting greenwashing strategies and refraining from "direct engagement with climate change and their contributions to it and towards strategic brand positioning through language and visuals that establish green, innovative, charitable brand identities."[78] These findings were echoed in a 2023 report on the fossil fuel industry released by the Center for American Progress, underscoring long-standing measures implemented to deflect accountability while "fueling democratic backsliding" and eroding "public trust in scientific consensus and genuine solutions to the climate crisis."[79] Evidence draws attention to deliberate obstructionist actions and conspiring to mislead the public by reducing, undermining and blocking efforts geared toward climate change policymaking through lobbying, public relations firms, supporting legislation, false advertising and ultimately the lack of corporate accountability and transparency.[80]

Additional examples are plentiful, all of which are indicative of a range of maneuvers Amy Westervelt and Kyle Pope have described, namely that the "increasingly sophisticated and better-funded disinformation is making climate coverage trickier both for journalists to produce and for the public to fully understand and trust."[81] A cursory glance at the public-facing websites of a handful of the "Big Oil" companies corroborates all the above-mentioned research, whereby Chevron has sought to rebrand itself as a "new energy company," ExxonMobil embraces "advanced climate solutions," Shell Global has implemented an "energy transition strategy" and BP claims to be committed to "sustainability advocacy activities."[82] The disingenuous nature of these statements is disquieting and one can only conclude that those most *responsible* for global warming are also the most *irresponsible*.

Imre Szeman and Dominic Boyer, trailblazers in the field of energy humanities, have argued that "while the story of modernity isn't reducible to the use of energy on an ever-greater scale, an account of its developments, transgressions, and contradictions that fails to address the role played by energy in shaping its infrastructures [...] and its subjectivities [...] can't help but misrepresent the forces and processes shaping historical development, especially over the past two centuries."[83] Afterall, as they succinctly state, "*the link between energy use and global warming is, at its core, an energy problem.*"[84] In *No More Fossils*, Dominic Boyer extends his earlier argument and gives prominence to the ways in which "Everything and everyone else was a fossil according to late nineteenth-century Europe, a historical leftover to be trampled or swept aside by the juggernaut of European modernity. Not incidentally, this juggernaut depended wholly on fossil fuels for its operation and expansion."[85] Adopting the term "petroknowledge," he goes on to demonstrate how "the petrocultural world order" is "the original post-truth."[86] Carbopolitics is symbiotically linked to "plastics," which "is also what makes petroculture so difficult to resist. One is no longer resisting a fossil fuel but instead a fundamental aspect of one's material environment."[87] This dimension has been widely exploited in the education sector in what researchers Emily M. Eaton and Nick A. Day call "petro-pedagogy,"[88] striking reminders of the propagandist measures deployed in European schools during the colonial era.

On December 9, 2022, the U.S. Committee on Oversight and Reform released a report assessing the effects of disinformation in the fossil fuel sector, "showing how the fossil fuel industry engages in 'greenwashing' to obscure its massive long-term investments in fossil fuels and failure to meaningfully reduce emissions."[89] Children are increasingly targeted by climate denialism propaganda.[90] One of the most striking examples of intrusion in the education system is that of the Oklahoma Energy Resources Board, an agency funded by oil and gas producers that since 1993 has subsidized the development of educational resources in schools in their jurisdictions. They have defined their role in terms of a responsibility "to tell the story of our industry. From high-paying jobs to infrastructure, providing money for education, restoring our land and helping lead the way to America's energy independence."[91] Several U.S. states rely heavily on tax revenues from fossil fuels, and these industries are therefore inextricably connected to the economic, political and social fabric of the communities in which they operate. According to Jie Jenny Zou, there is "a tightly woven network of organizations that works in concert with the oil and gas industry to paint a rosy picture of fossil fuels in America's classrooms" while "touting an industry that plays a central role in climate change and air pollution."[92] Through these actions, they seek to obfuscate "the central role that fossil fuel corporations have been playing, not just in causing global climate crisis, but in obstructing action and education that can address this crisis."[93] This situation is of course compounded by the broader national ideological context in which schools are increasingly becoming the battleground over a wide range of societal issues, including critical race theory, DEI initiatives and anti-LGBTQ+ policies.

Among the most notable initiatives are the illustrated children's literature albums in the Petro Pete's Adventures series. Let us consider the fourth volume in the series, *Petro Pete's Big Bad Dream*.[94] The eponymous young protagonist attends Elementary School in his hometown of Petroville, a metonymic reference to the state of Oklahoma where these books are distributed free of charge. His universe is defined by the dominant local industry. Even his friends have names associated with this context—Sammy Shale and Oliver Oilpatch—and their schoolteacher is none other than Mrs. Rigwell. The iconographic material is all the more relevant. For example, the pictures on his bedroom wall depict miners and oil wells, and in this interplay between text and image, the visual apparatus supports the narrative. Similarly, his favorite toys and objects are made from oil and natural gas, plastic or their derivatives: "Pete drifts off to sleep and wonders what life would be like if we didn't have petroleum." When he wakes up the next morning, he has to confront a newfound nightmarish reality, one in which "many of his belongings were missing" [...] At school, the lesson of the day is "The Story of Oil," aimed at sensitizing the class to the indispensability of fossil fuels in their daily lives, simultaneously promoting a lifestyle based on the importance of by-products, but also a rhetoric fostering a deep appreciation for them. Implicit in this instructional model is an anti-ecological discourse aimed at persuading and mobilizing arguments in favor of the positive attributes and contributions of the energy sector. Warnings about the harmful impact on the environment and global warming are absent. Petro Pete is invited to adopt an anthropocentric perspective that neglects to consider human contributions to climate change. With the adventures of Petro Pete, the objective is clear, unambiguous in fact as Mrs. Rigwell, responding to Pete's concern for the disappearance of the objects in his life, explains: "It sounds like you are missing all your petroleum by-products today!" The goal is to target an impressionable demographic group while allowing the companies most responsible for climate change to deflect responsibility.

There are obvious constraints and limitations to thinking differently given that the community in which Petro Pete resides is dependent on industrial activity. However, one has to wonder how the oil industry can serve as a vehicle with which to advance knowledge when that goal is hindered from the beginning by a mechanism concerned only with the intentional diffusion of false or misleading information that is subsequently repeated by successive generations as misinformation. Petro Pete cannot conceive of nature outside the parameters of extraction, and any invocation of ecological crisis is immediately downplayed in favor of the accelerated and exponential depletion of planetary resources at the service of entertainment and individual and collective fulfillment, pleasure and functionality. Education, as in the colonial context, is designed to indoctrinate and maintain ignorance and obscurantism rather than fostering analytic and critical thinking, prerequisites to understanding and countering the ecological degradation and global warming that will continue to impact their lives. Instead, young people in Pete's class are not mobilized to seek solutions that would mitigate the impending environmental catastrophe. At the end of the school day, Pete is grateful to his teacher and classmates for having solved the mystery of his disappearing objects, concluding that "Having no petroleum is like a nightmare!" As Jim Zeigler has argued, "His experience has taught him that he is always using petroleum; it is integral to most things he needs and enjoys," and the ecosystem demands recognition as a beneficiary.[95]

Nationalist and protectionist politics have driven efforts at consolidating the ramparts of Fortress Europe. But analogous phenomena have also informed a number of responses to global warming. British writer J. G. Ballard devoted several novels to forms of enclosure and exploited the metaphor of gated communities. The novel *High-Rise* (1975) charted the violent disintegration and conflict between wealthy residents in a luxury high-rise building. In *Super-Cannes* (2001), the stage was set in a futuristic utopian business park called Eden-Olympia, a residential gated community in which it soon became apparent that something was "rotten" as residents engaged in forays outside the gates to beat up (Arab) immigrants as "set tasks, assigned to them as part of a continuing program of psychotherapy."[96] As Milena Škobo and Jovana Đukić have shown, it is the "denatured environment that conditions their behavior, generating people whose counternatural actions and illicit deeds make them become 'waste' themselves," and "the gated communities are a manifestation of social and psychological entropy because they isolate the residents from the natural environment and promote a technologically dominant order that causes harm to both individuals and the community as a whole."[97]

J. G. Ballard's work connects with a prevalent response to immigration and global warming narratives, namely isolationism, revealing a deep-seated desire to avoid confrontation with environmental and political questions. These have been explored by other authors. The Egyptian writer Ahmed Khaled Towfik offers a dystopian futuristic fiction in the novel *Utopia* that juxtaposes two populations, separated but not isolated, though symbolic of growing economic, climatic and social disparities.[98] Brian Aldiss, in *Super-State: A Novel of a Future Europe*, turns to science fiction in order to explore climate breakdown and its impact on migration.[99] Indeed, if J. G. Ballard's fictional world featured a "vertical city," a recent Saudi Arabian architectural project promises to build a 110-mile horizontal linear megacity called "The Line,"[100] home to 9 million residents in "hyperconnected communities stretching from the mountains of northwest Saudi Arabia to the Red Sea" and "powered by 100 per cent clean energy," scheduled for completion in 2030.[101] The promotional YouTube video opens with the statement: "For too long, humanity has existed within dysfunctional and polluted cities that ignore nature. [...] Imagine a traditional city and consolidating its footprint. Designed to protect and enhance nature."[102] The city is, in actuality, amputated from nature rather than privileging a shared ecosystem in which interdependence is paramount for survival. The project presentation is narrated by a female voice, and the intonation deliberately aimed at fostering comforting and nurturing associations. One is reminded of the figure of Marianne, the personification of the French Republic since the Revolution, the benevolent face of French colonialism that appears on the official poster by Leonetto Cappiello of the 1922 Exposition Coloniale in Marseille, an allegory of Empire in which she is featured front and center draped in the national colors with the representatives of the colonies at her feet. That image obfuscated colonial violence much in the same way as the Saudi Arabian project elects to ignore scientific climate solutions that privilege multispecies interconnectivity. As Andreas Malm and the Zetkin Collective have argued in *White Skin, Black Fuel: On the Danger of Fossil Fascism*—conclusions that are pertinent to the mindset shaping the conceptualization of "The Line" project—this is the "time when mitigation could make the largest difference" or "everyone will be inside the furnace and see their shared destiny only when it's far too late to do anything about it."[103]

Oppositional Narratives and Accountability

This chapter has thus far focused on the ways in which propaganda in its various incarnations has furthered anti-ecological agendas.[104] Our attention will now shift to a consideration of various strategies that have been deployed in order to advance pro-ecological positions and promote awareness. One immediate example that comes to mind, and that is diametrically opposed to the adventures of Petro Pete we just considered, concerns the nonprofit Sesame Workshop, which announced in May 2024 that it planned to "partner with the global charity Save the Children to 'foster young children's climate resilience'."[105] Central to this discussion are also ethical and moral questions, a dimension that is often overlooked or one at least that does not receive the attention it deserves. As Genevieve Guenther has argued in *The Language of Climate Politics: Fossil-Fuel Propaganda and How to Fight It*, the call for climate justice must refrain from narrowing in on the "danger to the affluent without centering the fact that their prosperity was built on relations of colonial domination [that] in the name of growth, Global North capital forcibly opened markets, enslaved people, extracted resources, and left behind its waste and its harms—including the increasingly devastating harms of greenhouse gas emissions—in the poorer regions of the world."[106]

How then does one begin to counter disinformation? What examples are there of effective strategies? There is, of course, no dearth of environmental organizations. In fact, there are hundreds worldwide, located on every continent, including governmental, non-governmental, intergovernmental and global agencies engaged in local, regional, national and transnational projects. They include Just Stop Oil, Letzte Generation, Greenpeace, Environmental Defense Fund, Scientist Rebellion, Extinction Rebellion, Earthjustice, Natural Resources Defense Council, Conservation International, Sierra Club, World Wildlife Fund, Oceana and Climate Justice, among many others. What they have in common is their commitment to the protection of the natural environment, a focus on ocean safeguarding, forests and reforestation, wildlife conservation, social and environmental justice, climate action and regenerative agriculture, as well as the shared experience of being criticized and menaced in an effort to discredit their agendas and positions.[107]

What distinguishes them are the strategies they have adopted in order to raise public awareness. Some have engaged in acts of civil disobedience and have been labeled "eco-terrorists" and radicals.[108] As we know, there is no consensus on the effectiveness of such steps given, as Byung-Chul Han has argued, that "conspiracy theories are resistant to fact-checking because they are stories that, despite their fictional nature, base perception on reality."[109] Jonas Staal, in *Climate Propagandas: Stories of Extinction and Regeneration*, proposes five classifications: Liberal climate propaganda, Libertarian climate propaganda, Conspiracist climate propaganda, Ecofascist climate propaganda and Transformative climate propaganda.[110] The last connects with what we are considering here and outlines how we need to "approach the climate crisis as a colonial crisis resulting from 500 years of extinction wars," and also offers a roadmap that contains the potential to "install a different cultural imaginary, cultivating a new behavioral response" and enabling "a propagation of the realities that could become possible through disaster care and repair."[111]

As for Genevieve Guenther, each chapter of her book concludes with a "How to section" that provides readers with approaches, solutions and talking points to assist them in formulating responses to climate skeptics and denialists and to counter propaganda. The book reveals the extent to which dismissive positions have "shape[d] the dominant consensus" and the degree to which "fossil-energy interests have mined the language of climate advocates for material they can use for propaganda purposes, extracting, twisting, and deploying their words to entrap those advocates into unwittingly normalizing fossil-fuel disinformation. This dynamic turns fossil-fuel propaganda into a bipartisan consensus—the common-sense position."[112] In 2024, the Canadian government "rolled out a new propaganda campaign to build greater support for its climate and energy policies," and the multipronged effort, "Raising the Bar," included instructional videos, suggestions on lifestyle adjustments, informational tools and a dedicated website.[113] The Environmental Defense Fund is an American NGO that operates in partnership with the New Zealand Space Agency and is planning to launch a "satellite" whose mission will be to "name and shame" the worst methane polluters in the oil and gas industry.[114] Similarly, other organizations have launched dedicated outreach campaigns: the UN's *Actions for a Healthy Planet*, the World Wildlife Fund's *How We're Tackling Climate Change* and the Nature Conservancy's *Tackling Climate Change*.

Rethinking Our Relationships

In an interview in *Philosophie Magazine*, French philosopher Baptiste Morizot offered a path forward:

We cannot stop this ecological catastrophe, and so how might we give our actions a meaning that is irreducible? The answer that came to me is based on a verb: resist. We are going to enter a world that will become chaotic, complicated, where things that we hold dear will be weakened, such as social protection institutions, democratic institutions, living environments, thought in its most beautiful and honest form. [...] To resist is to work quietly, even at times as a minority and powerless, to defend everything that deserves to be defended. This is why I put forward the idea of a culture of struggle for the living: in all imaginable futures, all of them, from the worst to the luckiest, from the most preserved to the most catastrophic, this idea will be necessary and relevant, and will make life more livable for humans and non-humans alike, since the time has come for us to rethink our relationships.[115]

This assessment is rational and provides a remedy to the potentially debilitating impact of climate anxiety and eco-anxiety. But it also contains the possibility of "developing strong social networks of supportive relationships, and a living relationship with the natural world" whereby "community is crucial for collective resilience."[116] This is an expanding medical field, one in which research has defined concrete psychological symptoms and physical ailments and in which there is growing consensus that it represents a major global health threat for which "psychotherapists and clinical psychologists are coming to terms with ecological loss, anxiety and guilt in their patients, and also among themselves, as they come to grips with the faltering biosphere."[117] Energy has been weaponized in global conflicts in new and unforeseen ways that have "render[ed] the principles of international security and ecological sustainability inseparable."[118]

The future also brings uncertainty. But the problem with uncertainty projected into the future is that it fails to reckon with the immediacy of the threat, a threat that is already impacting many communities in the present. The current situation is simply untenable. Ultimately, we face what Pierre Charbonnier describes as an "ecological contradiction," because the land "literally cannot withstand in the long term and without serious pathologies the techno-scientific pressures to which it is subjected."[119] What we also know is that "the planet is going to continue to heat up until greenhouse gases stop being added to the atmosphere" and that "the forecasted acceleration of global warming will have severe effects on production and livelihoods and the overall stability of planetary ecosystems, which may reach a dangerous tipping point. Urgent action is needed to prevent irreparable damage."[120] This will necessitate coordinated alliances on a planetary scale and methodical attention to strategies and arguments that encourage radical lifestyle adjustments, a daunting challenge given the acute level of polarization that defines the quotidian political climate.[121]

As I delved into existing research on new technologies and disinformation, I collaborated with a designer (Adam Lomeli) on Midjourney's V5 model of their AI generation architecture creation tools in conjunction with ChatGPT (GPT-4) in order to generate images. I established an inventory of 142 of the prominent concepts and terms examined in *Climates of Migration*. Among these, one finds colonialism, climate change, global warming, algorithms, alternative facts, environment, indigenous cultures, populism, racial justice, disinformation, misinformation, extraction, post-truth, social media, immigration, ecosystems, climate denialism, pollution, capitalism, neoliberalism, nature, greenwashing, derangement, cosmocide, deforestation, refugees, migration, autocracy, fossil fuel, propaganda, eco-criticism and empire. Although the prompt engineering formula partially delineates the contours of the outcome, I was nevertheless interested in how new artificial intelligence technologies would connect with various processes of engineering propaganda and some of the principles found in the ecolonial games and online games explored in earlier chapters.[122] My goal was to gauge how AI image generation and algorithms would replicate the racial hierarchies, migrantphobia, xenophobia and disinformation mechanisms explored in the interplay between climate and migration in this book, given that "the authenticity and quality of AI-generated images heavily depend on the datasets used to train the models," leaving the door open to "bias."[123] Indeed, as Safiya Noble demonstrated in *Algorithms of Oppression: How Search Engines Reinforce Racism*, "On the Internet and in our everyday uses of technology, discrimination is also embedded in computer code and, increasingly, in artificial intelligence technologies," and in *Ethics of the Algorithm: Digital Humanities and Holocaust Memory*, Todd Presner studied how "algorithms and computational processes overlap insofar as the former are embedded within the latter in various programs, tools, and software. Together, they help construct methods, in the sense of forging pathways, to explore problems and offer possible solutions."[124]

AI and AI image generation place us in uncharted territory with unpredictable and unforeseen consequences and outcomes. In the images generated, as Alastair Johnstone-Hack has explained, one finds that they tend to "mimic a number of classic visual stereotypes—lone victims in the face of catastrophic climate change impacts, an overwhelming sense of disaster, destruction and death. The images are hopeless and devastating."[125] Although we cannot determine with any degree of certainty what algorithmic data sets the AI generated images were "trained on," what we can confidently say is that the process of amalgamating data reproduces widely disseminated alternative facts and disinformation and misinformation data that permeates the internet and social media platforms.[126]

For the purposes of this particular book, we initially generated 20 images—the decision to restrict the incorporation of images to the cover of *Climates of Migration* rather than reproduce all of them was motivated by respect for the reality pertaining to the undefined ethical terrain on which AI image generation currently resides. However, the abstract image included can be considered indicative of a broader argument given that the "AI image generators utilize trained artificial neural networks to create images from scratch" and "this mechanism transforms the input text into high-dimensional *vectors* that capture the semantic meaning and context of the text."[127] The AI-powered image description on the cover is of an evocative scene capturing the interplay between ecology and propaganda and generated through the following input criteria: *medium*: watercolor painting; *style*: a combination of surrealism and political satire, reminiscent of the works of René Magritte and Banksy; *lighting*: stark contrasts of light and shadow to emphasize the manipulation of information; *colors*: primarily monochromatic with splashes of vibrant reds, blues and greens; and *composition*: using a standard lens with a balanced perspective capturing the relationship between nature and the spreading of misleading messages. The divergence between AI-generated descriptions in the other images generated was striking, but what they all shared was an amalgamation of the arguments and ideas explored in *Climates of Migration*, emphasizing both the interconnectedness between environmental and migration questions *and* ecology and propaganda: pollution and atmospheric changes, dystopian urban sprawl, the stark reality of an ecological hellscape, ravaged landscapes and the remnants of natural habitats succumbing to climate change, images of a deteriorating environment emphasizing the role of information and disinformation in shaping our perception of the climate crisis, multilayered visual explorations of the dual impact of technology and propaganda on democratic institutions and ecological issues, and finally the struggle between human, nature and technology in a world grappling with climate change and political tensions. Ultimately, these descriptive elements reinforce terminological associations and tensions rather than transforming our perspective, stimulating our sense of justice and equipping us with the tools with which to navigate and traverse the fragile landscape of emotional sensibility and cultivate empathy and relationality as the various works of artists and authors considered have done.

Planetary Reparability

Colonial-era agricultural practices examined in Chapter 1 were premised on inexhaustible resources and "it wasn't so long ago that resource reproduction outstripped resource depletion," as David Theo Goldberg has reminded us.[128] This raises serious questions pertaining to coexistence among "the community of earthly inhabitants"[129] as we begin the process of assessing planetary reparability.[130] The world is also more unpredictable because, as Salman Rushdie has argued, "We're facing another old enemy, which is authoritarianism."[131] Many far-right parties claim to have been elected democratically, asserting that they did not actually *seize* power. Yet, increasingly, such claims have become questionable given that the path to power is paved with undemocratic actions, downward pressure on voting, disinformation and polarization. The intense battle and determination to gain control should never be underestimated. In some instances, combating demagoguery may even feel like one is swimming against the current. For, as Yanis Varoufakis has argued in *Technofeudalism: What Killed Capitalism*, "given capitalism's inherent tendency to deplete the commons, it was always going to take an enormous one [miracle] for our species to escape climate catastrophe. Technofeudalism's advances make this miracle even more improbable […] the greater the power of the cloudalist class, and the faster the march of technofeudalism, the less we, the demos, can do to avert climate catastrophe."[132] This is the "culture of struggle for the living" evoked earlier by Baptiste Morizot, "since the time has come for us to rethink our relationships."[133] Global warming will continue, if unchecked, and no species will be spared, similarly to the now oft-referenced metaphor of the *runaway greenhouse effect* or the *runaway train of climate change* over which we have collectively lost our hold. Those primarily responsible for global warming are also those on whom sustainable measures and climate change mitigation will depend. Relationality is not therefore negotiable since, as Achille Mbembe has argued, "One of the major effects of the accelerated combustion of the Earth is that there will be no more outside" and that "we now share the ordeal of extremes with many others who will not be able to be protected in the future by any wall, any border, any bubble or enclave."[134] For global warming doesn't care about fortresses, ramparts, fortifications or defensive walls.

EPILOGUE

The New Conquistadors

Silicon Valley engineers have long since stopped programming computers to become programmers of human behavior [and] have an interest in fueling the warming of the social climate.

Giuliano da Empoli[1]

Were one to be invited to participate in the design of a twenty-first-century version of ecolonial board games, tiles would be needed in order to capture new geopolitical configurations and incorporate visual display techniques equipped to accurately personify and convey power dynamics and transactional asymmetries. These should not be understood as innocuous changes, but rather as significant modifications with analogous adverse effects. Contemporary practices share with their historical predecessors a range of raptorial actions, profiteering motives, and extortionist orchestrations, as well as reckless and transgressive behaviors. As Giuliano da Empoli has convincingly shown, the "tech conquistadors" have transported us into an "era of digital colonization" and "the age of predators."[2]

Arguably, no world leader has, at the time of writing, more than Donald Trump, exploited and instrumentalized the nefarious and algorithmic potential of new technologies, and "the new American president has led a motley procession of unashamed autocrats, tech conquistadors, reactionaries and conspiracy theorists eager to do battle."[3] There has been no hesitation in rewriting history and privileging alternative narratives. Furthermore, the question of narrative is especially relevant to the rhetoric of Donald Trump and other far-right, populist or extremist politicians and thinkers, since recourse to narrative authority inserts itself into governance strategy. As the Colombian novelist Juan Gabriel Vásquez has explained, they "cannot exercise [...] power without convincing society, without making it believe in a story, which is, so to speak, always necessarily a fiction."[4] Naturally, the fabricated authoritarian narrative cannot survive scrutiny or scientific research data given that such evidence deviates from the story that is being recounted.

In order to be operative, it necessarily relies on silencing contradictory versions, whose expurgation becomes a condition of survivability in the social realm.

The resurgence of disquieting nationalist tendencies is therefore inseparable from these ideological strands, and has exacerbated tensions between historical allies and multilateral partners. In order to understand why such developments are the source of such tremendous concern, Austrian writer and political observer Robert Menasse has reminded us that the supranational economic and political configuration that is the European Union was the *direct outgrowth* of consensus among European citizens of the crucial necessity of embracing a "common postnational process."[5] This is an arrangement premised on the abandonment and rejection of a clearly defined and identified "aggressor," namely *nationalism*, to whom responsibility for the "crimes against humanity" that had "ravaged the continent" in the mid-twentieth century had been unambiguously attributed.[6] Therefore, newfound indicators of "renationalization" and backtracking on this commitment by, and under relentless pressure from, far-right and extremist "ethnonationalist" groups have heightened anxiety.[7]

Together, these factors have introduced uncertainty and unpredictability. Indeed, what is so striking about Donald Trump's second presidential term has been the scale and speed of policy changes and the significant impact of these on Africa and Europe. In the case of the former, this has translated into the progressive elimination of development aid, ambivalence regarding the renewal of the African Growth and Opportunity Act (AGOA) that had made it possible for more than two decades for several African countries to export duty-free, and plans to dramatically reduce the U.S. diplomatic presence through the gradual closing of consulates and embassies. With regard to the latter, presidential surrogates (Vice President JD Vance and Secretary of State Marco Rubio) have formulated multiple critiques that have included false accusations that Europe is retreating from democratic values, failing to uphold free speech and falling short of meeting NATO obligations, and together these have raised serious concerns about the U.S. commitment to transatlantic security. These interventions stand in addition to repeated statements in support of extending the footprint in the EU Parliament of right-wing populist, national conservative, euroskeptic positions, such as those adhered to by the Patriots for Europe, European Conservatives and Reformists or the Europe of Sovereign Nations Group. And these have been compounded by the actions taken by Elon Musk on his social networking and microblogging service X to meddle in German elections, and exploit a fragmented political landscape by interjecting himself by platforming co-chairwoman Alice Weidel of the far-right Alternative for Germany (AfD) party, a group officially labeled "rightwing extremist."[8]

To these examples, one could add the disparaging comments made by President Donald Trump himself about numerous world leaders, and contrast these with the positive and supportive words aimed at an expanding circle of far-right leaders and detractors. The reluctance to engage productively with long-standing partners, preferring instead to privilege bilateral relations that are themselves often inherently inequitable, has disrupted the existing world order. However, although launched in a seemingly disorganized and uncontrolled fashion, one should not underestimate the degree to which these actions are in actuality the product of systematic planning aimed at a comprehensive overhaul of institutions. These are, after all, outlined in the Heritage Foundation's *Project 2025: Mandate for Leadership: The Conservative Promise*, in what Spencer Chretien has described as a "Playbook," an "implementation plan for each agency to advocate to the incoming administration."[9]

Twenty-first-century conditions share points of commonality with historical antecedents. Colonialism was defined by a number of descriptors—domination, exploitation, displacement, racism, extraction, dehumanization—terms which remain applicable to the contemporary landscape. The disruption to the global trade order has caused a temporary blurring, and the reality that is materializing is coming into sharp definition. What is distinct is the recognition that planetary resources are not infinite (paradoxically because of resource depletion, global warming and climate change, and environmental degradation), thus the imperative and motivation to secure critical and rare minerals essential for the technology and defense industries. These factors are entangled with policies aimed at reducing environmental regulations, reorienting research programs away from climate change concerns, eliminating "climate extremism" in U.S. foreign aid programs while also reducing environmental safeguards.[10]

Competing interests are shaping the scramble for territorial and land rights, notably in terms of national security. The Executive Order "Unleashing America's offshore critical minerals and resources" dated April 25, 2025, announced that "the United States has a core national security and economic interest in maintaining leadership in deep sea science and technology and seabed mineral resources. The United States faces unprecedented economic and national security challenges in securing reliable supplies of critical minerals independent of foreign adversary control."[11] Pierre-Cyrille Hautcœur has drawn attention to "the insurmountable rivalry over natural resources that are the oceans (areas of maritime trade and fishing and mineral resources), land (arable and shelters for mining resources) and human labor. It aims at the appropriation—essentially by force and ultimately sanctioned by law—of these resources by actors powerful enough to do so."[12] These observations are corroborated by another related Executive Order dated April 15, 2025, in which one could read that "processed critical minerals and their derivative products face significant global supply chain vulnerabilities and market distortions due to reliance on a small number of foreign suppliers. These vulnerabilities and distortions have led to significant United States import dependencies. The dependence of the United States on imports and the vulnerability of our supply chains raises the potential for risks to national security, defense readiness, price stability, and economic prosperity and resilience."[13]

These decisions have also been motivated by what Achille Mbembe and Ruth Wilson Gilmore have described in the South African context as an "explicitly white supremacist twist, focused on the country's efforts to redress the compounded, multi-generational inequalities of apartheid. Trump has long supported the far-right conspiracy theory that falsely claims white farmers in South Africa are subject to a government-backed campaign of violence."[14] These point to a coalescence of far-right talking points: immigration, nationalist and protectionist economic measures, climate change denialism and the easing of environmental requirements. On February 7, 2025, an Executive Order "Addressing Egregious Actions of The Republic of South Africa" claimed that the South African government had "[seized] ethnic minority Afrikaners' agricultural property without compensation. This Act follows countless government policies designed to dismantle equal opportunity in employment, education, and business, and hateful rhetoric and government actions fueling disproportionate violence against racially disfavored landowners."[15] These claims cannot be substantiated, but align with similar measures whereby "From Mexico to Greenland, Panama to Ukraine, the Trump administration is bullying allies to align with its vision of national primacy and ethnic supremacy."[16]

The Trump administration has endeavored to foster asymmetrical power dynamics in which partners are obligated to be deferential. A compelling example is to be found in the peace agreement between the Democratic Republic of Congo and Rwanda that facilitates U.S. access to critical minerals through bilateral deals, efforts that, as an editorial in *The Guardian* newspaper demonstrated, have resulted in "a sovereign state cornered, at a weak moment, into accepting colonial-style terms without soldiers or flags. The tools are different—security deals, trade exemptions, private investment. But the logic is familiar."[17] And certainly, as if further evidence was necessary, the U.S. Department of the Treasury announcement on April 30, 2025, of the contours of the United States-Ukraine Reconstruction Investment Fund presented irrefutable confirmation as to what the rules of the game will henceforth correspond to, whereby "In recognition of the significant financial and material support that the people of the United States have provided to the defense of Ukraine since Russia's full-scale invasion, this economic partnership positions our two countries to work collaboratively and invest together to ensure that our mutual assets, talents, and capabilities can accelerate Ukraine's economic recovery."[18]

Good governance and transparency are prerequisites in ensuring accountability and equitable societies. Downplaying or deemphasizing these will have predictable outcomes, distracting from crucial issues, and only aggravating the kind of infrastructural disparities that fuel populism and encourage misguided policymaking rather than addressing the deeper systemic economic and social anxieties that shape them. Similarly, countering the agenda of far-right and extreme-right-wing groups cannot be achieved by mainstreaming and normalizing their positions. Alternative narratives must be forged, while emphasizing how the weakening of executive, judicial and legislative branches of government remains unacceptable. Their independence and the autonomy of the press are fundamental to the longevity of democratic institutions. Likewise, highlighting how xenophobic and racist speech can be inscribed in the transhistorical nationalist frameworks that informed colonial hierarchies, racial segregation and apartheid is essential, because these were also successfully combated and defeated in the past. We are at a crossroads. New directions will have to be explored, new paths taken and these will entail rethinking existing parameters, reimagining long-term security arrangements, disentangling from certain relationships, while finding innovative ways of forging sustainable communities and environments and relinquishing any inclination to see an inevitability in unfolding events, rather than countering a *warming* of *the social climate*.

NOTES

Prologue

1. George Orwell, *1984* (London: Secker & Warburg, 1949), 78.
2. Lesley Lokko, Venice Architecture biennale 2023, cited in Oliver Wainwright, "The Toxic Landscape of Colonialism: Venice's Architecture Biennale Spotlights Africa", *The Guardian*, May 19, 2023.
3. Dipesh Chakrabarty, 'Nous assistons à une prise de conscience: la planète a une histoire', Interview on *Radio France*, January 28, 2023, https://www.radiofrance.fr /franceculture/podcasts/l-invite-e-et-maintenant/dipesh-chakrabarty-nous-assis-tons-a-une-prise-de-conscience-la-planete-a-une-histoire-2375921. This history has been methodically documented in Jean-Baptiste Fressoz and Fabien Locher, *Les Révoltes du ciel. Une histoire du changement climatique XVe-XXe siècle* (Paris: Seuil, 2020).
4. Steffen Mau, *La réinvention de la frontière au XXIè siècle*, trans. C. Lucchese (Paris: Éditions de la Maison des sciences de l'homme, 2023), 61, emphasis added. See Matthias Rothe, "'Hidden Stockpiles of Words and Images': An Interview with Thomas Heise', in *Representing Social Precarity in German Literature and Film*, edited by Sophie Duvernoy, Karsten Olson and Ulrich Plass (New York: Bloomsbury Academic, 2024), 236–53.
5. Götz Aly, *The Magnificent Boat: The Colonial Theft of a South Seas Cultural Treasure*, trans. J. Chase (Cambridge, MA: The Belknap Press of Havard University Press, 2023 [2021]), 99–100.
6. Michael Kimmermann, 'Rebuilding a Palace May Become a Grand Blunder', *New York Times*, December 31, 2018.
7. Aly, *The Magnificent Boat*, 5 and 4.
8. Ibid., 137.
9. John M. Coetzee, *Disgrace* (New York: Viking, 1999), 172.
10. Dominic Boyer, 'Ostlagie and the Politics of the Future in East Germany', *Public Culture* 18, no. 2 (2006): 363.
11. Daniel Jütte, "Transparency: A German kaleidoscope", *The Berlin Journal* 38 (2024–2025): 11. See also Daniel Jütte, *Transparency: The Material History of an Idea* (New Haven, CT: Yale University Press, 2023).
12. Ibid., 9.
13. Jenny Erpenbeck, *Go, Went, Gone*, trans. S. Bernofsky (New York: New Directions Book, 2017 [2015]), 72.
14. Christoph Tannert, 'There Is No Absolute Truth', in *Claas Gutsche: Changing Truth* (Berlin: Claas Gutsche and Galerie Wagner + Partner, 2014), n.p.

15. Anna Wesle, 'Architectures of Memory: Claas Gutsche's Recent Linocuts', in *Claas Gutsche: Risse im Beton / Cracks in Concrete*, Kabinett Editions, no. 5 (Burgdorf: Museum Franz Gertsch, 2016), 11-12.

16. Ibid., 13.

17. Stefanie Gerke, 'On Berlin's Palace of the Republic – A New, Transitory Ruin Motif in Contemporary Art?', *View: Theories and Practices of Visual Culture* 4 (2013): 6, https://www.pismowidok.org/assets/files/article-pdf/issue-04/gerke.pdf.

18. Judith Schalansky, 'East Germany: Palace of the Republic', in *An Inventory of Losses* by Judith Schalansky, trans. J. Smith (New York: New Directions Publishing Corporation, 2020[2018]), 15-16

19. As Matthew Longo has described in *The Picnic: A Rush for Freedom and the Collapse of Communism* (New York: W. W. Norton, 2024), "The totalizing power of the Wall is captured most clearly on GDR-issued maps. The Wall didn't just tear across the cartographic city, it literally deleted the other half of it—West Berlin streets went unnamed, its parks and administrative buildings vanished into a monochrome nothingness. It was as though the mapmakers had tipped over an inkwell, blotting out the entire western portion of the city into undifferentiated blackness. This fed the ideology of the state: if the West disappeared, maybe people would give up trying to go there. If the citizens couldn't see it, maybe they would forget it existed", 73.

20. Jenny Erpenbeck, *Not a Novel: Collected Writings and Reflections*, trans. K. Beals (London: Granta, 2020 [2018]), 173 and 180.

21. Wendy Brown, *Walled States, Waning Sovereignty* (New York: Zone Books, 2014), 41, emphasis added.

22. See Sandrine Lemaire, Pascal Blanchard, Nicolas Bancel, Alain Mabanckou and Dominic Thomas, *Colonisation et Propagande. Le pouvoir de l'image* (Paris: Le cherche midi, 2022), 7.

23. Orwell, *1984*, 85.

24. Ibid., 162.

25. Alessandro Dal Lago, *Non-Persons: The Exclusion of Migrants in a Global Society*, trans. M. Orton (Milan: IPOC Press, 2009), 81.

26. Saskia Sassen, 'Migration policy from control to governance', *Open Democracy*, 12 July 2006, https://www.opendemocracy.net/en/militarising_borders_3735jsp/.

27. Hakim Abderrezak, 'The Mediterranean Sieve, Spring and Seametery', in *Refugee Imaginaries: Research Across the Humanities*, edited by Emma Cox, Sam Durrant, David Farrier, Lyndsey Stonebridge and Agnes Woolley (Edinburgh: Edinburgh University Press, 2020), 372-91. There is a parallel to be made with Jason De León's and Maite Zubiaurre's research on migrants, and to the way in which migrant deaths in the desert are ascribed to natural elements rather than blaming the state's immigration policies. See Jason De León, *The Land of Open Graves: Living and Dying on the Migrant Trail* (Oakland: University of California Press, 2015) and Maite Zubiaurre, *Talking Trash: Cultural Uses of Waste* (Nashville: Vanderbilt University Press, 2019).

28. Claire Rodier, *Xénophobie Business. À quoi servent les contrôles migratoires?* (Paris: La Découverte, 2012).

29. Abderrezak, 'The Mediterranean Sieve, Spring and Seametery', 383.

30. Erpenbeck, *Not a Novel*, 175.

31. Aly, *The Magnificent Boat*, 156.

32. Sarah Lea, 'Crossing Waters: Where to from here,' in *Entangled Pasts: 1768–Now: Art, Colonialism and Change* (London: Royal Academy Publications, 2024), February 3 to April 28, 2024, 180.

33. National Maritime Museum, 'Nelson's Ship in a Bottle', https://www.rmg.co.uk/sites/default/files/Ship_AW.pdf.

34. Ibid., emphasis added.

35. Wole Soyinka, *Climate of Fear: The Quest for Dignity in a Dehumanized World* (New York: Random House, 2005), 3 and Dipesh Chakrabarty, *The Climate of History in a Planetary Age* (Chicago, IL: University of Chicago Press, 2021).

36. Malcom Ferdinand, *Decolonial Ecology: Thinking from the Caribbean World*, trans. A. P. Smith (Cambridge: Polity Press, 2022), 124, emphasis added.

37. Estelle Zhong Mengual, *Apprendre à voir. Le point de vue du vivant* (Arles: Actes Sud, 2021), Achille Mbembe, *La communauté terrestre* (Paris: La Découverte, 2023), Ferdinand, *Decolonial Ecology*, Philippe Rahm, *Histoire naturelle de l'architecture: Comment le climat, les épidémies et l'énergie ont façonné la ville et les bâtiments* (Paris: Pavillon de l'Arsenal, 2020), Baptiste Morizot, *Ways of Being*, trans. A. Brown (Cambridge: Polity Press, 2022 [2020]) and Ursula K. Heise, *Sense of Place and Sense of Planet: The Environmental Imagination of the Global* (New York: Oxford University Press, 2008), 62. See also Imre Szeman and Dominic Boyer, eds., *Energy Humanities: An Anthology* (Baltimore, MD: Johns Hopkins University Press, 2017).

38. Macarena Gómez-Barris, 'The Colonial Anthropocene: Damage, Remapping, and Resurgent Resources: Book Review Essay', *Antipode Online*, March 19, 2019, https://antipodeonline.org/2019/03/19/the-colonial-anthropocene/.

39. Amitav Ghosh, *The Great Derangement: Climate Change and the Unthinkable* (Chicago: University of Chicago Press, 2016), 62.

40. See Françoise d'Eaubonne, *Naissance de l'écoféminisme* (Paris: Presses Universitaires de France, 2021) and Catherine Larrère, *L'écoféminisme* (Paris: La Découverte, 2023).

41. Sara de Wit, 'Gender and climate change as new development tropes of vulnerability for the Global South: essentializing gender discourses in Maasailand, Tanzania', *Tapuya: Latin American Science, Technology and Society* 4 (2021), 3.

42. Ferdinand, *Decolonial Ecology*, 234.

43. Morizot, *Ways of Being*, 10.

44. Chakrabarty, *The Climate of History in a Planetary Age*, 7.

45. Mengual, *Apprendre à voir*, 35.

46. Morizot, *Ways of Being*, 5.

47. Mbembe, *La communauté terrestre*, 203.

48. Arnaud Orain, *Le monde confisqué: Essai sur le capitalisme de la finitude (XVIᵉ- XXIᵉ)* (Paris: Flammarion, 2025), 8.

49. Amitav Ghosh, *The Nutmeg's Curse: Parables for a Planet in Crisis* (Chicago: University of Chicago Press, 2021), 140.

50. Cited in Wainwright, 'The toxic landscape of colonialism'.

51. Wainwright, 'The toxic landscape of colonialism'.

52. See Thomas Piketty, "Le national-capitalisme trumpiste aime étaler sa force, mais il est, en réalité, fragile et aux abois', *Le Monde*, February 15, 2025.

53. Roger Caillois, *Man, Play and Games*, trans. M. Barash (Urbana and Chicago: University of Illinois Press, 2001 [1958]), 58.

54. Amitav Ghosh, *The Great Derangement*, 115.

55. See Donna J. Haraway, *Staying with the Trouble: Making Kin in the Chthulucene* (Durham, NC: Duke University Press, 2016).

56. Daniel Macmillen Voskoboynik, *The Memory We Could Be: Overcoming Fear to Create Our Ecological Future* (Gabriola Island: New Society Publishers, 2018), 3-35, emphasis added.

57. Aimé Césaire, *Notebook of a Return to a Native Land*, trans. C. Eshleman and A. Smith (Middletown, CT: Wesleyan University Press, 2001 [1939]), 34.

58. Ferdinand, *Decolonial Ecology*, 206.

59. Ghosh, *The Nutmeg's Curse*, 53 and 54.

60. Bruno Latour, *Down to Earth: Politics in the New Climatic Regime*, trans. C. Porter (Cambridge: Polity Press, 2018), 2.

61. Hein de Haas, *How Migration Really Works: The Facts About the Most Divisive Issue in Politics* (New York: Basic Books, 2023), 19.

62. Latour, *Down to Earth*, 6.

63. Maya Goodfellow, '"You can't shoot climate change": Richard Seymour on how far right exploits environmental crisis', *The Guardian*, October 30, 2024. See Richard Seymour, *Disaster Nationalism: The Downfall of Liberal Civilisation* (London: Verso Books, 2024).

64. Haas, *How Migration Really Works*, 36.

65. Mbembe, *La communauté terrestre*, 7.

66. Haas, *How Migration Really Works*, 343.

67. Ghosh, *The Nutmeg's Curse*, 158.

68. Mengual, *Apprendre à voir*, 19.

69. Achille Mbembe 'The Earthly Community', The Holberg Lecture, June 5, 2024, https://holbergprize.org/en/news/holberg-prize/2024-holberg-lecture-achille -mbembe.

70. T.J. Demos, *Beyond the World's End: Arts of Living at the Crossing* (Durham and London: Duke University Press, 2020), 84. See also T. J. Demos, *Decolonizing Nature: Contemporary Art and the Politics of Ecology* (Berlin: Sternberg Press, 2016), an important work in which 'political ecology' operates in such a way that it 'acknowledges approaches to the environment that, although potentially divergent, nevertheless insist on environmental matters of concern as inextricable from social, political, and economic forces', 1.

71. Cheryll Glotfelty, 'Literary Studies in an Age of Environmental Crisis', in *The Ecocriticism Reader: Landmarks in Literary Ecology*, edited by Cheryll Glotfelty and Harold Fromm (Athens, GA: University of Georgia Press, 1996), xix. Strong indicators as to the extent to which this is a burgeoning field of research tare provided by two recent books: Sara Buekens, *Écologies littéraires africaines. L'imaginaire de l'environnement dans la littérature francophone postcoloniale* (Leiden and Boston, MA: Brill, 2025), Nsah Mala and Nicki Hitchcott, eds., *Ecotexts in the Postcolonial Francosphere* (Liverpool: Liverpool University Press, 2025), and Kirk Bryan Sides, *Environmental Entanglements: African Literature's Ecological Imaginary* (New York: Oxford University Press, 2025).

72. Mirca Madianou, 'Technocolonialism: Digital Innovation and Data Practices in the Humanitarian Response to Refugee Crises', *Social Media + Society* 5, no. 3 (July 2019), https://journals.sagepub.com/doi/10.1177/2056305119863146. See Mirca Madianou, *Technocolonialism; When Technology for Good is Harmful* (Hoboken, NJ: John Wiley and Sons Ltd, 2024).

73. Jenny Odell, *How to Do Nothing: Resisting the Attention Economy* (Brooklyn and London: Melville House, 2019), xviii.
74. Erpenbeck, *Not a Novel*, 177.
75. David Van Reybrouk, *Nous colonisons l'avenir*, trans. B.-T. Standaert (Arles: Actes Sud, 2023), 15.
76. David Theo Goldberg, 'Parting Waters: Seas of Movement', in *Life Adrift: Climate Change, Migration, Critique*, edited by Andrew Baldwin and Giovanni Bettini (London and New York: Rowman & Littlefield International, Ltd., 2017), 107
77. Haas, *How Migration Really Works*, 5 and 8.
78. Mbembe, *La communauté terrestre*, 184.
79. Esther Romeyn, 'Das Boot ist voll, The Boat is Full: Genealogy and Policy Consequences of an Ecological-Nativist Paradigm', in *The Politics of Replacement: Demographic Fears, Conspiracy Theories, and Race Wars*, edited by Sarah Bracke and Luis Manuel Hernández Aguilar (London and New York: Routledge, 2024), 38-50.
80. Nathacha Appanah, *La mémoire delavée* (Paris: Mercure de France, 2023), 18.

Chapter 1

1. Aimé Césaire, *Discourse on Colonialism*, trans. J. Pinkham (New York: Monthly Review Press, 1972 [1955]), 42.
2. Rebecca Solnit, 'Call Climate Change What It Is: Violence', *The Guardian*, April 7, 2014.
3. Baptiste Morizot, *Ways of Being Alive*, trans. A. Brown (Cambridge: Polity Press, 2022), 4.
4. Achille Mbembe, *La communauté terrestre* (Paris: La Découverte, 2023), 203.
5. Adam Hochschild, *King Leopold's Ghost: A Story of Greed, Terror, and Heroism in Colonial Africa* (Boston, MA: Houghton Mifflin Company, 1998), 57–8.
6. General Act of the Berlin Conference on West Africa, 'German Federal Foreign Office Political Archive', accessed February 21, 2025, https://archiv.diplo.de/arc-en/the-political-archive/2684468-2684468.
7. Eric Holt-Giménez, 'Introduction: Agrarian Questions and the Struggle for Land Justice in the United States', in *Land Justice: Re-Imagining Land, Food, and the Commons in the United States*, edited by Justine M. Williams and Eric Holt-Giménez (Oakland, CA: Food First Books, 2017), 4–5.
8. Daniel Macmillen Voskoboynik, *The Memory We Could Be: Overcoming Fear to Create Our Ecological Future* (Gabriola Island: New Society Publishers, 2018), 35 and 35–7, citing Richard Henry Drayton, *Nature's Government: Science, Imperial Britain and the 'Improvement' of the World* (New Haven, CT: Yale University Press, 2000).
9. Ibid., 35-37.
10. Amitav Ghosh, *The Great Derangement: Climate Change and the Unthinkable* (Chicago, IL: University of Chicago Press, 2016) and Dipesh Chakrabarty, *The Climate of History in a Planetary Age* (Chicago, IL: University of Chicago Press, 2021).
11. Jessica L. Horton, 'Ecolonial Holism', *Panorama: Journal of the Association of Historians of American Art* 5, no. 1 (Spring 2019), https://journalpanorama.org/article/ecocriticism/ecolonial-holism/.
12. T.J. Demos, *Beyond the World's End: Arts of Living at the Crossing* (Durham and London: Duke University Press, 2020), 16.

13. Kathryn Yusoff, *A Billion Black Anthropocenes or None* (Minneapolis: University of Minnesota Press, 2018), 30.

14. Achille Mbembe, *Critique of Black Reason*, trans. L. Dubois (Durham, NC: Duke University Press, 2017), 137.

15. Chakrabarty, *The Climate of History in a Planetary Age*, 31.

16. T.J. Demos, *Against the Anthropocene: Visual Culture and the Environment Today* (London: Sternberg Press, 2017), 85 and 87.

17. Amitav Ghosh, *The Nutmeg's Curse: Parables for a Planet in Crisis* (Chicago: University of Chicago Press, 2021), 36. See Jérôme Gaillardet, *La terre habitable ou l'épopée de la zone critique* (Paris: La Découverte, 2023).

18. Lynn White, 'The Historical Roots of Our Ecologic Crisis', *Science* 155, no. 3767 (1967): 1203.

19. Jan Nederveen Pieterse, *White on Black: Images of Africa and Blacks in Western Popular Culture* (New Haven: Yale University Press, 1992), 76, citing Basil Davidson, *Africa in Modern History: The Search for a New Society* (New York: Penguin Books, 1978).

20. Sandrine Lemaire, 'Spreading the Word: *The Agence Générale des Colonies (1920-1931)*', in *Colonial Culture in France Since the Revolution*, edited by Pascal Blanchard, Sandrine Lemaire, Nicolas Bancel and Dominic Thomas (Bloomington, IN: Indiana University Press, 2014), 166.

21. See Elizabeth Heath, 'Child's Play? Colonial commodities, ephemera, and the construction of the greater French family: *Apprendre l'Empire, un jeu d'enfants?*', *CLIO: Women, Gender, History* 40, no. 2 (2014), 69-87 and Charles Forsdick, 'Fragments of Empire: Ephemera, Toys, and the Dynamics of Colonial Memory', in *Visualizing Empire: Africa, Europe, and the Politics of Representation*, edited by Rebecca Peabody, Steven Nelson and Dominic Thomas (Los Angeles: Getty Publications, 2021), 50-67.

22. Pieterse, *White on Black*, 92.

23. Estelle Zhong Mengual, *Apprendre à voir: Le point de vue du vivant* (Arles: Actes Sud, 2021), 39.

24. Mohamad Amer Meziane, *The States of the Earth: An Ecological and Racial History of Secularization*, trans. J. Adjemian (New York: Verso, 2024), xiii and xv.

25. Morizot, *Ways of Being Alive*, 21–3.

26. William Cronon, 'The Trouble with Wilderness: Or, Getting Back to the Wrong Nature', *Environmental History* 1, no. 1 (January 1996): 17 and 7. This paradigm has survived into the postcolonial era and shapes the "green colonialism," as Guillaume Blanc has so convincingly shown in *The Invention of Green Colonialism*, trans. H. Morrison (Cambridge: Polity Press, 2022).

27. Malcom Ferdinand, *Decolonial Ecology: Thinking from the Caribbean World* (Cambridge: Polity Press, 2022), 4.

28. Ibid., 40 and 22.

29. See Tamiru Lemi, 'The Role of Traditional Ecological Knowledge (TEK) for Climate Change Adaptation', *International Journal of Environmental Sciences & Natural Resources* 18, no. 1 (2019), https://juniperpublishers.com/ijesnr/IJESNR .MS.ID.555980.php, Nadzirah Hosen, Hitoshi Nakamura and Amran Hamzah, 'Adaptation to Climate Change: Does Traditional Ecological Knowledge Hold the Key?', *Sustainability* 12, no. 676 (2020), https://www.mdpi.com/2071-1050/12 /2/676 and Kyle Powys Whyte, 'Is it Colonial Déjà vu? Indigenous Peoples and Climate Injustice', in *Humanities for the Environment: Integrating Knowledge, Forging*

New Constellations of Practice, edited by Joni Adamson and Michel Davis (London: Routledge, 2018), 88–104.

30. Kyle Powys Whyte, '"Our Ancestors" Dystopia Now: Indigenous Conservation and the Anthropocene', in *Routledge Companion to the Environmental Humanities*, edited by Ursula K. Heise, Jon Christensen and Michelle Niemann (New York: Routledge, 2017), 206-16. See also Kate Rigby, *Meditations on Creation in an Era of Extinction* (Maryknoll: Orbis Books, 2023).

31. Harriet Mercer and Thomas Simpson, 'Imperialism, colonialism, and climate change science', *WIREs Climate Change* 14, Issue 6, 6, https://wires.onlinelibrary.wiley.com/doi/full/10.1002/wcc.851

32. Morizot, *Ways of Being Alive*, 19.

33. Pascal Blanchard, Sandrine Lemaire, Nicolas Bancel and Dominic Thomas, 'The Creation of a *Colonial Culture* in France, from the Colonial Era to the "Memory Wars"', in *Colonial Culture in France Since the Revolution*, edited by Blanchard, Lemaire, Bancel and Thomas, 2.

34. Ibid., 3.

35. Ibid., 16.

36. Heath, 'Child's Play?', 76.

37. Lemaire, 'Spreading the Word,' 168.

38. Ibid., 162 and 165–7.

39. Sandrine Lemaire, 'Promotion: Creating the Colonial (1930–1940)', in *Colonial Culture in France Since the Revolution*, edited by Blanchard, Lemaire, Bancel and Thomas, 265.

40. Ulrike Ktetzchmar, 'Foreword', in *German Colonialism: Fragments Past and Present*, edited by Sebastian Gottschalk and Heike Hartmann (Berlin: Deutsches Historishes Museum, 2016), 10–11.

41. Wendeline Flores and Wayne Modest, eds., *Our Colonial Inheritance* (Tielt: Lannoo Publishers, 2024).

42. https://amsterdam.wereldmuseum.nl/en/whats-on/exhibitions/our-colonial-inheritance

43. Susan Legène and Janneke Van Dijk, eds., *The Netherlands East Indies at the Tropenmuseum: A Colonial History* (Amsterdam: KIT Publishers, 2011), 6.

44. Wendeline Flores and Wayne Modest, "This (Terrible) Inheritance," in Wendeline Flores and Wayne Modest, eds., *Our Colonial Inheritance* (Tielt: Lannoo Publishers, 2024), 17.

45. Ibid.,13.

46. See, for example, Nicolas Bancel, Pascal Blanchard and Dominic Thomas, eds., *The Colonial Legacy in France: Fracture, Rupture, and Apartheid* (Bloomington: Indiana University Press, 2017) and Pascal Blanchard, Nicolas Bancel, Sandrine Lemaire and Dominic Thomas, eds., *Histoire Globale de la France coloniale* (Paris: Philippe Rey, 2022).

47. Palais de la Porte Dorée and the Museum of the History of Immigration, 'Janniot's bas-relief', accessed January 30, 2025, https://monument.palais-portedoree.fr/en/the-settings/janniot-s-bas-relief.

48. Dominique Taffin, 'Le musée des colonies et l'imaginaire colonial', in *Images et colonies (1880–1962),* edited by Nicolas Bancel, Pascal Blanchard and Laurent Gervereau (Paris: ACHAC, 1993), 142.

49. Maureen Murphy, *Un Palais pour une cité: Du musée des colonies à la Cité nationale de l'histoire de l'immigration* (Paris: Réunion des musées nationaux, 2007), 29 and 33.

50. See Elise Pape, 'Postcolonial Debates in Germany—An Overview', *African Sociological Review / Revue Africaine de Sociologie* 21, no. 2 (2017): 2–14, Thomas Thiemeyer, 'Cosmopolitanizing Colonial Memories in Germany', *Critical Inquiry* 45, no. 4 (Summer 2019): 967–90, Jürgen Zimmerer, eds., *Climate Change and Genocide: Environmental Violence in the 21st Century* (New York: Routledge, 2021) and Thomas Rogers, 'The Long Shadow of German Colonialism', *New York Review of Books*, March 9, 2023.

51. Götz Aly, *The Magnificent Boat: The Colonial Theft of a South Seas Cultural Treasure*, trans. J. Chase (Cambridge: The Belknap Press of Harvard University Press, 2023), 132-33 and 137.

52. Jacques Chirac, 'Speech by M. Jacques Chirac, President of the Republic, at the opening of the Quai Branly Museum', June 20, 2006.

53. Felwine Sarr and Bénédicte Savoy, *The Restitution of African Cultural Heritage: Toward a New Relational Ethics* (Paris: Ministère de la culture, 2018).

54. Ghosh, *The Nutmeg's Curse*.

55. Ibid., 190.

56. Ibid., 184-86. See Sven Lindquist, *"Exterminate All the Brutes": One Man's Odyssey into the Heart of Darkness and the Origins of European Genocide*, trans. J. Tate (New York: New Press, 2007).

57. Ghosh, *The Nutmeg's Curse*, 183.

58. Olivette Otele, *African Europeans: An Untold History* (London: Hurst & Company, 2020), 12.

59. Catherine Coquery-Vidrovitch, 'Selling the Economic Myth (1900-1940)', in *Colonial Culture in France Since the Revolution*, edited by Blanchard, Lemaire, Bancel and Thomas, 180.

60. Yann Holo, 'L'œuvre civilisatrice de l'idée à l'image', in *Images et colonies (1880–1962)*, edited by Bancel, Blanchard and Gervereau, 58.

61. Coquery-Vidrovitch, 'Selling the Economic Myth', 181-86.

62. Nathacha Appanah, *La mémoire délavée* (Paris: Mercure de France, 2023), 17–8.

63. Blanc, *The Invention of Green Colonialism*, 28.

64. Mengual, *Apprendre à voir*, 43.

65. Ferdinand, *Decolonial Ecologies*, 47.

66. Max Liboiron, *Pollution is Colonialism* (Durham, NC: Duke University Press, 2021).

67. Alice L. Conklin, *A Mission to Civilize: The Republican Idea of Empire in France and West Africa, 1895-1930* (Stanford, CA: Stanford University Press, 1997).

68. Lori M. Hunter and Raphael J. Nawrotzki, 'Migration and the Environment', in *Handbook of Migration and Population Distribution*, edited by Michael J. White (Dordrecht: Springer, 2015), 479 and 467. The authors cite the important research of Rafael Reuveny and Will H. Moore on these questions, 'Does Environmental Degradation Influence Migration? Emigration to Developed Countries in the Late 1980s and 1990s', *Social Science Quarterly* 90, no. 3 (2009): 461–79.

69. Philippe Rahm, *Le style anthropocène* (Geneva: Head Publishing, 2023).

70. Blanc, *The Invention of Colonialism*, 29.

71. Deborah Coen, *Climate in Motion: Science, Empire, and the Problem of Scale* (Chicago, IL: University of Chicago Press, 2018), 4 and 6.

72. See Lynn E. Palermo, 'L'Exposition Anticolonialie: Political or Aesthetic Protest?', *French Cultural Studies* 20, no. 1 (2009): 27-46.

73. Lemaire, Blanchard, Bancel, Mabanckou and Thomas, *Colonisation et Propagande*, 7.
74. Blanchard, Lemaire, Bancel and Thomas, 'The Creation of a *Colonial Culture* in France', 8. See also Nicolas Bancel, 'The Colonial Bath: Sources of Popular *Colonial Culture* (1918-1931)', in *Colonial Culture in France Since the Revolution*, edited by Blanchard, Lemaire, Bancel and Thomas, 200-08.
75. Lemaire, Blanchard, Bancel, Mabanckou and Thomas, *Colonisation et Propagande*, 7.
76. Rebecca Peabody, Steven Nelson and Dominic Thomas, eds., *Visualizing Empire: Africa, Europe, and the Politics of Representation* (Los Angeles: Getty Publications, 2021), 1.
77. See Robert W. Rydell, *World of Fairs: The Century-of-Progress Expositions* (Chicago, IL: University of Chicago Press, 1993), Patricia A. Morton, *Hybrid Modernities: Architecture and Representation at the 1931 Colonial Exposition, Paris* (Cambridge, MA: MIT Press, 2000) and Caroline A. Jones, *Sensorium: Embodied Experience, Technology, and Contemporary Art* (Cambridge, MA: MIT Press, 2006).
78. Peabody, Nelson and Thomas, eds., *Visualizing Empire*, 1
79. Lemaire, Blanchard, Bancel, Mabanckou and Thomas, *Colonisation et Propagande*, 168.
80. Ibid.
81. Ibid., 14. See Jean Garrigues, *Banania: Histoire d'une passion française* (Paris: Du May, 1991).
82. Sandrine Lemaire, 'Manipulation: Conquering Taste (1931-1939)', in *Colonial Culture in France Since the Revolution*, edited by Blanchard, Lemaire, Bancel and Thomas, 289.
83. Sandrine Lemaire, Catherine Hodeir and Pascal Blanchard, 'The Colonial Economy: Between Propaganda Myths and Economic Reality (1940-1955)', in *Colonial Culture in France Since the Revolution*, edited by Blanchard, Lemaire, Bancel and Thomas, 323.
84. Mariana P. Candido, 'This is your land: Legislating dispossession in colonial West Africa', *The Berlin Journal*, no. 37 (2023-2024): 6.
85. John MacKenzie, *Propaganda and Empire: The Manipulation of British Public Opinion, 1880-1960* (Manchester: Manchester University Press, 1984), 100.
86. Ibid., 228 and 258.
87. Robin Wall Kimmerer, *Braiding Sweetgrass: Indigenous Wisdom, Scientific Knowledge and the Teachings of Plants* (Minneapolis: Milkweed Editions, 2013), 9.
88. Françoise Vergès, 'Colonizing, Educating, Guiding: A Republican Duty', in *Colonial Culture in France Since the Revolution*, edited by Blanchard, Lemaire, Bancel and Thomas, 252-53.
89. Aly, *The Magnificent Boat*.
90. Ibid., 1 and 3.
91. Baptiste Lanaspeze, *Nature* (Paris: Paris: Anamosa, 2022), 66.
92. Aly, *The Magnificent Boat*, 131, 5 and 132.
93. Hochschild, *King Leopold's Ghost* and David Van Reybrouck, *Congo: The Epic History of a People*, trans. S. Garrett (New York: HarperCollins Publishers, 2014).
94. Hochschild, *King Leopold's Ghost*, 27 and 160.
95. Ibid., 301.
96. Jean-Pierre Stroobants, 'Belgium prime minister officially apologizes for the death of Patrice Lumumba', *Le Monde*, June 21, 2022.
97. Ferdinand, *Decolonial Ecology*, 44.

98. Bill Gammage, 'Colonists upended Aboriginal farming, growing grain and running sheep on rich yamfields, and cattle on arid grainland', *The Conversation*, September 19, 2023.

99. Nicolas Bancel and Daniel Denis, 'Education: Becoming "Homo Imperialis" (1910-1940)', in *Colonial Culture in France Since the Revolution*, edited by Blanchard, Lemaire, Bancel and Thomas, 276–284 and Gilles Boyer, Pascal Clerc and Michelle Zancarini-Fournel, eds., *L'école aux colonies, les colonies à l'école* (Lyon: ENS, 2013).

100. Pieterse, *White on Black*, 76, himself citing Davidson, *Africa in Modern History*, 75.

101. Lemaire, 'Spreading the Word', 422.

102. Nicolas Bancel and Pascal Blanchard, 'The Republican Origins of the Colonial Fracture', in *Colonial Culture in France Since the Revolution*, edited by Blanchard, Lemaire, Bancel and Thomas, 47.

103. Nicolas Bancel and Pascal Blanchard, 'The Pitfalls of Colonial Memory', in *Colonial Culture in France Since the Revolution*, edited by Blanchard, Lemaire, Bancel and Thomas, 157.

104. Sandrine Lemaire, 'Colonization and Immigration: "Blind Spots" in the History Classroom?', in *Colonial Culture in France Since the Revolution*, edited Pascal Blanchard, Lemaire, Bancel and Thomas, 78-88.

105. Ibid., 78-88.

106. Alain Ruscio, 'Toward a Real History of French Colonialism', in *Colonial Culture in France Since the Revolution*, edited by Blanchard, Lemaire, Bancel and Thomas, 386-394.

107. Gloria Wekker, *White Innocence: Paradoxes of Colonialism and Race* (Durham: Duke University Press, 2016), 44.

108. Bancel and Blanchard, 'The Pitfalls of Colonial Memory', 153–64.

109. Kehinde Andrews, *The New Age of Empire: How Racism and Colonialism Still Rule the World* (London: Allen Lane, 2021), 90.

110. Bancel, 'The Colonial Bath', 201–2.

111. Ibid., 207.

112. Ibid., 200.

113. Ian Bogost, *Persuasive Games: The Expressive Power of Videogames* (Cambridge and London: The MIT Press, 2007), 46.

114. Carly A. Kocurek, 'Walter Benjamin on the Video Screen: Storytelling and Game Narratives', *Arts* 7, no. 4 (2018): 2–3.

115. Forsdick, 'Fragments of Empire', 58.

116. Yann Holo, "Jeux et jouets," in *Images et colonies (1880-1962)*, edited by Bancel, Blanchard and Gervereau, 125.

117. MacKenzie, *Propaganda and Empire*, 28 and 185–6.

118. David D. Hamlin, *Work and Play: The Production and Consumption of Toys in Germany, 1870-1914* (Ann Arbor: University of Michigan Press, 2007), 52.

119. Jeff Bowersox, *Raising Germans in the Age of Empire: Youth and Colonial Culture, 1871-1914* (Oxford University Press, 2013), 21.

120. Collection inventory, Getty Research Institute, Los Angeles, CA, accessed 2 May 2015, http://archives2.getty.edu:8082/xtf/view?docId=ead/970031/970031.xml ;chunk.id=ref1093;brand=default;query=deutsche%20kolonien.

121. Bowersox, *Raising Germans in the Age of Empire*, 72.

122. Alice L. Conklin and Julia Clancy-Smith, 'Introduction: Writing Colonial Histories', *French Historical Studies* 27, no. 3 (Summer 2004): 498.

123. Pieterse, *White on Black*, 64.

124. Lemaire, Hodeir and Blanchard, 'The Colonial Economy', 322.

125. Pascal Blanchard and Ruth Ginio, 'Imperial Revolution: Vichy's Colonial Myth (1940-1944)', in *Colonial Culture in France Since the Revolution*, edited Pascal Blanchard, Lemaire, Bancel and Thomas, 307.

126. Joseph Fèvre and Henri Hauser, *Précis de géographie* (Paris: F. Alcan, 1913), 838, cited in Gilles Manceron, 'School, Pedagogy, and the Colonies (1870–1914)', in *Colonial Culture in France Since the Revolution*, edited by Blanchard, Lemaire, Bancel and Thomas, 124. Translation altered slightly.

127. Conklin and Clancy-Smith, 'Introduction', 497.

128. See Claude Lamboley, "Les jeux de l'oie. Longue histoire et grande collection" (2023), accessed February 21, 2025, https://www.jouetsanciens.fr/les-jeux-de-loie/.

129. See Isotta Poggi, 'Colorful Board Game Turns the French Colonies into Child's Play', February 24, 2014, http://blogs.getty.edu/iris/colorful-board-game-turns-the-french-colonies-into-childs-play/.

130. Cognitive Science is not my field of research specialization. The language and concepts I draw upon here in order to better understand the various techniques employed by game designers come from this field, for example in the scholarship of Roger E. Beaty and Yoed N. Kenett, 'Associative Thinking at the Core of Creativity', *Trends in Cognitive Sciences* 27, no. 7 (2023), 671–83.

131. Ambroise Jeanneney, *Ce que produisent nos colonies: leçons de choses et lectures* (Paris: Librairie Ch. Delagrave, 1896), 6.

132. See Anne Hugon, 'Conquête et exploration en Afrique noire,' in *Images et colonies (1880-1962)*, edited by Bancel, Blanchard and Gervereau, 19.

133. See Yves Gaulupeau, 'L'Afrique en images dans les manuels élémentaires d'histoire (1880-1969)', in *Images et colonies (1880-1962)*, edited by Bancel, Blanchard and Gervereau, 66-9.

134. Didier Daeninckx, *L'école des colonies* (Paris: Hoëbeke, 2015).

135. Ibid., 7.

136. Arjun Appadurai, *Modernity at Large: Cultural Dimensions of Globalization* (Minneapolis: University of Minnesota Press, 1996), 28 and Eric Holt-Giménez, *A Foodie's Guide to Capitalism: Understanding the Political Economy of What We Eat* (New York: Monthly Review Press, 2017), 33 and 36.

137. Collectible albums included: Chocolat Cémoi, *L'Afrique équatoriale* (Grenoble, France, 1935, 240, photomechanical prints: https://bm-grenoble.fr/detailstatic.aspx?RSC_BASE=SYRACUSE&RSC_DOCID=1037433&TITLE=historique-des-colonies-francaises-album-n-5-l-afrique-equatoriale-francaise-cemoi&_lg=fr-FR); Chocolat Suchard, *La France pittoresque* (Paris, France, 1930, 300, photomechanical prints: https://www.getty.edu/research/collections/component/10Z6JD); and Chocolat Pupier, L'Afrique, (Saint-Étienne, France, 1938, 252, photomechanical prints: https://bastaire.msh.uca.fr/s/ICB/item/10247#?xywh=-895%2C0%2C4467%2C3568&cv=4).

138. Sonia Shah, *The Next Great Migration: The Beauty and Terror of Life on the Move* (New York: Bloomsbury Publishing, 2021), 10.

139. Philipp Lehmann, *Desert Edens: Colonial Climate Engineering in the Age of Anxiety* (Princeton: Princeton University Press, 2022), cited here in Mercer and Simpson, 'Imperialism, colonialism, and climate change science', 6.

140. Lemaire, Hodeir and Blanchard, 'The Colonial Economy', 323.

141. Pieterse, *White on Black*, 85.

142. Scott Rigby and Richard Ryan, 'Rethinking Carrots: A New Method for Measuring What Players Find Most Rewarding and Motivating about Your Game', January 16, 2007, http://www.gamasutra.com/view/feature/130155/rethinking_carrots_a _new_method_.php.
143. Holo, 'Jeux et jouets', 125.
144. Morton, *Hybrid Modernities*, 17.
145. Pascale Joassart-Marcelli, *Food Geographies: Social, Political, and Ecological Connections* (London: Rowman & Littlefield, 2022), 49.
146. Séverine Kodjo-Grandvaux, *Devenir vivants* (Paris: Philippe Rey, 2021), 52.
147. Joassart-Marcelli, *Food Geographies*, 58–68.
148. Van Reybrouk, *Nous colonisons l'avenir*, 18.
149. Achille Mbembe, 'Provincializing France?', trans. J. Roitman, *Public Culture* 23, no. 1 (2011): 110.
150. See François-Xavier Verschave, *La Françafrique. Le plus long scandale de la République* (Paris: Stock, 1998), Xavier Harel and Thomas Hofnung, *Le scandale des biens mal acquis. Enquête sur les milliards volés de la françafrique* (Paris: La Découverte, 2011) and Achille Mbembe, 'Afrique-France: neuf thèses sur la fin d'un cycle', *Le Grand Continent*, September 3, 2023.
151. Dominic Thomas, 'Bibliodiversity: Denationalizing and Defrancophonizing Francophonie', in *Reframing Postcolonial Studies: Concepts – Methodologies - Scholarly Activisms*, edited by David Kim (New York: Palgrave, 2021), 97 and 100.
152. Nicholas Niarcos, 'In Congo's Cobalt Mines,' *New York Review of Books*, December 7, 2023.
153. Blanc, *The Invention of Green Colonialism*, 13. See also Guillaume Blanc, *La nature des hommes. Une mission écologique pour "sauver" l'Afrique* (Paris: La Découverte, 2024).
154. Priyadarshi R. Shukla and Jim Skea, eds., *Mitigation of Climate Change: Working Group III Contribution to the Sixth Assessment Report of the Intergovernmental Panel on Climate Change*, Intergovernmental Panel on Climate Change (2022), https://www.ipcc.ch/ report/ar6/wg3/downloads/report/IPCC_AR6_WGIII_FullReport.pdf.
155. Harriet Mercer, 'Colonialism: why leading climate scientists have finally acknowledged its link with climate change', *The Conversation*, April 22, 2022.
156. Ibid.
157. Hans-Otto Pörtner et al., *Climate Change 2022: Impacts, Adaptation and Vulnerability. Contribution of Working Group Il to the Sixth Assessment Report of the Intergovernmental Panel on Climate Change* (Cambridge: Cambridge University Press, 2022), https://www.ipcc .ch/report/ar6/wg2/downloads/report/IPCC_AR6_WGII_SummaryForPolic ymakers.pdf, 12.
158. "Making Climate History," Cambridge University, https://www.geog.cam.ac.uk/ research/projects/makingclimatehistory/.
159. Mercer and Simpson, "Imperialism, colonialism, and climate change science." This research builds on an earlier *WIREs Climate Change* article, Martin Mahony and Georgina Endfield, 'Climate and colonialism', *WIREs Climate Change* 9, Issue 2, (2018), https://doi.org/10.1002/wcc.510.
160. Ibid., 12.
161. Ibid., 13.
162. Nishtha Singh, 'Climate Justice in the Global South: Understanding the Environmental Legacy of Colonialism', *E-International Relations*, February 2, 2023, https://www.e-ir.info/2023/02/02/climate-justice-in-the-global-south-understand ing-the-environmental-legacy-of-colonialism/.

163. Ghosh, *The Nutmeg's Curse*, 75 and 83.

164. Ghosh, *The Great Derangement*, 115.

165. Neel Ahuja, *Planetary Specters: Race, Migration, and Climate Change in the Twenty-First Century* (Chapel Hill: The University of North Carolina Press, 2021), 17 and 16.

166. See Ernest Breleur, Patrick Chamoiseau, Gérard Delver, Serge Domi, Édouard Glissant, Guillaume Pigeard de Gurbert, Olivier Porteop, Olivier Pular and Jean-Claude William, *Manifeste pour les "produits" de haute nécessité* (Paris: Éditions Galaade and the Institut du Tout-Monde in March 2009) and Édouard Glissant and Patrick Chamoiseau, "Manifesto for "products" of dire need," in *Manifestos*, trans. B. Wing and M. Reeck (London: Goldsmiths Press, 2022), 57–65.

167. Yarimar Bonilla, *Non-Sovereign Futures: French Caribbean Politics in the Wake of Disenchantment* (Chicago: University of Chicago Press, 2015), 61 and 65.

168. Anouch Missirian and Wolfram Schlenker, 'Asylum Applications Respond to Temperature Fluctuations', *Science* 358, no. 6370 (December 2017): 1610–4 and Nicole Greenfield, 'Climate Migration and Equity', Natural Resources Defense Council, May 9, 2022, https://www.nrdc.org/stories/climate-migration-equity.

169. Saskia Sassen, 'A Massive Loss of Habitat: New Drivers for Migration', *Sociology of Development* 2, no. 2 (2016): 213.

170. Bruno Latour, *Down to Earth: Politics in the New Climatic Regime*, trans. C. Porter (Cambridge: Polity Press, 2018), 106.

171. Jeremy Bentham, 'Of the Limits of the Penal Branch of Jurisprudence', in *An Introduction to the Principles of Morals and Legislation* by Jeremy Bentham (Oxford: The Clarendon Press, 1907 [1789]), 311.

172. Philippe Descola, *Beyond Nature and Culture*, trans. J. Lloyd (Chicago: University of Chicago Press, 2013), 193.

173. Aimé Césaire, *Notebook of a Return to a Native Land*, trans. C. Eshleman and A. Smith (Middletown, CT: Wesleyan University Press, 2001 [1939]), 13.

Chapter 2

1. Bruno Latour, *Down to Earth: Politics in the New Climatic Regime*, trans. C. Porter (Cambridge: Polity Press, 2018), 2.

2. Chimamanda Ngozi Adichie, 'The Danger of a Single Story', *TEDGlobal*, July 23, 2009.

3. Neel Ahuja, *Planetary Specters: Race, Migration, and Climate Change in the Twenty-First Century* (Chapel Hill, NC: University of North Carolina Press, 2021), 15.

4. Achille Mbembe, 'Scrap the Borders that Divide Africans', *Mail & Guardian*, May 17, 2017.

5. Quoted in Rajeev Syal, 'Suella Braverman Claims "Hurricane" of Mass Migration Coming to UK', *The Guardian*, October 3, 2023.

6. Katherine E. Russo, 'Floating Signifiers, Transnational Affect Flows: Climate-induced Migrants in Australian News Discourse', in *Life Adrift: Climate Change, Migration, Critique*, edited by Andrew Baldwin and Giovanni Bettini (London and New York: Rowman & Littlefield International, Ltd., 2017), 206 and 207-8.

7. Enoch Powell, 'Speech at Birmingham', April 20, 1968, https://www.enochpowell.net/fr-79.html.

8. Bayo Akomolafe, "Homo Icarus: The Depreciating Value of Whiteness and the Place of Healing," August 19, 2017, https://www.bayoakomolafe.net/post/homo-icarus-the-depreciating-value-of-whiteness-and-the-place-of-healing.

9. Latour, *Down to Earth*, 2.
10. Ibid., 3.
11. Patrick Chamoiseau, *Migrant Brothers: A Poet's Declaration of Human Dignity*, trans. M. Amos and F. Rönnbäck (New Haven, CT: Yale University Press, 2018), 93.
12. Felwine Sarr, *Habiter le monde. Essai de politique relationnelle* (Montreal: Mémoire d'encrier, 2017), 12 and 19.
13. Latour, *Down to Earth*, 7.
14. Eric Holt-Giménez, 'Introduction: Agrarian Questions and the Struggle for Land Justice in the United States', in *Land Justice: Re-Imagining Land, Food, and the Commons in the United States*, edited by Justine M. Williams and Eric Holt-Giménez (Oakland, CA: Food First Books, 2017), 2.
15. Eric Holt-Giménez, *A Foodie's Guide to Capitalism: Understanding the Political Economy of What We Eat* (New York: Monthly Review Press, 2017), 52.
16. Ravi Kanbur, 'The theory of structural adjustment and trade policy', in *Trade and development in sub-Saharan Africa*, edited by Jonathan H. Frimpong-Ansah, Ravi Kanbur and Peter Svedberg (Manchester: Manchester University Press, 1991), 188-202.
17. T.J. Demos, *The Migrant Image: The Art and Politics of Documentary during Global Crisis* (Durham, NC: Duke University Press, 2013), 205.
18. See François Boye, 'Economic Mechanisms in Historical perspective', in *Senegal: Essays in Statecraft*, edited by Momar Coumba Diop (Dakar: CODESRIA, 1993), 28-84.
19. Saskia Sassen, 'A Massive Loss of Habitat: New Drivers for Migration', *Sociology of Development* 2, no. 2 (2016): 207.
20. Intergovernmental Panel on Climate Change, *Climate Change 2022: Impacts, Adaptation and Vulnerability Working Group II Contribution to the Sixth Assessment Report of the Intergovernmental Panel on Climate Change*, 2022, https://report.ipcc.ch/ar6/wg2/IPCC_AR6_WGII_FullReport.pdf, 12.
21. Cajetan Iheka, *African Ecomedia: Network Forms, Planetary Politics* (Durham, NC: Duke University Press, 2021), 4 and 11.
22. Parag Khanna, *Move: The Forces Uprooting Us* (New York: Scribner, 2021), 272. See Ranabir Samaddar, 'The Ecological Migrant in Postcolonial Time', in *Life Adrift*, edited by Baldwin and Bettini, 177-93, and Ghosh, *The Great Derangement*, 62.
23. Philippe Rahm, *The Anthropocene Style* (Geneva: HEAD Publishing, 2023), 13.
24. Roger Zetter, 'Protecting People Displaced by Climate Change: Some Conceptual Challenges', in *Climate Change and Displacement: Multidisciplinary Perspectives*, edited by Jane McAdam (Oxford and Portland, OR: Hart Publishing, 2012), 140.
25. Maurice Stierl, 'Migration: Let us put the "pull factor" myth finally to rest', *euobserver*, October 4, 2023.
26. Hervé Le Bras, *L'Âge des migrations* (Paris: Autrement, 2017), 77.
27. Hein de Haas, Stephen Castles and Mark J. Miller, *The Age of Migration: International Population Movements in the Modern World* (New York and London: The Guilford Press, 2020), 38.
28. Ahuja, *Planetary Specters*, 12-13.
29. Andrew Baldwin and Giovanni Bettini, 'Introduction: Life Adrift', in *Life Adrift*, edited by Baldwin and Bettini, 6.
30. Amitav Ghosh, *The Nutmeg's Curse: Parables for a Planet in Crisis* (Chicago: University of Chicago Press, 2021), 154 and 157.

31. See Samuel Huckstep and Helen Dempster, 'The 'Climate Migration' Narrative Is Inaccurate, Harmful, and Pervasive. We Need an Alternative', Center for Global Development, December 5, 2023, https://www.cgdev.org/blog/climate-migration -narrative-inaccurate-harmful-and-pervasive-we-need-alternative.

32. Climate Change Group of the World Bank, 'Preparing for Internal Climate Migration', 2018, https://openknowledge.worldbank.org/entities/publication /2be91c76-d023-5809-9c94-d41b71c25635.

33. Climate Change Group of the World Bank, 'Acting on Internal Climate Migration', 2021, https://openknowledge.worldbank.org/entities/publication/2c9150df-52c3 -58ed-9075-d78ea56c3267.

34. Hein de Haas, *How Migration Really Works: The Facts About the Most Divisive Issue in Politics* (New York: Basic Books, 2023), 350, emphasis added. See Ian Smith and Lottie Limb, 'Will climate change really lead to more immigration? Here's what the experts think', Euronews, June 25, 2024, https://www.euronews.com/green /2024/06/25/will-climate-change-really-lead-to-more-immigration-heres-what -the-experts-think.

35. Ahuja, *Planetary Specters*, 45.

36. Sarah Bracke and Luis Manuel Hernández Aguilar, 'The Politics of Replacement: From "Race Suicide" to the "Great Replacement"', in *The Politics of Replacement: Demographic Fears, Conspiracy Theories, and Race Wars*, edited by Sarah Bracke and Luis Manuel Hernández Aguilar (London and New York: Routledge, 2024), 3.

37. Judith Butler, *Bodies that Matter: On the Discursive Limits of 'Sex'* (New York: Routledge, 1993), Elsa Dorlin, *La matrice de la race: généalogie sexuelle et coloniale de la nation Française* (Paris: La Découverte, 2006) and Françoise Vergès, *The Wombs of Women: Race, Capital, Feminism*, trans. K. L. Glover (Durham: Duke University Press, 2020).

38. Brown, *Migration and Climate Change*, 34-5. See Saskia Sassen, 'Women's Burden: Counter-geographies of Globalization: The Feminization of Survival', *Journal of International Affairs* 53, no. 2 (2000): 503-24. See Marjorie Cohen, ed., *Climate Change and Gender in Rich Countries* (London and New York: Routledge, 2017).

39. Carolyn Merchant, *The Death of Nature: Women, Ecology and the Scientific Revolution* (New York: Harper & Row, 1990 [1980]).

40. Ibid., 2.

41. See, for example, the work of Lorena Cabnal, who co-founded the community-ter-ritorial feminist movement in Guatemala and who, as Atamhi Cawayu and Sigrid Vertommen explain, has staged "the gendered interconnections between Indigenous bodies and lands as pivotal sites, battlefields or 'territories' of colonial control, extrac-tion, and exploitation and anticolonial resistance." See Atamhi Cawayu and Sigrid Vertommen, "Cuerpo-Territory/Body-Territory," *Kohl: a Journal for Body and Gender Research* 11, no. 1 (2025), https://kohljournal.press/cuerpo-territorio.

42. Frances Pine and Haldis Haukanes, 'Reconceptualising borders and boundaries: gender, movement, reproduction, regulation', in *Intimacy and Mobility in an Era of Hardening Borders: Gender, reproduction, regulation*, edited by Haldis Haukanes and Frances Pine (Manchester: Manchester University Press, 2021), 16.

43. Kyle Whyte, 'Indigenous Climate Change Studies: Indigenizing Futures, Decolonizing the Anthropocene', *English Language Notes* 55, no. 1-2 (Fall 2017): 156.

44. https://www.unhcr.org/us/what we do/how we work/safeguarding-individuals/ women.

45. Nicole Greenfield, 'What Is Climate Feminism?', Natural Resources Defense Council, March 18, 2021, https://www.nrdc.org/stories/what-climate-feminism.
46. Camille Schmoll, *Les damnées de la terre. Femmes et frontières en Méditerranée* (Paris: La Découverte, 2020).
47. See Smaïn Laacher, *De la violence à la persécution, femmes sur la route de l'exil* (Paris: La Dispute, 2010).
48. International Organization for Migration, 'Gender and Migration: Trends, Gaps and Urgent Action. Current context: from the feminization of migration to the growing global gap in migration,' 2024, https://worldmigrationreport.iom.int/what-we-do/world-migration-report-2024-chapter-6/current-context-feminization-migration-growing-global-gender-gap-migration. See Schmoll, *Les damnées de la terre*, 190-2.
49. Schmoll, *Les damnées de la terre*, 136.
50. Ursula Biemann, 'Performing the Border', in *Rethinking Marxism* 14, no.1 (2002): 29.
51. Schmoll, *Les damnées de la terre*, 169.
52. Ibid., 195.
53. See Claire Audhuy, *Les migrantes* (Strasbourg: Rodéo d'âme, 2016), Fatou Diome, *Celles qui attendent* (Paris: Flammarion, 2010), Marie NDiaye, *Three Strong Women*, trans. J. Fletcher (New York: Alfred A. Knopf, 2012) and Louis-Philippe Dallembert, *Mediterranean Wall*, trans. M. de Jager (Ashland: Schaffner Press, 2021).
54. As T.J. Demos has argued, 'figures can appear abstracted from complex determinants, detached from the vector of intersectionality that is migration [...] while the structural causes remain invisible', *Beyond the World's End: Arts of Living at the Crossing* (Durham, NC and London: Duke University Press, 2020), 82.
55. Christian Parenti, *Tropic of Chaos: Climate Change and the New Geography of Violence* (New York: Bold Type Books, 2012), 7.
56. Achille Mbembe, *La communauté terrestre* (Paris: La Découverte, 2023), 137 and 135. See Caroline Zickgraf, 'Where Are All the Climate Migrants? Explaining Immobility amid Environmental Change', Migration Policy Institute, October 4, 2023, https://www.migrationpolicy.org/article/climate-change-trapped-populations.
57. Haas, *How Migration Really Works*, 5 and 8. See Hein De Haas, 'Changing the Migration Narrative: On the Power of Discourse, Propaganda and Truth Distortion', IMI Working Paper Number 181/PACES Project Working Paper Number 3 (Amsterdam: University of Amsterdam, May 2024).
58. Christopher Priest, *Fugue for a Darkening Island* (London: Gollancz, 2011 [1972]), 54 and 20-1. See Anthony Mangeon, *L'Afrique au futur. Le renversement des mondes* (Paris: Hermann, 2022) for an in-depth analysis of a vast array of such dystopian narratives of this kind.
59. Priest, *Fugue for a Darkening Island*, 63 and vii.
60. Haas, *How Migration Really Works*, 16 and 16–7, emphasis added.
61. Ibid., 44 and 16.
62. Paul Gilroy, 'Foreword: Migrancy, Culture, and a New Map of Europe', in *Blackening Europe: The African American Presence*, edited by Heike Raphael-Hernandez (London: Routledge, 2004), xv. See Alec G. Hargreaves, *Multi-Ethnic France: Immigration, Politics, Culture and Society* (New York and London: Routledge,2007).
63. Elizabeth DeLoughrey, *Allegories of the Anthropocene* (Durham, NC: Duke University Press, 2019), 103.

64. Valeria Bello, *International Migration and International Security: Why Prejudice Is a Global Security Threat* (London and New York: Routledge, 2017), 3.

65. David Olusoga, 'There can be no excuses. The UK riots were violent racism fomented by populism', *The Guardian*, August 10, 2024.

66. Alessandro Dal Lago, *Non-Persons: The Exclusion of Migrants in a Global Society*, trans. M. Orton (Milan: IPOC Press, 2009), 69.

67. Ibid., 81.

68. Claire Rodier, *Xénophobie Business: À quoi servent les contrôles migratoires?* (Paris: La Découverte, 2012), 48 and 45.

69. Ibid., 14.

70. Achille Mbembe, 'Figures du Multiple: La France peut-elle réinventer son identité?', *Le Messager*, November 24, 2005.

71. Ghosh, *The Nutmeg's Curse*, 140 and Kathryn Yusoff, *A Billion Black Anthropocenes or None* (Minneapolis, MN: University of Minnesota Press, 2018), 60.

72. Chamoiseau, *Migrant Brothers*, 25 and 42.

73. Mangeon, *L'Afrique au futur*, 90. Matthew Carr explains that '"invasion" narratives were often based on hypotheses and fantasies rather than actual numbers', *Fortress Europe: Dispatches from a Gated Continent* (New York: The New Press, 2012), 22.

74. Paul Gilroy, *Postcolonial Melancholia* (New York: Columbia University Press, 2005), 2.

75. Nicolas Bancel, Pascal Blanchard and Ahmed Boubeker, *Le Grand Repli* (Paris: La Découverte, 2015), 167.

76. Caryl Phillips, *The European Tribe* (New York: Farrar Straus Giroux, 1987), 121 and 129.

77. See Étienne Balibar, *We, the People of Europe? Reflections on Transnational Citizenship*, trans. J. Swenson (Princeton, NJ: Princeton University Press, 2004).

78. See Fatima El-Tayeb, *European Others: Queering Ethnicity in Postnational Europe* (Minneapolis, MN: University of Minnesota Press, 2011).

79. See Jean-Yves Camus and Nicolas Lebourg, *Far-Right Politics in Europe*, trans. J. M. Todd (Cambridge, MA: The Belknap Press of Harvard University Press, 2017).

80. Cas Mudde, 'Geert Wilders' win shows we are in a new phase for the far right in western Europe', *The Guardian*, November 30, 2023.

81. Cas Mudde, *On Extremism and Democracy in Europe* (London and New York: Routledge, 2017).

82. David Smith, 'How Trump's Anti-immigrant Rhetoric is Taking Over the Republican Party', *The Guardian*, December 22, 2023. See Simon Hix et al., 'Immigration and Brexit', May 30, 2017, https://blogs.lse.ac.uk/politicsandpolicy/non-eu-migration-is -what-uk-voters-care-most-about/.

83. Rajeev Syal and Peter Walker, 'Suella Braverman: small boats plan will push boundaries of international law', *The Guardian*, March 7, 2023.

84. Suella Braverman, 'Keynote Address by UK Home Secretary Suella Braverman: UK-US Security Priorities for the 21st Century', American Enterprise Institute for Public Policy Research, Washington, DC, September 26, 2023.

85. Phillips, *The European Tribe*, 9. See Caryl Phillips, *Colour Me English* (London: Harvill Secker, 2011).

86. See Soumaya Majdoub, 'Malthusian Fears in Current Immigration Debates: Contemporary Manifestations of Malthusianization', in *The Politics of Replacement*, edited by Bracke and Aguilar, 23-36

87. Pascal Blanchard, 'Le passé colonial, un sujet incontournable de campagne', *Le NouvelObs*, March 29, 2022.

88. Adam Gabbatt, '"We're facing another old enemy": Rushdie warns against global authoritarianism', *Guardian*, September 13, 2023.

89. Gabbatt, '"We're facing another old enemy"'.

90. Douglas Murray, *The Strange Death of Europe: Immigration, Identity, Islam* (London: Bloomsbury Publishing, 2017).

91. Sonia Shah, *The Next Great Migration: The Beauty and Terror of Life on the Move* (New York: Bloomsbury Publishing, 2021), 12 and 14.

92. Ibid., 308.

93. Nicolas Bancel, Thomas David and Dominic Thomas, eds., *The Invention of Race: Scientific and Popular Representations* (New York and London: Routledge, 2014), 2.

94. Frantz Fanon, *The Wretched of the Earth*, trans. R. Philcox (New York: Grove Press, 2004 [1961]), 5.

95. Margaret Thatcher, *World in Action*, January 27, 1978, https://www.margaretthatcher .org/document/103485. See Evan Smith, '"Rather Swamped": Thatcher, Moral Panics and Racist hetoric', November 1, 2022, https://hatfulofhistory.wordpress .com/2022/11/01/rather-swamped-thatcher-moral-panics-and-racist-rhetoric/.

96. Brigitte Nehrlich, 'Invasion as a metaphor', November 4, 2022, https://blogs.nottingham.ac.uk/makingsciencepublic/2022/11/04/invasion-as-a-metaphor/.

97. Haas, *How Migration Really Works*, 31.

98. Ibid., 345 and 347.

99. Ahuja, *Planetary Specters*, 10-11.

100. See Claire Rodier with Catherine Portevin, *Migrants & Réfugiés. Réponse aux indécis, aux inquiets, aux réticents* (Paris: La Découverte, 2016).

101. Baldwin and Bettini, 'Introduction: Life Adrift', 3.

102. See Stephen Brain and Viktor Pál, eds., 'Introduction', in *Environmentalism under Authoritarian Regimes: Myth, Propaganda, Reality*, edited by Stephen Brain and Viktor Pál (Abington and New York, 2019).

103. Antoine Dubiau, *Écofascismes* (Caen: Grevis, 2023), 6.

104. Parenti, *Tropic of Chaos*, 223.

105. Balša Lubarda, *Far-Right Ecologism: Environmental Politics and the Far Right in Hungary and Poland* (London and New York: Routledge, 2024), 2.

106. Bernard Forchtner, 'Far-Right articulations of the natural environment: An introduction', in *The Far Right and the Environment: Politics, Discourse and Communication*, edited by Bernard Forchtner (London and New York: Routledge, 2020), 3 and 1-2.

107. Andreas Malm and the Zetkin Collective, *White Skin, Black Fuel: On the Danger of Fossil Fascism* (London and New York: Verso, 2021), 154. See Stéphane François, *La nouvelle droite et ses dissidences: identité, écologie et paganisme* (Lormont: Le Bord de l'Eau, 2021).

108. Lise Benoist, 'Nationalisme vert. Peut-on concilier nationalisme et écologie', in *Green Washing. Manuel pour dépolluer le débat public*, edited by Aurélien Berlan, Guillaume Carbou and Laure Teulières (Paris: Seuil, 2022), 146.

109. Salomi Boukala and Eirini Tountasaki, 'From black to green: Analysing Le Front National's "patriotic ecology"', in *The Far Right and the Environment*, edited by Forchtner, 72. See Hortense Chauvin and Clémence Michels, 'Marine Le Pen, à l'extrême opposé de l'écologie', *Reporterre*, April 20, 2022, https://reporterre.net/ Marine-Le-Pen-a-l-extreme-oppose-de-l-ecologie.

110. Boukala and Eirini Tountasaki, 'From black to green', 84.

111. David Theo Goldberg, *Dread: Facing Futureless Futures* (Cambridge: Polity Press, 2021), 164.

112. Lubarda, *Far-Right Ecologism*, 124.

113. Rassemblement National, *L'environnement pour une écologie française*, 2022, https://rassemblementnational.fr/documents/projet/projet-lecologie.pdf, 5 and 17.

114. Sindre Bangstad and Maria Darwish, 'Ecofascism and the Politics of Replacement in the Discourse of the Nordic Resistance Movement (NRM)', in *The Politics of Replacement*, edited by Bracke and Aguilar, 97.

115. Bangstad and Darwish, 'Ecofascism and the Politics of Replacement', 98. See Lou Mousset, '"Reverse Colonization", Early Narratives of Decline in the French New Right', in *The Politics of Replacement*, edited by Bracke and Aguilar, 66-81.

116. See Cas Mudde, 'The Hungary PM Made a "Rivers of Blood" Speech ... and No One Cares', *The Guardian*, July 30, 2015 and Michael Savage, 'Fifty Years On, What Is the Legacy of Enoch Powell's "Rivers of Blood" Speech?', *The Guardian*, April 14, 2018.

117. See Cécile Alduy, *Ce qu'ils disent vraiment. Les politiques pris aux mots* (Paris: Seuil, 2017).

118. Julia Ebner, *Going Dark: The Secret Lives of Extremists* (London: Bloomsbury, 2019), 247.

119. Éric Zemmour, *Le suicide français* (Paris: Albin Michel, 2014), a work that extends conclusions made previously by Jean Raspail, *Le Camp des saints* (Paris: Robert Laffont, 2011 [1973]). See Renaud Camus, *Le grand remplacement. Introduction au remplacisme global* (Paris: La Nouvelle Librairie, 2021 [2011]), Thilo Sarrazin *Deutschland schafft sich ab: Wie wir unser Land aufs Spiel setzen* (Munich: Deutsche Verlags-Anstalt 2010) and Murray, *The Strange Death of Europe*.

120. See Julia Ebner, "Conspiracy Theorists. Incels. White Nationalists. Dara Research and Technological Change," Distinguished Lecture in the Digital Humanities, University of California, Los Angeles, May 29, 2025. See Jakob Guhl, Julia Ebner and Jan Rau, "The Online Ecosystem of the German Far-Right," London, ISD, 2020: https://www.isdglobal.org/wp-content/uploads/2020/02/ISD-The-Online-Ecosystem-of-the-German-Far-Right-English-Draft-11.pdf.

121. Soumaya Majdoub, 'Malthusian Fears in Current Immigration Debates: Contemporary Manifestations of Malthusianization', in *The Politics of Replacement*, edited by Bracke and Aguilar, 23. See Hervé Le Bras, *Il n'y a pas de grand remplacement* (Paris: Grasset, 2022).

122. As Cécile Alduy has shown, 'Language, drained of its ability to make us think, listen and debate, becomes an instrument of anti-democratic perversion', *La Langue de Zemmour* (Paris: Seuil, 2022), 49.

123. Bram Frouws, 'Negative narratives, mistaken metaphors. The need for careful language on migration', Mixed Migration Center, March 8, 2021.

124. Sam Moore and Alex Roberts, *The Rise of Ecofascism: Climate Change and The Far Right* (Cambridge: Polity Press, 2022), 57.

125. Betsy Hartmann, 'The Ghosts of Malthus: Narratives and Mobilizations of Scarcity in the US Political Context', in *The Limits to Scarcity: Contesting the Politics of Allocation*, edited by Lyla Mehta (London and Washington, DC: Earthscan, 2010), 50 and Moore and Roberts, *The Rise of Ecofascism*, 126. See Larry Lohmann, 'Malthusianism and the terror of scarcity', in *Making Threats, Biofears and Environmental Anxieties*, edited by Betsy Hartmann, Banu Subramaniam and Charles Zerner (Lanham: Rowman and Littlefield, 2005), 81-98.

126. Carolin Emcke, *Against Hate*, trans. T. Crawford (Cambridge: Polity Press, 2019), 33.

127. Michel Agier, *La peur des autres. Essai sur l'indésirabilité* (Paris: Payot & Rivages, 2022), 44. See Karine Parrot, *Carte blanche: L'État contre les étrangers* (Paris: La Fabrique, 2023) and Karine Parrot, *Étranger* (Paris: Anamosa, 2023).

128. See Alexandra Minna Stern, *Proud Boys and the White Ethnostate: How the Alt-Right Is Warping the American Imagination* (Boston, MA: Beacon Press, 2020).

129. Gloria Wekker, *White Innocence: Paradoxes of Colonialism and Race* (Durham: Duke University Press, 2016), 4.

130. Ahuja, *Planetary Specters*, 15.

131. Ibid., 3.

132. Zygmunt Bauman, *Liquid Fear* (Cambridge: Polity Press, 2006), 2 and 15.

133. Ibid., 83.

134. Ibid., 15, translation slightly altered to align with the published translation of Jean-Pierre Dupuy, *How to Think About Catastrophe: Toward a Theory of Enlightened Doomsaying*, trans. M. B. DeBevoise and M. R. Anspach (East Lansing: Michigan State University Press, 2022 [2002]).

135. Cécile Alduy, Annie Collovald and Jean-Yves Pranchère, 'Les faillites du langage', *L'Esprit*, no. 502 (2023): 76. See Juli Zeh and Ilia Trojanow, *Atteinte à la liberté. Les dérives de l'obsession sécuritaire*, trans. P. Charbonneau (Arles: Actes Sud, 2010).

136. See Catherine et Raphaël Larrère, *Le pire n'est pas certain. Essai sur l'aveuglement catastrophiste* (Paris: Premier Parallèle, 2020).

137. Todd Miller, *Storming the Wall: Climate Change, Migration, and Homeland Security* (San Francisco, CA: City Lights Books, 2017), 27. British journalist and novelist John Lanchester has offered a dystopian synthesis of the multiple ways in which climate change and migration have emerged in the imaginative and political realm in his novel, *The Wall* (London: Faber & Faber, 2019). A ten thousand kilometer-long concrete wall (officially the National Coastal Defence Structure) divides the world between the 'Others' (climate migrants) and the 'Defenders' (commissioned for two years of national service to protect the homeland).

138. Hartmann, "The Ghosts of Malthus, 55.

139. Ibid., 30. See Harsha Walia, *Undoing Border Imperialism* (Oakland: AK Press, 2013) and Wendy Brown, *Walled States, Waning Sovereignty* (New York: Zone Books, 2014).

140. Kira Walker, 'As climate displacement increases, migration myths fuel fears', *Equal Times*, February 10, 2021. See Nicole Bates-Eamer, 'Border and Migration Controls and Migrant Precarity in the Context of Climate Change', *Social Sciences* 8, no. 7 (2019), https://www.mdpi.com/2076-0760/8/7/198.

141. United Nations, 'United Nations 1951 Convention and 1967 Protocol', accessed February 2, 2025, https://www.unhcr.org/sites/default/files/legacy-pdf/4ec262df9 .pdf, 3.

142. Simon Behrman and Avidan Kent, 'Overcoming the Legal Impasse: Setting the scene', in *'Climate Refugees': Beyond the Legal Impasse?*, edited by Simon Behrman and Avidan Kent (London and New York: Routledge, 2018), 6.

143. Sumudu Anopama Atapattu, 'A New category of Refugees? "Climate refugees" and a gaping hole in international law', in *'Climate Refugees*, edited by Behrman and Kent, 36. See Frank Biermann, 'Global Governance to Protect Future Climate Refugees', in *'Climate Refugees'*, edited by Behrman and Kent, 265-77.

144. Joanna Apap with Sami James Harju, 'The Concept of 'Climate Refugee': Towards a Possible Definition', European Union, 2023, https://www.europarl.europa.eu/ RegData/etudes/BRIE/2021/698753/EPRS_BRI(2021)698753_EN.pdf, 2 and 1.

145. International Organization for Migration, 'Migration and the Environment', November 1, 2007, https://www.iom.int/sites/g/files/tmzbdl486/files/jahia/webdav/shared/shared/mainsite/about_iom/en/council/94/MC_INF_288.pdf, 8 and 1-2.
146. Mariam Traore Chazalnoël and Dina Ionesco, 'Advancing the Global Governance of Climate Migration Through the United Nations Framework Convention on Climate Change and the Global Compact on Migration', in *'Climate Refugees'?*, edited by Behrman and Kent, 105–6.
147. International Organization for Migration, 'Environmental Migration', 2025, https://environmentalmigration.iom.int/environmental-migration.
148. Demos, *Beyond the World's End*, 80-81.
149. Ursula von der Leyen, 'Answering the Call of History: 2023 State of the Union Address', September 13, 2023, https://ec.europa.eu/commission/presscorner/detail/ov/speech_23_4426.
150. See Rüdiger K. W. Wurzel, Duncan Liefferink and James Connelly, 'Introduction: European Union climate leadership', in *The European Union in International Climate Change Politics*, edited by Rüdiger K. W. Wurzel, James Connelly and Duncan Liefferink (London and New York: Routledge, 2017), 3-19 and Jos Delbeke and Peter Vis, *EU Climate Policy Explained* (London and New York: Routledge, 2015).
151. European Commission, 'The European Green Deal: Striving to be the first climate-neutral continent,' 2024, https://commission.europa.eu/strategy-and-policy/priorities-2019-2024/european-green-deal_en.
152. European Environment Agency, European Climate Risk Assessment Executive summary, January 2024, 5 and 6, https://www.eea.europa.eu/publications/european-climate-risk-assessment.
153. Josep Borrell, 'European Diplomatic Academy: Opening Remarks by High Representative Josep Borrell at the Inauguration of the Pilot Programme', October 13, 2022, https://www.eeas.europa.eu/eeas/european-diplomatic-academy-opening-remarks-high-representative-josep-borrell-inauguration-pilot_en.
154. https://migrantsrights.org.uk/projects/wordsmatter/colonialism/
155. Walker, 'As climate displacement increases, migration myths fuel fears,'
156. Nehrlich, 'Invasion as a metaphor'.
157. Bram Frouws, 'Negative Narratives, Mistaken Metaphors. The Need for Careful Language on Migration', *Mixed Migration Centre*, March 8, 2021.
158. Dominic Thomas, 'Into the Jungle: Migration and Grammar in the New Europe', in *Postcolonial Cultures, Migration, and Racism* (Bloomington: Indiana University Press, 2013), 171.
159. Adrian Favell, *Philosophies of Integration: Immigration and the Idea of Citizenship in France and Britain* (New York: Palgrave, 2001), 105.
160. Frouws, "Negative narratives, mistaken metaphors."
161. Council of the European Union, 'European Pact on Immigration and Asylum', September 24, 2008, https://data.consilium.europa.eu/doc/document/ST-13440-2008-INIT/en/pdf.
162. https://www.frontex.europa.eu.
163. Frontex, Annual Risk Analysis 2024/2025, May 2024, https://www.frontex.europa.eu/assets/Publications/Risk_Analysis/Annual_Risk_Analysis_2024-2025.pdf.
164. Frontex, Annual Risk Analysis, 7 and 17.
165. Charles Heller, Nicholas De Genova, Maurice Stierl, Martina Tazzioli and Huub van Baar, 'Crisis', in *Europe/Crisis: New Keywords of 'the Crisis' in and of 'Europe'*, 2016,

https://nearfuturesonline.org/wp-content/uploads/2016/01/New-Keywords
-Collective_12.pdf., 22.

166. Louis Imbert, *Immigration: Fabrique d'un discours de crise* (Paris: 10/18, 2022), 87-8.

167. Ibid., 99 and 95.

168. Vincent Geisser, 'Le Pacte européen sur l'immigration et l'asile ou le triomphe de la "frontexisation" des esprits', *Migrations Société* 5, no. 119 (2008): 3-12.

169. European Commission, 'Pact on Migration and Asylum', May 21, 2024, https://home-affairs.ec.europa.eu/policies/migration-and-asylum/pact-migration-and-asylum_en.

170. Ankita Dutta, 'Unpacking the EU's migration deal', Observer Research Foundation, July 4, 2023.

171. Council of the European Union, 'Migration Policy: Council Reaches Agreement on Key Asylum and Migration Laws', June 8, 2023, https://home-affairs.ec.europa.eu/policies/migration-and-asylum/common-european-asylum-system/country-responsible-asylum-application-dublin-regulation_en.

172. European Commission, 'A humane and effective return and readmission policy', 2024, https://home-affairs.ec.europa.eu/policies/migration-and-asylum/irregular-migration-and-return/humane-and-effective-return-nd-readmission-policy_en. See Thomas, *Africa and France*, 49 and 84.

173. European Commission, '10-point Plan for Lampedusa', September 17, 2023, https://ec.europa.eu/commission/presscorner/detail/en/IP_23_4503.

174. See Philippe Jacqué, 'The EU Wants to Outsource Immigration Management', *Le Monde*, November 20, 2023.

175. Rodier, *Xénophobie Business*, 108.

176. Ibid., 184.

177. Francesca De Benedetti, 'Ursula von der Leyen Is Taking Europe to the Right', *Jacobin*, September 24, 2023.

178. Francesca De Benedetti, 'Giorgia Meloni Is Orbánizing the European Union', *Jacobin*, February 2, 2024.

179. Leyen, 'Answering the Call of History'.

180. Stéphane Foucart, 'Pour la première fois, toute l'Union européenne a enclenché la marche arrière sur l'environnement', *Le Monde*, November 26, 2023.

181. 'L'extrême droite en Europe abattra-t-elle le Pacte vert? Une carte inédite', *Le Grand Continent*, September 16, 2023.

182. Presidential Transition Project (Project 2025), accessed February 2, 2025, https://www.project2025.org.

183. Andy Bounds, 'Climate regulation is driving support for populism, says EU parliament chief', *Financial Times*, September 7, 2023.

184. International Organization for Migration, 'Strategy on Migration, Environment and Climate Change, 2021-2030.' https://environmentalmigration.iom.int/iom-strategy-migration-environment-and-climate-change-2021-2030.

185. Apap with Harju, 'The concept of "climate refugee"', 10.

186. Arjun Appadurai, *Modernity at Large: Cultural Dimensions of Globalization* (Minneapolis, MN: University of Minnesota Press, 1996), 156.

187. Achille Mbembe, 'Bodies as Borders', *From the European South*, no. 4 (2019), 5.

188. See Nicole Greenfield, 'Climate Migration and Equity', Natural Resources Defense Council, May 9, 2022, https://www.nrdc.org/stories/climate-migration-equity.

189. See Astrid Mignon Colombet and Alfred Reboul, 'Justice climatique: les limites du *name and shame*', *L'Esprit*, no. 502 (2023): 10-13.
190. Jenny Erpenbeck, *Go, Went, Gone*, trans. S. Bernofsky (New York: New Directions Books, 2017). See James Wood, 'A Novelist's Powerful Response to the Refugee Crisis', *The New Yorker*, September 25, 2017.
191. Juli Zeh, *About People*, trans. A. L. Price (New York: World Editions, 2023), 102.
192. Ibid., 312.
193. Baptiste Morizot, *Ways of Being Alive*, trans. A. Brown (Cambridge: Polity Press), 187.
194. Ibid., 13.
195. Claire Rodier, 'Migrations: choix politique ou responsabilité collective', *France Culture Radio*, October 8, 2013, https://www.dailymotion.com/video/x15ojw5.
196. Brown, *Walled States, Waning Sovereignty*, 7.
197. Mbembe, 'Scrap the borders that divide Africans'.
198. Mbembe, 'Bodies as Borders', 16.
199. Pope Francis, 'Moment of Reflection with Religious Leaders Near the Memorial Dedicated to Sailors and Migrants Lost at Sea', September 22, 2023, https://www .vatican.va/content/francesco/en/speeches/2023/september/documents/20230922 -marsiglia-leaderreligiosi.html.
200. Adichie, 'The Danger of a Single Story'.

Chapter 3

1. Susan Sontag, 'The Art of Fiction', interviewed by Edward Hirsch, *The Paris Review*, Issue 137 (Winter 1995), https://www.theparisreview.org/interviews/1505/the-art -of-fiction-no-143-susan-sontag.
2. Patrick Chamoiseau, *Migrant Brothers: A Poet's Declaration of Human Dignity*, trans. M. Amos and F. Rönnbäck (New Haven, CT: Yale University Press, 2018 [2017]), 8.
3. Estelle Zhong Mengual, *Apprendre à voir. Le point de vue du vivant* (Arles: Actes Sud, 2021), 19.
4. Kehinde Wiley, 'An Archaeology of Silence: Exhibition', The Museum of Fine Arts, Houston, TX, November 19, 2023 to May 27, 2024.
5. Tate Britain, 'Six Ways J.M.W. Turner Painted a Changing World', Turner's Modern World Exhibition, October 28, 2020 to September 12, 2021.
6. In *Africa and France: Postcolonial Cultures, Migration, and Racism* (Bloomington:Indiana University Press, 2013), I previously argued that works of literature focusing on Mediterranean migrations compelled us 'to reflect additionally on the limits of empathy and tolerance and how literature can articulate such frameworks, particularly as a way of countering the debasing official discourse and accompanying claims that Europe is being invaded and its social fabric eroded', 166.
7. Ariel Dorfman and Viet Thanh Nguyen, 'The Displaced: Refugee Writers Ariel Dorfman and Viet Thanh Nguyen on Migration, US Wars & Resistance', *Democracy Now!*, May 4, 2018, https://z.umn.edu/44c6.
8. Viet Thanh Nguyen, 'Introduction', in *The Displaced: Refugee Writers on Refugee Lives*, edited by Viet Thanh Nguyen (New York: Abrams Press, 2018), 17.
9. See Jørgen Bruhn and Niklas Salmose, eds., *Intermedial Ecocriticism: The Climate Crisis Through Art and Media* (Lanham: Lexington Books, 2023).

10. David Palumbo-Liu, *The Deliverance of Others: Reading Literature in a Global Age* (Durham, NC: Duke University Press, 2012), 2.

11. Ibid., 1.

12. Ibid., 8.

13. Amy Coplan and Peter Goldie, 'Introduction', in *Empathy: Philosophical and Psychological Perspectives*, edited by Amy Coplan and Peter Goldie (New York: Oxford University Press, 2014), xxxii and xxxi.

14. Graham McFee, 'Empathy: Interpersonal vs Artistic', in *Empathy*, edited by Coplan and Goldie, 192.

15. Martha Nussbaum, *Upheavals of Thought: The Intelligence of Emotions* (New York: Cambridge University Press, 2001), 302.

16. In *Arendt's Solidarity: Anti-Semitism & Racism in the Atlantic World* (Stanford, CA: Stanford University Press, 2024), David Kim interrogates notions of equality, freedom and violence in Hannah Arendt's work, highlighting an especially relevant dimension: 'in a globalized world, it was essential to transcend borders via imagination and to judge political experiences from even greater pluralistic perspectives', 164.

17. Johannes Lang, 'Explaining Genocide: Hannah Arendt and the Social-Scientific Concept of Dehumanization', in Peter Baehr and Philip Walsh, eds., *The Anthem Companion to Hannah Arendt* (New York: Anthem Press,2017), 187 and 188.

18. Rebecca Adami, 'Human rights for more than one voice: rethinking political space beyond the global/local divide', *Ethics & Global Politics* 7, no. 4 (2014): 168.

19. Coplan and Goldie, 'Introduction', xxxvii.

20. See Karen Akofa, *L'Asile et l'Exil. Une histoire de la distinction réfugié/migrants* (Paris: La Découverte, 2020).

21. Deborah R. Coen, *Climate in Motion: Science, Empire, and the Problem of Scale* (Chicago: University of Chicago Press, 2018), 360.

22. Anat Tzom Ayalon, 'A Tiny Boat Lost at Sea: Trauma and Ethics in *Havarie* [*Collision*] by Philip Scheffner (Germany, 2016)', *Ekphrasis* 23, no. 3 (2020): 33 and 36.

23. Brigitta Wagner, 'A Shared Space at Eye Level: An Interview with Documentary Filmmaker Philip Scheffner', *Senses of Cinema*, Issue 78, March 2016, https://www.sensesofcinema.com/2016/feature-articles/philip-scheffner-interview/.

24. Ibid.

25. T.J. Demos, *The Migrant Image: The Art and Politics of Documentary during Global Crisis* (Durham, NC: Duke University Press, 2013), 208.

26. Isabella Nathani-Alexander, *The Burning: The Untold Story of the Africa's Migrant Crisis* (2023), accessed September 12, 2024, https://www.smallworldfilms.org.

27. Brad Evans, 'Dead in the Waters', in *Life Adrift: Climate Change, Migration, Critique*, edited by Andrew Baldwin and Giovanni Bettini (London and New York: Rowman & Littlefield International, Ltd., 2017), 60-1.

28. Felwine Sarr, *Habiter le monde. Essai de politique relationnelle* (Montreal: Mémoire d'encrier, 2017), 13-14. Byung-Chul Han has evoked how "Stories unite people by promoting their capacity for empathy," in *The crisis of narration*, trans. D. Steuer (Cambridge: Polity Press, 2024 [2023]), x-xi.

29. Federica Mazzara, *Reframing Migration: Lampedusa, Border Spectacle and aesthetics of Subversion* (Oxford: Peter Lang, 2019), 44.

30. T. J. Demos, *Beyond the World's End: Arts of Living at the Crossing* (Durham, NC and London: Duke University Press, 2020), 76–7.

31. Christine Ross, *Art for Coexistence: Unlearning the Way We See Migration* (Cambridge, MA and London: The MIT Press, 2022), 9.
32. Mazzara, *Reframing Migration*, 51.
33. Susan Sontag, *Regarding the Pain of Others* (New York: Farrar, Straus and Giroux, 2003), 102–3.
34. Mazzara, *Reframing Migration*, 134.
35. Demos, *Beyond the World's End*, 69.
36. Mieke Bal, 'Documenting What? Auto-Theory and Migratory Aesthetics', in *A Contemporary Guide to Documentary Film*, edited by Alexandra Juhasz and Alisa Lebow (Chichester: John Wiley & Sons, Inc., 2015), 132. Though indebted to Mieke Bal's term, Glenda R. Carpio, does not embrace the 'emphasis on identity' and instead privileges 'the political and social realities of migration, focusing on the aesthetic forms through which it is represented', *Migrant Aesthetics: Contemporary Fiction, Global Migration, and the Limits of Empathy* (New York: Columbia University Press, 2023), 24.
37. Ross, *Art for Coexistence*, 16. See Sam Durrant and Catherine M. Lord, eds., *Essays in Migratory Aesthetics: Cultural Practices Between Migration and Art-Making* (Amsterdam: Rodopi, 2007).
38. Michael Rothberg, *Multidirectional Memory: Remembering the Holocaust in the Age of Decolonization* (Stanford, CA: Stanford University Press, 2009), 6. See Karina Horsti and Ilaria Tucci, 'Performance of Memory: Testimonies of Survival and Rescue at Europe's Border', in *A Contemporary Guide to Documentary Film*, edited by Johan Schimanski and Jopi Nyman (Manchester: Manchester University Press, 2021), 225–41.
39. Achille Mbembe, *Critique of Black Reason*, trans. L. Dubois (Durham, NC: Duke University Press, 2017 [2013]), 1 and 2.
40. Pierre Tevanian and Jean-Charles Stevens, *"On ne peut accueillir toute la misère du monde": En finir avec une sentence de mort* (Paris: Anamosa, 2022), 7 and 13.
41. Achille Mbembe, 'Thoughts on the Planetary', 2019, https://www.newframe.com/thoughts-on-the-planetary-an-interview-with-achille-mbembe/.
42. Mengual, *Apprendre à voir*, 19.
43. Baptiste Morizot, *Ways of Being Alive*, trans. R. Powers (Cambridge: Polity, 2022 [2020]), 46, cited here in Mengual, *Aprendre à voir*, 229.
44. Ibid., 5.
45. Ibid., 207.
46. Ibid., 225.
47. Ato Quayson, 'Stories and Empathy in a Time of Crisis: An African Viewpoint', *African Studies Review* 65, no. 4 (2022): 967.
48. Wole Soyinka, *Climate of Fear: The Quest for Dignity in a Dehumanized World* (New York: Random House, 2005), xxi and xiv.
49. Michel Agier, *La peur des autres. Essai sur l'indésirabilité* (Paris: Payot & Rivages, 2022), 63 and 61. See Thomas, *Africa and France*, 156-68.
50. Massama Mbaye, 'Senegal', in *Foreigners Everywhere - Stranieri Ovunque Volume 2*, edited by Flavia Fossa Margutti, Venice Biennale, 2024, 144.
51. Patrick Chamoiseau and Michel Le Bris, 'Introduction: "Là où littérature ne peut"', in *Osons la fraternité. Les écrivains aux côtés des migrants*, edited by Patrick Chamoiseau and Michel Le Bris (Paris: Philippe Rey, 2018), 10.
52. Wilfried N'Sondé, 'Sang frontières,' in *Osons la fraternité*, edited by Chamoiseau and Le Bris, 55-62.

53. See T.J. Demos, *Radical Futurisms: Ecologies of Collapse, Chronopolitics, and Justice-to-Come* (New York: Sternberg Press, 2023).

54. Fatima Bhutto, 'Flesh and Sand', in *The Displaced*, edited by Nguyen, 43.

55. Susan Feagin, 'Empathizing as Simulating', in *Empathy*, edited by Coplan and Goldie, 150-1.

56. Gregory Currie, 'Empathy for Objects', in *Empathy*, edited by Coplan and Goldie, 88. This is among the works explored in Ross, *Art for Coexistence*, 196-210.

57. Nguyen, 'Introduction', in *The Displaced*, 2–13.

58. Frances Stonor Saunders, 'Where on Earth are you', *London Review of Books* 38, no. 5, March 3, 2016.

59. Ai Weiwei, 'The Refugee Crisis Isn't About Refugees. It's About Us', *The Guardian*, February 2, 2018.

60. See Hans-Jürgen Schlamp, 'Flüchtlingsdrama vor Lampedusa: Europas Versagen,' *Der Spiegel*, October 3, 2013 and Vincent Delecroix, *Naufrage* (Paris: Gallimard: 2023).

61. Václav Havel, 'Speech to United States Congress,' *Washington Post*, February 21, 1990.

62. Jiř í Fajt and Adam Budak, 'Ai Weiwei: Law of the Journey', Národní galerie v Praze (Prague National Gallery, March 17, 2017 to July 1, 2018), https://www.ngprague.cz /en/event/153/aj-wej-wej.

63. See Dina Siegel, 'The 'Crises' of Lesbos', *Utrecht Law Review* 17, no. 4 (2021): 10–8.

64. Fajt and Budak, 'Ai Weiwei: Law of the Journey.'

65. Ibid.

66. Ai Weiwei, *1000 Years of Joys and Sorrows: A Memoir*, trans. A. H. Barr (New York: Crown, 2021), 368.

67. Demos, *The Migrant Image*, 209.

68. Ibid., xiv and xv.

69. Ibid., 208.

70. Morizot, *Ways of Being Alive*, 213.

71. Valérie Marin La Meslée, 'Achille Mbembe: L'insurrection se fera par l'éducation', *Le Point Afrique*, February 3, 2018.

72. Martha Nussbaum, *Poetic Justice: Literary Imagination and Public Life* (Boston, MA: Beacon Press, 1995), 66.

73. Fajt and Budak, 'Ai Weiwei: Law of the Journey.' N.B. 'Das Gesetz der Fahrt' translates as 'law of travel', but Franz Kafka's original work was published in 1915 as 'Vor dem Gesetz', which translates as 'before the Law'.

74. Aimee Dawson, 'Interview with Ai Weiwei', *The Art Newspaper*, March 27, 2018.

75. Gualtiero Zambonini, 'The Evolution of German Media Coverage of Migration', Migration Policy Institute, 2009, https://www.migrationpolicy.org/sites/default/ files/publications/TCM-GermanMedia.pdf, 1 and 3.

76. Ross, *Art for Coexistence*, 191.

77. Chiara Brambilla, 'In/visibilities beyond the Spectacularisation: Young People, Subjectivity and Revolutionary Border Imaginations in the Mediterranean Borderscape', in *Border Images, Border Narratives*, edited by Schimanski and Nyman, 84.

78. Ross, *Art for Coexistence*, 187 and 191.

79. Ibid., 187.

80. Demos, *Beyond the World's End*, 85.

81. Carpio, *Migrant Aesthetics*, 8.

82. Ibid., 11 and 13.

83. Ai Weiwei, *Dans la peau de l'étranger*, trans. B. Commengé (Arles: Actes Sud, 2020 [2019]), 39.

84. Sontag, 'The Art of Fiction'.

85. Weiwei, *Dans la peau de l'étranger*, 38. As Ai Weiwei has argued, this entails a reckoning with the degree to which 'our prejudices are man-made', in Ai Weiwei and Hans Ulrich Obrist, *Ai Weiwei Speaks with Hans Ulrich Obrist* (London: Penguin Books, 2016),156.

86. Juan Gabriel Vásquez, *La traduction du monde*, trans. I. Gugnon (Paris: Seuil, 2025), 43.

87. Vásquez, *La traduction du monde*, 45 and Hannah Arendt, 'Truth and Politics', in *Between past and Future: Eight Exercises in Political Thought* (New York: Penguin Books, 1977) [1967], 237.

88. Michel Agier, Filippo Furri et Carolina Kobelinsky, 'L'indifférence face aux morts en Méditerranée est le signe d'un effondrement en humanité', *Le Monde*, July 25, 2023.

89. Demos, *Beyond the World's End*, 38 and Jacques Rancière, *The Emancipated Spectator*, trans. G. Eliot (London: Verso, 2009 [2008]).

90. Bruno David, ed., *Manifeste du muséum: Migrations* (Paris: Muséum National d'Histoire Naturelle, 2018), 76.

91. See Hakim Abderrezak, *Ex-Centric Migrations: Europe and the Maghreb in Mediterranean Cinema, Literature, and Music* (Bloomington, IN: Indiana University Press, 2016).

92. Hakim Abderrezak, 'The Mediterranean Sieve, Spring and Seametery', in *Refugee Imaginaries: Research Across the Humanities*, edited by Emma Cox, Sam Durrant, David Farrier, Lyndsey Stonebridge and Agnes Woolley (Edinburgh: Edinburgh University Press, 2020), 373, emphasis added.

93. Ibid., 379.

94. Maite Zubiaurre, *Talking Trash: Cultural Uses of Waste* (Nashville: Vanderbilt University Press, 2019), 95.

95. Ibid., 98.

96. See the analysis of the interaction between 'border studies' and 'border poetics' by Nyman and Schimanski, 'Introduction: images and narratives on the border', in *Border Images, Border Narratives*, edited by Schimanski and Nyman, 6. See also Chiara Brambilla, 'Exploring the Critical Potential of the Borderscapes Concept', *Geopolitics* 20, no. 1 (2015): 14-34 and Elena Dell'Agnese and Anne-Laure Amilhat Szary, 'Borderscapes: From border landscapes to border aesthetics', *Geopolitics* 20, no. 1 (2015): 4-13.

97. Susan D. Moeller, *Compassion Fatigue: How the Media Sell Disease, Famine, War and Death* (New York: Routledge, 1999).

98. Abderrezak, 'The Mediterranean Sieve, Spring and Seametery', 372.

99. Chamoiseau, *Migrant Brothers*, 69.

100. http://www.zalab.org/en/.

101. Ibid.

102. Mbembe, *Critique of Black Reason*, 173.

103. Erri De Luca, 'Saving Lives at Sea: Onboard a Migrant Rescue Ship in the Mediterranean', June 6, 2017, https://lithub.com/saving-lives-at-sea-onboard-a-migrant-rescue-ship-in-the-mediterranean/.

104. Nathacha Appanah, *Tropic of Violence*, trans. G. Strachan (Minneapolis, MN. Graywolf Press, 2020 [2016]).

105. Mohamed Mbougar Sarr, *The Silence of the Choir*, trans. A. Anderson (New York: Europa editions 2024 [2017]).
106. Ibid., 58.
107. Ibid., 58.
108. https://underwatersculpture.com/projects/museo-atlantico-lanzarote/.
109. Susan Smillie, 'Drowned world: welcome to Europe's first undersea sculpture museum', *The Guardian*, February 2, 2016.
110. Chamoiseau, *Migrant Brothers*, 103.
111. Lucinda Joly, 'The many extraordinary iterations of The Raft of the Medusa', *Daily Maverick*, October 24, 2022.
112. Ross, *Art for Coexistence*, 2-3.
113. Ibid., 15.
114. Heather Stewart and Rowena Mason, "Nigel Farage's Anti-migrant Poster Reported to Police," *The Guardian*, June 16, 2026.
115. See Paulus Kaufmann, Hannes Kuch, Christian Neuhaüser and Elaine Webster, eds., *Humiliation, Degradation, Dehumanization: Human Dignity Violated* (New York: Springer, 2011).
116. Demos, *Beyond the World's End*, 21.
117. Saskia Sassen, 'A Massive Loss of Habitat: New Drivers for Migration', *Sociology of Development* 2, no. 2 (2016): 223.
118. Achille Mbembe 'The Earthly Community', The Holberg Lecture, June 5, 2024, https://holbergprize.org/en/news/holberg-prize/2024-holberg-lecture-achille-mbembe
119. Philippe Descola, *Beyond Nature and Culture*, trans. Janet Lloyd (Chicago: University of Chicago Press, 2013), 307 and 310.
120. Amanda Gorman, 'In Memory of Those Still in the Water', *New York Times*, July 15, 2023.
121. Ibid.
122. Ibid.
123. Ibid.

Chapter 4

1. Ken Saro-Wiwa, 'The Call', in *Silence Would be Treason: Last writings of Ken Saro-Wiwa*, edited by Íde Corley, Helen Fallon and Laurence Cox (Nairobi: Daraja Press, 2018), 167.
2. Édouard Glissant, *Caribbean Discourse: Selected Essays*, trans. J. M. Dash (Charlottesville, VA: University Press of Virginia, 1989 [1981]), 105, emphasis added.
3. Cheryll Glotfelty, 'Literary Studies in an Age of Environmental Crisis', in *The Ecocriticism Reader: Landmarks in Literary Ecology*, edited by Cheryll Glotfelty and Harold Fromm (Athens, GA: University of Georgia Press, 1996), xix.
4. See Byron Caminero-Santangelo, *Different Shades of Green: African Literature, Environmental Justice, and Political Ecology* (Charlotteville: University of Virginia Press, 20.
5. Baptiste Morizot, *Ways of Being Alive*, trans. A. Brown (Cambridge: Polity, 2022 [2020]), 4.
6. Ursula K. Heise, *Sense of Place and Sense of Planet: The Environmental Imagination of the Global* (New York: Oxford University Press, 2008), 205.
7. Étienne Goyémidé, *Le silence de la forêt* (Paris: Hatier, 1984) and Cheikh C. Sow, *Cycle de sécheresse* (Paris: Hatier, 1983), 23. Other indicative works (among numerous

others) would include Assitou Ndinga, *Les Marchands du développement durable* (Paris: L'Harmattan, 2006) and El Yezid Yezid, *Tazadit la mine de fer* (Paris: L'Harmattan, 2021).

8. Kathryn Yusoff, *A Billion Black Anthropocenes or None* (Minneapolis, MN: University of Minnesota Press, 2018), 34.

9. Tanella Boni, 'The Polluting of the World and the Silence of African Writer', *Journal of the African Studies Association* 5, no. 1 (2010): 25-36.

10. Janice Spleth, 'Exploring the Gendered Nature of National Violence: The Intersection of Patriarchy and Civil Conflict in Tanella Boni's *Matins de couvre-feu (Mornings Under Curfew)*', *Wagadu: A Journal of Transnational Women's & Gender Studies* 18, Issue 1 (2017): 141.

11. Boni, 'The Polluting of the World', 27.

12. Morizot, *Ways of Being Alive*, 5.

13. Estelle Zhong Mengual, *Apprendre à voir: Le point de vue du vivant* (Arles: Actes Sud, 2021), 239 and 16-17.

14. Pierre Schoentjes, *Littérature et écologie: Le Mur des abeilles* (Paris: Corti, 2020), 83 and 14.

15. Pascale Casanova, *The World Republic of Letters*, trans. M. B. DeBevoise (Cambridge, MA: Harvard University Press, 2004) and 'Toward a World Literature in French', trans. D. Simon, *World Literature Today* 83, no. 2 (March-April 2009), 54-6.

16. Michel Collot, *Un nouveau sentiment de la nature* (Paris: Corti, 2022), 177.

17. Alexandre Gefen, 'De l'écologie à l'écocritique', *Revue Esprit* 472 (March 2021): 149. See Alexandre Gefen, *Réparer le monde. La littérature française face au XXIᵉ siècle* (Paris: Corti, 2017).

18. Heise, *Sense of Place and Sense of Planet*, 62.

19. Mongo Beti, 'Romancing Africa', in *Cruel City* by Mongo Béti, trans. P. Higginson (Bloomington: Indiana University Press, 2013 [1955]), xxi.

20. Alex A. Moulton and Inge Salo, 'Black Geographies and Black Ecologies as Insurgent Ecocriticism', *Environment and Society: Advances in Research* 13 (2022): 156.

21. Guy Ossito Midiohouan, 'Le créateur négro-africain et l'environnement: de la contemplation à l'engagement', *Mots Pluriels* 11 (September 1999), https://motspluriels.arts.uwa.edu.au/MP1199gom.html.

22. Ibid.

23. Amitav Ghosh, *The Great Derangement: Climate Change and the Unthinkable* (Chicago: University of Chicago Press, 2016), 128.

24. See James P. Daughton, *In the Forest of No Joy: The Tragedy of the Congo-Océan Railroad and the Tragedy of French Colonialism* (New York: W. W. Norton, 2021).

25. A digital platform, 'Anthologie écopoétique située des arts et des littératures', developed at the University of Paris Sorbonne Nouvelle, offers a search engine in which two filters (*artistic forms* and *environmental issues*) provide information on different works (fiction and non-fiction) focusing (primarily) on African countries: https://ecopoetique.huma-num.fr/.

26. Emma Carenini, *Soleil: Mythes, histoire et sociétés* (Paris: Le Pommier / Humensis, 2022), 149.

27. Alain Romestaing, Pierre Schoentjes and Anne Simon, 'Essor d'une conscience littéraire de l'environnement', *Revue critique de fixxion française contemporaine* 11 (2015), https://journals.openedition.org/fixxion/8389.

28. Ato Quayson, "Anatomizing a Postcolonial Tragedy: Ken Saro Wiwa and the Ogoni," *Performance Research* 1, no. 2 (1996): 83-92.

29. Ben De Bruyn, 'The Great Displacement: Reading Migration Fiction at the End of the World', *Humanities* 9, no. 25 (2020): 4.

30. Gwennäel Gaffric, *La Littérature à l'ère de l'Anthroposcène. Une étude écocritique autour des œuvres de l'écrivain taïwanais Wu Ming-yi* (Le Pré-Saint-Gervais: L'Asiathèque, 2019), 25. See Jennifer Wenzel, *The Disposition of Nature: Environmental Crisis and World Literature* (New York: Fordham University Press, 2019).

31. Khalil Diallo, *L'odyssée des oubliés* (Paris: Emmanuelle Colas, 2021), 15-16, Djali Amadou Amal, *Cœur du Sahel* (Paris: Emmanuelle Collas, 2022) and Diadié Dembélé, *Deux grands hommes et demi* (Paris: Jean-Claude Lattès, 2024), 60.

32. See Andrew Curley and Sara Smith, 'The Cene Scene: Who Gets to Theorize Global Time and How Do We Center Indigenous and Black Futurities?', *Environment and Planning E: Nature and Space* 7, no. 1 (2024): 169.

33. Amitav Ghosh, *The Nutmeg's Curse: Parables for a Planet in Crisis* (Chicago: University of Chicago Press, 2021), 204.

34. Gauz', *Comrade Papa*, trans. F. Wynne (Windsor: Biblioasis, 2024 [2018]) and Gauz', *Cocoaïans (naissance d'une nation chocolat)* (Paris: L'arche, 2022).

35. The Congo Basin's rainforests have been compromised, leaving little hope of climate mitigation. Henri Djombo's and Osée Colin Koagne's play *Le Cri de la forêt* (Paris: LC Éditions / Éditions Hermar, 2015) explores these circumstances.

36. See Sean Mobray, 'Delectable but destructive: Tracing chocolate's environmental life cycle', *Mongabay*, August 1, 2022.

37. Food and Agriculture Organization of the United Nations, 'Construire une culture cacaoyère résiliente en Côte d'Ivoire', July 22, 2022, https://www.fao.org/cote-divoire/actualites/detail-events/fr/c/1601694/.

38. Gauz', "Les rêves de Kong de Binger," in *Penser et écrire l'Afrique aujourd'hui*, edited by Alain Mabanckou (Paris: Seuil, 2017), 182–7.

39. Ibid., 182, emphasis added.

40. Ibid., 183, emphasis added.

41. Ibid., 186.

42. Ibid., 187.

43. Ninon Chavoz, 'From the *Roi de Kahel* to *Camarade Papa*: The Itinerary of a Spoiled Colonial', trans. J. Angell, *Politika*, April 24, 2023, https://www.politika.io/en/article/from-the-roi-kahel-to-camarade-papa-the-itinerary-of-a-spoiled-colonial.

44. Ibid. See Pascal Blanchard, Nicolas Bancel, Gilles Böetsch, Christelle Taraud and Dominic Thomas, eds., *Sexe, race et colonies: La domination des corps du XVè siècle à nos jours* (Paris: La Découverte, 2018).

45. Marie Poinsot, 'Gauz, *Camarade Papa*', *Hommes & Migrations* 1, no. 1324 (2019): 173-74.

46. Frantz Fanon, *Black Skin, White Masks*, trans. R. Philcox (New York: Grove Press, 2008 [1952]).

47. David Murphy, 'Representations of the *tirailleur sénégalais* and World War I', in *Visualizing Empire: Africa, Europe, and the Politics of Representation*, edited by Rebecca Peabody, Steven Nelson and Dominic Thomas (Los Angeles: Getty Publications, 2021), 118.

48. Chavoz, 'From the *Roi de Kahel* to *Camarade Papa*.'

49. Gauz', *Comrade Papa*, 68.

50. Ibid.,69.

51. Ibid., 81.
52. Gauz', *Cocoaïans*, 20.
53. Ibid., 51.
54. Ibid., 19.
55. Camara Laye, *The Dark Child*, trans. J. Kirkup and E. Jones (New York: Farrar, Straus & Giroux, 1954), 75.
56. Gauz', *Cocoaïans*, 75.
57. Ibid., 18.
58. Jean-Louis Kouakou, Sery Gonedelé Bi, Eloi Anderson Bitty, Célestin Kouakou, Alphonse Kouassi Yao, Kouadio Bénoîtype Kassé and Soulemane Ouattara, 'Ivory Coast without ivory: Massive extinction of African forest elephants in Côte d'Ivoire', *PloS One* 15, no. 10 (2020), 1.
59. Gauz', *Cocoaïans*, 82 and 35.
60. Ibid., 104.
61. Ibid., 75.
62. Ibid., 13.
63. Elara Bertho, 'Du chocolat, du sang et des larmes *(Cocoaïans)*', *Diacritik*, October 13, 2022, https://diacritik.com/2022/10/13/gauz-du-chocolat-du-sang-et-des-larmes-cocoaians/.
64. Ibid., emphasis added.
65. Caroline Meva, *La science des sorciers de Koba* (Paris: Saint-Honoré, 2021), 86.
66. Baltazar Atanganga, 'Discours sur l'environnement: Entretien avec Caroline Meva', *La Pépinière*, November 30, 2023, https://lapepinieregeneve.ch/discours-sur-lenvironnement-entretien-avec-caroline-meva/.
67. Samy Manga, *Chocolaté. Le goût amer de la culture du cacao* (Montreal: Écosociété, 2023).
68. Chanelle Leclerc, 'Samy Manga and the bitter taste of the cacao culture in Africa', *Cacao Source*, 2023, https://www.sourcecacao.com/es_GT/blog/viajes-1/samy-manga-and-the-bitter-taste-of-the-cacao-culture-in-africa-46
69. Manga, *Chocolaté*, 110.
70. Ibid., 103.
71. Ibid., 87.
72. Ibid., 106. This is a variation of the proverb according to which "Until the lion tells the story, the hunter will always be the hero."
73. Samy Manga, *La dent de Lumumba: Régicide contre la Colonie* (Brussels: Météores, 2024).
74. Véronique Clette-Gakuba and David Jamar, 'Preface', in *La dent de Lumumba: Régicide contre la Colonie* by Samy Manga (Brussels: Météores, 2024), 30.
75. Manga, *La dent de Lumumba*, 52
76. Manga, *Chocolaté*, 94.
77. See Daniel Tödt, *The Lumumba Generation African Bourgeoisie and Colonial Distinction in the Belgian Congo* (Berlin and Boston: De Gruyter, 2021).
78. Adam Hochschild, *King Leopold's Ghost: A Story of Greed, Terror, and Heroism in Colonial Africa* (New York: Houghton Mifflin Company, 1998), 301.
79. Manga, *Chocolaté*, 95 and 96.
80. Saro-Wiwa, 'The Call', 167.
81. Manga, *Chocolaté*, 101–2.

82. Cajetan Iheka, *African Ecomedia: Network Forms, Planetary Politics* (Durham, NC: Duke University Press, 2021), 110-11.

83. In Koli Jean Bofane, *Congo Inc.: Bismarck's Testament*, trans. M. De Jaeger (Bloomington: Indiana University Press, 2018 [2014]).

84. Analogous questions are also to be found in In Koli Jean Bofane, *Nation cannibale* (Paris: Denoël, 2025).

85. Bofane, *Congo Inc.*, 7.

86. Xavier Garnier, *Écopoétiques africaines. Une expérience décoloniale des lieux* (Paris: Karthala, 2022), 214.

87. Bofane, *Congo Inc.*, 174-5.

88. David Van Reybrouck, *Congo: The Epic History of a People*, trans. S. Garrett (New York: HarperCollins, 2014 [2010]), 119.

89. Kossi Efoui, *La Fabrique des cérémonies* (Paris: Seuil, 2001), 62.

90. Blaise Ndala, *In the Belly of the Congo*, trans. A. B. Reid (New York: Other Press, 2023 [2021]), 376 and ix.

91. See Nicolas Bancel, Pascal Blanchard, Gilles Boëtsch, Eric Deroo, Sandrine Lemaire and Charles Forsdick, eds., *Human Zoos: Science and Spectacle in the Age of Colonial Empires* (Liverpool: Liverpool University Press, 2008) and Pascal Blanchard, Gilles Boëtsch and Nanette Jacomijn Snoep, eds., *Human Zoos: The Invention of the Savage* (Paris: Musée du Quai Branly and Arles: Actes Sud, 2011).

92. Nicolas Michel, 'RDC: In Koli Jean Bofane, le satyricongolais', *Jeune Afrique*, April 9, 2014.

93. Bofane, *Congo Inc.*, 186.

94. Christopher L. Miller, *Nationalists and Nomads: Essays on Francophone African Literature and Culture* (Chicago: University of Chicago Press, 1998).

95. Bofane, *Congo Inc.*, 6.

96. Ibid., 113.

97. Ibid., 22.

98. Ibid., 43.

99. Lieve Joris, *Sur les ailes du dragon: Voyages entre l'Afrique et la Chine*, trans. A. Ounanian (Arles: Actes Sud, 2014 [2013]).

100. See Macarena Gómez-Barris, *The Extractive Zone: Social Ecologies and Decolonial Perspectives* (Durham, NC: Duke University Press, 2017).

101. T.J. Demos, *Beyond the World's End: Arts of Living at the Crossing* (Durham and London: Duke University Press, 2020), 96-97.

102. Pierre-Philippe Fraiture, 'État présent: Congolese cultural production in Africa and the world', *French Studies* LXXVIII, no. 1 (2024): 106.

103. Malcom Ferdinand, *Decolonial Ecology: Thinking from the Caribbean World* (Cambridge: Polity Press, 2022), 47.

104. Bofane, *Congo Inc.*, 127–8.

105. Ibid., 146.

106. Achille Mbembe, 'The age of humanism is ending', *Mail & Guardian*, December 22, 2016.

107. Bofane, *Congo Inc.*, 160.

108. Mélanie Talcott, 'Sinzo Aanza: Interview', *L'Ombre du regard*, July 12, 2016.

109. Sinzo Aanza, *Généalogie d'une banalité* (La Roque d'Anthéron: Vents d'ailleurs, 2015).

110. Iheka, *African Ecomedia*, 145.

111. Justin Bisanswa, *Généalogie d'une banalité* de Sinzo Aanza. Le roman des moins-que-rien et des héros médiocres', *Présence Francophone: Revue internationale de langue et de littérature* 94, no. 1 (2020): 40.

112. Pierre-Philippe Fraiture, 'Tracking the Potholes of Colonial History: Sinzo Aanza's *Généalogie d'une banalité* and Fiston Mwanza Mujila's *Tram 83*', in *Unfinished Histories: Empire and Postcolonial Resonance in Central Africa and Belgium*, edited by Pierre-Philippe Fraiture (Leuven: Leuven University Press, 2022), 360.

113. Aanza, *Généalogie d'une banalité*, 185 and 26

114. Ibid., 185.

115. Sony Labou Tansi, *Conscience de tracteur* (Dakar and Yaoundé: NEA/CLÉ, 1979), 17. See Sony Labou Tansi, 'Lettre ouverte aux riches ou SOS Afrique', in *Encre, sueur, salive et sang*, edited by Greta Rodriguez-Antoniotti (Paris: Seuil, 2015), 124–7.

116. Sony Labou Tansi, *Le Commencement des douleurs* (Paris: Seuil, 1995), 90.

117. Sara Buekens, 'Le monde postcolonial de Sony Labou Tansi: entre magie et science', *RELIEF – Revue électronique de littérature française* 16, no. 1 (2022): 154 and 155.

118. Alice Desquilbet, 'Polémiques congolaises: les armes discursives de Sony Labou Tansi et Sinzo Aanza', *Revue des Sciences Humaines* 351 (2023): 149–62.

119. Alice Desquilbet, 'De la matière et des trous: l'envers du décor de la coopération sino-congolaise contemporaine,' *Études littéraires africaines*, no. 52 (2021): 113 and 107.

120. James Putnam and Michele Gervasuti, 'Democratic Republic of Congo," in *Foreigners Everywhere - Stranieri Ovunque, Volume 2*, edited by Flavia Fossa Margutti, Venice Biennale, 2024, 40.

121. https://www.hainesgallery.com/news/89-aime-mpane-biennale-vibranium-national-pavilion-of-the-democratic-republic-of/.

122. Fiston Mwanza Mujila, *Tram 83*, trans. R. Glasser (Dallas, TX: Deep Vellum, 2015 [2014]).

123. Fraiture, 'Tracking the Potholes of Colonial History', 362.

124. Ibid., 359 and 362.

125. Dominic Thomas, *Nation-Building, Propaganda, and Literature in Francophone Africa* (Bloomington: Indiana University Press, 2002), 87-8.

126. Fraiture, 'Tracking the Potholes of Colonial History', 367.

127. Xavier Garnier, 'Writings of the Subsoil in the Contemporary Congolese Novel', *Journal of World Literature* 6 (2021): 133-47. See Achille Mbembe, 'Le Monde-zéro: matière et machine / De nulwereld: materie en machine / The Zero-World: Materials and Machine', in *Mémoire/Kolwezi*, edited by Sammy Baloji (Oostkamp: Stichting Kunstboek, 2014), 73-79.

128. Mujila, *Tram 83*, 40-41.

129. Ibid., 109.

130. Pierre-Philippe Fraiture, 'Digging Holes, Excavating the Present, Mining the Future: Extractivism, Time, and Memory in Fiston Mwanza Mujila's and Sammy Baloji's Works', *Modern and Contemporary France* 32, no. 1 (2024): 140.

131. Fiston Mwanza Mujila, *The Villains's Dance*, trans. R. Glasser (Dallas: Deep Vellum, 2024 [2020]).

132. Ibid., 49-50.

133. Ibid., 7 and 11.

134. Ibid., 51.

135. Ato Quayson, 'Shakara Baby-chicks and Locomotive Tales: Fiston Mwanza Mujila's *Tram 83*', *Arcade: The Humanities in the World*, May 23, 2016, https://shc.stanford.edu/arcade/interventions/shakara-baby-chicks-and-locomotive-tales-fiston-mwanza-mujilas-tram-83.

136. Fiston Mwanza Mujila, 'Solitude 19', in *The River in the Belly*, trans. J. B. Maney (Dallas, TX: Deep Vellum, 2021), 42.

137. Filip De Boeck and Sammy Baloji, *Suturing the City: Living Together in Congo's Urban World* (London: Autograph ABP, 2016).

138. Pierre-Philippe Fraiture, 'Beyond images of war: Sammy Baloji's work captures DR Congo's vibrant arts and culture, challenging western views', *The Conversation*, April 15, 2024.

139. Vincent van Velsen, *A Blueprint for Toads and Snakes: A solo exhibition by Sammy Baloji* (Amsterdam: Framer Framed Gallery, 2018), 4, https://framerframed.nl/wp-content/uploads/2018/06/ABFTAS-HANDOUT-DIGITAAL_C.pdf.

140. Fraiture, 'État présent', 109 and 125.

141. Iheka, *African Ecomedia*, 110.

142. Gómez-Barris, *The Extractive Zone*.

143. Roy Doron and Toyin Falola, *Ken Saro-Wiwa* (Athens, OH: Ohio University Press, 2016), 88.

144. Saskia Sassen, 'A Massive Loss of Habitat: New Drivers for Migration', *Sociology of Development* 2, no. 2 (2016): 206 and 208.

145. https://www.mosop.org.

146. Doron and Falola, *Ken Saro-Wiwa*, 'Activism and the Politics of Oil, the Environment, and Genocide', 77–99.

147. Saro-Wiwa, 'Ogoni! Ogoni', in *Silence Would be Treason*, edited by Corley, Fallon and Cox, 152.

148. Collectif Des Auteurs Africains, eds., *Nos vers en vert* (Libreville: GNK éditions, 2021)

149. Fath Kumbe Manduku, 'La forêt', in *Nos vers en vert*, edited by Collectif Des Auteurs Africains, 15.

150. Doron and Falola, *Ken Saro-Wiwa*, 80 and 82. See Wole Soyinka, *The Open Sore of a Continent: A Personal Narrative of the Nigerian Crisis* (Oxford: Oxford University Press, 1996).

151. Daisy Pullman, 'A Rich Inheritance': An Ecocritical Reading of Ken Saro-Wiwa's Short Stories and Poetry', *Green Letters* 27, no. 3 (2023): 303–16.

152. Doron and Falola, *Ken Saro-Wiwa*, 101-102.

153. Mark Dummett, 'Afterword', in *Silence Would be Treason*, edited by Corley, Fallon and Cox, 173.

154. Helon Habila, *Oil on Water* (New York: W. W. Norton & Company, Inc., 2010), 125.

155. Olarotimi Ogungbemi, 'Literature as Resistance: The Pragmatics of Ecological Advocacy in "Oil and Water" by Helon Habila', *Journal Arbitrer* 10, no. 4 (2023): 362.

156. Imbolo Mbue, *How Beautiful We Were* (New York: Random House, 2020).

157. Sandrine Nan-Nguema [Bessora], *Mémoires pétrolières au Gabon*, Doctoral Thesis, University of Paris 7, 2002, https://theses.fr/2002PA070076.

158. Bessora, *Petroleum* (Paris: Denoël, 2004).

159. Giulia Champion, 'Pervasive extractivism: Petroculture and sedimented histories in Sandrine Bessora's *Petroleum*', *Journal of Energy History/Revue d'Histoire de l'Énergie*, no. 10 (3 August 2023): 14 and 3.

160. See Alexandra Perisic, 'Life after Oil: The Politics of Labor in Bessora's *Petroleum*', *Cambridge Journal of Postcolonial Literary Inquiry* 5, no. 3 (2018): 406-22.

161. Wilfried N'Sondé, *Femme du ciel et des tempêtes* (Arles: Actes Sud, 2021).

162. Ibid., 20.

163. Ibid., 156.

164. Stéphane Gladieu, *Homo Detritus* (photographs), text by Wilfried N'Sondé, trans. C. Penswarden (Arles: Actes Sud, 2022), 44 and 50

165. Jean-Michel André, *Borders* (photographs), text by Wilfried N'Sondé, trans. K. Lindo (Arles: Actes Sud, 2021), 76-7.

166. Wilfried N'Sondé, *Héliosphéra, fille des abysses, d'amour et de plancton* (Arles: Actes Sud, 2022).

167. Stéphane Durand, 'Preface', in *Héliosphéra* by N'Sondé, 11.

168. Morizot, *Ways of Being Alive*, 24 and 195.

169. Ghosh, *The Nutmeg's Curse*, 58.

170. Timothy Morton, *Dark Ecology: For a Logic of Future Coexistence* (New York: Columbia University Press, 2016), 35.

171. https://fondationtaraocean.org/en/foundation/.

172. Nicolas Michel, 'Environnement: du Cap à Dakar, la goélette Tara prend le pouls de l'Atlantique Sud', *Jeune Afrique*, May 8, 2022.

173. See Gregory T. Cushman, 'Humboldtian science, creole meteorology, and the discovery of human-caused climate change in South America', *Osiris* 26, no. 1 (2011): 19-44 and Harriet Mercer and Thomas Simpson, 'Imperialism, colonialism, and climate change science', *WIREs Climate Change* 14, Issue 6, June 21, 2023, https://wires.onlinelibrary.wiley.com/doi/10.1002/wcc.851.

174. Aaron Sachs, *The Humboldt Current: Nineteenth-Century Exploration and the Roots of American Environmentalism* (New York: Viking Penguin, 2007), 150.

175. https://fondationtaraocean.org/en/expedition/mission-microbiomes/#objectives.

176. Nicolas Michel, 'Congo: Wilfried N'Sondé et ses amours planctoniques', *Jeune Afrique*, October 23, 2022.

177. Ibid.

178. Wilfried N'Sondé, Fondation Tara Océan, 2021, https://fondationtaraocean.org/en/artists/wilfried-nsonde/.

179. Ghosh, *The Nutmeg's Curse*, 204.

180. Wilfried N'Sondé, 'Recherchons ce qui nous unit', *Afrique Magazine*, May 3, 2023, https://www.youtube.com/watch?v=NLflMiXSfx8.

181. N'Sondé, *Héliosphéra*, 131.

182. Wilfried N'Sondé, 'Ethnidentité', in *Je est un autre. Pour une identité-monde*, edited by Michel Le Bris and Jean Rouaud (Paris: Gallimard, 2010), 100.

183. David Bornstein, 'Héliosphéra, fille des abysses, amour planctonique', *Libération*, December 16, 2022.

184. This information is augmented with the detailed descriptions available on the comprehensive National Marine Ecosystem Status Website on marine life: https://ecowatch.noaa.gov/about.

185. N'Sondé, *Héliosphéra*, 21.

186. See Benjamin Schmidt, 'Exotic Allies: The Dutch-Chilean Encounter and the (Failed) Conquest of America', *Renaissance Quarterly* 52, no. 2 (1999): 440-73.

187. N'Sondé, *Héliosphéra*, 60 and 87.

188. See Mark Meuwese, *Brothers in Arms, Partners in Trade: Dutch-Indigenous Alliances in the Atlantic World, 1595–1674* (Leiden: Brill, 2012) and Mark Meuwese, *To the Shores of Chile: The Journal and History of the Brouwer Expedition to Valdivia in 1643* (University Park, PA: Penn State University Press, 2019).

189. N'Sondé, *Héliosphéra*, 70.

190. See Séverine Kodjo-Grandvaux, *Devenir vivants* (Paris: Philippe Rey, 2021), 30.

191. David Theo Goldberg, *Dread: Facing Futureless Futures* (Cambridge: Polity Press, 2021), 142.

192. N'Sondé, *Héliosphéra*, 79.
193. The work of the Dutch Plastic Soup Foundation concentrates on highlighting the links between plastics and human health: https://www.plasticsoupfoundation.org/en/.
194. Elizabeth M. DeLoughrey, *Allegories of the Anthropocene* (Durham, NC: Duke University Press, 2019), 138 and 28.
195. N'Sondé, *Héliosphéra*, 70.
196. Ibid., 90.
197. David Theo Goldberg, 'Parting Waters: Seas of Movement', in *Life Adrift: Climate Change, Migration, Critique*, edited by Andrew Baldwin and Giovanni Bettini (London and New York: Rowman & Littlefield International, Ltd., 2017), 107.
198. N'Sondé, *Héliosphéra*, 16.
199. Achille Mbembe, *La communauté terrestre* (Paris: La Découverte, 2023), 8.
200. Jeff Goodell, *The Heat Will Kill You First: Life and Death on a Scorched Planet* (New York: Little, Brown and Company, 2023).
201. N'Sondé, *Héliosphéra*, 36.
202. Ibid., 20.
203. Ibid., 113.
204. Ibid., 120.
205. Ibid., 124.
206. Ibid., 105.
207. Ibid., 108.
208. Ato Quayson, 'Stories and Empathy in a Time of Crisis: An African Viewpoint', *African Studies Review* 65, no. 4 (2022): 980.

Chapter 5

1. Jenny Erpenbeck, *Kairos*, trans. M. Hofmann (New York: New Directions Publishing Corporation, 2023 [2021]), 177.
2. Sibylle Berg, *Grime*, trans. T. Mohr (New York: St. Martin's Griffin, 2022 [2019]), 141.
3. See Helier Cheung, 'What Does Trump Actually Believe on Climate Change?', *BBC News*, January 23, 2020, https://www.bbc.com/news/world-us-canada-51213003.
4. Sam Moore and Alex Roberts, *The Rise of Ecofascism: Climate Change and The Far Right* (Cambridge: Polity Press, 2022), 52 and 56 and Peter K. Fallon, *Propaganda 2.1: Understanding Propaganda in the Digital Age* (Eugene: Cascade Books, 2022), 64-5.
5. Edward Bernays, *Propaganda* (New York: Liveright Publishing Corporation, 1928), 52.
6. Ibid., 139.
7. Ibid., 37.
8. Julia Ebner, *The Rage: The Vicious Circle of Islamists and Far-Right Extremism* (London and New York: I. B. Tauris, 2017), 103-4, emphasis added.
9. Edward S. Herman and Noam Chomsky, *Manufacturing Consent: The Political Economy of the Mass Media* (New York: Pantheon Books, 1988), 18.
10. Marshall McLuhan, *Understanding Media: The Extensions of Man* (Boston: The MIT Press, 1994 [1964]), 18.
11. Jacques Ellul, *Propaganda: The Formation of Men's Attitudes*, trans. K. Kellen and J. Lerner (New York: Vintage, 1968).
12. Peter Pomerantsev, *How to Win an Information War: The Propagandist Who Outwitted Hitler* (New York: Public Affairs, 2024), 223.

13. Timothy Snyder, *The Road to Unfreedom: Russia, Europe, America* (New York: Tim Duggan Books, 2018), 229.

14. Timothy Snyder, 'Ukraine Holds the Future: The War Between Democracy and Nihilism', *Foreign Affairs*, September 6, 2022.

15. Fallon, *Propaganda 2.1*, 168.

16. Pankaj Mishra, *The Age of Anger: A History of the Present* (New York: Picador, 2017), 13.

17. George Monbiot and Peter Hutchison, *The Invisible Doctrine: The Secret History of Neoliberalism (& How It Came to Control Your Life)* (London: Allen Lane, 2024), 102.

18. Eva Illouz, *The Emotional Life of Populism: How Fear, Disgust, Resentment, and Love Undermine Democracy* (Cambridge: Polity Press, 2023).

19. Ebner, *The Rage*, 104.

20. Shoshana Zuboff, *The Age of Surveillance Capitalism: The Fight for a Human Future at the New Frontier of Power* (New York: PublicAffairs, 2020).

21. Giuliano da Empoli, *Les ingénieurs du chaos* (Paris: Jean-Claude Lattès, 2019), 21.

22. Sandrine Lemaire, 'Manipulation: Conquering Taste (1931-1939)', in *Colonial Culture in France Since the Revolution*, edited by Pascal Blanchard, Sandrine Lemaire, Nicolas Bancel and Dominic Thomas (Bloomington: Indiana University Press, 2014), 289.

23. Empoli, *Les ingénieurs du chaos*, 22 and 25.

24. Hein de Haas, *How Migration Really Works: The Facts About the Most Divisive Issue in Politics* (New York: Basic Books, 202), 8 and 5.

25. Anne Applebaum, *The Dictators Who Want to Run the World* (New York: Doubleday, 2024), 96-97.

26. Haas, *How Migration Really Works*, 357. See Francis Rawlinson, *How Press Propaganda Paved the Way to Brexit* (Cham: Palgrave Macmillan, 2019) and Hannah Marshall and Alena Drieschova, 'Post-Truth Politics in the UK's Brexit Referendum', *New Perspectives* 26, no. 3 (2018): 89–106.

27. Haas, *How Migration Really Works*, 355.

28. Gloria Oladipo, '"Racism Is Embedded in Our Society": How Attacks on Immigrants in Ohio Highlight US Disinformation Crisis', *The Guardian*, September 18, 2024.

29. Pierre Tevanian and Jean-Charles Stevens, *"On ne peut accueillir toute la misère du monde": En finir avec une sentence de mort* (Paris: Anamosa, 2022), 62 and 64.

30. Amitav Ghosh, *The Great Derangement: Climate Change and the Unthinkable* (Chicago, IL: University of Chicago Press, 2016), 137.

31. Berg, *Grime*, 151.

32. Moisés Naím, *The Revenge of Power: How Autocrats Are Reinventing Politics for the 21st Century* (New York: St. Martin's Griffin, 2022), xv.

33. Ibid., xii and xv.

34. Ibid., xvi-xvii.

35. Ibid., xviii.

36. Juli Zeh, *About People*, trans. A. L. Price (New York: World Editions, 2023 [2021]), 33.

37. See Catherine Beauvais, 'Fake News: Why Do We Believe It?', *Joint Bone Spine* 89 (March 2022): 1–2, https://www.sciencedirect.com/science/article/pii/S1297319X22000306?via%3Dihub.

38. Bálsa Lubarda, *Far-Right Ecologism: Environmental Politics and the Far Right in Hungary and Poland* (London and New York, Routledge, 2024), 125.

39. Daniel Macmillen Voskoboynik, *The Memory We Could Be: Overcoming Fear to Create Our Ecological Future* (Gabriola Island: New Society Publishers, 2018), 97-8.

40. Stella Levantesi, '"Enemies of Society": How the Media Portray Climate Activists', *Green European Journal*, October 17, 2023, Adam Forest, 'Greta Thunberg: Right Wing French MPs Insult and Boycott Teenage Climate Activist', *The Independent*, 24 July 2019 and Tom Phillips, 'Greta Thunberg Labelled a 'Brat' by Brazil's Far-right Leader Jair Bolsonaro', *The Guardian*, December 19, 2019.

41. Cara Daggett, 'Petro-masculinity and the politics of climate refusal', Autonomy Institute, May 1, 2022, https://autonomy.work/portfolio/petro-masculinity-climate -refusal/.

42. Cited in Fiona Harvey, 'Demagogues imperiling global fight against climate breakdown, says Kerry', *The Guardian*, February 28, 2024.

43. Peter Schwartz and Doug Randall, 'An Abrupt Climate Change Scenario and Its Implications for United States National Security', Global Business Network for the Department of Defense, October 2003, https://www.iatp.org/sites/default/files/An _Abrupt_Climate_Change_Scenario_and_Its_Impl.pdf.

44. Amitav Ghosh, *The Nutmeg's Curse: Parables for a Planet in Crisis* (Chicago: University of Chicago Press, 2021), 127.

45. Claire Rodier, *Xénophonie Business. À quoi servent les contrôles migratoires* (Paris: La Découverte, 2012) and Matt McDonald, 'Ecological Security', *E-International Relations*, November 28, 2015, https://www.e-ir.info/2015/11/28/ecological -security/.

46. Ghosh, *The Nutmeg's Curse*, 133 and 145.

47. Betsy Hartmann, 'The Ghosts of Malthus: Narratives and Mobilizations of Scarcity in the US Political Context', in *The Limits to Scarcity: Contesting the Politics of Allocation*, edited by Lyla Mehta (London and Washington, DC: Earthscan, 2010), 57-8.

48. Laurence Tubiana, 'Polariser pour mieux masquer l'inaction climatique', *La Croix*, July 5, 2023.

49. Mathieu Rigouste, *La police du futur. Le marché de la violence et ce qui lui résiste* (Paris: 10/18, 2022), 50-1.

50. Regulation of the European Parliament and of the Council of 30 June 2021 establishing the framework for achieving climate neutrality and amending Regulations (EC) No 401/2009 and (EU) 2018/1999 ('European Climate Law'), *Official Journal of the European Union*, July 9, 2021, https://eur-lex.europa.eu/legal-content/EN/TXT/ HTML/?uri=CELEX:32021R1119.

51. Virginie Malingre, 'La Commission européenne propose une nouvelle PAC avec beaucoup moins de contraintes environnementales', *Le Monde*, March 15, 2024.

52. Genevieve Guenther, *The Language of Climate Politics: Fossil-Fuel Propaganda and How to Fight It* (New York: Oxford University Press, 2024), 5.

53. Fred Pearce, 'Why Is Britain Retreating from Global Leadership on Climate Action?', *YaleEnvironment360*, Yale School of the Environment, October 17, 2023, https://e360.yale.edu/features/ungreening-britain-sunak-climate-change.

54. Quoted in Fiona Harvey and Damian Carrington, 'UK absent from key international statement on climate action', *The Guardian*, September 20, 2023.

55. Harriet Mercer and Thomas Simpson, 'Imperialism, Colonialism, and Climate Change Science', *WIREs Climate Change* 14, no. 6, https://wires.onlinelibrary.wiley .com/doi/full/10.1002/wcc.851.

56. David Van Reybrouck, *Revolusi: Indonesia and the Birth of the Modern World*, trans. D. Colmer and D. McKay (New York: W. W. Norton & Company, 2024), cited by Philip

Oltermann, *The Guardian*, 'End fossil-fuel era to address colonial injustices, urges prominent historian', February 15, 2024.

57. Kelvin Chan, 'Musk's X is the Largest Source of Disinformation, EU Official Says', *PBS News*, September 26, 2023.

58. Zac Gershberg and Sean Illing, *The Paradox of Democracy: Free Speech, Open Media, and Perilous Persuasion* (Chicago, IL: University of Chicago Press, 2022), 1.

59. See Matteo Wong, 'We Haven't Seen the Worst of Fake News. Deepfakes still might be poised to corrupt the basic ways we process reality – or what's left of it', *Atlantic*, December 20, 2022.

60. European Commission, 'The Digital Services Act,' 2024, https://commission .europa.eu/strategy-and-policy/priorities-2019-2024/europe-fit-digital-age/digital -services-act_en.

61. Julia Ebner, *Going Mainstream: How Extremists Are Taking Over* (London: Ithaca Press, 2023), viii and ix.

62. Ibid., 47.

63. Ibid., 76.

64. Carlos Diaz Ruiz, 'Disinformation on Digital Media Platforms: A Market-shaping Approach', *New Media & Society* (2023): 2, https://journals.sagepub.com/doi/10.1177 /14614448231207644.

65. Ibid., 7 and 3.

66. See David Chavalarias, *Toxic data. Comment les réseaux sociaux manipulent nos opinions* (Paris: Flammarion, 2022).

67. Ruiz, 'Disinformation on digital media platforms', 15.

68. Climate Action Against Disinformation Coalition (CAAD), 'Climate of Misinformation: Ranking Big Tech', September 2023, https://caad.info/wp-content /uploads/2023/09/Climate-of-Misinformation.pdf, 2.

69. Google Ads Team, 'Updating our ads and monetization policies on climate change', October 7, 2021, https://support.google.com/google-ads/answer/11221321.

70. Climate Action Against Disinformation Coalition (CAAD), 'Climate of Misinformation: Ranking Big Tech', 3.

71. Fabio Duarte, 'X (Formerly Twitter) User Age, Gender, & Demographic Stats (2024)', *Exploding Topics*, April 25, 2024, https://explodingtopics.com/blog/x-user -stats.

72. See Stéphane Foucart, 'L'aggravation récente des effets du réchauffement coïncide, et c'est une autre cause de sidération, avec un retour apparent du climatoscepti- cisme', *Le Monde*, September 10, 2023.

73. See Joëlle Zask, *Écologie et démocratie* (Paris: Premier Parallèle, 2022) and Michiko Kakutani, *The Death of Truth: Notes on Falsehood in the Age of Trump* (New York: Tim Duggan Press, 2018).

74. Moore and Roberts, *The Rise of Ecofascism*, 129.

75. Climate Intelligence Foundation (CLINTEL), https://clintel.org/world-climate -declaration/. See Jacques Laurentie, *Climat de peur: Enquête sur le changement climatique, de l'alarmisme aux faits* (Alençon: Bien Commun, 2023).

76. Geoffrey Supran and Cameron Hickey and the Algorithmic Transparency Institute, 'Three Shades of Green(washing): Content Analysis of Social Media Discourse by European Oil, Car, and Airline Companies', Working Paper, September 21, 2022, https://ati.io/wp-content/uploads/2022/09/ThreeShadesofGreenwashingv2.pdf, 4

77. Ibid., 3.

78. Ibid., 4 and 48.

79. Chris Martinez, Laura Kilbury, Joel Martinez, Calee White, Mariel Lutz, Kat So, Kate Petosa, Allison McManus and Anne Christianson, 'These Fossil Fuel Industry Tactics Are Fueling Democratic Backsliding', Center for American Progress, December 5, 2023, https://www.americanprogress.org/article/these-fossil-fuel-industry-tactics-are-fueling-democratic-backsliding/.

80. See Aurélien Berlan, Guillaume Carbou and Laure Teulières, eds., *Green Washing. Manuel pour dépolluer le débat public* (Paris: Seuil, 2022), 143-50.

81. Amy Westervelt and Kyle Pope, 'How to Spot Five of the Fossil Fuel Industry's Biggest Disinformation Tactics', *The Guardian*, April 14, 2024.

82. https://www.chevron.com, https://corporate.exxonmobil.com, https://www.shell.com, https://www.bp.com.

83. Imre Szeman and Dominic Boyer, eds., *Energy Humanities: An Anthology* (Baltimore, MD: Johns Hopkins University Press, 2017), 2.

84. Ibid., emphasis added.

85. Dominic Boyer, *No More Fossils* (Minneapolis: University of Minnesota Press, 2023), 6-7.

86. Ibid., 60.

87. Ibid., 24 and 40.

88. Emily M. Eaton et Nick A. Day, 'Petro-pedagogy: fossil fuel interests and the obstruction of climate justice in public education', *Environmental Education Research* 26, no. 4 (2020): 457-73.

89. Carolyn B. Maloney and Ro Khanna, 'Oversight Committee Releases New Documents Showing Big Oil's Greenwashing Campaign and Failure to Reduce Emissions', December 9, 2022, https://oversightdemocrats.house.gov/news/press-releases/oversight-committee-releases-new-documents-showing-big-oil-s-greenwashing.

90. See Keerti Gopal, 'Kids and families: the latest targets of climate denialism propaganda', *Bulletin of the Atomic Scientists*, August 10, 2023.

91. Oklahoma Oil & Natural Gas, https://oerb.com.

92. Jie Jenny Zou, 'Pipeline to the classroom: how big oil promotes fossil fuels to America's children', *The Guardian*, June 15, 2017.

93. Stuart Tannock, 'The oil industry in our schools: From Petro Pete to science capital in the age of climate crisis', *Environmental Education Research* 26, no. 4 (2020): 475.

94. Carla Schaeperkoetter, *Petro Pete's Big Bad Dream*, illustrated by Cameron Eagle (Oklahoma, OK: Oklahoma Energy Resources Board, 2016).

95. Jim Zeigler, 'Petro Pete, Plastic Mascot for Plausible Denial', *Inhabiting the Anthropocene*, April 10, 2019, https://inhabitingtheanthropocene.com/2019/04/10/petro-pete-plastic-mascot-for-plausible-denial/.

96. James G. Ballard, *High-Rise* (New York and London: Liveright Publishing Corporation, 2012 [1975] and James G. Ballard, *Super-Cannes* (London: Flamingo, 2001), 250.

97. Milena Škobo and Jovana Đukić, 'Urban Landscape as the Embodiment of Social and Psychological Entropy in J. G. Ballard's *Cocaine Nights* and *Super-Cannes*', *Interfaces*, no. 2, Year 13 (2023), 4.

98. Ahmed Khaled Towfik, *Utopia*, trans. R. Jacquemond (Paris: Flammarion, 2013 [2008]).

99. Brian Aldiss, *Super-State: A Novel of a Future Europe* (London: Orbit Books, 2002).
100. https://www.neom.com/en-us/regions/theline.
101. Dan Avery, 'Saudi Arabia Building 100-Mile-Long "Linear" City', *Architectural Digest*, January 26, 2021
102. https://www.youtube.com/watch?v=0kz5vEqdaSc.
103. Andreas Malm and the Zetkin Collective, *White Skin, Black Fuel: On the Danger of Fossil Fascism* (London and New York: Verso, 2021), 320.
104. See Hermas Abudu, Presley K. Wesseh and Boqiang Lin, 'Does Political Propaganda Matter in Mitigating Climate Change? Insights from the United States of America', *Journal of Management Science and Engineering* 8, no. 3 (2023): 386–97.
105. Sammy Roth, 'Column: How "Sesame Street" can prepare kids for climate disasters', *Los Angeles Times*, May 23, 2024.
106. Guenther, *The Language of Climate Politics*, 107.
107. See Green Dreamer, '35 Environmental Organizations and Nonprofits For a Sustainable Future (List and Ways You Can Get Involved)', https://www.greendreamer.com/journal/environmental-organizations-nonprofits-for-a-sustainable-future.
108. See Jacques Pezet, 'Dernière Rénovation, Just Stop Oil, Scientist Rebellion... La nouvelle galaxie des mouvements écolos radicaux', *Libération*, November 4, 2022.
109. Byung-Chul Han, *Infocracy. Digitization and the Crisis of Democracy*, trans. Daniel Steuer (Cambridge: Polity Books, 2022 [2021]), 96. *Le Monde* newspaper offers its readers a (regularly updated) guide with which to address climate skeptics. See William Audureau, Manon Romain and Thomas Steffen, 'Le guide critique des arguments et intox climatosceptiques', *Le Monde*, May 8, 2023.
110. Jonas Staal, *Climate Propagandas: Stories of Extinction and Regeneration* (Boston: MIT Press, 2024), 167-71.
111. Ibid., 27, 125, and 171.
112. Guenther, in *The Language of Climate Politics*, 189 and 3.
113. Kenneth Green, 'Trudeau government ratchets up "climate" propaganda', *The Toronto Star*, February 13, 2024.
114. Damian Carrington, 'Satellite to "name and shame" worst oil and gas methane polluters', *The Guardian*, March 4, 2024.
115. Alexandre Lacroix, "Interview with Baptiste Morizot: Le monde va devenir chaotique, mais nous pouvons entrer en résistance', *Philosophie Magazine* 164 (November 2022): 68.
116. See Joseph Dodds, 'The Psychology of Climate Anxiety', *BJPsych Bulletin* 45, no. 4 (2021): 225.
117. Ibid., 222.
118. Pierre Charbonnier, 'Introduction: Après l'invasion de l'Ukraine: géopolitique de l'anthropocène', *GREEN: Géopolique, réseaux, énergie, environnement, nature*, no. 2 (September 2022), 6.
119. Pierre Charbonnier, *Abondance et liberté. Une histoire environnementale des idées politiques* (Paris: La Découverte, 2020), 265 and 266. Arnaud Orain, *Les savoirs perdus de l'économie. Contribution à l'équilibre du vivant* (Paris: Gallimard, 2023), has described this in terms of a 'rupture', 296.
120. Guenther, in *The Language of Climate Politics*, 44 and Haas, *How Migration Really Works*, 357.
121. See Szeman and Boyer, *Energy Humanities*, 3.

122. Altexsoft Software R&D Engineering, 'AI Image Generation Explained: Techniques, Applications, and Limitations', *Newsletter*, July 9, 2023, https://www.altexsoft.com/blog/ai-image-generation/.

123. Ibid.

124. Safiya Noble, *Algorithms of Oppression: How Search Engines Reinforce Racism* (New York: New York University Press, 2018), 1 and Todd Presner, *Ethics of the Algorithm: Digital Humanities and Holocaust Memory* (Princeton and Oxford: Princeton University Press, 2024), 19.

125. Alastair Johnstone-Hack, 'What Does AI Imagery Mean for Climate Change Photography?', *Climate Outreach*, March 6, 2024.

126. Ibid.

127. Altexsoft Software R&D Engineering, 'AI Image Generation Explained'.

128. David Theo Goldberg, 'Parting Waters: Seas of Movement', in *Life Adrift: Climate Change, Migration, Critique*, edited by Andrew Baldwin and Giovanni Bettini (London and New York: Rowman & Littlefield International, Ltd., 2017), 107.

129. Achille Mbembe, *La communauté terrestre* (Paris: La Découverte, 2023), 18.

130. Achille Mbembe, Rémy Rioux and Séverine Kodjo-Grandvaux, *Pour un monde en commun. Regards croisés entre l'Afrique et l'Europe* (Arles: Actes Sud / Paris: Agence française de développement, 2022), 159.

131. Adam Gabbatt, '"We're facing another old enemy": Rushdie warns against global authoritarianism', *The Guardian*, September 13, 2023.

132. Yanis Varoufakis, *Technofeudalism: What Killed Capitalism* (New York: Melville House Publishing, 2023), 171. See Cédric Durand, *Techno-féodalisme. Critique de l'économie numérique* (Paris: La Découverte, 2023).

133. Lacroix, 'Interview with Baptiste Morizot,' 68.

134. Mbembe, *La communauté terrestre*, 192 and 8.

Epilogue

1. Giuliano da Empoli, *L'Heure des prédateurs* (Paris: Gallimard, 2025), 93.

2. Ibid., 12, 117, and 75.

3. Ibid., 49. See 'Giuliano da Empoli : "La formule des ingénieurs du chaos est toujours la même: la colère et la frustration, démultipliées par l'algorithme"', Interview with Nicolas Truong, *Le Monde*, April 21, 2025.

4. Juan Gabriel Vásquez, *La traduction du monde*, trans. I. Gugnon (Paris: Seuil, 2025), 128.

5. Robert Menasse, *Le monde de demain: Une Europe souveraine et démocratique – et ses ennemis*, trans. O. Mannoni (Lagrasse: Éditions Verdier, 2025), 17.

6. Ibid., 18.

7. Ibid., 37.

8. See Maya Yang, 'Germany Hits Back at Marco Rubio after He Panned Labeling of AfD as "Extremist"', *The Guardian*, May 3, 2025.

9. Spencer Chretien, 'Project 2025', accessed May 5, 2025, https://www.heritage.org/conservatism/commentary/project-2025.

10. See Center for Law, Energy, and the Environment, 'A Guide to Major Climate and Environmental Excerpts in the Project 2025 Report', University of California Berkeley, accessed March 11, 2025, https://www.law.berkeley.edu/wp-content

/uploads/2024/08/Index-and-Summary-Annotated-of-Project-2025-Report -Aug1424.pdf.

11. Executive Order, 'Unleashing America's Offshore Critical Minerals and Resources', accessed May 5, 2025, https://www.whitehouse.gov/presidential-actions/2025/04/ unleashing-americas-offshore-critical-minerals-and-resources/.

12. Pierre-Cyrille Hautcœur, 'Le monde entre dans une nouvelle ère de domination du capitalisme de la finitude', *Le Monde*, January 15, 2025.

13. Executive Order, 'Ensuring National Security and Economic Resilience through section 232 Actions on Processed Critical Minerals and Derivative Products', accessed May 5, 2025, https://www.whitehouse.gov/presidential-actions/2025/04 /ensuring-national-security-and-economic-resilience-through-section-232-actions -on-processed-critical-minerals-and-derivative-products/. See Ravi Agrawal, 'Trump Is Ushering In a More Transactional World', *Foreign Policy*, January 7, 2025.

14. Achille Mbembe and Ruth Wilson Gilmore, 'Trump's Attacks on South Africa Are a Punishment for Independence', *The Guardian*, March 7, 2025.

15. See Executive Order, 'Addressing Egregious Actions of The Republic of South Africa', accessed April 20, 2025, https://www.whitehouse.gov/presidential-actions /2025/02/addressing-egregious-actions-of-the-republic-of-south-africa/.

16. Mbembe and Gilmore, 'Trump's attacks on South Africa are a punishment for independence'.

17. Editorial, 'The Guardian View on Donald Trump's Congo Deal: Mineral Riches for Protection', *The Guardian*, April 13, 2025.

18. U.S. Department of the Treasury, 'Treasury Announces Agreement to Establish United States-Ukraine Reconstruction Investment Fund', accessed May 1, 2025, https://home.treasury.gov/news/press-releases/sb0126.

BIBLIOGRAPHY

Aanza, Sinzo. *Généalogie d'une banalité*. La Roque d'Anthéron: Vents d'ailleurs, 2015.

Abderrezak, Hakim. *Ex-Centric Migrations: Europe and the Maghreb in Mediterranean Cinema, Literature, and Music*. Bloomington, IN: Indiana University Press, 2016.

———. 'The Mediterranean Sieve, Spring and Seametery'. In *Refugee Imaginaries: Research Across the Humanities*, edited by Emma Cox, Sam Durrant, David Farrier, Lyndsey Stonebridge and Agnes Woolley, 372–91. Edinburgh: Edinburgh University Press, 2020.

Abudu, Hermas, Presley K. Wesseh and Boqiang Lin. 'Does Political Propaganda Matter in Mitigating Climate Change? Insights from the United States of America'. *Journal of Management Science and Engineering* 8, no. 3 (2023): 386–97.

Adami, Rebecca. 'Human Rights for More Than One Voice: Rethinking Political Space beyond the Global/Local Divide'. *Ethics & Global Politics* 7, no. 4 (2014): 163–80.

Adichie, Chimamanda Ngozi. 'The Danger of a Single Story'. TEDGlobal, Oxford, July 23, 2009.

Agier, Michel. *La peur des autres. Essai sur l'indésirabilité*. Paris: Payot & Rivages, 2022.

Agier, Michel, Filippo Furri and Carolina Kobelinsky. 'L'indifférence face aux morts en Méditerranée est le signe d'un effondrement en humanité'. *Le Monde*, July 25, 2023.

Agrawal, Ravi. 'Trump Is Ushering In a More Transactional World'. *Foreign Policy*, January 7, 2025.

Ahuja, Neel. *Planetary Specters: Race, Migration, and Climate Change in the Twenty-First Century*. Chapel Hill, NC: University of North Carolina Press, 2021.

Akofa, Karen. *L'Asile et l'Exil. Une histoire de la distinction réfugié/migrants*. Paris: La Découverte, 2020.

Aldiss, Brian. *Super-State: A Novel of a Future Europe*. London: Orbit Books, 2002.

Alduy, Cécile. *Ce qu'ils disent vraiment. Les politiques pris aux mots*. Paris: Seuil, 2017.

———. *La Langue de Zemmour*. Paris: Seuil, 2022.

Alduy, Cécile, Annie Collovald and Jean-Yves Pranchère. 'Les faillites du langage'. *L'Esprit* 502 (2023): 65–79.

Altexsoft software R&D engineering. 'AI Image Generation Explained: Techniques, Applications, and Limitations'. *Newsletter*, July 9, 2023. https://www.altexsoft.com/blog/ai-image-generation/.

Aly, Götz. *The Magnificent Boat: The Colonial Theft of a South Seas Cultural Treasure*. Trans. J. Chase. Cambridge, MA: The Belknap Press of Havard University Press, 2023 [2021].

Amal, Djali Amadou. *Cœur du Sahel*. Paris: Emmanuelle Collas, 2022.

Andrews, Kehinde. *The New Age of Empire: How Racism and Colonialism Still Rule the World*. London: Allen Lane, 2021.

'Anthologie écopoétique située des arts et des littératures'. University of Paris Sorbonne Nouvelle. Accessed January 30, 2025. https://ecopoetique.huma-num.fr/.

Apap, Joanna with Sami James Harju. 'The concept of "climate refugee": Towards a possible definition'. European Union, 2023. https://www.europarl.europa.eu/RegData/etudes/BRIE/2021/698753/EPRS_BRI(2021)698753_EN.pdf.

Appadurai, Arjun. *Modernity at Large: Cultural Dimensions of Globalization*. Minneapolis, MN: University of Minnesota Press, 1996.

Appanah, Nathacha. *Tropic of Violence*. Trans. G. Strachan. Minneapolis, MN: Graywolf Press, 2020 [2016].

———. *La mémoire delavée*. Paris: Mercure de France, 2023.

Applebaum, Anne. *The Dictators Who Want to Run the World*. New York: Doubleday, 2024.

Arendt, Hannah. 'Truth and Politics'. In *Between past and Future: Eight Exercises in Political Thought*, by Hannah Arendt, 223–59. New York: Penguin Books, 1977 [1967].

Atangana, Baltazar. 'Discours sur l'environnement: Entretien avec Caroline Meva'. *La Pépinière*, November 30, 2023. https://lapepinieregeneve.ch/discours-sur-lenvironnement-entretien-avec-caroline-meva/.

Atapattu, Sumudu Anopama. 'A New Category of Refugees? "Refugees" and a Gaping Hole in International Law'. In *'Climate Refugees': Beyond the Legal Impasse?*, edited by Simon Behrman and Avidan Kent, 34–51. London and New York: Routledge, 2018.

Audhuy, Claire. *Les migrantes*. Strasbourg: Rodéo d'âme, 2016.

Audureau, William, Manon Romain and Thomas Steffen. 'Le guide critique des arguments et intox climatosceptiques'. *Le Monde*, May 8, 2023.

Avery, Dan. 'Saudi Arabia Building 100-Mile-Long "Linear" City'. *Architectural Digest*, January 26, 2021.

Ayalon, Anat Tzom. 'A Tiny Boat Lost at Sea: Trauma and Ethics in *Havarie [Collision]* by Philip Scheffner (Germany, 2016)'. *Ekphrasis* 23, no. 3 (2020): 29–49.

Bal, Mieke. 'Documenting What? Auto-Theory and Migratory Aesthetics'. In *A Contemporary Guide to Documentary Film*, edited by Alexandra Juhasz and Alisa Lebow, 124–44. Chichester: John Wiley & Sons, Inc., 2015.

Baldwin, Andrew and Giovanni Bettini. 'Introduction: Life Adrift'. In *Life Adrift: Climate Change, Migration, Critique*, edited by Andrew Baldwin and Giovanni Bettini, 1–21. London and New York: Rowman & Littlefield International, 2017.

Balibar, Étienne. *We, the People of Europe? Reflections on Transnational Citizenship*. Trans. J. Swenson. Princeton, NJ: Princeton University Press, 2004.

Ballard, James G. *High-Rise*. New York and London: Liveright Publishing Corporation, 2012 [1975].

———. *Super-Cannes*. London: Flamingo, 2001.

Bancel, Nicolas. 'The Colonial Bath: Sources of Popular *Colonial Culture* (1918-1931)'. In *Colonial Culture in France Since the Revolution*, edited by Pascal Blanchard, Sandrine Lemaire, Nicolas Bancel and Dominic Thomas, 200–8. Bloomington, IN: Indiana University Press, 2014.

Bancel, Nicolas and Pascal Blanchard. 'The Colonial Issue is the Last Taboo of France's 19th and 20th Century History'. *Le Monde*, November 5, 2023.

Bancel, Nicolas and Pascal Blanchard. 'The Pitfalls of Colonial Memory'. In *The Colonial Legacy in France: Fracture, Rupture, and Apartheid*, edited by Nicolas Bancel, Pascal Blanchard and Dominic Thomas, 153–64. Bloomington, IN: Indiana University Press, 2017.

Bancel, Nicolas and Pascal Blanchard. 'The Republican Origins of the Colonial Fracture'. In *The Colonial Legacy in France: Fracture, Rupture, and Apartheid*, edited by Nicolas Bancel, Pascal Blanchard and Dominic Thomas, 43–52. Bloomington, IN: Indiana University Press, 2017.

Bancel, Nicolas, Pascal Blanchard, Gilles Boëtsch, Eric Deroo, Sandrine Lemaire and Charles Forsdick, eds. *Human Zoos: Science and Spectacle in the Age of Colonial Empires*. Liverpool: Liverpool University Press, 2008.

Bancel, Nicolas, Pascal Blanchard and Ahmed Boubeker. *Le Grand Repli*. Paris: La Découverte, 2014.

Bancel, Nicolas, Pascal Blanchard, Sandrine Lemaire and Dominic Thomas, eds. *Histoire globale de la colonisation française*. Paris: Philippe Rey, 2022.

Bancel, Nicolas, Pascal Blanchard and Dominic Thomas, eds. *The Colonial Legacy in France: Fracture, Rupture, and Apartheid*. Bloomington, IN: Indiana University Press, 2017.

Bancel, Nicolas, Thomas David and Dominic Thomas, eds. *The Invention of Race: Scientific and Popular Representations*. New York: Routledge, 2014.

Bancel, Nicolas and Daniel Denis. 'Education: Becoming "Homo Imperialis" (1910-1940)'. In *Colonial Culture in France Since the Revolution*, edited by Pascal Blanchard, Sandrine Lemaire, Nicolas Bancel and Dominic Thomas, 276–84. Bloomington, IN: Indiana University Press, 2014.

Bangstad, Sindre and Maria Darwish. 'Ecofascism and the Politics of Replacement in the Discourse of the Nordic Resistance Movement (NRM)'. In *The Politics of Replacement: Demographic Fears, Conspiracy Theories, and Race Wars*, edited by Sarah Bracke and Luis Manuel Hernández Aguilar, 95–106. London and New York: Routledge, 2024.

Bates-Eamer, Nicole. 'Border and Migration Controls and Migrant Precarity in the Context of Climate Change'. *Social Sciences* 8, no. 7 (2019). https://www.mdpi.com/2076-0760/8/7/198.

Bauman, Zygmunt. *Liquid Fear*. Cambridge: Polity Press, 2006.

Beaty, Roger E. and Yoed N. Kenett. 'Associative Thinking at the Core of Creativity'. *Trends in Cognitive Sciences* 27, no. 7 (2023): 671–83.

Beauvais, Catherine. 'Fake News: Why Do We Believe It?'. *Joint Bone Spine* 89 (March 2022). https://www.sciencedirect.com/science/article/pii/S1297319X22000306?via%3Dihub.

Behrman, Simon and Avidan Kent. 'Overcoming the Legal Impasse: Setting the Scene'. In *'Climate Refugees': Beyond the Legal Impasse?*, edited by Simon Behrman and Avidan Kent, 3–15. London and New York: Routledge, 2018.

Bello, Valeria. *International Migration and International Security: Why Prejudice Is a Global Security Threat*. London and New York: Routledge, 2017.

Benedetti, Francesca De. 'Giorgia Meloni Is Orbánizing the European Union'. *Jacobin*, February 2, 2024.

———. 'Ursula von der Leyen Is Taking Europe to the Right'. *Jacobin*, September 24, 2023.

Benoist, Lise. 'Nationalisme vert. Peut-on concilier nationalisme et écologie'. In *Green Washing. Manuel pour dépolluer le débat public*, edited by Aurélien Berlan, Guillaume Carbou and Laure Teulières, 143–9. Paris: Seuil, 2022.

Bentham, Jeremy. 'Of the limits of the penal branch of jurisprudence'. In *An Introduction to the Principles of Morals and Legislation*, by Jeremy Bentham. Oxford: Clarendon Press, 1907 [1789]

Berg, Sibylle. *Grime*. Trans. T. Mohr. New York: St. Martin's Griffin, 2022 [2019].

Berlan, Aurélien, Guillaume Carbou and Laure Teulières, eds. *Green Washing. Manuel pour dépolluer le débat public.* Paris: Seuil, 2022.

Bernays, Edward. *Propaganda.* New York: Liveright Publishing Corporation, 1928.

Bertho, Elara. 'Du chocolat, du sang et des larmes *(Cocoaïans)*'. *Diacritik*, October 13, 2022. https://diacritik.com/2022/10/13/gauz-du-chocolat-du-sang-et-des-larmes-cocoaians/.

Bessora, *Petroleum.* Paris: Denoël, 2004.

Beti, Mongo. 'Romancing Africa.' In *Cruel City* by Mongo Béti. Trans. P. Higginson, xi–xxiii. Bloomington, IN: Indiana University Press, 2013 [1955].

Bhutto, Fatima. 'Flesh and Sand'. In *The Displaced: Refugee Writers on Refugee Lives*, edited by Viet Thanh Nguyen, 43–51. New York: Abrams Press, 2018.

Biemann, Ursula. 'Performing the Border: On Gender, Transnational Bodies, and Technology'. In *Globalization on the Line: Gender, Nation, and Capital at U.S. Borders*, edited by Claudia Sadowsky, 99–120. New York: Palgrave Macmillan, 2002.

———. 'Performing the Border'. *Rethinking Marxism* 14, no. 1 (2002): 29–47.

Biermann, Frank. 'Global Governance to Protect Future Climate Refugees'. In *'Climate Refugees': Beyond the Legal Impasse?*, edited by Simon Behrman and Avidan Kent, 265–77. London and New York: Routledge, 2018.

Bisanswa, Justin. '*Généalogie d'une banalité* de Sinzo Aanza. Le roman des moins-que-rien et des héros médiocres'. *Présence Francophone: Revue internationale de langue et de littérature* 94, no. 1 (2020): 35–57.

Blanc, Guillaume. *The Invention of Green Colonialism.* Trans. H. Morrison. Cambridge: Polity Press, 2022.

———. *La nature des hommes. Une mission écologique pour "sauver" l'Afrique.* Paris: La Découverte, 2024.

Blanchard, Pascal. 'Le passé colonial, un sujet incontournable de campagne'. *Le NouvelObs*, March 29, 2022.

Blanchard, Pascal, Nicolas Bancel, Gilles Böetsch, Christelle Taraud and Dominic Thomas, eds. *Sexe, race et colonies: La domination des corps du XVè siècle à nos jours.* Paris: La Découverte, 2018.

Blanchard, Pascal, Gilles Boëtsch and Nanette Jacomijn Snoep, eds. *Human Zoos: The Invention of the Savage.* Paris: Musée du Quai Branly and Arles: Actes Sud, 2011.

Blanchard, Pascal and Ruth Ginio. 'Imperial Revolution: Vichy's Colonial Myth (1940-1944)'. In *Colonial Culture in France Since the Revolution*, edited by Pascal Blanchard, Sandrine Lemaire, Nicolas Bancel and Dominic Thomas, 307–19. Bloomington, IN: Indiana University Press, 2014.

Blanchard, Pascal, Sandrine Lemaire, Nicolas Bancel and Dominic Thomas. 'The Creation of a *Colonial Culture* in France, from the Colonial Era to the "Memory Wars"'. In *Colonial Culture in France Since the Revolution*, edited by Pascal Blanchard, Sandrine Lemaire, Nicolas Bancel and Dominic Thomas, 1–47. Bloomington, IN: Indiana University Press, 2014.

Boeck, Filip De and Sammy Baloji. *Suturing the City: Living Together in Congo's Urban World.* London: Autograph ABP, 2016.

Bofane, In Koli Jean. *Congo Inc.: Bismarck's Testament.* Trans. M. De Jaeger. Bloomington, IN: Indiana University Press, 2018 [2014].

———. *Nation cannibale.* Paris: Denoël, 2025.

Bogost, Ian. *Persuasive Games: The Expressive Power of Videogames.* Cambridge, MA and London: The MIT Press, 2007.

Boni, Tanella. 'The Polluting of the World and the Silence of African Writer'. *Journal of the African Studies Association* 5, no. 1 (2010): 25–36.

Bonilla, Yarimar. *Non-Sovereign Futures: French Caribbean Politics in the Wake of Disenchantment.* Chicago, IL: University of Chicago Press, 2015.

Bornstein, David. 'Héliosphéra, fille des abysses, amour planctonique'. *Libération*, December 16, 2022.

Borrell, Josep. 'European Diplomatic Academy: Opening Remarks by High Representative Josep Borrell at the Inauguration of the Pilot Programme.' October 13, 2022. https://www.eeas.europa.eu/eeas/european-diplomatic-academy-opening -remarks-high-representative-josep-borrell-inauguration-pilot_en.

Boukala, Salomi and Eirini Tountasaki. 'From Black to Green: Analysing Le Front National's "Patriotic Ecology"'. In *The Far Right and the Environment: Politics, Discourse and Communication*, edited by Bernard Forchtner, 72–87. London and New York: Routledge, 2020.

Bounds, Andy. 'Climate Regulation is Driving Support for Populism, Says EU Parliament Chief'. *Financial Times*, September 7, 2023.

Bowersox, Jeff. *Raising Germans in the Age of Empire: Youth and Colonial Culture, 1871–1914.* Oxford: Oxford University Press, 2013.

Boye, François. 'Economic Mechanisms in Historical perspective'. In *Senegal: Essays in Statecraft*, edited by Momar Coumba Diop, 28–84. Dakar: CODESRIA, 1993.

———. *No More Fossils*. Minneapolis, MN: University of Minnesota Press, 2023.

Boyer, Dominic. 'Ostlagie and the Politics of the Future in East Germany'. *Public Culture* 18, no. 2 (2006): 361–81.

Boyer, Gilles, Pascal Clerc and Michelle Zancarini-Fournel, eds. *L'école aux colonies, les colonies à l'école*. Lyon: ENS, 2013.

Bracke, Sarah and Luis Manuel Hernández Aguilar. 'The Politics of Replacement: From "Race Suicide" to the "Great Replacement"'. In *The Politics of Replacement: Demographic Fears, Conspiracy Theories, and Race Wars*, edited by Sarah Bracke and Luis Manuel Hernández Aguilar, 1–19. London and New York: Routledge, 2024.

Brain, Stephen and Viktor Pál, eds. *Environmentalism under Authoritarian Regimes: Myth, Propaganda, Reality*. Abingdon and New York: Routledge, 2019.

———. 'Introduction'. In *Environmentalism under Authoritarian Regimes: Myth, Propaganda, Reality*, edited by Stephen Brain and Viktor Pál, 1–10. Abingdon and New York: Routledge, 2019.

Brambilla, Chiara. 'Exploring the Critical Potential of the Borderscapes Concept'. *Geopolitics* 20, no. 1 (2015): 14–34.

———. 'In/visibilities beyond the Spectacularisation: Young People, Subjectivity and Revolutionary Border Imaginations in the Mediterranean Borderscape'. In *Border Images, Border Narratives: The Political Aesthetics of Boundaries and Crossings*, edited by Johan Schimanski and Jopi Nyman, 83–104. Manchester: Manchester University Press, 2021.

Braverman, Suella. 'Keynote Address by UK Home Secretary Suella Braverman: UK-US Security Priorities for the 21st Century'. American Enterprise Institute for Public Policy Research, Washington, DC, September 26, 2023.

Breleur, Ernest, Patrick Chamoiseau, Gérard Delver, Serge Domi, Édouard Glissant, Guillaume Pigeard de Gurbert, Olivier Porteop, Olivier Pular and Jean-Claude William. *Manifeste pour les "produits" de haute nécessité*. Paris: Éditions Galaade and the Institut du Tout-Monde, 2009.

British Petroleum. https://www.bp.com.

Brown, Oli. *Migration and Climate Change*. IOM Migration Research Series, no. 31. Geneva: International Organization for Migration, 2008, 1–62.

Brown, Wendy. *Walled States, Waning Sovereignty*. New York: Zone Books, 2014.

Bruhn, Jørgen and Niklas Salmose, eds. *Intermedial Ecocriticism: The Climate Crisis Through Art and Media*. Lanham, MD: Lexington Books, 2023.

Bruyn, Ben De. 'The Great Displacement: Reading Migration Fiction at the End of the World'. *Humanities* 9, no. 25 (2020): 1–16.

Buekens, Sara. 'Le monde postcolonial de Sony Labou Tansi: entre magie et science'. *RELIEF – Revue électronique de littérature française* 16, no. 1 (2022): 150–65.

———. *Écologies littéraires africaines. L'imaginaire de l'environnement dans la littérature francophone postcoloniale*. Leiden and Boston, MA: Brill, 2025.

Butler, Judith. *Bodies that Matter: On the Discursive Limits of 'Sex'*. New York: Routledge, 1993.

Caillois, Roger. *Man, Play and Games*. Trans. M. Barash. Urbana and Chicago, IL: University of Illinois Press, 2001 [1958].

Camus, Jean-Yves and Nicolas Lebourg. *Far-Right Politics in Europe*. Trans. J. M. Todd. Cambridge, MA: The Belknap Press of Harvard University Press, 2017.

Camus, Renaud. *Le grand remplacement. Introduction au remplacisme global*. Paris: La Nouvelle Librairie, 2021 [2011].

Candido, Mariana P. 'This is your land: Legislating dispossession in colonial West Africa'. *The Berlin Journal* 37 (2023–2024): 6–9.

Carenini, Emma. *Soleil: Mythes, histoire et sociétés*. Paris: Le Pommier / Humensis, 2022.

Carpio, Glenda R. *Migrant Aesthetics: Contemporary Fiction, Global Migration, and the Limits of Empathy*. New York: Columbia University Press, 2023.

Carr, Matthew. *Fortress Europe: Dispatches from a Gated Continent*. New York: The New Press, 2012.

Carrington, Damian. 'Satellite to "Name and Shame" Worst Oil and Gas Methane Polluters'. *The Guardian*, March 4, 2024.

Casanova, Pascale. *The World Republic of Letters*. Trans. M. B. DeBevoise. Cambridge, MA: Harvard University Press, 2004.

Cawayu, Atmahi and Sigrid Vertommen. "Cuerpo-Territory/Body-Territory." *Kohl: a Journal for Body and Gender Research* 11, no. 1 (2025). https://kohljournal.press/cuerpo -territorio.

Center for Law, Energy, and the Environment. 'A Guide to Major Climate and Environmental Excerpts in the Project 2025 Report', University of California Berkeley. Accessed March 11, 2025. https://www.law.berkeley.edu/wp-content/uploads/2024 /08/Index-and-Summary-Annotated-of-Project-2025-Report-Aug1424.pdf.

Césaire, Aimé. *Discourse on Colonialism*. Trans. J. Pinkham. New York: Monthly Review Press, 1972 [1955].

———. *Notebook of a Return to a Native Land*. Trans. C. Eshleman and A. Smith. Middletown, CT: Wesleyan University Press, 2001 [1939].

Chakrabarty, Dipesh. *The Climate of History in a Planetary Age*. Chicago, IL: University of Chicago Press, 2021.

———. 'Nous assistons à une prise de conscience: la planète a une histoire'. Interview, *Radio France*, January 28, 2023. https://www.radiofrance.fr/franceculture/podcasts /l-invite-e-et-maintenant/dipesh-chakrabarty-nous-assistons-a-une-prise-de -conscience-la-planete-a-une-histoire-2375921.

Chamoiseau, Patrick. *Migrant Brothers: A Poet's Declaration of Human Dignity*. Trans. M. Amos and F. Rönnbäck. New Haven, CT: Yale University Press, 2018.

Chamoiseau, Patrick and Michel Le Bris. 'Introduction: "Là où littérature ne peut"'. In *Osons la fraternité. Les écrivains aux côtés des migrants*, edited by Patrick Chamoiseau and Michel Le Bris, 9–14. Paris: Philippe Rey, 2018.

Champion, Giulia. 'Pervasive Extractivism: Petroculture and Sedimented Histories in Sandrine Bessora's *Petroleum*'. *Journal of Energy History/Revue d'Histoire de l'Énergie* 10 (3 August 2023): 1–17.

Chan, Kelvin. 'Musk's X is the Largest Source of Disinformation, EU Official Says'. *PBS News*, September 26, 2023. https://www.pbs.org/newshour/politics/musks-x-is-the -largest-source-of-disinformation-eu-official-says.

Charbonnier, Pierre. *Abondance et liberté. Une histoire environnementale des idées politiques*. Paris: La Découverte, 2020.

———. 'Introduction: Après l'invasion de l'Ukraine: géopolitique de l'anthropocène'. *GREEN: Géopolique, Eéseaux, Énergie, Environnement, Nature* 2 (September 2022): 5–11.

Chauvin, Hortense and Clémence Michels. 'Marine Le Pen, à l'extrême opposé de l'écologie'. *Reporterre*, April 20, 2022. https://reporterre.net/Marine-Le-Pen-a-l -extreme-oppose-de-l-ecologie.

Chavalarias, David. *Toxic data. Comment les réseaux sociaux manipulent nos opinions*. Paris: Flammarion, 2022.

Chavoz, Ninon. 'From the *Roi de Kahel* to *Camarade Papa*: The Itinerary of a Spoiled Colonial'. Trans. J. Angell, *Politika*, April 24, 2023. https://www.politika.io/en/ article/from-the-roi-kahel-to-camarade-papa-the-itinerary-of-a-spoiled-colonial.

Chazalnoël, Mariam Traore and Dina Ionesco. 'Advancing the Global Governance of Climate Migration Through the United Nations Framework Convention on Climate Change and the Global Compact on Migration'. In *'Climate Refugees': Beyond the Legal Impasse?*, edited by Simon Behrman and Avidan Kent, 103–17. London and New York: Routledge, 2018.

Cheung, Helier. 'What Does Trump Actually Believe on Climate Change?' *BBC News*, January 23, 2020. https://www.bbc.com/news/world-us-canada-51213003.

Chevron. https://www.chevron.com.

Chirac, Jacques. 'Speech by M. Jacques Chirac, President of the Republic, at the Opening of the Quai Branly Museum'. June 20, 2006. https://ccbmn.culture.gouv.fr/Default /doc/SYRACUSE/927424/allocution-de-monsieur-jacques-chirac-a-l-occasion-de-l -inauguration-du-musee-du-quai-branly-paris-m.

Chretien, Spencer. 'Project 2025'. Accessed May 5, 2025. https://www.heritage.org/ conservatism/commentary/project-2025.

Clette-Gakuba, Véronique and David Jamar. 'Preface'. In *La dent de Lumumba: Régicide contre la Colonie*, edited by Samy Manga, 7–39. Brussels: Météores, 2024.

Clifford, James. 'Quai Branly in Process'. *October* 120 (2007): 3–23.

Climate Action Against Disinformation Coalition (CAAD). 'Climate of Misinformation: Ranking Big Tech'. September 2023. https://caad.info/wp-content/uploads/2023 /09/Climate-of-Misinformation.pdf.

Climate Change Group of the World Bank. 'Acting on Internal Climate Migration'. 2021. https://openknowledge.worldbank.org/entities/publication/2c9150df-52c3 -58ed-0075-d78ea56c3267.

Climate Change Group of the World Bank. 'Preparing for Internal Climate Migration'. 2018. https://openknowledge.worldbank.org/entities/publication/2be91c76-d023 -5809-9c94-d41b71c25635.

Climate Intelligence Foundation (CLINTEL). https://clintel.org/world-climate -declaration/.

Coen, Deborah. *Climate in Motion: Science, Empire, and the Problem of Scale.* Chicago, IL: University of Chicago Press, 2018.

Coetzee, John M. *Disgrace.* New York: Viking, 1999.

Cohen, Marjorie, ed. *Climate Change and Gender in Rich Countries.* London and New York: Routledge, 2017.

Collectif Des Auteurs Africains, eds. *Nos vers en vert.* Libreville: GNK éditions, 2021.

Collot, Michel. *Un nouveau sentiment de la nature.* Paris: Corti, 2022.

Colombet, Astrid Mignon and Alfred Reboul. 'Justice climatique: les limites du *name and shame*.' *L'Esprit* 502 (2023): 10–13.

Conklin, Alice L. *A Mission to Civilize: The Republican Idea of Empire in France and West Africa, 1895–1930.* Stanford, CA: Stanford University Press, 1997.

Conklin, Alice L. and Julia Clancy-Smith. 'Introduction: Writing Colonial Histories'. *French Historical Studies* 27, no. 3 (Summer 2004): 497–505.

Coplan, Amy and Peter Goldie, eds. *Empathy: Philosophical and Psychological Perspectives.* New York: Oxford University Press, 2014.

———. 'Introduction.' In *Empathy: Philosophical and Psychological Perspectives*, edited by Amy Coplan and Peter Goldie, ix–xlvii. New York: Oxford University Press, 2014.

Coquery-Vidrovitch, Catherine. 'Selling the Economic Myth (1900-1940).' In *Colonial Culture in France Since the Revolution*, edited by Pascal Blanchard, Sandrine Lemaire, Nicolas Bancel and Dominic Thomas, 180–8. Bloomington, IN: Indiana University Press, 2014.

Council of the European Union. 'European Pact on Immigration and Asylum'. Document 13440/08, September 24, 2008. https://data.consilium.europa.eu/doc/document/ ST-13440-2008-INIT/en/pdf.

———. 'Migration Policy: Council Reaches Agreement on Key Asylum and Migration Laws.' June 8, 2023. https://home-affairs.ec.europa.eu/policies/migration-and -asylum/common-european-asylum-system/country-responsible-asylum-application -dublin-regulation_en.

Cronon, William. 'The Trouble with Wilderness: Or, Getting Back to the Wrong Nature'. *Environmental History* 1, no. 1 (January 1996): 7–28.

Curley, Andrew and Sara Smith. 'The Cene Scene: Who Gets to Theorize Global Time and How Do We Center Indigenous and Black Futurities?' *Environment and Planning E: Nature and Space* 7, no. 1 (2024): 166–88.

Currie, Gregory. 'Empathy for Objects.' In *Empathy: Philosophical and Psychological Perspectives*, edited by Amy Coplan and Peter Goldie, 82–98. New York: Oxford University Press, 2014.

Cushman, Gregory T. 'Humboldtian Science, Creole Meteorology, and the Discovery of Human-Caused Climate Change in South America'. *Osiris* 26, no. 1 (2011): 19–44.

d'Eaubonne, Françoise. *Naissance de l'écoféminisme.* Paris: Presses Universitaires de France, 2021.

Daeninckx, Didier. *L'école des colonies.* Paris: Hoëbeke, 2015.

Daggett, Cara. 'Petro-masculinity and the Politics of Climate Refusal'. Autonomy Institute, May 1, 2022. https://autonomy.work/portfolio/petro-masculinity-climate -refusal/.

Dal Lago, Alessandro. *Non-Persons: The Exclusion of Migrants in a Global Society*. Trans. M. Orton. Milan: IPOC Press, 2009.

Dallembert, Louis-Philippe. *Mediterranean Wall*. Trans. M. de Jager. Ashland, OH: Schaffner Press, 2021.

Daughton, James P. *In the Forest of No Joy: The Tragedy of the Congo-Océan Railroad and the Tragedy of French Colonialism*. New York: W. W. Norton, 2021.

David, Bruno. ed. *Manifeste du muséum: Migrations*. Paris: Muséum National d'Histoire Naturelle, 2018.

David, Kim. *Arendt's Solidarity: Anti-Semitism & Racism in the Atlantic World*. Stanford, CA: Stanford University Press, 2024.

Davidson, Basil. *Africa in Modern History: The Search for a New Society*. New York: Penguin Books, 1978.

Dawson, Aimee. 'Interview with Ai Weiwei'. *The Art Newspaper*, March 27, 2018.

Delbeke, Jos and Peter Vis. *EU Climate Policy Explained*. London and New York: Routledge, 2015.

Delecroix, Vincent. *Naufrage*. Paris: Gallimard: 2023.

Dell'Agnese, Elena and Anne-Laure Amilhat Szary. 'Borderscapes: From Border Landscapes to Border Aesthetics'. *Geopolitics* 20, no. 1 (2015): 4–13.

DeLoughrey, Elizabeth. *Allegories of the Anthropocene*. Durham, NC: Duke University Press, 2019.

Dembélé, Diadié. *Deux grands hommes et demi*. Paris: Jean-Claude Lattès, 2024.

Demos, T. J. *Against the Anthropocene: Visual Culture and the Environment Today*. London: Sternberg Press, 2017.

———. *Beyond the World's End: Arts of Living at the Crossing*. Durham, NC and London: Duke University Press, 2020.

———. *Decolonizing Nature: Contemporary Art and the Politics of Ecology*. Berlin: Sternberg Press, 2016.

———. *Radical Futurisms: Ecologies of Collapse, Chronopolitics, and Justice-to-Come*. New York: Sternberg Press, 2023.

———. *The Migrant Image: The Art and Politics of Documentary during Global Crisis*. Durham, NC: Duke University Press, 2013.

Descola, Philippe. *Beyond Nature and Culture*. Trans. J. Lloyd. Chicago, IL: University of Chicago Press, 2013.

Desquilbet, Alice. 'De la matière et des trous: l'envers du décor de la coopération sino-congolaise contemporaine'. *Études littéraires africaines* 52 (2021): 103–17.

———. 'Polémiques congolaises: les armes discursives de Sony Labou Tansi et Sinzo Aanza.' *Revue des Sciences Humaines* 351 (2023): 149–62.

Diallo, Khalil. *L'odyssée des oubliés*. Paris: Emmanuelle Colas, 2021.

Diome, Fatou. *Celles qui attendent*. Paris: Flammarion, 2010.

Djombo, Henri and Osée Colin Koagne. *Le Cri de la forêt*. Paris: LC Éditions/Éditions Hermar, 2015.

Dodds, Joseph. 'The Psychology of Climate Anxiety'. *BJPsych Bulletin* 45, no. 4 (2021): 222–6.

Dorfman, Ariel and Viet Thanh Nguyen. 'The Displaced: Refugee Writers Ariel Dorfman and Viet Thanh Nguyen on Migration, US Wars & Resistance'. *Democracy Now!*, May 4, 2018. https://z.umn.edu/44c6.

Dorlin, Elsa. *La matrice de la race: généalogie sexuelle et coloniale de la nation Française*. Paris: La Découverte, 2006.

Doron, Roy and Toyin Falola. *Ken Saro-Wiwa*. Athens, OH: Ohio University Press, 2016.

Drayton, Richard Henry. *Nature's Government: Science, Imperial Britain and the 'Improvement' of the World*. New Haven, CT: Yale University Press, 2000.

Duarte, Fabio. 'X (Formerly Twitter) User Age, Gender, & Demographic Stats (2024)'. *Exploding Topics*, April 25, 2024. https://explodingtopics.com/blog/x-user-stats.

Dubiau, Antoine. *Écofascismes*. Caen: Grevis, 2023.

Dummett, Mark. 'Afterword'. In *Silence Would be Treason: Last writings of Ken Saro-Wiwa*, edited by Íde Corley, Helen Fallon and Laurence Cox, 173–5. Nairobi: Daraja Press, 2018.

Dupuy, Jean-Pierre. *How to Think About Catastrophe: Toward a Theory of Enlightened Doomsaying*. Trans. M. B. DeBevoise and M. R. Anspach. East Lansing, MI: Michigan State University Press, 2022 [2002].

Durand, Cédric. *Techno-féodalisme. Critique de l'économie numérique*. Paris: La Découverte, 2023.

Durand, Stéphane. 'Preface'. In *Héliosphéra, fille des abysses, d'amour et de plancton*, by Wilfried N'Sondé, 11. Arles: Actes Sud, 2022.

Durrant, Sam and Catherine M. Lord, eds. *Essays in Migratory Aesthetics: Cultural Practices Between Migration and Art-Making*. Amsterdam: Rodopi, 2007.

Dutch Plastic Soup Foundation. Accessed January 31, 2025. https://www.plasticsoup foundation.org/en/.

Dutta, Ankita. 'Unpacking the EU's Migration Deal'. Observer Research Foundation, July 4, 2023. https://www.orfonline.org/expert-speak/unpacking-the-eus-migration -deal.

Eaton, Emily M. and Nick A. Day. 'Petro-pedagogy: Fossil Fuel Interests and the Obstruction of Climate Justice in Public Education'. *Environmental Education Research* 26, no. 4 (2020): 457–73.

Ebner, Julia. *Going Dark: The Secret Lives of Extremists*. London: Bloomsbury, 2019.

———. *Going Mainstream: How extremists are taking over*. London: Ithaca Press, 2023.

———. "Conspiracy Theorists. Incels. White Nationalists. Dara Research and Technological Change." Distinguished Lecture in the Digital Humanities, University of California, Los Angeles, May 29, 2025.

———. *The Rage: The Vicious Circle of Islamists and Far-Right Extremism*. London and New York: I. B. Tauris, 2017.

Editorial. 'The Guardian View on Donald Trump's Congo Deal: Mineral Riches for Protection'. *The Guardian*, April 13, 2025.

Efoui, Kossi. *La Fabrique des cérémonies*. Paris: Seuil, 2001.

El-Tayeb, Fatima. *European Others: Queering Ethnicity in Postnational Europe*. Minneapolis, MN: University of Minnesota Press, 2011.

Ellul, Jacques. *Propaganda: The Formation of Men's Attitudes*. Trans. K. Kellen and J. Lerner. New York: Vintage Books, 1968.

Emcke, Carolin. *Against Hate*. Trans. T. Crawford. Cambridge: Polity Press, 2019.

Empoli, Giuliano da. *Les ingénieurs du chaos*. Paris: Jean-Claude Lattès, 2019.

———. *L'Heure des prédateurs*. Paris: Gallimard, 2025.

———. 'Giuliano da Empoli : "La formule des ingénieurs du chaos est toujours la même: la colère et la frustration, démultipliées par l'algorithme"'. Interview with Nicolas Truong. *Le Monde*, April 21, 2025.

Erpenbeck, Jenny. *Go, Went, Gone*. Trans. S. Bernofsky. New York: New Directions Books, 2017 [2015].

———. *Kairos*. Trans. M. Hofmann. New York: New Directions Publishing Corporation, 2023 [2021].

———. *Not a Novel: Collected Writings and Reflections*. Trans. K. Beals. London: Granta, 2020 [2018].

European Commission. '10-Point Plan for Lampedusa.' September 17, 2023. https://ec .europa.eu/commission/presscorner/detail/en/IP_23_4503.

———. 'A Humane and Effective Return and Readmission Policy'. 2024. https:// home-affairs.ec.europa.eu/policies/migration-and-asylum/irregular-migration-and -return/humane-and-effective-return-and-readmission-policy_en.

———. 'Pact on Migration and Asylum'. May 21, 2024, https://home-affairs.ec.europa .eu/policies/migration-and-asylum/pact-migration-and-asylum_en.

———. 'The Digital Services Act.' 2024. https://commission.europa.eu/strategy-and -policy/priorities-2019-2024/europe-fit-digital-age/digital-services-act_en.

———. 'The European Green Deal: Striving to be the First Climate-Neutral Continent'. 2024. https://commission.europa.eu/strategy-and-policy/priorities-2019-2024/ european-green-deal_en.

European Environment Agency. 'European Climate Risk Assessment Executive Summary'. January 2024. https://www.eea.europa.eu/publications/european -climate-risk-assessment.

Evans, Brad. 'Dead in the Waters'. In *Life Adrift: Climate Change, Migration, Critique*, edited by Andrew Baldwin and Giovanni Bettini, 59–78. London and New York: Rowman & Littlefield International, Ltd., 2017.

Executive Order. 'Addressing Egregious Actions of The Republic of South Africa'. Accessed April 20, 2025. https://www.whitehouse.gov/presidential-actions/2025/02 /addressing-egregious-actions-of-the-republic-of-south-africa/.

———. 'Ensuring National Security and Economic Resilience through section 232 Actions on Processed Critical Minerals and Derivative Products.' Accessed May 5, 2025. https://www.whitehouse.gov/presidential-actions/2025/04/ensuring-national -security-and-economic-resilience-through-section-232-actions-on-processed-critical -minerals-and-derivative-products/.

———. 'Unleashing America's Offshore Critical Minerals and Resources'. Accessed May 5, 2025. https://www.whitehouse.gov/presidential-actions/2025/04/unleashing -americas-offshore-critical-minerals-and-resources/.

Exxon Mobil. https://corporate.exxonmobil.com.

Fajt, Jiří and Adam Budak. 'Ai Weiwei: Law of the Journey'. Národní galerie v Praze (Prague National Gallery, March 17, 2017 to July 1, 2018. https://www.ngprague.cz /en/event/153/aj-wej-wej.

Fallon, Peter K. *Propaganda 2.1: Understanding Propaganda in the Digital Age*. Eugene, OR: Cascade Books, 2022.

Fanon, Frantz. *The Wretched of the Earth*. Trans. R. Philcox. New York: Grove Press, 2004 [1961].

Favell, Adrian. *Philosophies of Integration: Immigration and the Idea of Citizenship in France and Britain*. New York: Palgrave Macmillan, 2001.

Feagin, Susan. 'Empathizing as Simulating.' In *Empathy: Philosophical and Psychological Perspectives*, edited by Amy Coplan and Peter Goldie, 149–61. New York: Oxford University Press, 2014.

Ferdinand, Malcom. *Decolonial Ecology: Thinking from the Caribbean World*. Trans. A. P. Smith. Cambridge: Polity Press, 2022 [2019].

Fèvre, Joseph and Henri Hauser. *Précis de géographie*. Paris: F. Alcan, 1913.

Flores, Wendeline and Wayne Modest, eds. *Our Colonial Inheritance*. Tielt: Lannoo Publishers, 2024.

———. 'This (Terrible) Inheritance'. In *Our Colonial* Inheritance, edited by Wendeline Flores and Wayne Modest, 13–28. Tielt: Lannoo Publishers, 2024.

Food and Agriculture Organization of the United Nations. 'Construire une culture cacaoyère résiliente en Côte d'Ivoire'. July 22, 2022. https://www.fao.org/cote -divoire/actualites/detail-events/fr/c/1601694/.

Forchtner, Bernard. 'Far-Right Articulations of the Natural Environment: An Introduction'. In *The Far Right and the Environment: Politics, Discourse and Communication*, edited by Bernard Forchtner, 1–18. London and New York: Routledge, 2020.

Forest, Adam. 'Greta Thunberg: Right Wing French MPs Insult and Boycott Teenage Climate Activist'. *The Independent*, July 24, 2019.

Forsdick, Charles. 'Fragments of Empire: Ephemera, Toys, and the Dynamics of Colonial Memory'. In *Visualizing Empire: Africa, Europe, and the Politics of Representation*, edited by Rebecca Peabody, Steven Nelson and Dominic Thomas, 50–67. Los Angeles, CA: Getty Publications, 2021.

Foucart, Stéphane. 'L'aggravation récente des effets du réchauffement coïncide, et c'est une autre cause de sidération, avec un retour apparent du climatoscepticisme'. *Le Monde*, September 10, 2023.

———. 'Pour la première fois, toute l'Union européenne a enclenché la marche arrière sur l'environnement'. *Le Monde*, November 26, 2023.

Fraiture, Pierre-Philippe. 'Beyond Images of War: Sammy Baloji's Work Captures DR Congo's Vibrant Arts and Culture, Challenging Western Views'. *The Conversation*, April 15, 2024.

———. 'Digging Holes, Excavating the Present, Mining the Future: Extractivism, Time, and Memory in Fiston Mwanza Mujila's and Sammy Baloji's Works'. *Modern and Contemporary France* 32, no. 1 (2024): 139–59.

———. 'État Présent: Congolese Cultural Production in Africa and the World'. *French Studies* LXXVIII, no. 1 (2024): 101–27.

———. 'Tracking the Potholes of Colonial History: Sinzo Aanza's *Généalogie d'une banalité* and Fiston Mwanza Mujila's *Tram 83*'. In *Unfinished Histories: Empire and Postcolonial Resonance in Central Africa and Belgium*, edited by Pierre-Philippe Fraiture, 359–79. Leuven: Leuven University Press, 2022.

François, Stéphane. *La nouvelle droite et ses dissidences: identité, écologie et paganisme*. Lormont: Le Bord de l'Eau, 2021.

Fressoz, Jean-Baptiste and Fabien Locher. *Les Révoltes du ciel. Une histoire du changement climatique XVe-XXe siècle*. Paris: Seuil, 2020.

Frontex. https://www.frontex.europa.eu.

———. 'Annual Risk Analysis 2024/2025'. May 2024. https://www.frontex.europa.eu/ assets/Publications/Risk_Analysis/Annual_Risk_Analysis_2024-2025.pdf.

Frouws, Bram. 'Negative Narratives, Mistaken Metaphors. The Need for Careful Language on Migration.' Mixed Migration Center, March 8, 2021. https:// mixedmigration.org/op-ed-negative-narratives-mistaken-metaphors-the-need-for -careful-language-on-migration/.

Gabbatt, Adam. '"We're Facing Another Old Enemy": Rushdie Warns against Global Authoritarianism'. *The Guardian*, September 13, 2023.

Gaffric, Gwennäel. *La Littérature à l'ère de l'Anthroposcène. Une étude écocritique autour des œuvres de l'écrivain taïwanais Wu Ming-yi*. Le Pré-Saint-Gervais: L'Asiathèque, 2019.

Gaillardet, Jérôme. *La terre habitable ou l'épopée de la zone critique*. Paris: La Découverte, 2023.

Gammage, Bill. 'Colonists Upended Aboriginal Farming, Growing Grain and Running Sheep on Rich Yamfields, and Cattle on Arid Grainland'. *The Conversation*, September 19, 2023.

Garnier, Xavier. *Écopoétiques africaines. Une expérience décoloniale des lieux*. Paris: Karthala, 2022.

———. 'Writings of the Subsoil in the Contemporary Congolese Novel'. *Journal of World Literature* 6 (2021): 133–47.

Garrigues, Jean. *Banania: Histoire d'une passion française*. Paris: Du May, 1991.

Gaulupeau, Yves. 'L'Afrique en images dans les manuels élémentaires d'histoire (1880-1969)'. In *Images et colonies (1880-1962)*, edited by Nicolas Bancel, Pascal Blanchard and Laurent Gervereau, 66–69. Paris: ACHAC, 1993.

Gauz'. 'Les rêves de Kong de Binger'. In *Penser et écrire l'Afrique aujourd'hui*, edited by Alain Mabanckou, 182–7. Paris: Seuil, 2017.

———. *Cocoaïans (naissance d'une nation chocolat)*. Paris: L'arche, 2022.

———. *Comrade Papa*. Trans. F. Wynne. Windsor: Biblioasis, 2024 [2018].

Gefen, Alexandre. 'De l'écologie à l'écocritique'. *Revue Esprit* 472 (March 2021): 146–50.

———. *Réparer le monde. La littérature française face au XXIe siècle*. Paris: Corti, 2017.

Geisser, Vincent. 'Le Pacte européen sur l'immigration et l'asile ou le triomphe de la "frontexisation" des esprits'. *Migrations Société* 5, no. 119 (2008): 3–12.

General Act of the Berlin Conference on West Africa. 'German Federal Foreign Office Political Archive'. Accessed February 21, 2025. https://archiv.diplo.de/arc-en/the-political-archive/2684468-2684468.

Gerke, Stefanie. 'On Berlin's Palace of the Republic – A New, Transitory Ruin Motif in Contemporary Art?' *View: Theories and Practices of Visual Culture* 4 (2013). https://www.pismowidok.org/assets/files/article-pdf/issue-04/gerke.pdf.

Gershberg, Zac and Sean Illing. *The Paradox of Democracy: Free Speech, Open Media, and Perilous Persuasion*. Chicago, IL: University of Chicago Press, 2022.

Getty Research Institute. 'ACHAC Collection Inventory'. Accessed January 30, 2025. http://archives2.getty.edu:8082/xtf/view?docId=ead/970031/970031.xml;chunk.id=ref1093;brand=default;query=deutsche%20kolonien.

Ghosh, Amitav. *The Great Derangement: Climate Change and the Unthinkable*. Chicago, IL: University of Chicago Press, 2016.

———. *The Nutmeg's Curse: Parables for a Planet in Crisis*. Chicago, IL: University of Chicago Press, 2021.

Gilroy, Paul. 'Foreword: Migrancy, Culture, and a New Map of Europe'. In *Blackening Europe: The African American Presence*, edited by Heike Raphael-Hernandez, xi–xxii. London: Routledge, 2004.

———. *Postcolonial Melancholia*. New York: Columbia University Press, 2005.

Glissant, Édouard. *Caribbean Discourse: Selected Essays*. Trans. J. M. Dash. Charlottesville, VA: University Press of Virginia, 1989 [1981].

Glissant, Édouard and Patrick Chamoiseau. "Manifesto for "products" of dire need." In *Manifestos*, Trans. B. Wing and M. Reeck. London: Goldsmiths Press, 2022), 57–65.

Glotfelty, Cheryll. 'Literary Studies in an Age of Environmental Crisis'. In *The Ecocriticism Reader: Landmarks in Literary Ecology*, edited by Cheryll Glotfelty and Harold Fromm, xv–xxxvii. Athens, GA. University of Georgia Press, 1996.

Goldberg, David Theo. *Dread: Facing Futureless Futures.* Cambridge: Polity Press, 2021.

———. 'Parting Waters: Seas of Movement'. In *Life Adrift: Climate Change, Migration, Critique*, edited by Andrew Baldwin and Giovanni Bettini, 99–114. London and New York: Rowman & Littlefield International, Ltd., 2017.

Gómez-Barris, Macarena. 'The Colonial Anthropocene: Damage, Remapping, and Resurgent Resources: Book Review Essay.' *Antipode Online*, March 19, 2019. https://antipodeonline.org/2019/03/19/the-colonial-anthropocene/.

———. *The Extractive Zone: Social Ecologies and Decolonial Perspectives.* Durham, NC: Duke University Press, 2017.

Goodell, Jeff. *The Heat Will Kill You First: Life and Death on a Scorched Planet.* New York: Little, Brown and Company, 2023.

Goodfellow, Maya. '"You Can't Shoot Climate Change": Richard Seymour on How Far Right Exploits Environmental Crisis.' *The Guardian*, October 30, 2024.

Google Ads Team. 'Updating Our Ads and Monetization Policies on Climate Change'. October 7, 2021. https://support.google.com/google-ads/answer/11221321.

Gopal, Keerti. 'Kids and Families: The Latest Targets of Climate Denialism Propaganda'. *Bulletin of the Atomic Scientists*, August 10, 2023.

Gorman, Amanda. 'In Memory of Those Still in the Water'. *New York Times*, July 15, 2023.

Goyémidé, Étienne. *Le silence de la forêt.* Paris: Hatier, 1984.

Green Dreamer. '35 Environmental Organizations and Nonprofits for a Sustainable Future (List and Ways You Can Get Involved)'. https://www.greendreamer.com/journal/environmental-organizations-nonprofits-for-a-sustainable-future.

Green, Kenneth. 'Trudeau Government Ratchets Up 'Climate' Propaganda'. *The Toronto Star*, February 13, 2024.

Greenfield, Nicole. 'Climate Migration and Equity.' Natural Resources Defense Council, May 9, 2022. https://www.nrdc.org/stories/climate-migration-equity.

———. 'What Is Climate Feminism?'. Natural Resources Defense Council, March 18, 2021. https://www.nrdc.org/stories/what-climate-feminism.

Guenther, Genevieve. *The Language of Climate Politics: Fossil-Fuel Propaganda and How to Fight It.* New York: Oxford University Press, 2024.

Guhl, Jakob, Julia Ebner and Jan Rau. "The Online Ecosystem of the German Far-Right." London, ISD, 2020. https://www.isdglobal.org/wp-content/uploads/2020/02/ISD-The-Online-Ecosystem-of-the-German-Far-Right-English-Draft-11.pdf.

Haas, Hein de. 'Changing the Migration Narrative: On the Power of Discourse, Propaganda and Truth Distortion'. IMI Working Paper Number 181/PACES Project Working Paper Number 3. Amsterdam: University of Amsterdam, May 2024.

———. *How Migration Really Works: The Facts About the Most Divisive Issue in Politics.* New York: Basic Books, 2023.

Haas, Hein de, Stephen Castles and Mark J. Miller. *The Age of Migration: International Population Movements in the Modern World.* New York and London: The Guilford Press, 2020.

Habila, Helon. *Oil on Water.* New York: W. W. Norton & Company, Inc., 2010.

Hamlin, David D. *Work and Play: The Production and Consumption of Toys in Germany, 1870-1914.* Ann Arbor, MI: University of Michigan Press, 2007.

Han, Byung-Chul. *Infocracy. Digitization and the Crisis of Democracy.* Trans. D. Steuer. Cambridge: Polity Press, 2022 [2021].

———. *The Crisis of Narration.* Trans. D. Steuer. Cambridge: Polity Press, 2024 [2023].

Haraway, Donna J. *Staying with the Trouble: Making Kin in the Chthulucene*. Durham, NC: Duke University Press, 2016.

Harel, Xavier and Thomas Hofnung, *Le scandale des biens mal acquis. Enquête sur les milliards volés de la françafrique*. Paris: La Découverte, 2011.

Hargreaves, Alec G. *Multi-Ethnic France: Immigration, Politics, Culture and Society*. New York and London: Routledge, 2007.

Hartmann, Betsy. 'The Ghosts of Malthus: Narratives and Mobilizations of Scarcity in the US Political Context'. In *The Limits to Scarcity: Contesting the Politics of Allocation*, edited by Lyla Mehta, 49–68. London and Washington, DC: Earthscan, 2010.

Harvey, Fiona. 'Demagogues Imperiling Global Fight against Climate Breakdown, Says Kerry.' *The Guardian*, February 28, 2024.

Harvey, Fiona and Damian Carrington. 'UK Absent from Key International Statement on Climate Action'. *The Guardian*, September 20, 2023.

Hautcœur, Pierre-Cyrille. 'Le monde entre dans une nouvelle ère de domination du capitalisme de la finitude'. *Le Monde*, January 15, 2025.

Havel, Václav. 'Speech to United States Congress'. *Washington Post*, February 21, 1990.

Heath, Elizabeth. 'Child's Play? Colonial Commodities, Ephemera, and the Construction of the Greater French Family: *Apprendre l'Empire, un jeu d'enfants?*'. *CLIO: Women, Gender, History* 40, no. 2 (2014): 69–87.

Heise, Ursula K. *Sense of Place and Sense of Planet: The Environmental Imagination of the Global*. New York: Oxford University Press, 2008.

Heller, Charles, Nicholas De Genova, Maurice Stierl, Martina Tazzioli and Huub van Baar. 'Crisis'. In *Europe/Crisis: New Keywords of 'the Crisis' in and of 'Europe'*, 1–45, 2016. https://nearfuturesonline.org/wp-content/uploads/2016/01/New-Keywords-Collective_12.pdf.

Herman, Edward S. and Noam Chomsky. *Manufacturing Consent: The Political Economy of the Mass Media*. New York: Pantheon Books, 1988.

Hix, Simon et al. 'Immigration and Brexit'. May 30, 2017. https://blogs.lse.ac.uk/politicsandpolicy/non-eu-migration-is-what-uk-voters-care-most-about/.

Hochschild, Adam. *King Leopold's Ghost: A Story of Greed, Terror, and Heroism in Colonial Africa*. Boston, MA: Houghton Mifflin Company, 1998.

Holo, Yann. 'L'œuvre civilisatrice de l'idée à l'image'. In *Images et colonies (1880–1962)*, edited by Nicolas Bancel, Pascal Blanchard and Laurent Gervereau, 58–65. Paris: ACHAC, 1993.

Holt-Giménez, Eric. *A Foodie's Guide to Capitalism: Understanding the Political Economy of What We Eat*. New York: Monthly Review Press, 2017.

———. 'Introduction: Agrarian Questions and the Struggle for Land Justice in the United States'. In *Land Justice: Re-Imagining Land, Food, and the Commons in the United States*, edited by Justine M. Williams and Eric Holt-Giménez, 1–14. Oakland, CA: Food First Books, 2017.

Horsti, Karina and Ilaria Tucci. 'Performance of Memory: Testimonies of Survival and Rescue at Europe's Border'. In *Border Images, Border Narratives: The Political Aesthetics of Boundaries and Crossings*, edited by Johan Schimanski and Jopi Nyman, 225–41. Manchester: Manchester University Press, 2021.

Horton, Jessica L. 'Ecolonial Holism'. *Panorama: Journal of the Association of Historians of American Art* 5, no. 1 (Spring 2019). https://journalpanorama.org/article/ecocriticism/ecolonial-holism/.

Hosen, Nadzirah, Hitoshi Nakamura and Amran Hamzah. 'Adaptation to Climate Change: Does Traditional Ecological Knowledge Hold the Key?'. *Sustainability* 12, no. 676 (2020). https://www.mdpi.com/2071-1050/12/2/676.

Huckstep, Samuel and Helen Dempster. 'The "Climate Migration" Narrative Is Inaccurate, Harmful, and Pervasive. We Need an Alternative'. Center for Global Development, December 5, 2023. https://www.cgdev.org/blog/climate-migration -narrative-inaccurate-harmful-and-pervasive-we-need-alternative.

Hugon, Anne. 'Conquête et exploration en Afrique noire'. In *Images et colonies (1880– 1962),* edited by Nicolas Bancel, Pascal Blanchard and Laurent Gervereau, 18–23. Paris: ACHAC, 1993.

Hunter, Lori M. and Raphael J. Nawrotzki. 'Migration and the Environment'. In *Handbook of Migration and Population Distribution,* edited by Michael J. White, 465–84. Dordrecht: Springer, 2015.

Iheka, Cajetan. *African Ecomedia: Network Forms, Planetary Politics.* Durham, NC: Duke University Press, 2021.

Illouz, Eva. *The Emotional Life of Populism: How Fear, Disgust, Resentment, and Love Undermine Democracy.* Cambridge: Polity Press, 2023.

Imbert, Louis. *Immigration: Fabrique d'un discours de crise.* Paris: 10/18, 2022.

International Organization for Migration. 'Environmental Migration'. 2025. https://env ironmentalmigration.iom.int/environmental-migration.

———. 'Gender and Migration: Trends, Gaps and Urgent Action. Current Context: From the Feminization of Migration to the Growing Global Gap in Migration'. 2024. https://worldmigrationreport.iom.int/what-we-do/world-migration-report-2024 -chapter-6/current-context-feminization-migration-growing-global-gender-gap -migration.

———. 'Migration and the Environment'. November 1, 2007. https://www.iom.int/ sites/g/files/tmzbdl486/files/jahia/webdav/shared/shared/mainsite/about_iom/en /council/94/MC_INF_288.pdf.

———. 'Strategy on Migration, Environment, and Climate Change 2021-2030'. https:// environmentalmigration.iom.int/iom-strategy-migration-environment-and-climate -change-2021-2030.

Jacqué, Philippe. 'The EU Wants to Outsource Immigration Management'. *Le Monde,* November 20, 2023.

James, Erin. *Narrative in the Anthropocene.* Columbus, OH: The Ohio State University Press, 2022.

Jeanneney, Ambroise. *Ce que produisent nos colonies: leçons de choses et lectures.* Paris: Librairie Ch. Delagrave, 1896.

Joassart-Marcelli, Pascale. *Food Geographies: Social, Political, and Ecological Connections.* London: Rowman & Littlefield, 2022.

Johnstone-Hack, Alastair. 'What Does AI Imagery Mean for Climate Change Photography?'. *Climate Outreach,* March 6, 2024.

Joly, Lucinda. 'The Many Extraordinary Iterations of The Raft of the Medusa'. *Daily Maverick,* October 24, 2022.

Jones, Caroline A. *Sensorium: Embodied Experience, Technology, and Contemporary Art.* Cambridge, MA: MIT Press, 2006.

Joris, Lieve. *Sur les ailes du dragon: Voyages entre l'Afrique et la Chine.* Trans. A. Ounanian. Arles: Actes Sud, 2014 [2013].

Jütte, Daniel. 'Transparency: A German Kaleidoscope'. *The Berlin Journal* 38 (2024– 2025): 6–11.

————. *Transparency: The Material History of an Idea.* New Haven, CT: Yale University Press, 2023.

Kakutani, Michiko. *The Death of Truth: Notes on Falsehood in the Age of Trump.* New York: Tim Duggan Press, 2018.

Kanbur, Ravi. 'The Theory of Structural Adjustment and Trade Policy'. In *Trade and Development in Sub-Saharan Africa*, edited by Jonathan H. Frimpong-Ansah, Ravi Kanbur and Peter Svedberg, 188–202. Manchester: Manchester University Press, 1991.

Kaufmann, Paulus, Hannes Kuch, Christian Neuhäuser and Elaine Webster, eds. *Humiliation, Degradation, Dehumanization: Human Dignity Violated.* New York: Springer, 2011.

Khanna, Parag. *Move: The Forces Uprooting Us.* New York: Scribner, 2021.

Kimmerer, Robin Wall. *Braiding Sweetgrass: Indigenous Wisdom, Scientific Knowledge and the Teachings of Plants.* Minneapolis, MN: Milkweed Editions, 2013.

Kimmermann, Michael. 'Rebuilding a Palace May Become a Grand Blunder'. *New York Times*, December 31, 2018.

Kocurek, Carly A. 'Walter Benjamin on the Video Screen: Storytelling and Game Narratives'. *Arts* 7, no. 4 (2018). https://doi.org/10.3390/arts7040069.

Kodjo-Grandvaux, Séverine. *Devenir vivants.* Paris: Philippe Rey, 2021.

Kouakou, Jean-Louis, Sery Gonedelé Bi, Eloi Anderson Bitty, Célestin Kouakou, InKouassi Yao, Kouadio Bénoîtype Kassé and Soulemane Ouattara. 'Ivory Coast without Ivory: Massive Extinction of African Forest Elephants in Côte d'Ivoire'. *PLoS One* 15, no. 10 (2020). https://journals.plos.org/plosone/article?id=10.1371/journal.pone.0232993.

Ktetzchmar, Ulrike. 'Foreword.' In *German Colonialism: Fragments Past and Present*, edited by Sebastian Gottschalk and Heike Hartmann, 10–11. Berlin: Deutsches Historishes Museum, 2016.

La Meslée, Valérie Marin. 'Achille Mbembe: L'insurrection se fera par l'éducation'. *Le Point Afrique*, February 3, 2018.

Laacher, Smaïn. *De la violence à la persécution, femmes sur la route de l'exil.* Paris: La Dispute, 2010.

Lacroix, Alexandre. 'Interview with Baptiste Morizot: Le monde va devenir chaotique, mais nous pouvons entrer en résistance'. *Philosophie Magazine* 164 (November 2022): 64–8.

Lamboley, Claude. 'Les jeux de l'oie. Longue histoire et grande collection'. 2023. https://www.jouetsanciens.fr/les-jeux-de-loie/.

Lanaspeze, Baptiste. *Nature.* Paris: Anamosa, 2022.

Lanchester, John. *The Wall.* London: Faber & Faber, 2019.

Lang, Johannes. 'Explaining Genocide: Hannah Arendt and the Social-Scientific Concept of Dehumanization'. In *The Anthem Companion to Hannah Arendt*, edited by Peter Baehr and Philip Walsh, 175–96. New York: Anthem Press, 2017.

Larrère, Catherine. *L'écoféminisme.* Paris: La Découverte, 2023.

Larrère, Catherine and Raphaël. *Le pire n'est pas certain. Essai sur l'aveuglement catastrophiste.* Paris: Premier Parallèle, 2020.

Latour, Bruno. *Down to Earth: Politics in the New Climatic Regime.* Trans. C. Porter. Cambridge: Polity Press, 2018.

Laurentie, Jacques. *Climat de peur: Enquête sur le changement climatique, de l'alarmisme aux faits.* Alençon: Bien Commun, 2023.

Laye, Camara. *The Dark Child*. Trans. J. Kirkup and E. Jones. New York: Farrar, Straus & Giroux, 1954.

Le Bras, Hervé. *L'Âge des migrations*. Paris: Autrement, 2017.

———. *Il n'y a pas de grand remplacement*. Paris: Grasset, 2022.

Lea, Sarah. 'Crossing Waters: Where to From Here'. In *Entangled Pasts: 1768-Now: Art, Colonialism and Change*, edited by Dorothy Price, 179–81. London: Royal Academy Publications, 2024.

Leclerc, Chanelle. 'Samy Manga and the Bitter Taste of the Cacao Culture in Africa'. *Cacao Source*, 2023. https://www.sourcecacao.com/es_GT/blog/viajes-1/samy -manga-and-the-bitter-taste-of-the-cacao-culture-in-africa-46.

'L'extrême droite en Europe abattra-t-elle le Pacte vert? Une carte inédite'. *Le Grand Continent*, September 16, 2023.

Legène, Susan and Janneke Van Dijk, eds. *The Netherlands East Indies at the Tropenmuseum: A colonial history*. Amsterdam: KIT Publishers, 2011.

Lehmann, Philipp. *Desert Edens: Colonial Climate Engineering in the Age of Anxiety*. Princeton, NJ: Princeton University Press, 2022.

Lemaire, Sandrine. 'Colonization and Immigration: "Blind Spots" in the History Classroom?'. In *The Colonial Legacy in France: Fracture, Rupture, and Apartheid*, edited by Nicolas Bancel, Pascal Blanchard and Dominic Thomas, 78–88. Bloomington, IN: Indiana University Press, 2017.

———. 'Promotion: Creating the Colonial (1930-1940)'. In *Colonial Culture in France Since the Revolution*, edited by Pascal Blanchard, Sandrine Lemaire, Nicolas Bancel and Dominic Thomas, 257–67. Bloomington, IN: Indiana University Press, 2014.

———. 'Spreading the Word: *The Agence Générale des Colonies (1920-1931)*'. In *Colonial Culture in France Since the Revolution*, edited by Pascal Blanchard, Sandrine Lemaire, Nicolas Bancel and Dominic Thomas, 162–70. Bloomington, IN: Indiana University Press, 2014.

Lemaire, Sandrine, Pascal Blanchard, Nicolas Bancel, Alain Mabanckou and Dominic Thomas. *Colonisation et Propagande. Le pouvoir de l'image*. Paris: Le cherche midi, 2022.

Lemaire, Sandrine, Catherine Hodeir and Pascal Blanchard. 'The Colonial Economy: Between Propaganda Myths and Economic Reality (1940-1955)'. In *Colonial Culture in France Since the Revolution*, edited by Pascal Blanchard, Sandrine Lemaire, Nicolas Bancel and Dominic Thomas, 320–32. Bloomington, IN: Indiana University Press, 2014.

Lemi, Tamiru. 'The Role of Traditional Ecological Knowledge (TEK) for Climate Change Adaptation'. *International Journal of Environmental Sciences & Natural Resources* 18, no. 1 (2019). https://juniperpublishers.com/ijesnr/IJESNR.MS.ID.555980.php.

León, Jason De. *The Land of Open Graves: Living and Dying on the Migrant Trail*. Oakland, CA: University of California Press, 2015.

Levantesi, Stella. '"Enemies of Society": How the Media Portray Climate Activists.' *Green European Journal*, October 17, 2023. https://www.greeneuropeanjournal.eu/enemies -of-society-how-the-media-portray-climate-activists/.

Leyen, Ursula von der. 'Answering the Call of History'. 2023 State of the Union Address, September 13, 2023. https://ec.europa.eu/commission/presscorner/detail/en/ speech_23_4426.

Liboiron, Max. *Pollution is Colonialism*. Durham, NC: Duke University Press, 2021.

Lindquist, Sven. *"Exterminate All the Brutes": One Man's Odyssey into the Heart of Darkness and the Origins of European Genocide*. Trans. J. Tate. New York: New Press, 2007.

Lohmann, Larry. 'Malthusianism and the Terror of Scarcity'. In *Making Threats, Biofears and Environmental Anxieties,* edited by Betsy Hartmann, Banu Subramaniam and Charles Zerner, 81–98. Lanham, MD: Rowman and Littlefield, 2005.

Longo, Matthew. *The Picnic: A Rush for Freedom and the Collapse of Communism.* New York: W. W. Norton, 2024.

Lubarda, Balša. *Far-Right Ecologism: Environmental Politics and the Far Right in Hungary and Poland.* London and New York, Routledge, 2024.

Luca, Erri De. 'Saving Lives at Sea: Onboard a Migrant Rescue Ship in the Mediterranean'. June 6, 2017. https://lithub.com/saving-lives-at-sea-onboard-a-migrant-rescue-ship-in-the-mediterranean/.

MacKenzie, John. *Propaganda and Empire: The Manipulation of British Public Opinion, 1880-1960.* Manchester: Manchester University Press, 1984.

Madianou, Mirca. 'Technocolonialism: Digital Innovation and Data Practices in the Humanitarian Response to Refugee Crises'. *Social Media + Society* 5, no. 3 (July 2019). https://journals.sagepub.com/doi/10.1177/2056305119863146.

——— *Technocolonialism: When Technology for Good is Harmful.* Hoboken, NJ: John Wiley and Sons, 2024.

Mahony, Martin and Georgina Endfield. 'Climate and Colonialism'. *WIREs Climate Change* 9, no. 2 (2018). https://doi.org/10.1002/wcc.510.

Majdoub, Soumaya. 'Malthusian Fears in Current Immigration Debates: Contemporary Manifestations of Malthusianization'. In *The Politics of Replacement: Demographic Fears, Conspiracy Theories, and Race Wars,* edited by Sarah Bracke and Luis Manuel Hernández Aguilar, 23–36. London and New York: Routledge, 2024.

'Making Climate History'. Cambridge University. Accessed January 30, 2025. https://www.geog.cam.ac.uk/research/projects/makingclimatehistory/.

Mala, Nsah and Nicki Hitchcott, eds. *Ecotexts in the Postcolonial Francosphere.* Liverpool: Liverpool University Press, 2025.

Malingre, Virginie. 'La Commission européenne propose une nouvelle PAC avec beaucoup moins de contraintes environnementales'. *Le Monde,* March 15, 2024.

Malm, Andreas and the Zetkin Collective. *White Skin, Black Fuel: On the Danger of Fossil Fascism.* London and New York: Verso Books, 2021.

Maloney, Carolyn B. and Ro Khanna. 'Oversight Committee Releases New Documents Showing Big Oil's Greenwashing Campaign and Failure to Reduce Emissions'. December 9, 2022. https://oversightdemocrats.house.gov/news/press-releases/oversight-committee-releases-new-documents-showing-big-oil-s-greenwashing.

Manceron, Gilles. 'School, Pedagogy, and the Colonies (1870–1914)'. In *Colonial Culture in France Since the Revolution,* edited by Pascal Blanchard, Sandrine Lemaire, Nicolas Bancel and Dominic Thomas, 124–31. Bloomington, IN: Indiana University Press, 2014.

Manduku, Fath Kumbe. 'La forêt'. Collectif Des Auteurs Africains. *Nos vers en vert.* Libreville: GNK éditions, 2021, 15.

Manga, Samy. *Chocolaté. Le goût amer de la culture du cacao.* Montreal: Écosociété, 2023.

———. *La dent de Lumumba: Régicide contre la Colonie.* Brussels: Météores, 2024.

Mangeon, Anthony. *L'Afrique au futur. Le renversement des mondes.* Paris: Hermann, 2022.

Marshall, Hannah and Alena Drieschova. 'Post-Truth Politics in the UK's Brexit Referendum'. *New Perspectives* 26, no. 3 (2018): 89–106.

Martinez, Chris, Laura Kilbury, Joel Martinez, Calee White, Mariel Lutz, Kat So, Kate Petosa, Allison McManus and Anne Christianson. 'These Fossil Fuel Industry Tactics

Are Fueling Democratic Backsliding'. Center for American Progress, December 5, 2023. https://www.americanprogress.org/article/these-fossil-fuel-industry-tactics-are-fueling-democratic-backsliding/.

Mau, Steffen. *La réinvention de la frontière au XXIè siècle*. Trans. C. Lucchese. Paris: Éditions de la Maison des sciences de l'homme, 2023.

Mazzara, Federica. *Reframing Migration: Lampedusa, Border Spectacle and aesthetics of Subversion*. Oxford: Peter Lang, 2019.

Mbaye, Massama. 'Senegal.' In *Foreigners Everywhere - Stranieri Ovunque, Volume 2*, edited by Flavia Fossa Margutti, 144–5. Venice Biennale, 2024.

Mbembe, Achille. 'Afrique-France : neuf thèses sur la fin d'un cycle'. *Le Grand Continent*, September 3, 2023.

———. 'Bodies as Borders.' *From the European South* 4 (2019): 5–18.

———. *Critique of Black Reason*. Trans. L. Dubois. Durham, NC: Duke University Press, 2017 [2013].

———. 'Figures du Multiple: La France peut-elle réinventer son identité?'. *Le Messager*, November 24, 2005.

———. *La communauté terrestre*. Paris: La Découverte, 2023.

———. 'Le Monde-zéro: matière et machine / De nulwereld: materie en machine / The Zero-World: Materials and Machine'. In *Mémoire/Kolwezi*, edited by Sammy Baloji, 73–9. Oostkamp: Stichting Kunstboek, 2014.

———. 'Provincializing France?'. Trans. J. Roitman. *Public Culture* 23, no. 1 (2011): 85–119.

———. 'Scrap the Borders That Divide Africans'. *Mail & Guardian*, May 17, 2017.

———. 'The Age of Humanism Is Ending'. *Mail & Guardian*, December 22, 2016.

———. 'The Earthly Community'. The Holberg Lecture, June 5, 2024. https://holbergprize.org/en/news/holberg-prize/2024-holberg-lecture-achille-mbembe.

———. 'Thoughts on the Planetary.' 2019. https://www.newframe.com/thoughts-on-the-planetary-an-interview-with-achille-mbembe/.

Mbembe, Achille and Ruth Wilson Gilmore. 'Trump's attacks on South Africa are a punishment for independence'. *The Guardian*, March 7, 2025.

Mbembe, Achille, Rémy Rioux and Séverine Kodjo-Grandvaux. *Pour un monde en commun. Regards croisés entre l'Afrique et l'Europe*. Arles: Actes Sud / Agence française de développement, 2022.

Mbue, Imbolo. *How Beautiful We Were*. New York: Random House, 2020.

McDonald, Matt. 'Ecological Security'. *E-International Relations*, November 28, 2015. https://www.e-ir.info/2015/11/28/ecological-security/.

McFee, Graham. 'Empathy: Interpersonal vs Artistic'. In *Empathy: Philosophical and Psychological Perspectives*, edited by Amy and Peter Goldie, 185–208. New York: Oxford University Press, 2014.

McLuhan, Marshall. *Understanding Media: The Extensions of Man*. Boston, MA: The MIT Press, 1994 [1964].

Menasse, Robert. *Le monde de demain: Une Europe souveraine et démocratique – et ses ennemis*. Trans. O. Mannoni. Lagrasse: Éditions Verdier, 2025.

Mengual, Estelle Zhong. *Apprendre à voir. Le point de vue du vivant*. Arles: Actes Sud, 2021.

Mercer, Harriet. 'Colonialism: Why Leading Climate Scientists Have Finally Acknowledged Its Link With Climate Change'. *The Conversation*, April 22, 2022.

Mercer, Harriet and Thomas Simpson. 'Imperialism, Colonialism, and Climate Change Science'. *WIREs Climate Change* 14, no. 6 (June 21, 2023). https://wires.onlinelibrary.wiley.com/doi/full/10.1002/wcc.851.

Merchant, Carolyn. *The Death of Nature: Women, Ecology and the Scientific Revolution*. New York: Harper & Row, 1990 [1980].

Meuwese, Mark. *Brothers in Arms, Partners in Trade: Dutch-Indigenous Alliances in the Atlantic World, 1595–1674*. Leiden: Brill, 2012.

———. *To the Shores of Chile: The Journal and History of the Brouwer Expedition to Valdivia in 1643*. University Park, PA: Penn State University Press, 2019.

Meva, Caroline. *La science des sorciers de Koba*. Paris: Saint-Honoré, 2021.

Meziane, Mohamad Amer. *The States of the Earth: An Ecological and Racial History of Secularization*. Trans. J. Adjemian. New York: Verso Books, 2024.

Michel, Nicolas. 'Congo: Wilfried N'Sondé et ses amours planctoniques.' *Jeune Afrique*, October 23, 2022.

———. 'Environnement: du Cap à Dakar, la goélette Tara prend le pouls de l'Atlantique Sud'. *Jeune Afrique*, May 8, 2022.

———. 'RDC: In Koli Jean Bofane, le satyricongolais'. *Jeune Afrique*, April 9, 2014.

Midiohouan, Guy Ossito. 'Le créateur négro-africain et l'environnement: de la contemplation à l'engagement'. *Mots Pluriels* 11 (September 1999). https://motspluriels.arts.uwa.edu.au/MP1199gom.html.

Miller, Christopher L. *Nationalists and Nomads: Essays on Francophone African Literature and Culture*. Chicago, IL: University of Chicago Press, 1998.

Miller, Todd. *Storming the Wall: Climate Change, Migration, and Homeland Security*. San Francisco, CA: City Lights Books, 2017.

Mishra, Pankaj. *The Age of Anger: A History of the Present*. New York: Picador, 2017.

Missirian, Anouch and Wolfram Schlenker. 'Asylum Applications Respond to Temperature Fluctuations'. *Science* 358, no. 6370 (December 2017): 1610–4.

Mobray, Sean. 'Delectable but Destructive: Tracing Chocolate's Environmental Life Cycle'. *Mongabay*, August 1, 2022.

Moeller, Susan D. *Compassion Fatigue: How the Media Sell Disease, Famine, War and Death*. New York: Routledge, 1999.

Mohamed Mbougar. *The Silence of the Choir*. Trans. A. Anderson. New York: Europa Editions, 2024 [2017].

Monbiot, George and Peter Hutchison. *The Invisible Doctrine: The Secret History of Neoliberalism (& How It Came to Control Your Life)*. London: Allen Lane, 2024.

Moore, Sam and Alex Roberts. *The Rise of Ecofascism: Climate Change and The Far Right*. Cambridge: Polity Press, 2022.

Morizot, Baptiste. *Ways of Being*. Trans. A. Brown. Cambridge: Polity Press, 2022 [2020].

Morton, Patricia A. *Hybrid Modernities: Architecture and Representation at the 1931 Colonial Exposition, Paris*. Cambridge, MA: MIT Press, 2000.

Morton, Timothy. *Dark Ecology: For a Logic of Future Coexistence*. New York: Columbia University Press, 2016.

Moulton, Alex A. and Inge Salo. 'Black Geographies and Black Ecologies as Insurgent Ecocriticism'. *Environment and Society: Advances in Research* 13 (2022): 156–74.

Mousset, Lou. 'Geert Wilders' Win Shows We Are in a New Phase for the Far Right in Western Europe.' *The Guardian*, November 30, 2023.

———. *On Extremism and Democracy in Europe*. London and New York: Routledge, 2017.

———. '"Reverse Colonization": Early Narratives of Decline in the French New Right'. In *The Politics of Replacement: Demographic Fears, Conspiracy Theories, and Race Wars*, edited by Sarah Bracke and Luis Manuel Hernández Aguilar, 66–81. London and New York: Routledge, 2024.

Mudde, Cas. 'The Hungary PM Made a "Rivers of Blood" Speech … And No One Cares'. *The Guardian*, July 30, 2015.

Mujila, Fiston Mwanza. *Tram 83*. Trans. R. Glasser. Dallas, TX: Deep Vellum, 2015 [2014].

———. *The River in the Belly*. Trans. J. B. Maney. Dallas, TX: Deep Vellum, 2021.

———. *The Villains's Dance*. Trans. R. Glasser. Dallas, TX: Deep Vellum, 2024 [2020].

Murphy, David. 'Representations of the *tirailleur sénégalais* and World War I'. In *Visualizing Empire: Africa, Europe, and the Politics of Representation*, edited by Rebecca Peabody, Steven Nelson and Dominic Thomas, 118–35. Los Angeles, CA: Getty Publications, 2021.

Murphy, Maureen. *Un Palais pour une cité: Du musée des colonies à la Cité nationale de l'histoire de l'immigration*. Paris: Réunion des musées nationaux, 2007.

Murray, Douglas. *The Strange Death of Europe: Immigration, Identity, Islam*. London: Bloomsbury Publishing, 2021.

N'Sondé, Wilfried. 'Ethnidentité'. In *Je est un autre. Pour une identité-monde*, edited by Michel Le Bris and Jean Rouaud, 95–100. Paris: Gallimard, 2010.

———. 'Borders'. In *Borders*. by Jean-Michel André (photographs), 76–7. Trans. K. Lindo. London: Actes Sud, 2021.

———. *Femme du ciel et des tempêtes*. Arles: Actes Sud, 2021.

———. Fondation Tara Océan, 2021. https://fondationtaraocean.org/en/artists/wilfried-nsonde/.

———. *Héliosphéra, fille des abysses, d'amour et de plancton*. Arles: Actes Sud, 2022.

———. 'Homo Detritus'. In *Homo Detritus* by Stéphane Gladieu (photographs), 8–89. Trans. C. Penswarden. Arles: Actes Sud, 2022.

———. 'Recherchons ce qui nous unit'. *Afrique Magazine*, May 3, 2023. https://www.youtube.com/watch?v=NLflMiXSfx8.

———. 'Sang frontières'. In *Osons la fraternité. Les écrivains aux côtés des migrants*, edited by Patrick Chamoiseau and Michel Le Bris, 55–62. Paris: Philippe Rey, 2018.

Naím, Moisés. *The Revenge of Power: How Autocrats Are Reinventing Politics for the 21st Century*. New York: St. Martin's Griffin, 2022.

Nan-Nguema, Sandrine [Bessora]. *Mémoires pétrolières au Gabon*. Doctoral Thesis, University of Paris 7, 2002. https://theses.fr/2002PA070076.

Nathani-Alexander, Isabella. *The Burning: The Untold Story of the Africa's Migrant Crisis*, 2023. Accessed September 12, 2024. https://www.smallworldfilms.org.

National Maritime Museum. 'Nelson's Ship in a Bottle'. https://www.rmg.co.uk/sites/default/files/Ship_AW.pdf.

Ndala, Blaise. *In the Belly of the Congo*. Trans. A. B. Reid. New York: Other Press, 2023 [2021].

NDiaye, Marie. *Three Strong Women*. Trans. J. Fletcher. New York: Alfred A. Knopf, 2012.

Ndinga, Assitou. *Les Marchands du développement durable*. Paris: L'Harmattan, 2006.

Nehrlich, Brigitte. 'Invasion as a Metaphor'. November 4, 2022. https://blogs.nottingham.ac.uk/makingsciencepublic/2022/11/04/invasion-as-a-metaphor/.

Nguyen, Viet Thanh. 'Introduction'. In *The Displaced: Refugee Writers on Refugee Lives*, edited by Viet Thanh Nguyen, 11–22. New York: Abrams Press, 2018.

Niarcos, Nicholas. 'In Congo's Cobalt Mines'. *New York Review of Books*, December 7, 2023.

Noble, Safiya. *Algorithms of Oppression: How Search Engines Reinforce Racism*. New York: New York University Press, 2018.

Nussbaum, Martha. *Poetic Justice: Literary Imagination and Public Life*. Boston, MA: Beacon Press, 1995.

———. *Upheavals of Thought: The Intelligence of Emotions*. New York: Cambridge University Press, 2001.

Nyman, Jopi and Johan Schimanski. 'Introduction: Images and Narratives on the Border'. In *Border Images, Border Narratives: The Political Aesthetics of Boundaries and Crossings*, edited Johan Schimanski and Jopi Nyman, 1–20. Manchester: Manchester University Press, 2021.

Odell, Jenny. *How to Do Nothing: Resisting the Attention Economy*. Brooklyn, NY and London: Melville House, 2019.

Ogungbemi, Olarotimi. 'Literature as Resistance: The Pragmatics of Ecological Advocacy in 'Oil and Water' by Helon Habila'. *Journal Arbitrer* 10, no. 4 (2023): 360–70.

Oklahoma Oil & Natural Gas. https://oerb.com.

Oladipo, Gloria. '"Racism is Embedded in Our Society": How Attacks on Immigrants in Ohio Hhighlight US Disinformation Crisis'. *The Guardian*, September 18, 2024.

Oltermann, Philip. 'End Fossil-Fuel Era to Address Colonial Injustices, Urges Prominent Historian'. *The Guardian*, February 15, 2024.

Olusoga, David. 'There Can be No Excuses. The UK Riots Were Violent Racism Fomented by Populism'. *The Guardian*, August 10, 2024.

Orain, Arnaud. *Les savoirs perdus de l'économie. Contribution à l'équilibre du vivant*. Paris: Gallimard, 2023.

———. *Le monde confisqué: Essai sur le capitalisme de la finitude (XVIᵉ- XXIᵉ)*. Paris: Flammarion, 2025.

Orwell, George. *1984*. London: Secker & Warburg, 1949.

Otele, Olivette. *African Europeans: An Untold History*. London: Hurst & Company, 2020.

Palais de la Porte Dorée and the Museum of the History of Immigration. 'Janniot's Bas-relief'. Accessed January 30, 2025. https://monument.palais-portedoree.fr/en/the-settings/janniot-s-bas-relief.

Palermo, Lynn E. 'L'Exposition Anticolonialie: Political or Aesthetic Protest?'. *French Cultural Studies* 20, no. 1 (2009): 27–46.

Palumbo-Liu, David. *The Deliverance of Others: Reading Literature in a Global Age*. Durham, NC: Duke University Press, 2012.

Pape, Elise. 'Postcolonial Debates in Germany-An Overview'. *African Sociological Review / Revue Africaine de Sociologie* 21, no. 2 (2017): 2–14.

Parenti, Christian. *Tropic of Chaos: Climate Change and the New Geography of Violence*. New York: Bold Type Books, 2012.

Parrot, Karine. *Carte blanche: L'État contre les étrangers*. Paris: La Fabrique, 2023.

———. *Étranger*. Paris: Anamosa, 2023.

Peabody, Rebecca, Steven Nelson and Dominic Thomas, eds. *Visualizing Empire: Africa, Europe, and the Politics of Representation*. Los Angeles, CA: Getty Publications, 2021.

Pearce, Fred. 'Why Is Britain Retreating from Global Leadership on Climate Action?'. YaleEnvironment360, Yale School of the Environment, October 17, 2023. https://e360.yale.edu/features/ungreening-britain-sunak-climate-change.

Perisic, Alexandra. 'Life after Oil: The Politics of Labor in Bessora's *Petroleum*'. *Cambridge Journal of Postcolonial Literary Inquiry* 5, no. 3 (2018): 406–22.

Pezet, Jacques. 'Dernière Rénovation, Just Stop Oil, Scientist Rebellion... La nouvelle galaxie des mouvements écolos radicaux'. *Libération*, November 4, 2022.

Phillips, Caryl. *Colour Me English*. London: Harvill Secker, 2011.

————. *The European Tribe*. New York: Farrar Straus Giroux, 1987.

Phillips, Tom. 'Greta Thunberg Labelled a "Brat" by Brazil's Far-right Leader Jair Bolsonaro'. *The Guardian*, December 19, 2019.

Pieterse, Jan Nederveen. *White on Black: Images of Africa and Blacks in Western Popular Culture*. New Haven, CT: Yale University Press, 1992.

Piketty, Thomas. 'Le national-capitalisme trumpiste aime étaler sa force, mais il est, en réalité, fragile et aux abois'. *Le Monde*, February 15, 2025.

Pine, Frances and Haldis Haukanes. 'Reconceptualising Borders and Boundaries: Gender, Movement, Reproduction, Regulation'. In *Intimacy and Mobility in an Era of Hardening Borders: Gender, Reproduction, Regulation*, edited by Haldis Haukanes and Frances Pine, 7–30. Manchester: Manchester University Press, 2021.

Poggi, Isotta. 'Colorful Board Game Turns the French Colonies into Child's Play'. February 24, 2014. http://blogs.getty.edu/iris/colorful-board-game-turns-the-french -colonies-into-childs-play/.

Poinsot, Marie. 'Gauz, *Camarade Papa*'. *Hommes & Migrations* 1, no. 1324 (2019): 173–4.

Pomerantsev, Peter. *How to Win an Information War: The Propagandist Who Outwitted Hitler*. New York: Public Affairs, 2024.

Pope Francis. 'Moment of Reflection with Religious Leaders Near the Memorial Dedicated to Sailors and Migrants Lost at Sea'. September 22, 2023. https://www .vatican.va/content/francesco/en/speeches/2023/september/documents/20230922 -marsiglia-leaderreligiosi.html.

Pörtner, Hans-Otto et al. *Climate Change 2022: Impacts, Adaptation and Vulnerability. Contribution of Working Group Il to the Sixth Assessment Report of the Intergovernmental Panel on Climate Change*. Cambridge: Cambridge University Press, 2022. https://www.ipcc.ch/report /ar6/wg2/downloads/report/IPCC_AR6_WGII_SummaryForPolicymakers.pdf.

Powell, Enoch. 'Speech at Birmingham'. April 20, 1968. https://www.enochpowell.net /fr-79.html.

Presidential Transition Project (Project 2025). Accessed February 2, 2025. https://www .project2025.org.

Presner, Todd. *Ethics of the Algorithm: Digital Humanities and Holocaust Memory*. Princeton, NJ and Oxford: Princeton University Press, 2024.

Priest, Christopher. *Fugue for a Darkening Island*. London: Gollancz, 2011 [1972].

Pullman, Daisy. 'A Rich Inheritance: An Ecocritical Reading of Ken Saro-Wiwa's Short Stories and Poetry'. *Green Letters* 27, no. 3 (2023): 303–16.

Putnam, James and Michele Gervasuti. 'Democratic Republic of Congo.' In *Foreigners Everywhere – Stranieri Ovunque, Volume 2*, edited by Flavia Fossa Margutti, 40–1. Venice: Biennale, 2024.

Quayson, Ato. 'Anatomizing a Postcolonial Tragedy: Ken Saro-Wiwa and the Ogoni'. *Performance Research* 1, no. 2 (1996): 83–92.

————. 'Shakara Baby-chicks and Locomotive Tales: Fiston Mwanza Mujila's *Tram 83*'. *Arcade: The Humanities in the World*, May 23, 2016. https://shc.stanford.edu/arcade/ interventions/shakara-baby-chicks-and-locomotive-tales-fiston-mwanza-mujilas -tram-83.

————. 'Stories and Empathy in a Time of Crisis: An African Viewpoint'. *African Studies Review* 65, no. 4 (2022): 965–84.

Rahm, Philippe. *Histoire naturelle de l'architecture: Comment le climat, les épidémies et l'énergie ont façonné la ville et les bâtiments*. Paris: Pavillon de l'Arsenal, 2020.

————. *Le style anthropocène*. Geneva: Head Publishing, 2023.

Rancière, Jacques. *The Emancipated Spectator*. Trans. G. Eliot. London: Verso Books, 2009 [2008].

Raspail, Jean. *Le Camp des saints*. Paris: Robert Laffont, 2011 [1973].

Rassemblement National. *L'environnement pour une écologie française*, 2022. https://rassemblementnational.fr/documents/projet/projet-lecologie.pdf.

Rawlinson, Francis. *How Press Propaganda Paved the Way to Brexit*. Cham: Palgrave Macmillan, 2019.

Regulation of the European Parliament and of the Council of 30 June 2021 Establishing the Framework for Achieving Climate Neutrality and Amending Regulations (EC) No 401/2009 and (EU) 2018/1999 ('European Climate Law'). *Official Journal of the European Union*, July 9, 2021. https://eur-lex.europa.eu/legal-content/EN/TXT/HTML/?uri=CELEX:32021R1119.

Reuveny, Rafael, and Will H. Moore. 'Does Environmental Degradation Influence Migration? Emigration to Developed Countries in the Late 1980s and 1990s'. *Social Science Quarterly* 90, no. 3 (2009): 461–79.

Reybrouck, David Van. *Congo: The Epic History of a People*. Trans. S. Garrett. New York: HarperCollins Publishers, 2014.

———. *Nous colonisons l'avenir*. Trans. B.-T. Standaert. Arles: Actes Sud, 2023.

———. *Revolusi: Indonesia and the Birth of the Modern World*. Trans. D. Colmer and D. McKay. New York: W. W. Norton & Company, 2024.

Rigby, Kate. *Meditations on Creation in an Era of Extinction*. Maryknoll, NY: Orbis Books, 2023.

Rigby, Scott and Richard Ryan. 'Rethinking Carrots: A New Method for Measuring What Players Find Most Rewarding and Motivating about Your Game'. January 16, 2007. http://www.gamasutra.com/view/feature/130155/rethinking_carrots_a_new_method_.php.

Rigouste, Mathieu. *La police du futur. Le marché de la violence et ce qui lui résiste*. Paris: 10/18, 2022.

Rodier, Claire. 'Migrations: choix politique ou responsabilité collective'. *France Culture Radio*, October 8, 2013. https://www.dailymotion.com/video/x15ojw5.

———. *Xénophobie Business: À quoi servent les contrôles migratoires?* Paris: La Découverte, 2012.

Rodier, Claire with Catherine Portevin. *Migrants & Réfugiés. Réponse aux indécis, aux inquiets, aux réticents*. Paris: La Découverte, 2016.

Rogers, Thomas. 'The Long Shadow of German Colonialism'. *New York Review of Books*, March 9, 2023.

Romestaing, Alain, Pierre Schoentjes and Anne Simon. 'Essor d'une conscience littéraire de l'environnement'. *Revue critique de fixxion française contemporaine* 11 (2015). https://journals.openedition.org/fixxion/8389.

Romeyn, Esther. 'Das Boot ist voll, The Boat is Full: Genealogy and Policy Consequences of an Ecological-Nativist Paradigm'. In *The Politics of Replacement: Demographic Fears, Conspiracy Theories, and Race Wars*, edited by Sarah Bracke and Luis Manuel Hernández Aguilar, 38–50. London and New York: Routledge, 2024.

Ross, Christine. *Art for Coexistence: Unlearning the Way We See Migration*. Cambridge, MA and London: The MIT Press, 2022.

Roth, Sammy. 'Column: How "Sesame Street" Can Prepare Kids for Climate Disasters'. *Los Angeles Times*, May 23, 2024.

Rothberg, Michael. *Multidirectional Memory. Remembering the Holocaust in the Age of Decolonization*. Stanford, CA: Stanford University Press, 2009.

Rothe, Matthias. '"Hidden Stockpiles of Words and Images": An Interview with Thomas Heise'. In *Representing Social Precarity in German Literature and Film*, edited by Sophie Duvernoy, Karsten Olson and Ulrich Plass, 236–53. New York: Bloomsbury Academic, 2024.

Ruiz, Carlos Diaz. 'Disinformation on Digital Media Platforms: A Market-shaping Approach'. *New Media & Society* (2023). https://journals.sagepub.com/doi/10.1177/14614448231207644.

Ruscio, Alain. 'Toward a Real History of French Colonialism'. In *The Colonial Legacy in France: Fracture, Rupture, and Apartheid*, edited by Nicolas Bancel, Pascal Blanchard and Dominic Thomas, 386–94. Bloomington, IN: Indiana University Press, 2017.

Russo, Katherine E. 'Floating Signifiers, Transnational Affect Flows: Climate-induced Migrants in Australian News Discourse'. In *Life Adrift: Climate Change, Migration, Critique*, edited by Andrew Baldwin and Giovanni Bettini, 195–210. London and New York: Rowman & Littlefield International, Ltd., 2017.

Rydell, Robert W. *World of Fairs: The Century-of-Progress Expositions*. Chicago, IL: University of Chicago Press, 1993.

Sachs, Aaron. *The Humboldt Current: Nineteenth-Century Exploration and the Roots of American Environmentalism*. New York: Viking Penguin, 2007.

Samaddar, Ranabi. 'The Ecological Migrant in Postcolonial Time'. In *Life Adrift: Climate Change, Migration, Critique*, edited by Andrew Baldwin and Giovanni Bettini, 177–93. London and New York: Rowman & Littlefield International, Ltd., 2017.

Saro-Wiwa, Ken. 'Ogoni! Ogoni'. In *Silence Would be Treason: Last writings of Ken Saro-Wiwa*, edited by Íde Corley, Helen Fallon, and Laurence Cox, 152. Nairobi: Daraja Press, 2018.

———. 'The Call'. In *Silence Would be Treason: Last writings of Ken Saro-Wiwa*, edited by Íde Corley, Helen Fallon, and Laurence Cox, 167. Nairobi: Daraja Press, 2018.

Sarr, Felwine. *Habiter le monde. Essai de politique relationnelle*. Montreal: Mémoire d'encrier, 2017.

Sarr, Felwine and Bénédicte Savoy. *The Restitution of African Cultural Heritage: Toward a New Relational Ethics*. Trans. D. S. Burk. Paris: Ministère de la culture, 2018.

Sarrazin, Thilo. *Deutschland schafft sich ab: Wie wir unser Land aufs Spiel setzen*. Munich: Deutsche Verlags-Anstalt 2010.

Sassen, Saskia. 'A Massive Loss of Habitat: New Drivers for Migration'. *Sociology of Development* 2, no. 2 (2016): 204–33.

———. 'Migration Policy from Control to Governance'. *Open Democracy*, July 12, 2006. https://www.opendemocracy.net/en/militarising_borders_3735jsp/.

———. 'Women's Burden: Counter-geographies of Globalization: The Feminization of Survival'. *Journal of International Affairs* 53, no. 2 (2000): 503–24.

Saunders, Frances Stonor. 'Where on Earth Are You'. *London Review of Books* 38, no. 5 (March 3, 2016). https://www.lrb.co.uk/the-paper/v38/n05/frances-stonor-saunders/where-on-earth-are-you.

Savage, Michael. 'Fifty Years on, What is the Legacy of Enoch Powell's "Rivers of Blood" Speech?'. *The Guardian*, April 14, 2018.

Schaeperkoetter, Carla. *Petro Pete's Big Bad Dream*, illustrated by Cameron Eagle. Oklahoma Energy Resources Board, 2016.

Schalansky, Judith. 'East Germany: Palace of the Republic'. In *An Inventory of Losses*, edited by Judith Schalansky, 209–23. Trans. J. Smith. New York: New Directions Publishing Corporation, 2020 [2018].

Schlamp, Hans-Jürgen. 'Flüchtlingsdrama vor Lampedusa: Europas Versagen.' *Der Spiegel*, October 3, 2013.

Schmidt, Benjamin. 'Exotic Allies: The Dutch-Chilean Encounter and the (Failed) Conquest of America'. *Renaissance Quarterly* 52, no. 2 (1999): 440–73.

Schmoll, Camille. *Les damnées de la terre. Femmes et frontières en Méditerranée*. Paris: La Découverte, 2020.

Schoentjes, Pierre. *Littérature et écologie. Le Mur des abeilles*. Paris: Corti, 2020.

Schwartz, Peter and Doug Randall. 'An Abrupt Climate Change Scenario and Its Implications for United States National Security'. Global Business Network for the Department of Defense, October 2003. https://www.iatp.org/sites/default/files/An_Abrupt_Climate_Change_Scenario_and_Its_Impl.pdf.

Seymour, Richard. *Disaster Nationalism: The Downfall of Liberal Civilisation*. London: Verso Books, 2024.

Shah, Sonia. *The Next Great Migration: The Beauty and Terror of Life on the Move*. New York: Bloomsbury Publishing, 2021.

Shell. https://www.shell.com.

Shukla, Priyadarshi R. and Jim Skea, eds. *Mitigation of Climate Change: Working Group III Contribution to the Sixth Assessment Report of the Intergovernmental Panel on Climate Change*. Intergovernmental Panel on Climate Change, 2022. https://www.ipcc.ch/report/ar6/wg3/downloads/report/IPCC_AR6_WGIII_FullReport.pdf.

Sides, Kirk Bryan. *Environmental Entanglements: African Literature's Ecological Imaginary*. New York, NY: Oxford University Press, 2025.

Siegel, Dina. 'The "Crises" of Lesbos'. *Utrecht Law Review* 17, no. 4 (2021): 10–8.

Singh, Nishtha. 'Climate Justice in the Global South: Understanding the Environmental Legacy of Colonialism'. *E-International Relations*, February 2, 2023. https://www.e-ir.info/2023/02/02/climate-justice-in-the-global-south-understanding-the-environmental-legacy-of-colonialism/.

Škobo, Milena and Jovana Đukić. 'Urban Landscape as the Embodiment of Social and Psychological Entropy in J. G. Ballard's *Cocaine Nights* and *Super-Cannes*'. *Interfaces* 2, Year 13 (2023). https://www.sic-journal.org/Article/Index/729.

Smillie, Susan. 'Drowned World: Welcome to Europe's First Undersea Sculpture Museum'. *The Guardian*, February 2, 2016.

Smith, David. 'How Trump's Anti-immigrant Rhetoric is Taking Over the Republican Party'. *The Guardian*, December 22, 2023.

Smith, Evan. '"Rather Swamped": Thatcher, Moral Panics and Racist Rhetoric'. November 1, 2022. https://hatfulofhistory.wordpress.com/2022/11/01/rather-swamped-thatcher-moral-panics-and-racist-rhetoric/.

Smith, Ian and Lottie Limb. 'Will Climate Change Really Lead to More Immigration? Here's What the Experts Think'. *Euronews*, June 25, 2024. https://www.euronews.com/green/2024/06/25/will-climate-change-really-lead-to-more-immigration-heres-what-the-experts-think.

Snyder, Timothy. *The Road to Unfreedom: Russia, Europe, America*. New York: Tim Duggan Books, 2018.

———. 'Ukraine Holds the Future: The War Between Democracy and Nihilism'. *Foreign Affairs*, September 6, 2022.

Solnit, Rebecca. 'Call Climate Change What It Is: Violence'. *The Guardian*, April 7, 2014.

Sontag, Susan. *Regarding the Pain of Others*. New York: Farrar, Straus and Giroux, 2003.

————. 'The Art of Fiction'. Interviewed by Edward Hirsch. *The Paris Review* 137 (Winter 1995). https://www.theparisreview.org/interviews/1505/the-art-of-fiction-no-143-susan-sontag.

Sow, Cheikh C. *Cycle de sécheresse*. Paris: Hatier, 1983.

Soyinka, Wole. *Climate of Fear: The Quest for Dignity in a Dehumanized World*. New York: Random House, 2005.

————. *The Open Sore of a Continent: A Personal Narrative of the Nigerian Crisis*. Oxford: Oxford University Press, 1996.

Spleth, Janice. 'Exploring the Gendered Nature of National Violence: The Intersection of Patriarchy and Civil Conflict in Tanella Boni's *Matins de couvre-feu (Mornings Under Curfew)*'. *Wagadu: A Journal of Transnational Women's & Gender Studies* 18, no. 1 (2017): 125–47.

Staal, Jonas. *Climate Propagandas: Stories of Extinction and Regeneration*. Boston, MA: MIT Press, 2024.

Stern, Alexandra Minna. *Proud Boys and the White Ethnostate: How the Alt-Right Is Warping the American Imagination*. Boston, MA: Beacon Press, 2020.

Stewart, Heather and Rowena Mason. 'Nigel Farage's Anti-migrant Poster Reported to Police'. *The Guardian*, June 16, 2016.

Stierl, Maurice. 'Migration: Let Us Put the "Pull Factor" Myth Finally to Rest'. *EUobserver*, October 4, 2023.

Stierl, Maurice, Charles Heller and Nicholas De Genova. 'Numbers (or the Spectacle of Statistics in the Production of "Crisis"'. In *Europe/Crisis: New Keywords of 'the Crisis' in and of 'Europe'*, 1–45, 2016. https://nearfuturesonline.org/wp-content/uploads/2016/01/New-Keywords-Collective_12.pdf.

Stroobants, Jean-Pierre. 'Belgium Prime Minister Officially Apologizes for the Death of Patrice Lumumba'. *Le Monde*, June 21, 2022.

Supran, Geoffrey and Cameron Hickey. 'Three Shades of Green(washing): Content Analysis of Social Media Discourse by European Oil, Car, and Airline Companies'. Working Paper, The Algorithmic Transparency Institute, September 21, 2022. https://ati.io/wp-content/uploads/2022/09/ThreeShadesofGreenwashingv2.pdf.

Syal, Rajeev and Peter Walker. 'Suella Braverman Claims "Hurricane" of Mass Migration Coming to UK'. *The Guardian*, October 3, 2023.

————. 'Suella Braverman: Small Boats Plan Will Push Boundaries of International Law'. *The Guardian*, March 7, 2023.

Szeman, Imre and Dominic Boyer, eds. *Energy Humanities: An Anthology*. Baltimore, MD: Johns Hopkins University Press, 2017.

Taffin, Dominique. 'Le musée des colonies et l'imaginaire colonial'. In *Images et colonies (1880–1962)*, edited by Nicolas Bancel, Pascal Blanchard and Laurent Gervereau, 140–4. Paris: ACHAC, 1993.

Talcott, Mélanie. 'Sinzo Aanza: Interview'. *L'Ombre du regard*, July 12, 2016.

Tannert, Christoph. 'There Is No Absolute Truth'. In *Claas Gutsche: Changing Truth*, edited by Claas Gutsche and Galerie Wagner. Berlin: Claas Gutsche and Galerie Wagner + Partner, 2014, n.p.

Tannock, Stuart. 'The Oil Industry in Our Schools: From Petro Pete to Science Capital in the Age of Climate Crisis'. *Environmental Education Research* 26, no. 4 (2020): 474–90.

Tansi, Sony Labou. *Conscience de tracteur*. Dakar and Yaoundé: NEA/CLÉ, 1979.

————. *Le Commencement des douleurs*. Paris: Seuil, 1995.

————. 'Lettre ouverte aux riches ou SOS Afrique.' In *Encre, sueur, salive et sang*, edited by Greta Rodriguez-Antoniotti, 124–7. Paris: Seuil, 2015.

Tara Foundation. https://fondationtaraocean.org/en/foundation/.

Tate Britain. 'Six Ways J.M.W. Turner Painted a Changing World'. Turner's Modern World Exhibition, October 28, 2020 to September 12, 2021.

Tevanian, Pierre and Jean-Charles Stevens. *"On ne peut accueillir toute la misère du monde": En finir avec une sentence de mort*. Paris: Anamosa, 2022.

Thatcher, Margaret. *World in Action*, January 27, 1978. https://www.margaretthatcher.org/document/103485.

The 2025 Presidential Transition Project. 'Chapter 13: The Environmental Protection Agency'. https://static.project2025.org/2025_MandateForLeadership_CHAPTER-13.pdf.

Thiemeyer, Thomas. 'Cosmopolitanizing Colonial Memories in Germany'. *Critical Inquiry* 45, no. 4 (Summer 2019): 967–90.

Thomas, Dominic. *Africa and France: Postcolonial Cultures, Migration, and Racism*. Bloomington, IN: Indiana University Press, 2013.

————. 'Bibliodiversity: Denationalizing and Defrancophonizing Francophonie.' In *Reframing Postcolonial Studies: Concepts – Methodologies – Scholarly Activisms*, edited by David Kim, 93–110. New York: Palgrave Macmillan, 2021.

————. 'Into the Jungle: Migration and Grammar in the New Europe.' In *Postcolonial Cultures, Migration, and Racism* by Dominic Thomas. Bloomington, IN: Indiana University Press, 2013, 169–87.

————. *Nation-Building, Propaganda, and Literature in Francophone Africa*. Bloomington, IN: Indiana University Press, 2002.

Tödt, Daniel. *The Lumumba Generation African Bourgeoisie and Colonial Distinction in the Belgian Congo*. Berlin and Boston, MA: De Gruyter, 2021.

'Toward a World Literature in French'. Trans. D. Simon, *World Literature Today* 83, no. 2 (March–April 2009): 54–6.

Towfik, Ahmed Khaled. *Utopia*. Trans. R. Jacquemond. Paris: Flammarion, 2013 [2008].

Tubiana, Laurence. 'Polariser pour mieux masquer l'inaction climatique.' *La Croix*, July 5, 2023.

United Nations 1951 Convention and 1967 Protocol. Accessed February 2, 2025. https://www.unhcr.org/sites/default/files/legacy-pdf/4ec262df9.pdf.

U.S. Department of the Treasury. 'Treasury Announces Agreement to Establish United States-Ukraine Reconstruction Investment Fund'. Accessed May 1, 2025. https://home.treasury.gov/news/press-releases/sb0126.

Varoufakis, Yanis. *Technofeudalism: What Killed Capitalism*. New York: Melville House Publishing, 2023.

Vásquez, Juan Gabriel. *La traduction du monde*. Trans. I. Gugnon. Paris: Seuil, 2025.

Velsen, Vincent van. *A Blueprint for Toads and Snakes: A solo exhibition by Sammy Baloji*. Amsterdam: Framer Framed Gallery, 2018. https://framerframed.nl/wp-content/uploads/2018/06/ABFTAS-HANDOUT-DIGITAAL_C.pdf.

Vergès, Françoise. 'Colonizing, Educating, Guiding: A Republican Duty.' In *Colonial Culture in France Since the Revolution*, edited by Pascal Blanchard, Sandrine Lemaire, Nicolas Bancel and Dominic Thomas, 250–6. Bloomington, IN: Indiana University Press, 2014.

———— *The Wombs of Women: Race, Capital, Feminism*. Trans. K. L. Glover. Durham, NC: Duke University Press, 2020.

Verschave, François-Xavier. *La Françafrique. Le plus long scandale de la République*. Paris: Stock, 1998.

Voskoboynik, Daniel Macmillen. *The Memory We Could Be: Overcoming Fear to Create Our Ecological Future*. Gabriola Island: New Society Publishers, 2018.

Wagner, Brigitta. 'A Shared Space at Eye Level: An Interview with Documentary Filmmaker Philip Scheffner'. *Senses of Cinema*, Issue 78, March 2016. https://www.sensesofcinema.com/2016/feature-articles/philip-scheffner-interview/.

Wainwright, Oliver. 'The Toxic Landscape of Colonialism: Venice's Architecture Biennale Spotlights Africa'. *The Guardian*, May 19, 2024.

Walia, Harsha. *Undoing Border Imperialism*. Oakland, CA: AK Press, 2013.

Walker, Kira. 'As Climate Displacement Increases, Migration Myths Fuel Fears'. *Equal Times*, February 10, 2021.

Weiwei, Ai. *1000 Years of Joys and Sorrows: A Memoir*. Trans. A. H. Barr. New York: Crown, 2021.

———. *Dans la peau de l'étranger*. Trans. B. Commengé. Arles: Actes Sud, 2020 [2019].

———. 'The Refugee Crisis Isn't about Refugees. It's About Us'. *The Guardian*, February 2, 2018.

Weiwei, Ai and Hans Ulrich Obrist. *Ai Weiwei Speaks with Hans Ulrich Obrist*. London: Penguin Books, 2016.

Wekker, Gloria. *White Innocence: Paradoxes of Colonialism and Race*. Durham, NC: Duke University Press, 2016.

Wenzel, Jennifer. *The Disposition of Nature: Environmental Crisis and World Literature*. New York: Fordham University Press, 2019.

Wesle, Anna. 'Architectures of Memory: Claas Gutsche's Recent Linocuts'. In *Claas Gutsche: Risse im Beton / Cracks in Concrete*, edited by Anna Wesle, 10–5. Kabinett Editions, no. 5. Burgdorf: Museum Franz Gertsch, 2016.

Westervelt, Amy and Kyle Pope. 'How to Spot Five of the Fossil Fuel Industry's Biggest Disinformation Tactics'. *The Guardian*, April 14, 2024.

White, Lynn. 'The Historical Roots of Our Ecologic Crisis'. *Science* 5, no. 3767 (1967): 1203–7.

Whyte, Kyle Powys. 'Is it Colonial Déjà vu? Indigenous Peoples and Climate Injustice'. In *Humanities for the Environment: Integrating Knowledge, Forging New Constellations of Practice*, edited by Joni Adamson and Michel Davis, 88–104. London: Routledge, 2018.

———. '"Our Ancestors" Dystopia Now: Indigenous Conservation and the Anthropocene'. In *Routledge Companion to the Environmental Humanities*, edited by Ursula K. Heise, Jon Christensen and Michelle Niemann, 206–16. New York: Routledge, 2017.

Wiley, Kehinde. 'An Archaeology of Silence: Exhibition'. The Museum of Fine Arts, Houston, Texas, November 19, 2023 to May 27, 2024.

Wit, Sara de. 'Gender and Climate Change as New Development Tropes of Vulnerability for the Global South: Essentializing Gender Discourses in Maasailand, Tanzania'. *Tapuya: Latin American Science, Technology and Society* 4 (2021): 1–23.

Wolf, Christa. 'What Remains'. In *What Remains and Other Stories* by Christa Wolf. Trans. H. Schwarzbauer and R. Takvorian, 231–95. New York: Farrar, Straus and Giroux, 1993 [1990].

Wong, Matteo. 'We Haven't Seen the Worst of Fake News. Deepfakes Still Might be Poised to Corrupt the Basic Ways We Process Reality – Or What's Left of it'. *Atlantic*, December 20, 2022.

Wood, James. 'A Novelist's Powerful Response to the Refugee Crisis'. *The New Yorker*, September 25, 2017.

Wurzel, Rüdiger K. W., Duncan Liefferink and James Connelly. 'Introduction: European Union Climate Leadership'. In *The European Union in International Climate Change Politics*, edited by Rüdiger K. W. Wurzel, James Connelly and Duncan Liefferink, 3–19. London and New York: Routledge, 2017.

Yang, Maya. 'Germany Hits Back at Marco Rubio after He Panned Labeling of AfD as "Extremist"'. *The Guardian*, May 3, 2025.

Yezid, El Yezid. *Tazadit la mine de fer*. Paris: L'Harmattan, 2021.

Yusoff, Kathryn. *A Billion Black Anthropocenes or None*. Minneapolis, MN: University of Minnesota Press, 2018.

Zambonini, Gualtiero. 'The Evolution of German Media Coverage of Migration'. Migration Policy Institute, 2009. https://www.migrationpolicy.org/sites/default/files/publications/TCM-GermanMedia.pdf.

Zask, Joëlle. *Écologie et démocratie*. Paris: Premier Parallèle, 2022.

Zeh, Juli. *About People*. Trans. A. L. Price. New York: World Editions, 2023.

Zeh, Juli and Ilia Trojanow. *Atteinte à la liberté. Les dérives de l'obsession sécuritaire*. Trans. P. Charbonneau. Arles: Actes Sud, 2010.

Zeigler, Jim. 'Petro Pete, Plastic Mascot for Plausible Denial'. *Inhabiting the Anthropocene*, April 10, 2019. https://inhabitingtheanthropocene.com/2019/04/10/petro-pete-plastic-mascot-for-plausible-denial/.

Zemmour, Éric. *Le suicide français*. Paris: Albin Michel, 2014.

Zetter, Roger. 'Protecting People Displaced by Climate Change: Some Conceptual Challenges'. In *Climate Change and Displacement: Multidisciplinary Perspectives*, edited by Jane McAdam, 131–50. Oxford and Portland: Hart Publishing, 2012.

Zickgraf, Caroline. 'Where Are All the Climate Migrants? Explaining Immobility amid Environmental Change'. Migration Policy Institute, October 4, 2023. https://www.migrationpolicy.org/article/climate-change-trapped-populations.

Zimmerer, Jürgen, eds. *Climate Change and Genocide: Environmental Violence in the 21st Century*. New York: Routledge, 2021.

Zou, Jie Jenny. 'Pipeline to the Classroom: How Big Oil Promotes Fossil Fuels to America's Children'. *The Guardian*, June 15, 2017.

Zubiaurre, Maite. *Talking Trash: Cultural Uses of Waste*. Nashville, TN: Vanderbilt University Press, 2019.

Zuboff, Shoshana. *The Age of Surveillance Capitalism: The Fight for a Human Future at the New Frontier of Power*. New York: PublicAffairs, 2020.

INDEX

Note: Page numbers in **bold** indicate text within a table or figure